ALSO FROM JOE BOOKS

GRAVITY FALLS

CINESTORY COMIC

VOLUME 4

JOE BOOKS LTD

Published simultaneously in the United States and Canada by Joe Books Ltd,
489 College Street, Suite 203, Toronto, ON M6G 1A5.

www.joebooks.com

First Joe Books Edition: April 2018

ISBN: 978-1-77275-672-2

Library and Archives Canada Cataloguing in Publication
information is available upon request.

Printed and bound in Canada

1 3 5 7 9 10 8 6 4 2

CINESTORY COMIC

VOLUME 4

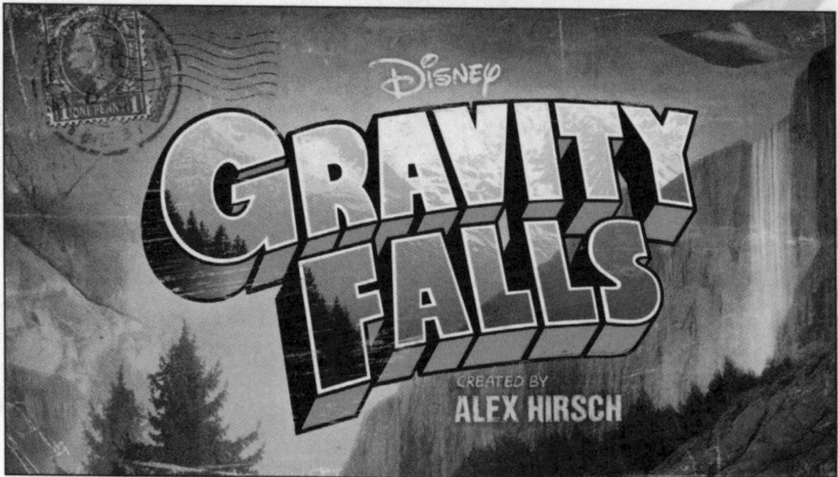
Disney
GRAVITY FALLS
CREATED BY
ALEX HIRSCH

FIGHT FIGHTERS
EPISODE 10

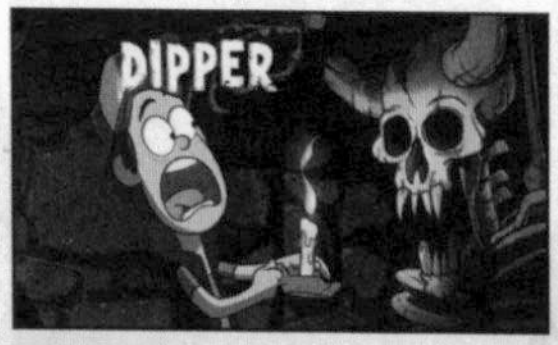
DIPPER

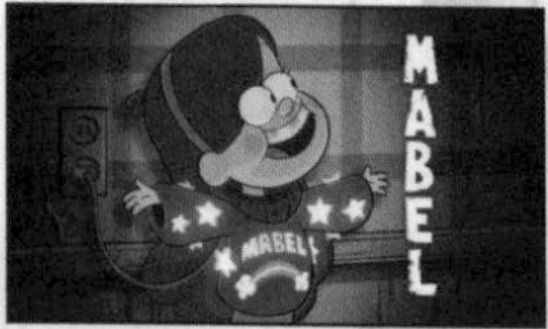
MABEL

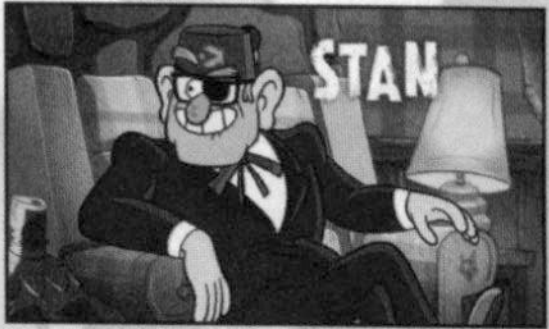
STAN

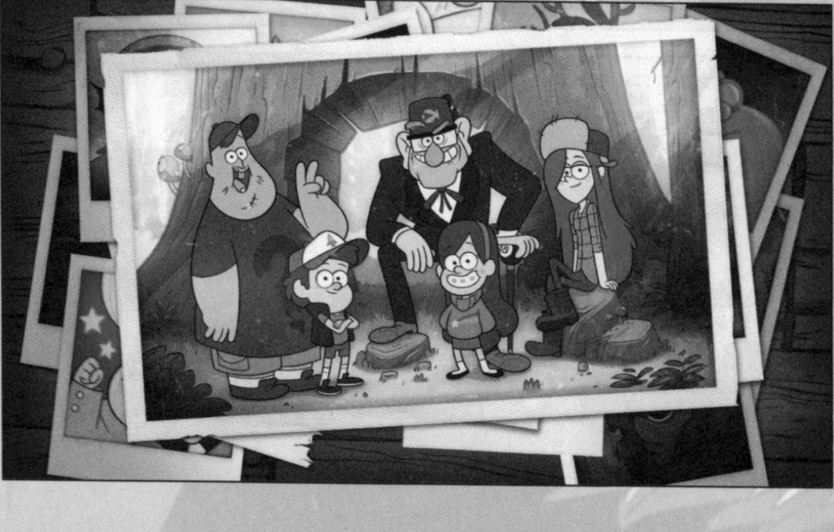

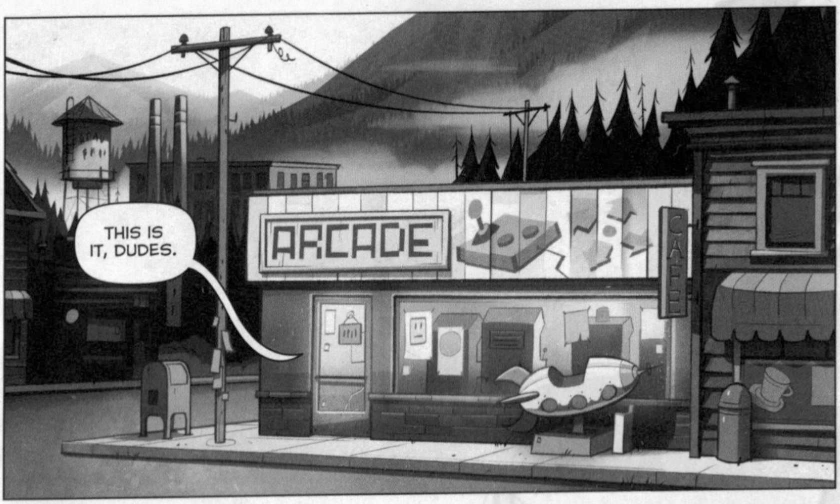
ARCADE
CAFE
THIS IS IT, DUDES.

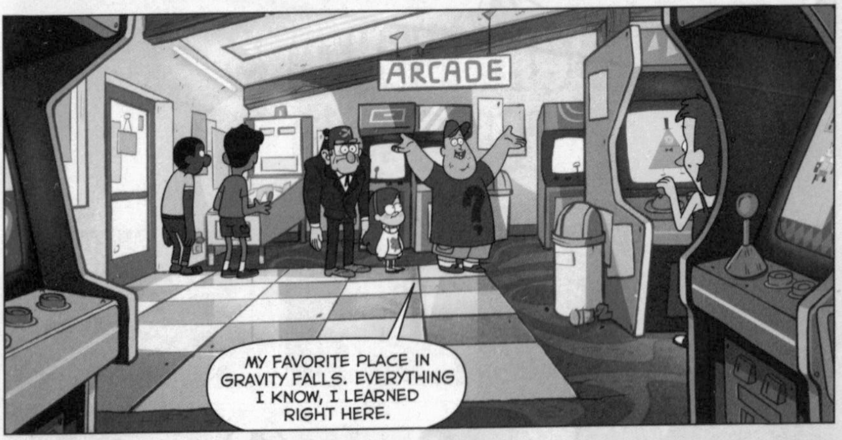
ARCADE
MY FAVORITE PLACE IN GRAVITY FALLS. EVERYTHING I KNOW, I LEARNED RIGHT HERE.

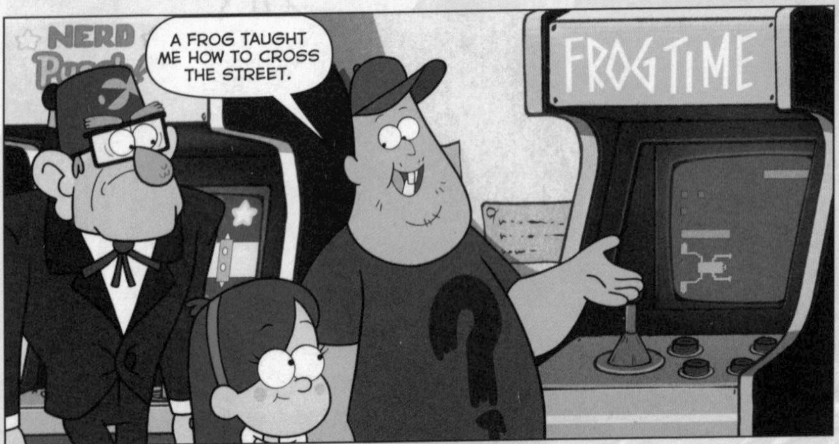
NERD
A FROG TAUGHT ME HOW TO CROSS THE STREET.
FROGTIME

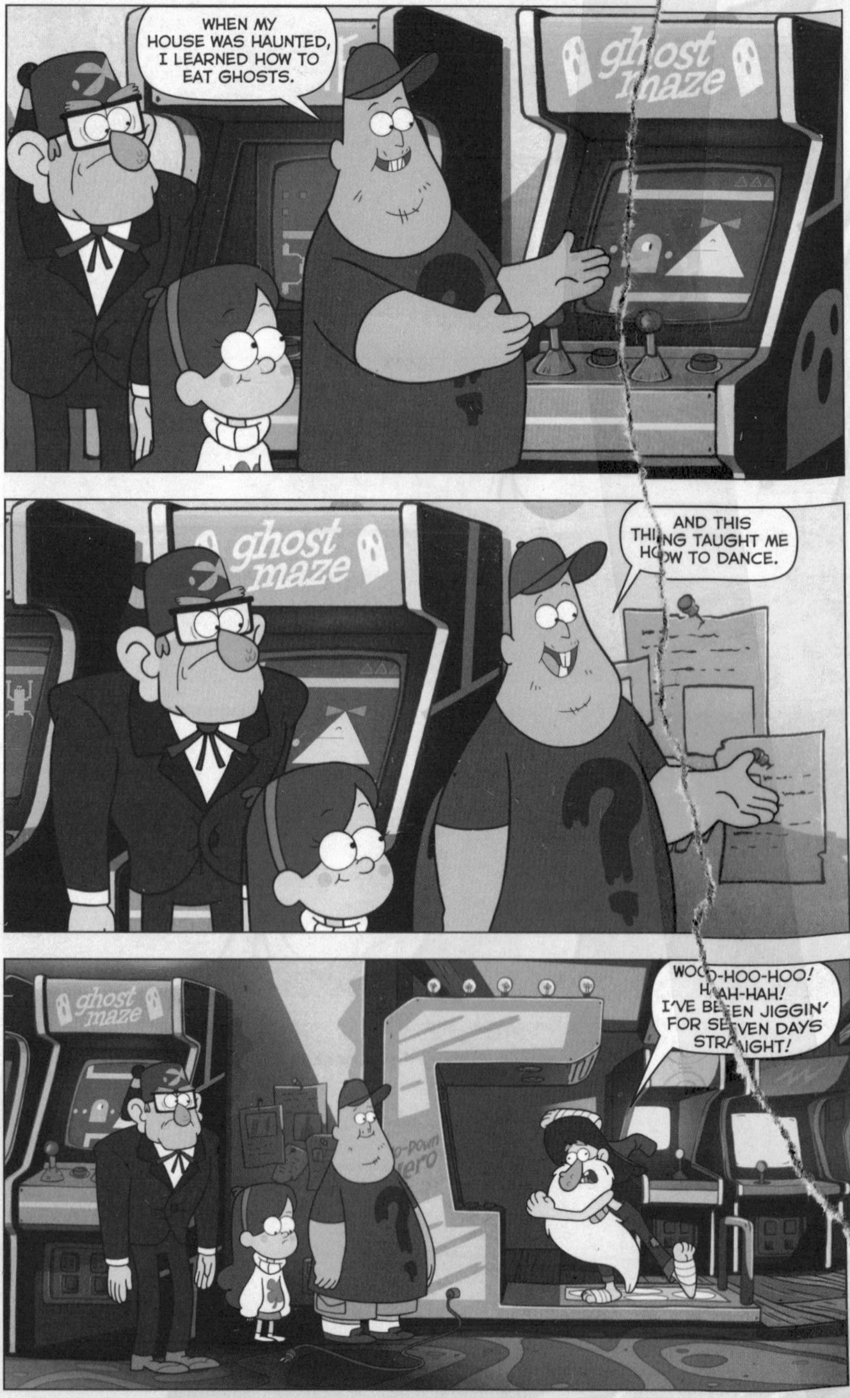
WHEN MY HOUSE WAS HAUNTED, I LEARNED HOW TO EAT GHOSTS.
ghost maze
AND THIS THING TAUGHT ME HOW TO DANCE.
ghost maze
WOO-HOO-HOO! HAH-HAH! I'VE BEEN JIGGIN' FOR SEVEN DAYS STRAIGHT!

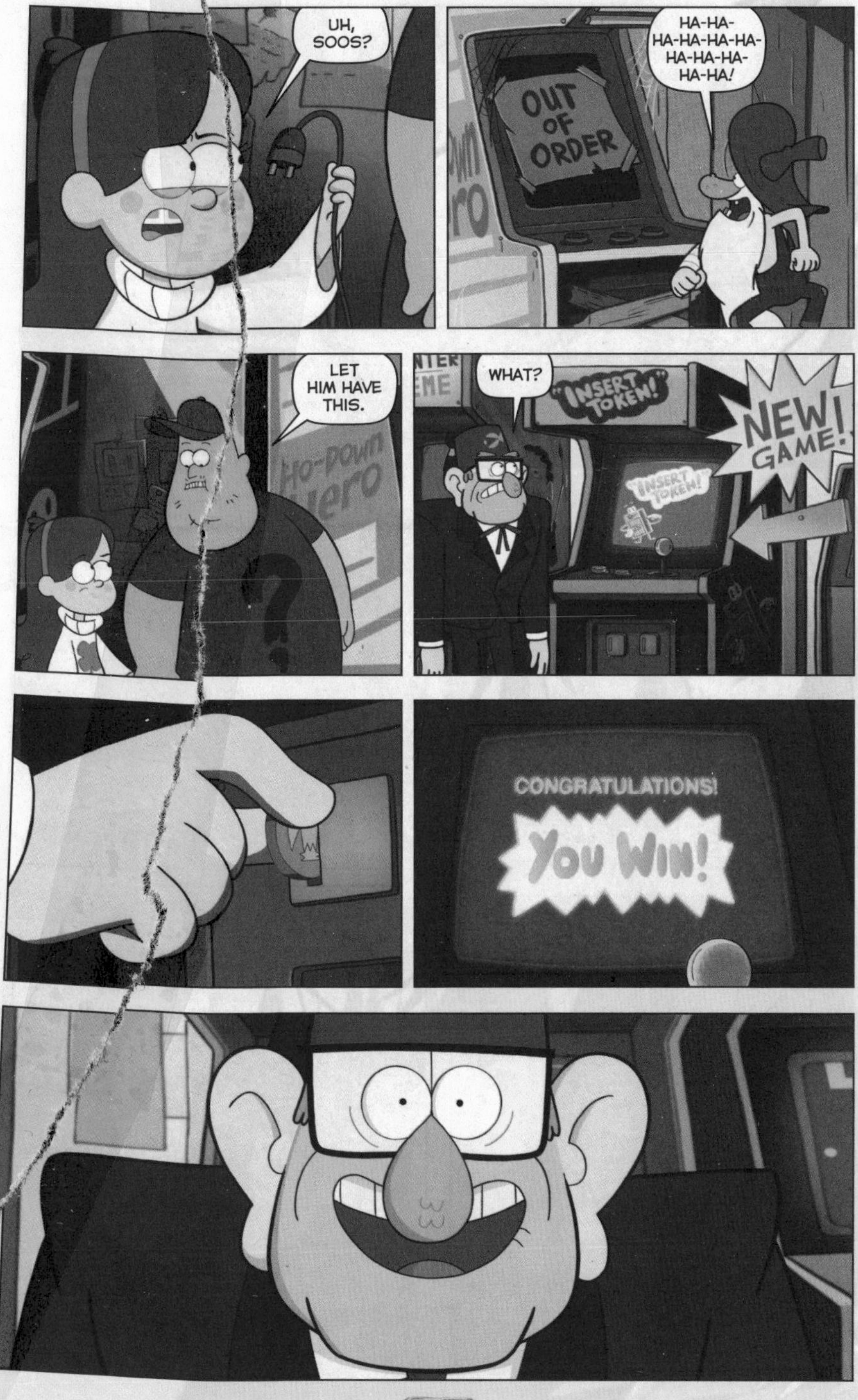
UH, SOOS?
OUT OF ORDER
HA-HA-HA-HA-HA-HA-HA-HA-HA-HA-HA-HA!
LET HIM HAVE THIS.
Ho-Down Hero
WHAT?
"INSERT TOKEN!"
NEW! GAME!
"INSERT TOKEN!"
CONGRATULATIONS!
You Win!

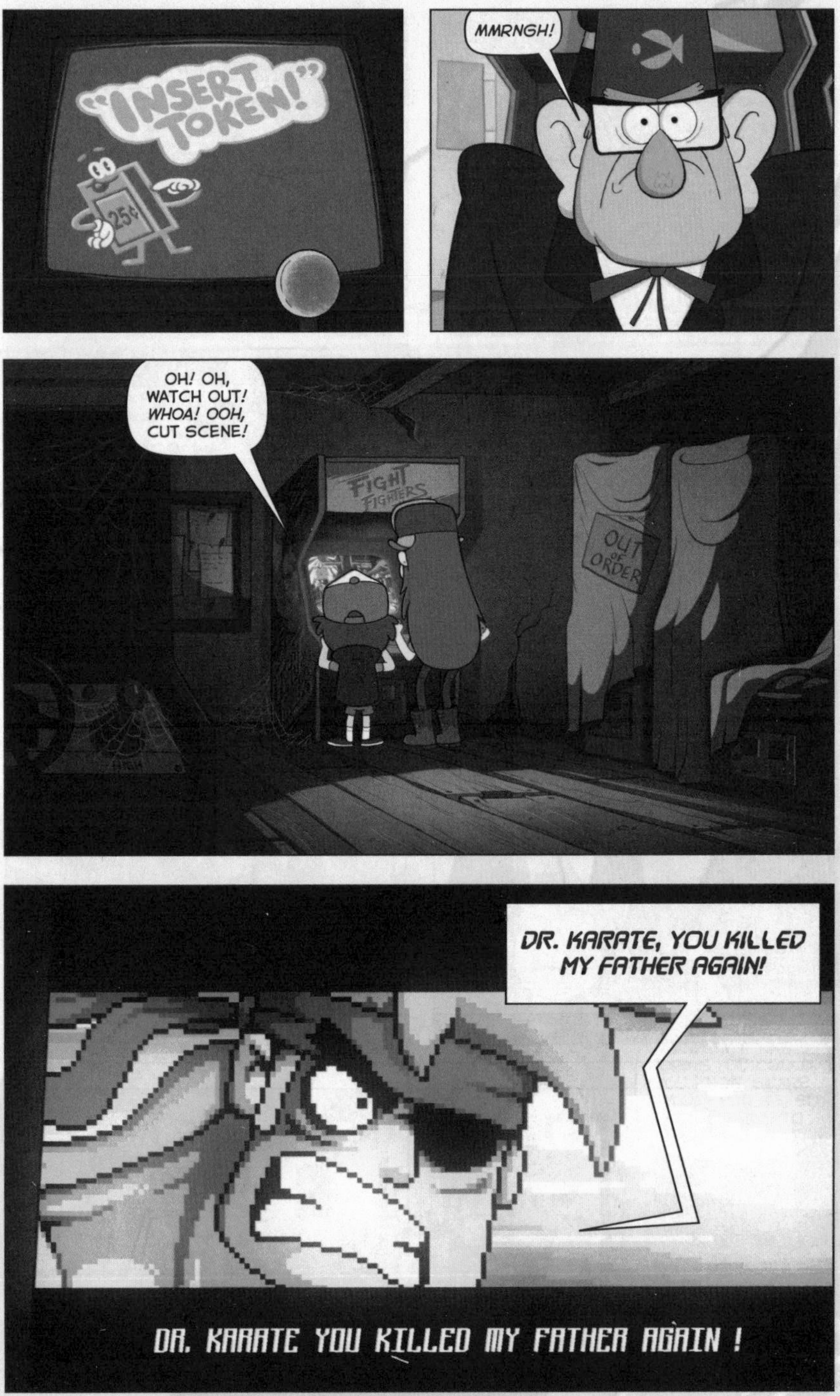
"INSERT TOKEN!"
25¢
MMRNGH!
OH! OH, WATCH OUT! WHOA! OOH, CUT SCENE!
FIGHT FIGHTERS
OUT of ORDER
DR. KARATE, YOU KILLED MY FATHER AGAIN!
DR. KARATE YOU KILLED MY FATHER AGAIN !

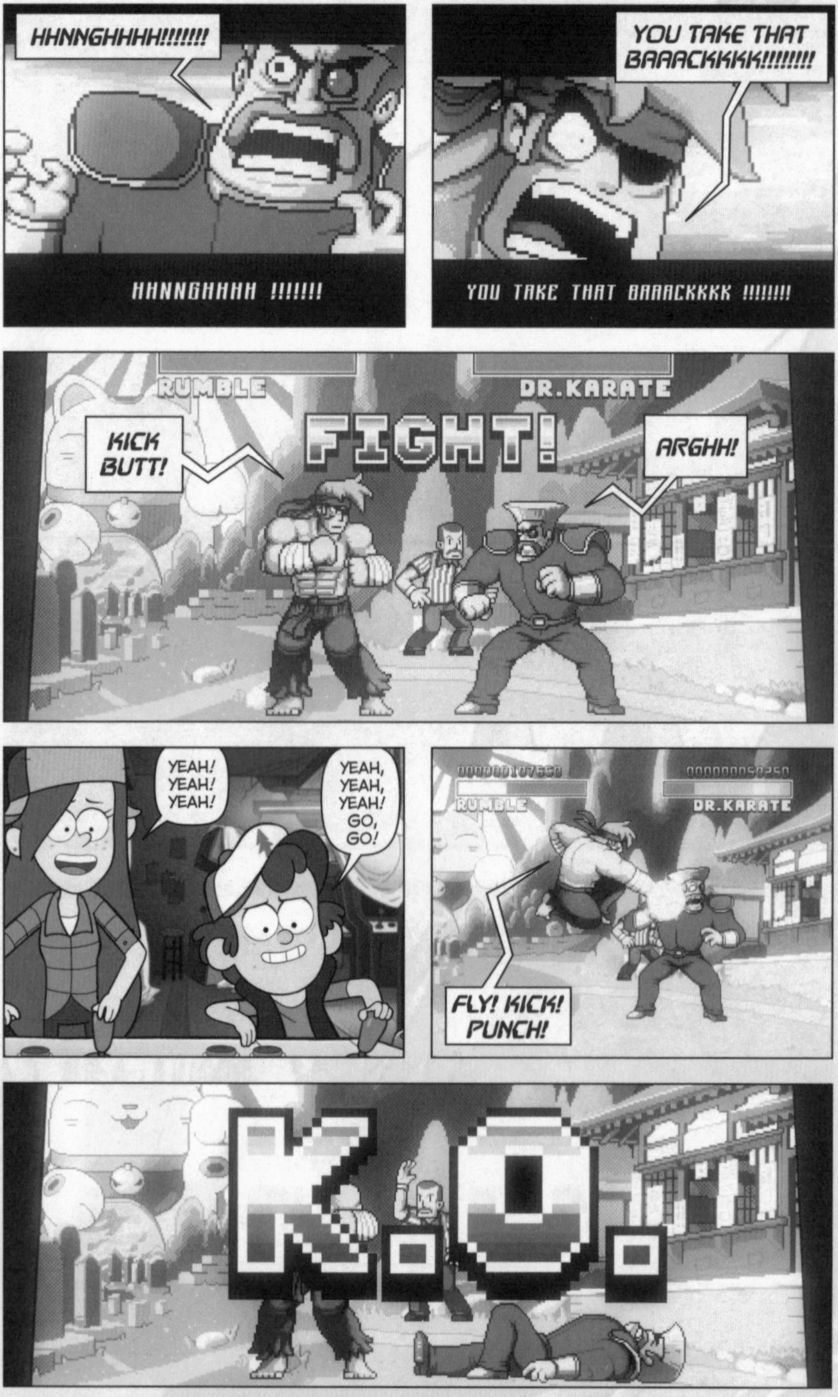
HHNNGHHHH!!!!!!!
HHNNGHHHH !!!!!!!
YOU TAKE THAT BAAACKKKK!!!!!!!!
YOU TAKE THAT BAAACKKKK !!!!!!!
RUMBLE
DR.KARATE
FIGHT!
KICK BUTT!
ARGHH!
YEAH! YEAH! YEAH!
YEAH, YEAH, YEAH! GO, GO!
RUMBLE
DR.KARATE
FLY! KICK! PUNCH!
K.O.

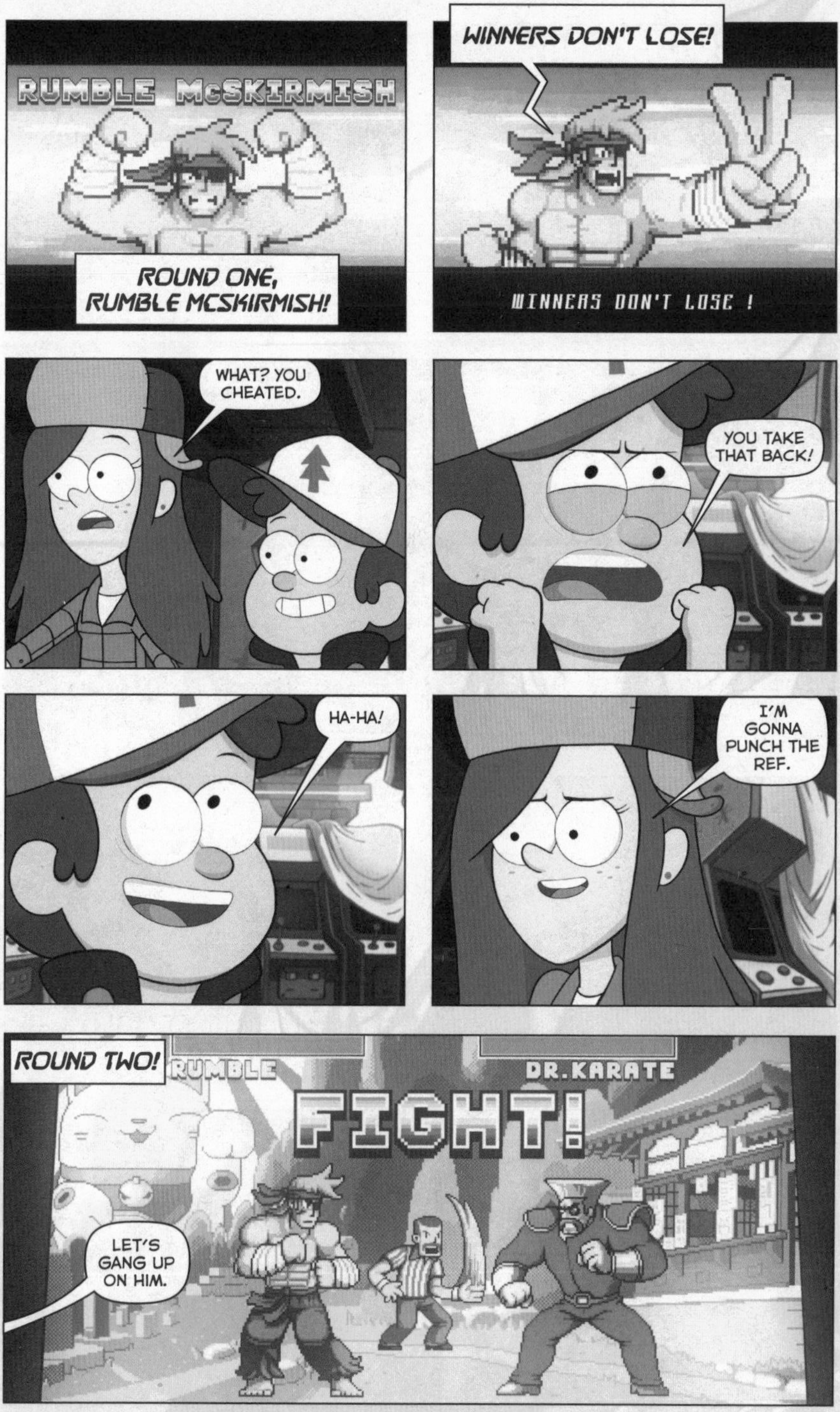
RUMBLE McSKIRMISH
ROUND ONE, RUMBLE MCSKIRMISH!
WINNERS DON'T LOSE!
WINNERS DON'T LOSE !
WHAT? YOU CHEATED.
YOU TAKE THAT BACK!
HA-HA!
I'M GONNA PUNCH THE REF.
ROUND TWO!
RUMBLE
DR.KARATE
FIGHT!
LET'S GANG UP ON HIM.

ROBBIE V
AND THE TOMBSTONES

"YOU'RE DEAD!"

HA-HA!

WHOA!

WENDY! WHAT'S UP, BABE? YEAH, JUST PUTTIN' UP SOME FLYERS FOR MY BAND. I'M LEAD GUITAR. NO BIGGIE.

ARE YOU WEARING MASCARA?

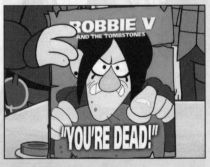

ROBBIE V
AND THE TOMBSTONES

"YOU'RE DEAD!"

IT'S EYE PAINT FOR MEN!

OH, HEY, ROBBIE, DIPPER WAS JUST SHOWING ME THIS GREAT GAME.

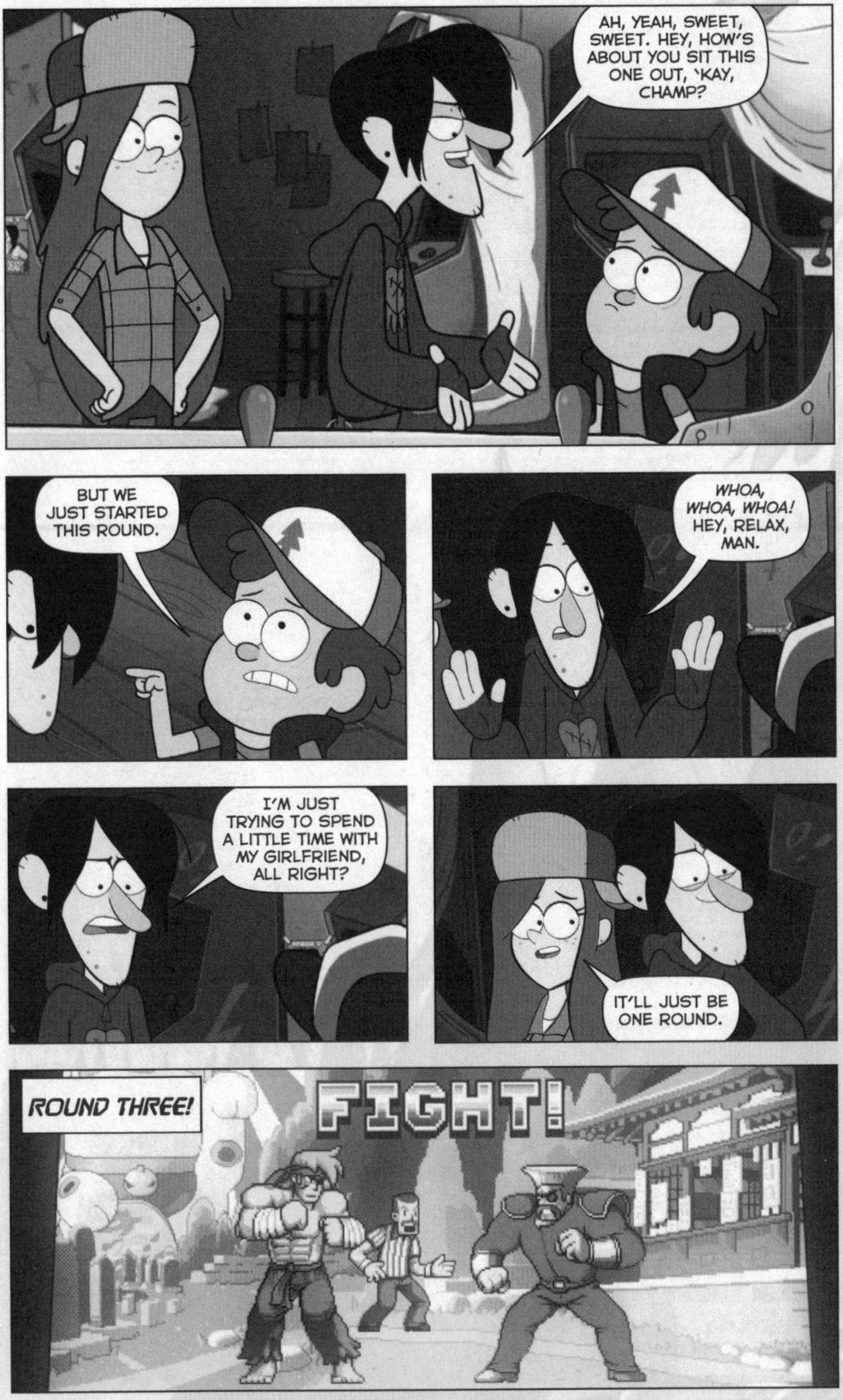
AH, YEAH, SWEET, SWEET. HEY, HOW'S ABOUT YOU SIT THIS ONE OUT, 'KAY, CHAMP?
BUT WE JUST STARTED THIS ROUND.
WHOA, WHOA, WHOA! HEY, RELAX, MAN.
I'M JUST TRYING TO SPEND A LITTLE TIME WITH MY GIRLFRIEND, ALL RIGHT?
IT'LL JUST BE ONE ROUND.
ROUND THREE!
FIGHT!

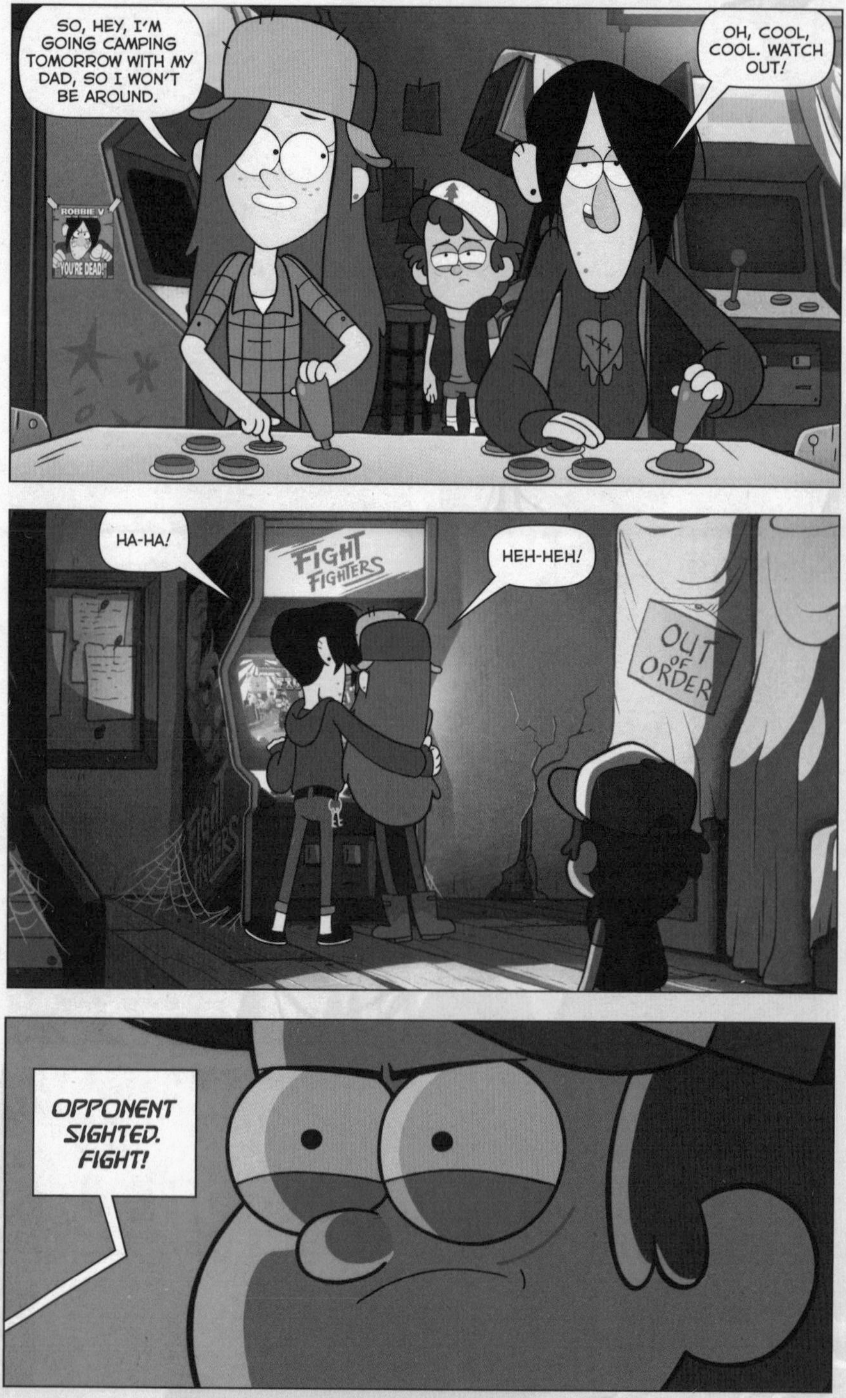
SO, HEY, I'M GOING CAMPING TOMORROW WITH MY DAD, SO I WON'T BE AROUND.
ROBBIE V
YOU'RE DEAD!
OH, COOL, COOL. WATCH OUT!
HA-HA!
FIGHT FIGHTERS
HEH-HEH!
OUT of ORDER
OPPONENT SIGHTED. FIGHT!

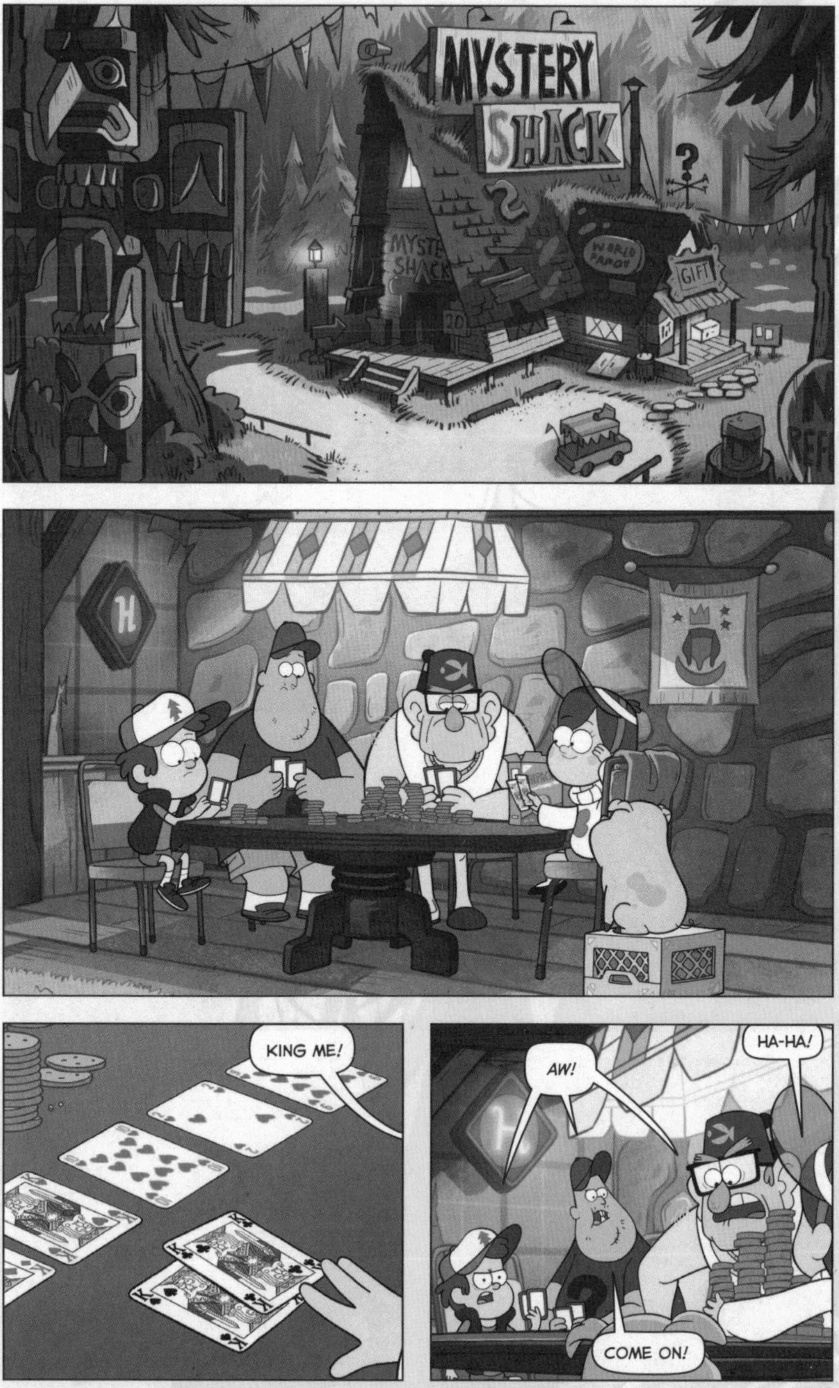
MYSTERY
SHACK
GIFT
KING ME!
AW!
HA-HA!
COME ON!

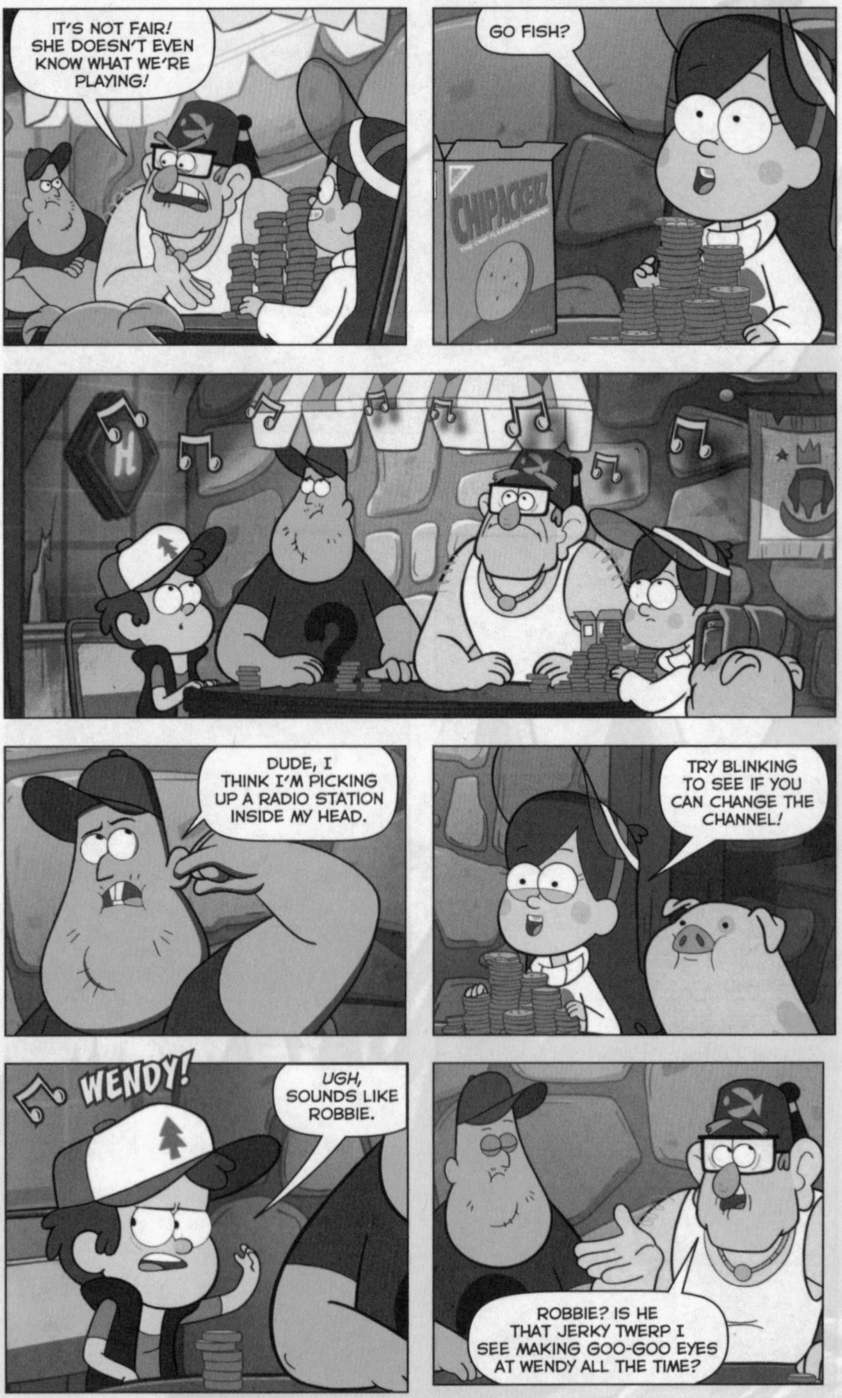
IT'S NOT FAIR! SHE DOESN'T EVEN KNOW WHAT WE'RE PLAYING!
GO FISH?
CHIPACKERZ
DUDE, I THINK I'M PICKING UP A RADIO STATION INSIDE MY HEAD.
TRY BLINKING TO SEE IF YOU CAN CHANGE THE CHANNEL!
WENDY!
UGH, SOUNDS LIKE ROBBIE.
ROBBIE? IS HE THAT JERKY TWERP I SEE MAKING GOO-GOO EYES AT WENDY ALL THE TIME?

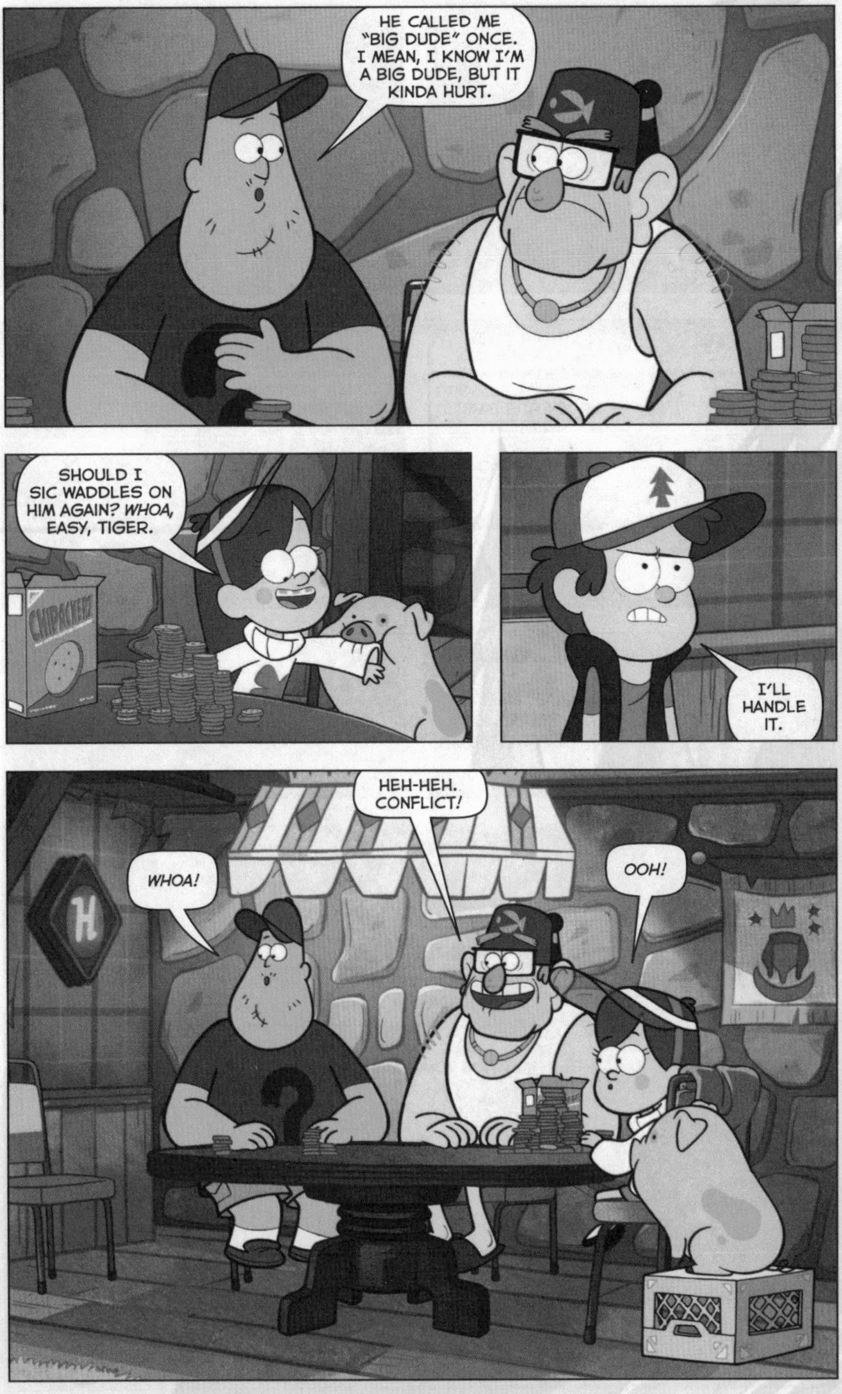

HE CALLED ME "BIG DUDE" ONCE. I MEAN, I KNOW I'M A BIG DUDE, BUT IT KINDA HURT.
SHOULD I SIC WADDLES ON HIM AGAIN? *WHOA*, EASY, TIGER.
CHIPACKERZ
I'LL HANDLE IT.
HEH-HEH. CONFLICT!
WHOA!
OOH!

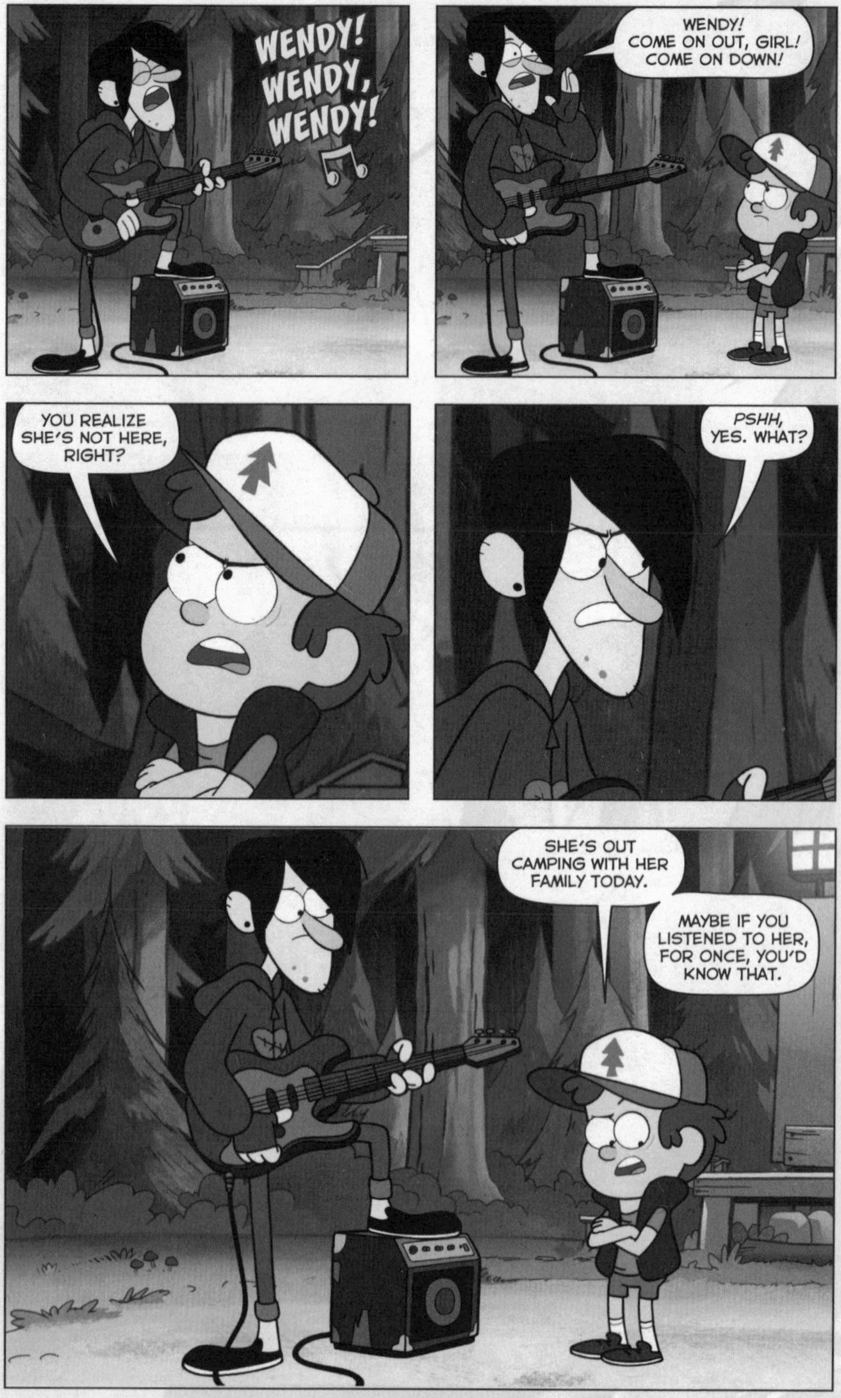
WENDY! WENDY, WENDY!
WENDY! COME ON OUT, GIRL! COME ON DOWN!
YOU REALIZE SHE'S NOT HERE, RIGHT?
PSHH, YES. WHAT?
SHE'S OUT CAMPING WITH HER FAMILY TODAY.
MAYBE IF YOU LISTENED TO HER, FOR ONCE, YOU'D KNOW THAT.

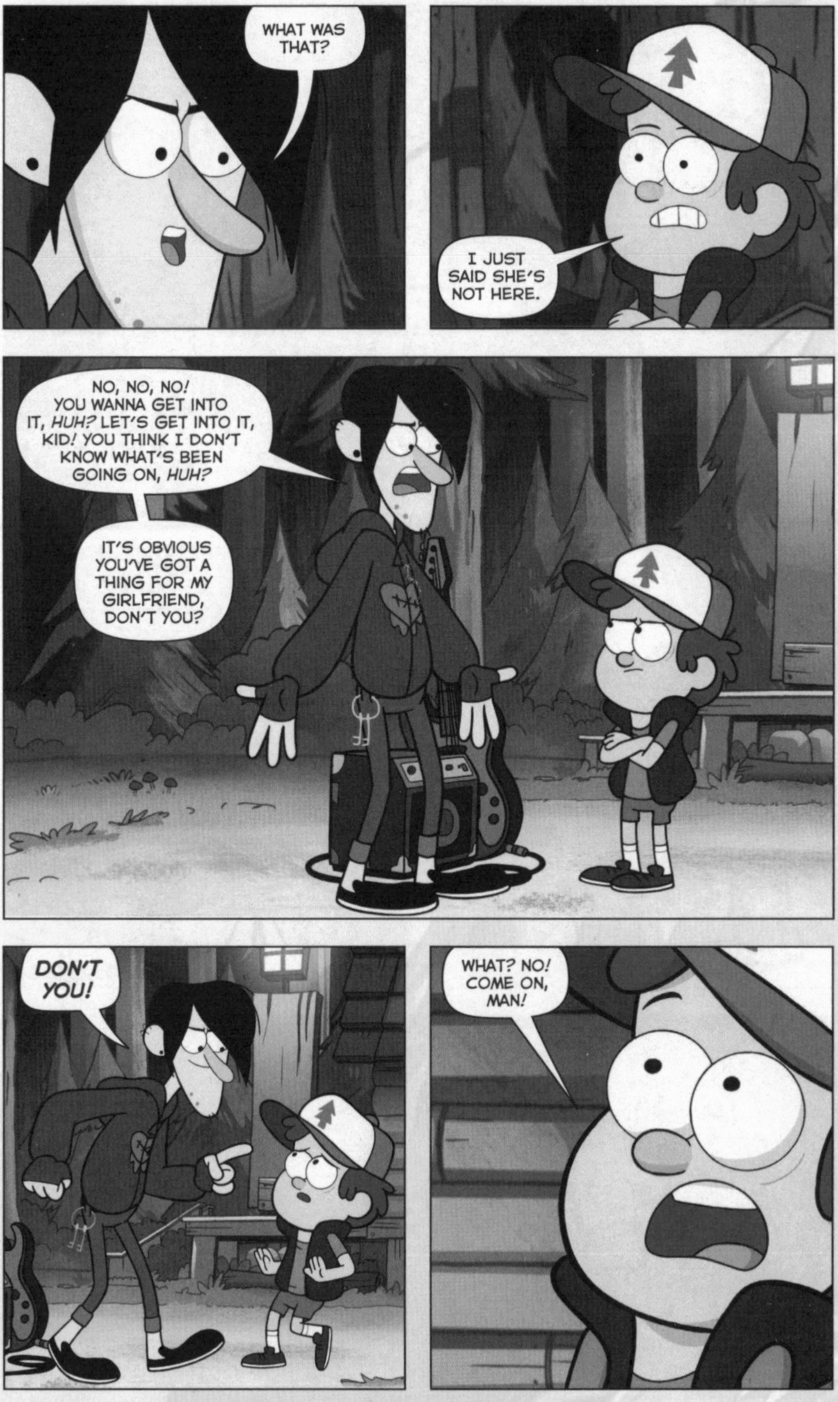
WHAT WAS THAT?
I JUST SAID SHE'S NOT HERE.
NO, NO, NO! YOU WANNA GET INTO IT, *HUH?* LET'S GET INTO IT, KID! YOU THINK I DON'T KNOW WHAT'S BEEN GOING ON, *HUH?*
IT'S OBVIOUS YOU'VE GOT A THING FOR MY GIRLFRIEND, DON'T YOU?
DON'T YOU!
WHAT? NO! COME ON, MAN!

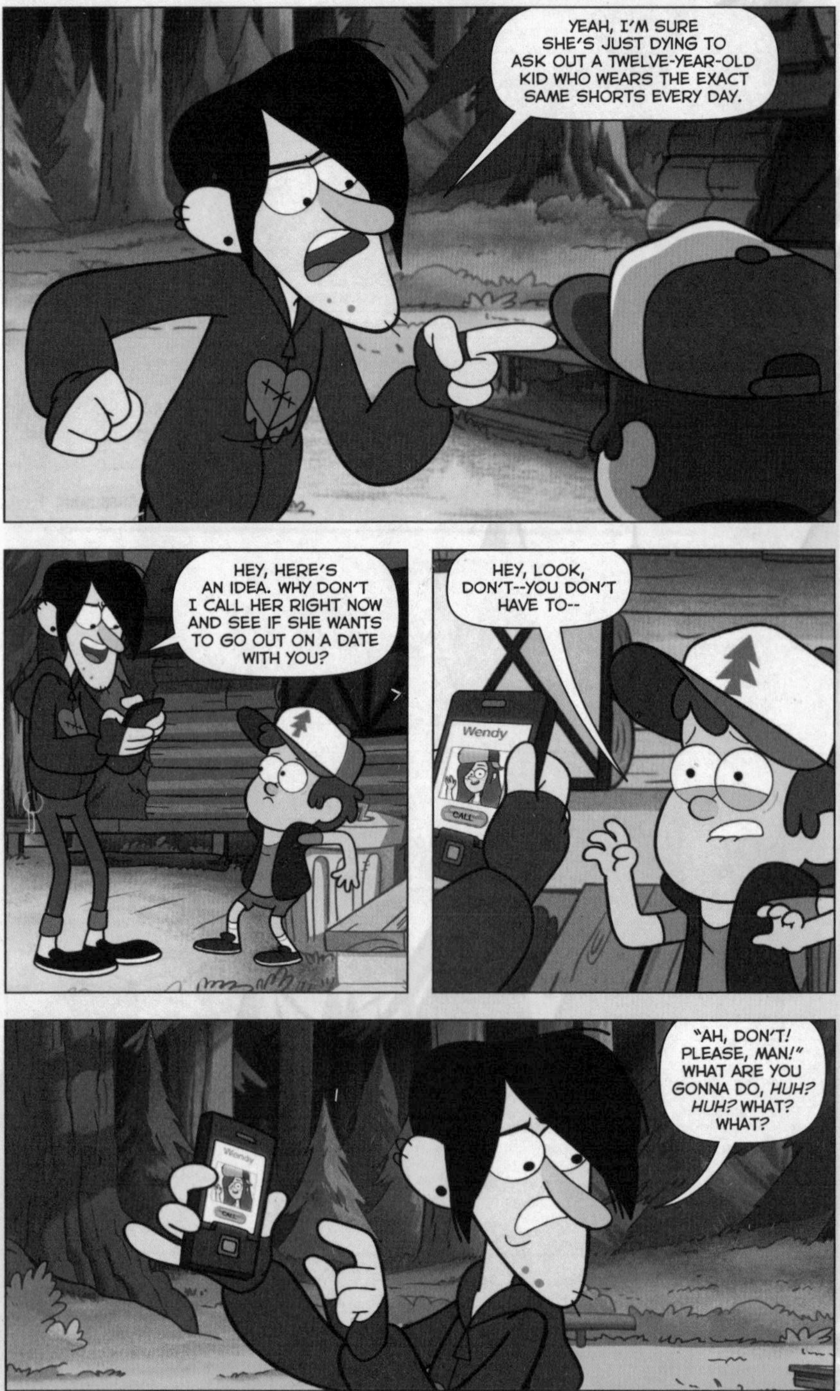
YEAH, I'M SURE SHE'S JUST DYING TO ASK OUT A TWELVE-YEAR-OLD KID WHO WEARS THE EXACT SAME SHORTS EVERY DAY.
HEY, HERE'S AN IDEA. WHY DON'T I CALL HER RIGHT NOW AND SEE IF SHE WANTS TO GO OUT ON A DATE WITH YOU?
HEY, LOOK, DON'T--YOU DON'T HAVE TO--
Wendy
CALL
"AH, DON'T! PLEASE, MAN!" WHAT ARE YOU GONNA DO, *HUH? HUH?* WHAT? WHAT?
Wendy

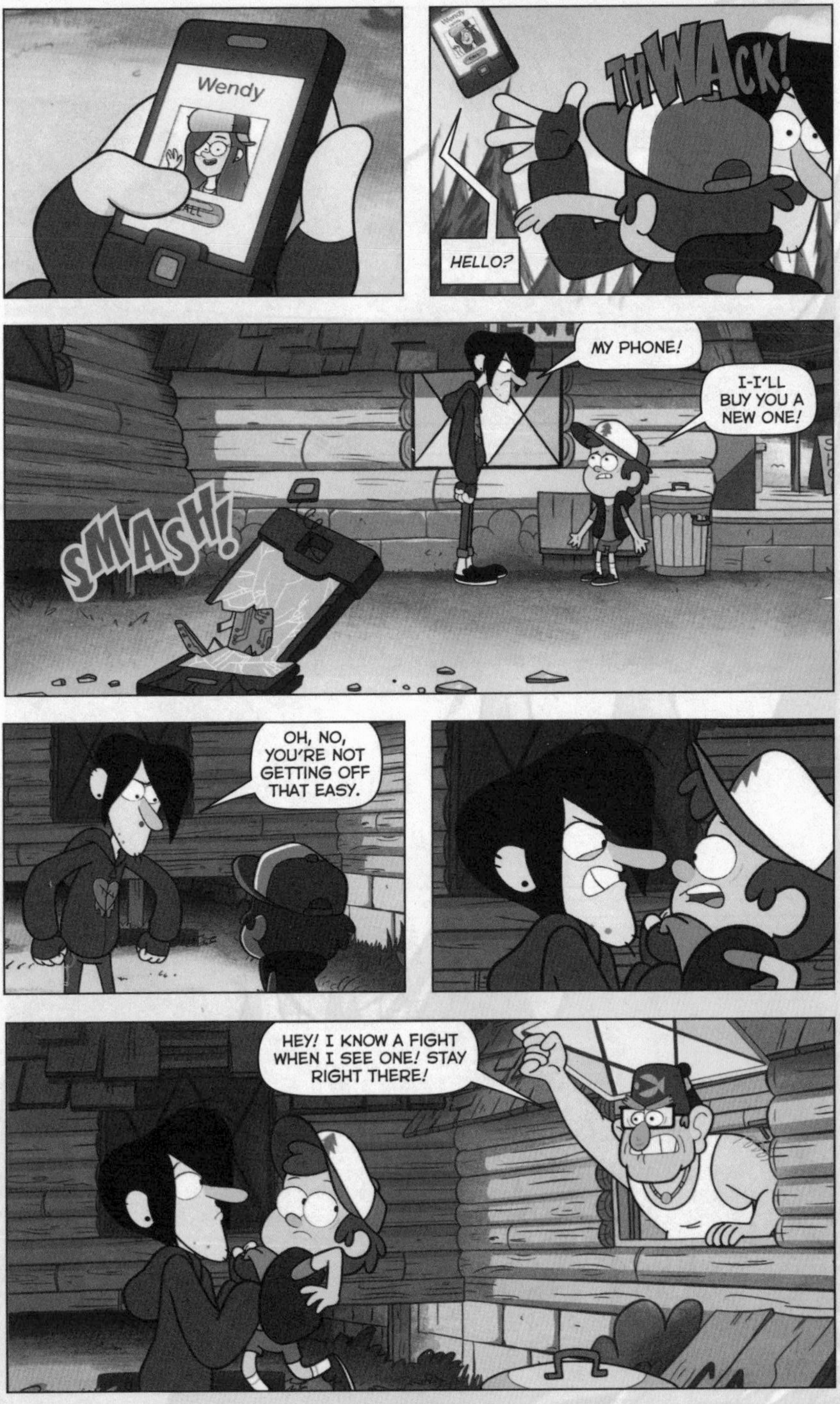
Wendy
THWACK!
HELLO?
MY PHONE!
I-I'LL BUY YOU A NEW ONE!
SMASH!
OH, NO, YOU'RE NOT GETTING OFF THAT EASY.
HEY! I KNOW A FIGHT WHEN I SEE ONE! STAY RIGHT THERE!

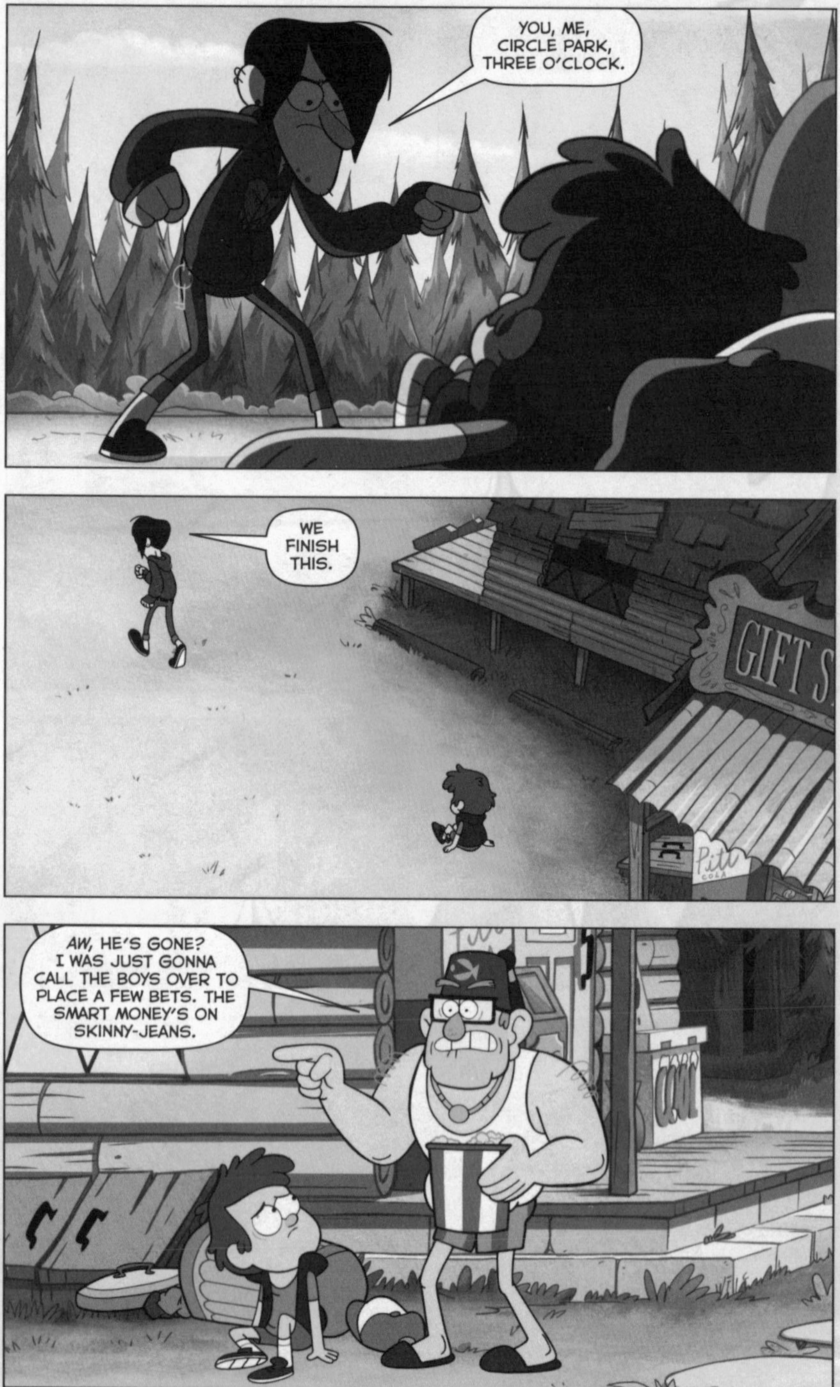
YOU, ME, CIRCLE PARK, THREE O'CLOCK.
WE FINISH THIS.
GIFT S
Pitt COLA
AW, HE'S GONE? I WAS JUST GONNA CALL THE BOYS OVER TO PLACE A FEW BETS. THE SMART MONEY'S ON SKINNY-JEANS.

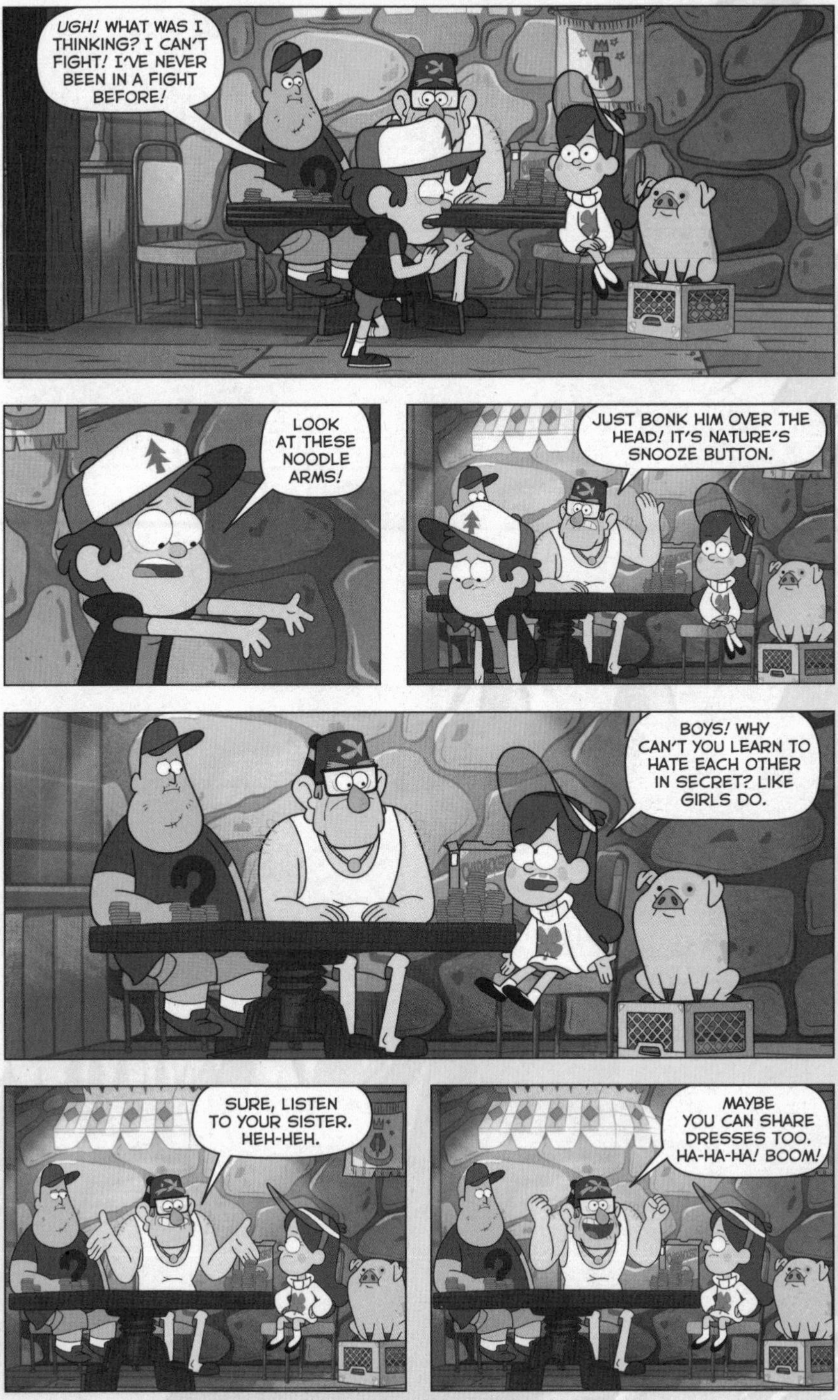
UGH! WHAT WAS I THINKING? I CAN'T FIGHT! I'VE NEVER BEEN IN A FIGHT BEFORE!
LOOK AT THESE NOODLE ARMS!
JUST BONK HIM OVER THE HEAD! IT'S NATURE'S SNOOZE BUTTON.
BOYS! WHY CAN'T YOU LEARN TO HATE EACH OTHER IN SECRET? LIKE GIRLS DO.
SURE, LISTEN TO YOUR SISTER. HEH-HEH.
MAYBE YOU CAN SHARE DRESSES TOO. HA-HA-HA! BOOM!

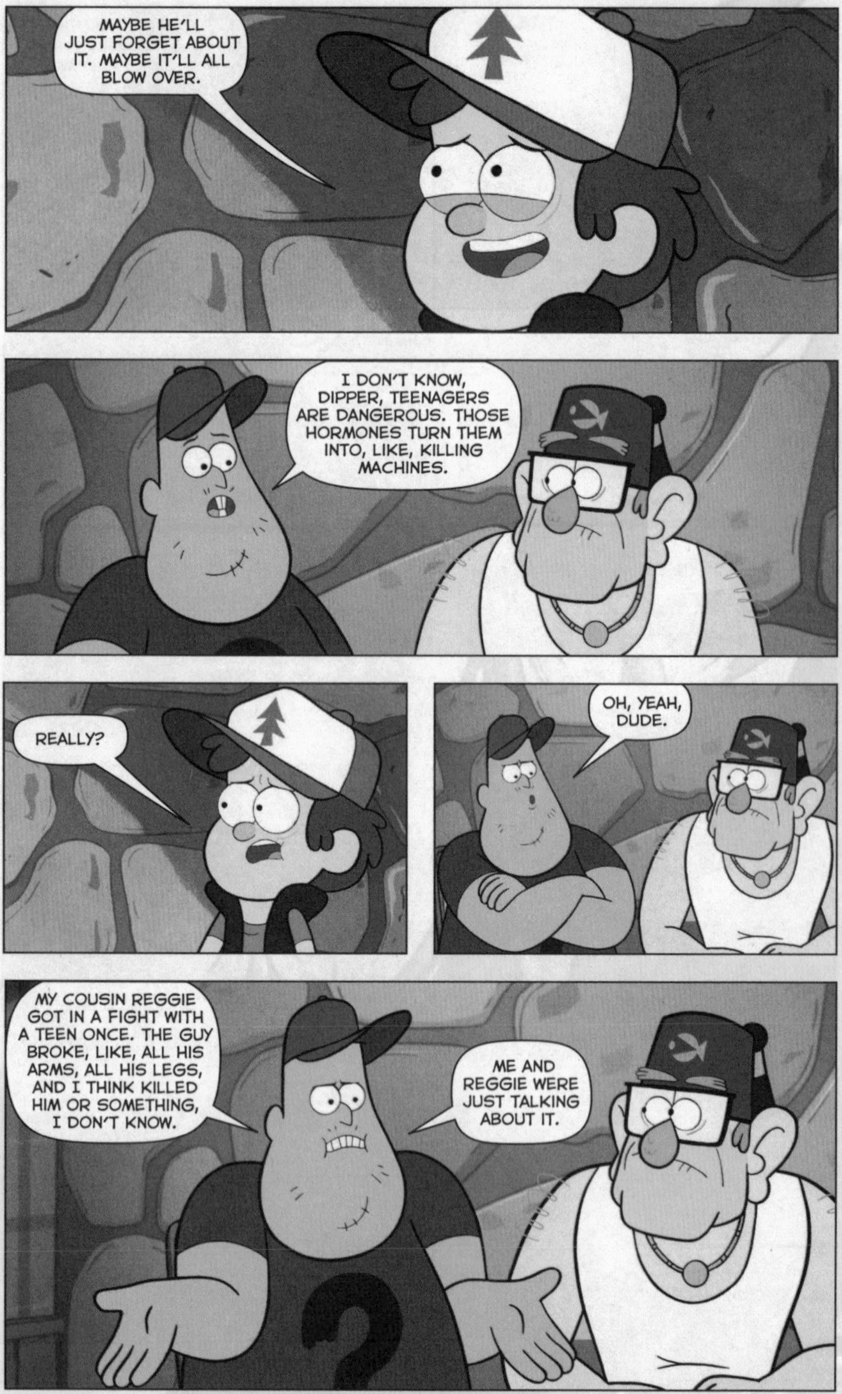
MAYBE HE'LL JUST FORGET ABOUT IT. MAYBE IT'LL ALL BLOW OVER.
I DON'T KNOW, DIPPER, TEENAGERS ARE DANGEROUS. THOSE HORMONES TURN THEM INTO, LIKE, KILLING MACHINES.
REALLY?
OH, YEAH, DUDE.
MY COUSIN REGGIE GOT IN A FIGHT WITH A TEEN ONCE. THE GUY BROKE, LIKE, ALL HIS ARMS, ALL HIS LEGS, AND I THINK KILLED HIM OR SOMETHING, I DON'T KNOW.
ME AND REGGIE WERE JUST TALKING ABOUT IT.

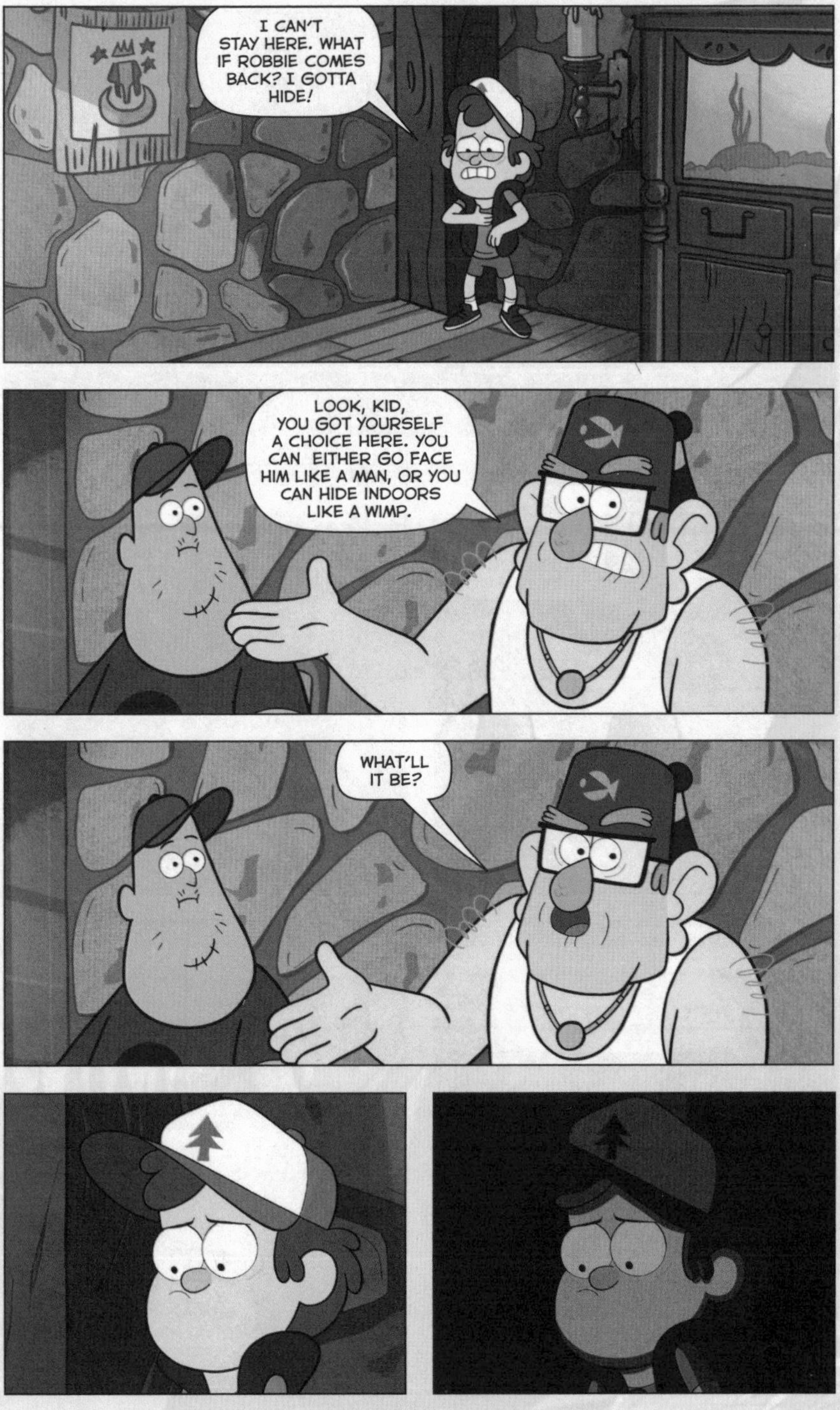
I CAN'T STAY HERE. WHAT IF ROBBIE COMES BACK? I GOTTA HIDE!
LOOK, KID, YOU GOT YOURSELF A CHOICE HERE. YOU CAN EITHER GO FACE HIM LIKE A MAN, OR YOU CAN HIDE INDOORS LIKE A WIMP.
WHAT'LL IT BE?

WIMP IT IS!

LAZER WIZARD

00.928 998.251

COME ON, SOOS, ROBBIE'S, LIKE, TWICE MY SIZE!

LAZER WIZARD

00.928 998.251

I MEAN, WHAT WOULD GETTING MYSELF KILLED ACCOMPLISH?

LAZER WIZARD

I JUST NEED TO HIDE HERE UNTIL THREE O'CLOCK PASSES.

LAZER WIZARD

11:29

UGH! THIS DAY WILL NEVER END!

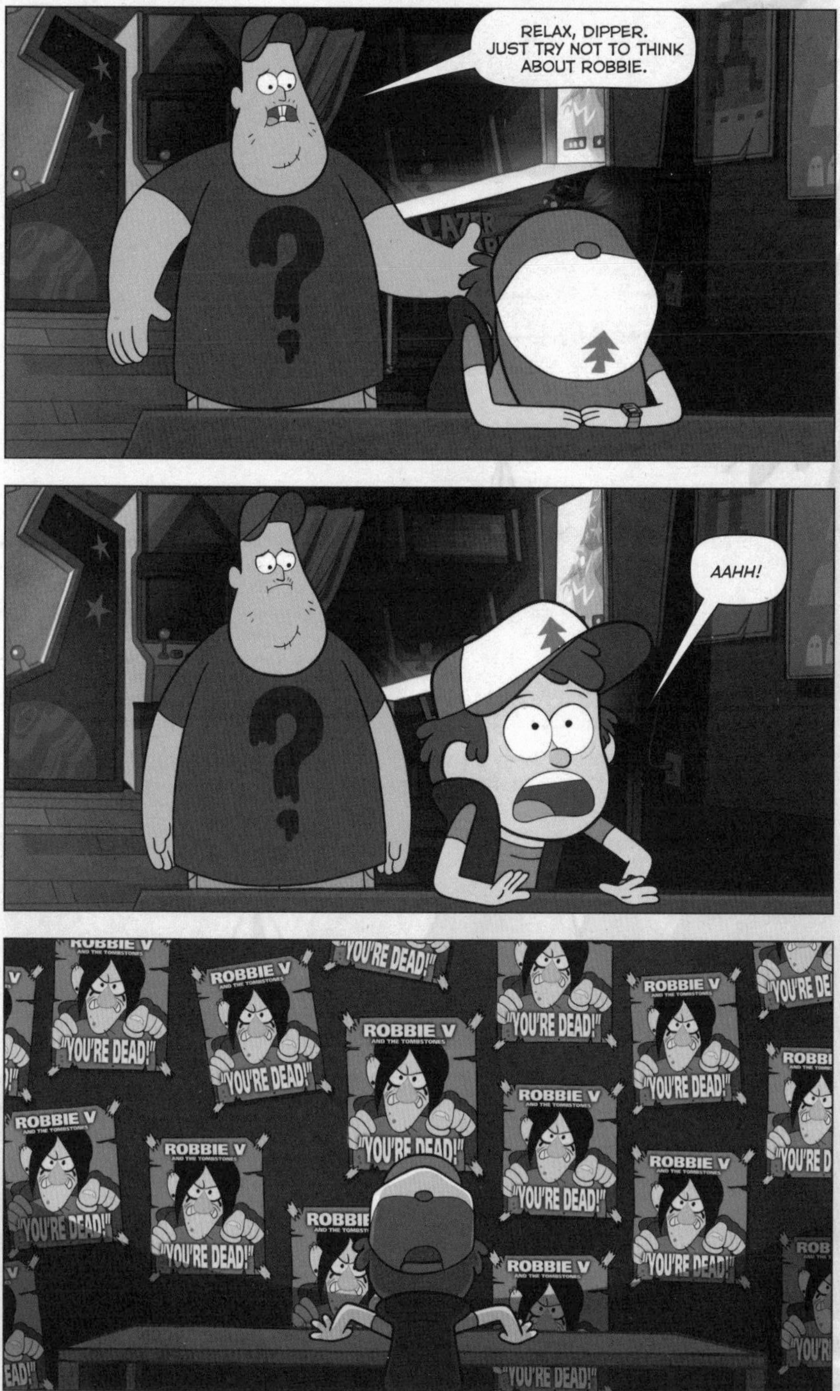
RELAX, DIPPER. JUST TRY NOT TO THINK ABOUT ROBBIE.
AAHH!
ROBBIE V
AND THE TOMBSTONES
"YOU'RE DEAD!"

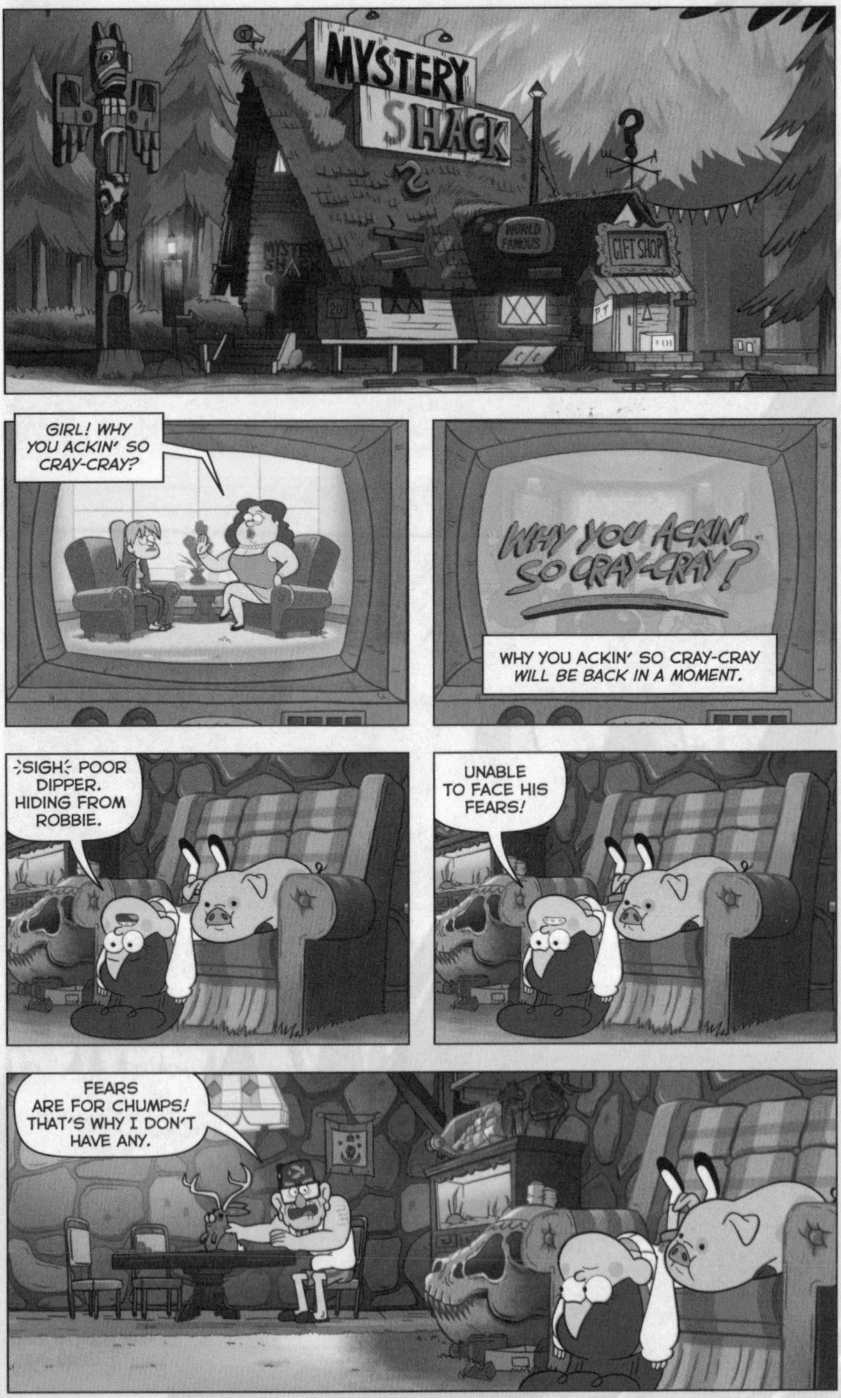
MYSTERY SHACK
GIFT SHOP
GIRL! WHY YOU ACKIN' SO CRAY-CRAY?
WHY YOU ACKIN' SO CRAY-CRAY?
WHY YOU ACKIN' SO CRAY-CRAY WILL BE BACK IN A MOMENT.
-SIGH- POOR DIPPER. HIDING FROM ROBBIE.
UNABLE TO FACE HIS FEARS!
FEARS ARE FOR CHUMPS! THAT'S WHY I DON'T HAVE ANY.

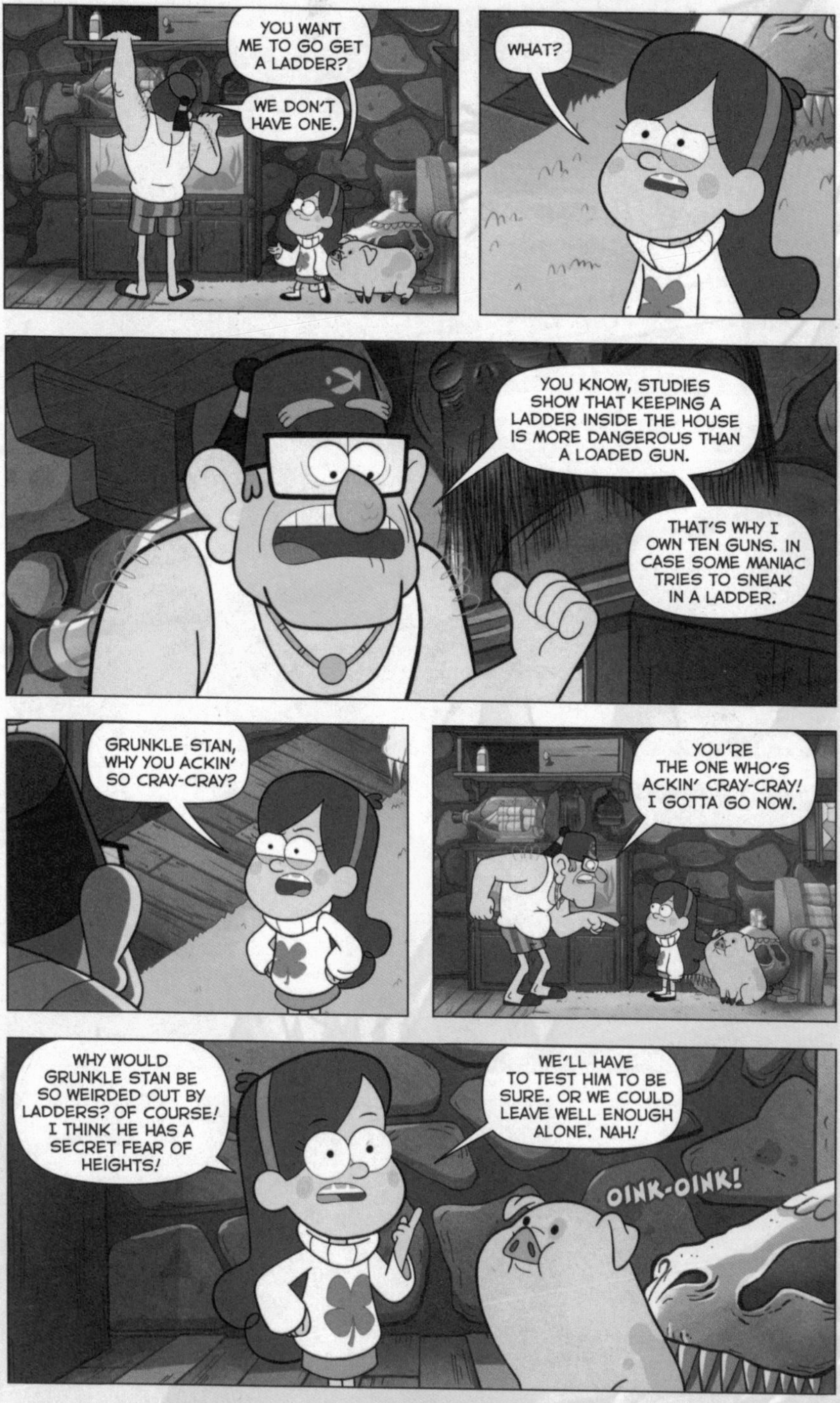
YOU WANT ME TO GO GET A LADDER?
WE DON'T HAVE ONE.
WHAT?
YOU KNOW, STUDIES SHOW THAT KEEPING A LADDER INSIDE THE HOUSE IS MORE DANGEROUS THAN A LOADED GUN.
THAT'S WHY I OWN TEN GUNS. IN CASE SOME MANIAC TRIES TO SNEAK IN A LADDER.
GRUNKLE STAN, WHY YOU ACKIN' SO CRAY-CRAY?
YOU'RE THE ONE WHO'S ACKIN' CRAY-CRAY! I GOTTA GO NOW.
WHY WOULD GRUNKLE STAN BE SO WEIRDED OUT BY LADDERS? OF COURSE! I THINK HE HAS A SECRET FEAR OF HEIGHTS!
WE'LL HAVE TO TEST HIM TO BE SURE. OR WE COULD LEAVE WELL ENOUGH ALONE. NAH!
OINK-OINK!

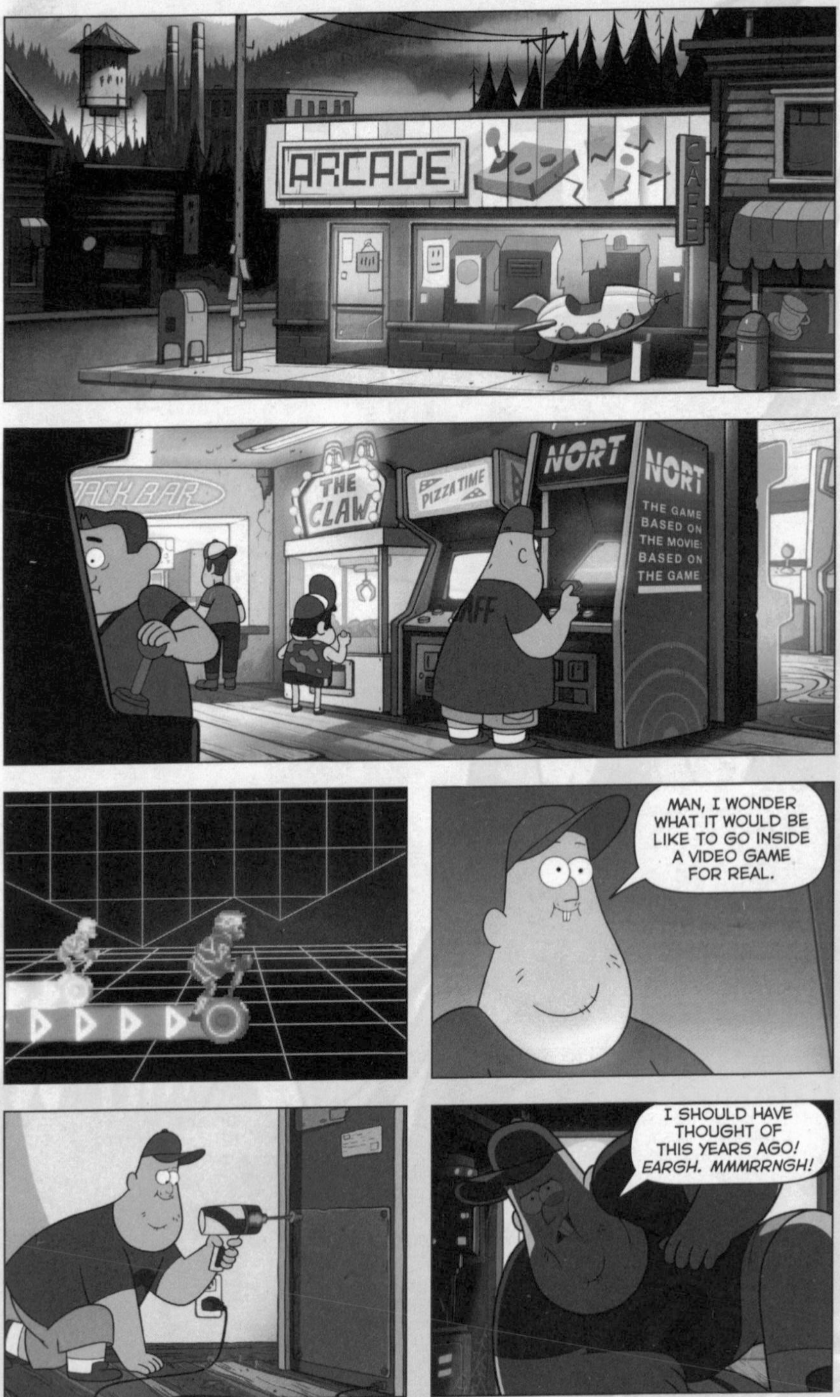
ARCADE
CAFE
THE CLAW
PIZZA TIME
NORT
NORT
THE GAME BASED ON THE MOVIE: BASED ON THE GAME
MAN, I WONDER WHAT IT WOULD BE LIKE TO GO INSIDE A VIDEO GAME FOR REAL.
I SHOULD HAVE THOUGHT OF THIS YEARS AGO! *EARGH. MMMRRNGH!*

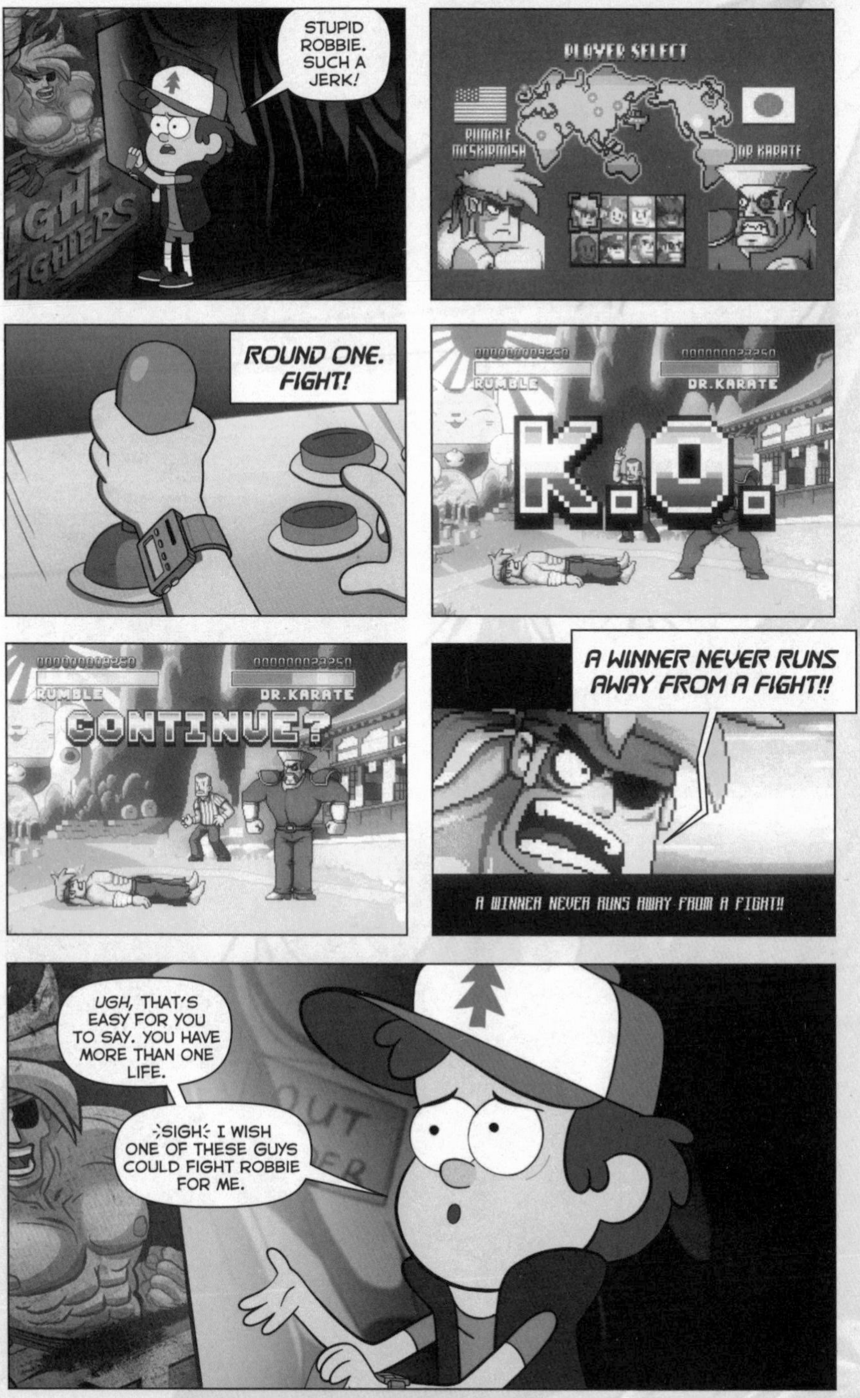

STUPID ROBBIE. SUCH A JERK!
PLAYER SELECT
RUMBLE McSKIRMISH
DR KARATE
ROUND ONE. FIGHT!
RUMBLE
DR.KARATE
K.O.
RUMBLE
DR.KARATE
CONTINUE?
A WINNER NEVER RUNS AWAY FROM A FIGHT!!
A WINNER NEVER RUNS AWAY FROM A FIGHT!!
UGH, THAT'S EASY FOR YOU TO SAY. YOU HAVE MORE THAN ONE LIFE.
SIGH I WISH ONE OF THESE GUYS COULD FIGHT ROBBIE FOR ME.

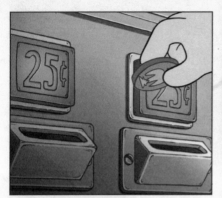

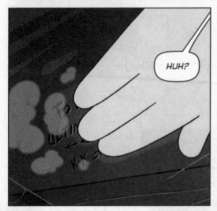

HUH?

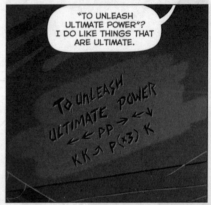

"TO UNLEASH ULTIMATE POWER"? I DO LIKE THINGS THAT ARE ULTIMATE.

TO UNLEASH ULTIMATE POWER
<< PP >< ↓
KK ↗ P(×3) K

BACK, BACK, HOLD, FORWARD, BACK, FORWARD, DOWN, HOLD, QUARTER CIRCLE, FORWARD, TRIPLE PUNCH!

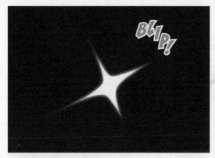

BLIP!

I GUESS IT DIDN'T WORK.

FIGHT FIGHTERS

...SOOS?

SELECT YOUR CHARACTER!

UM, RUMBLE MCSKIRMISH?

FEET– FEET–FEET– SPINNING– KICK!

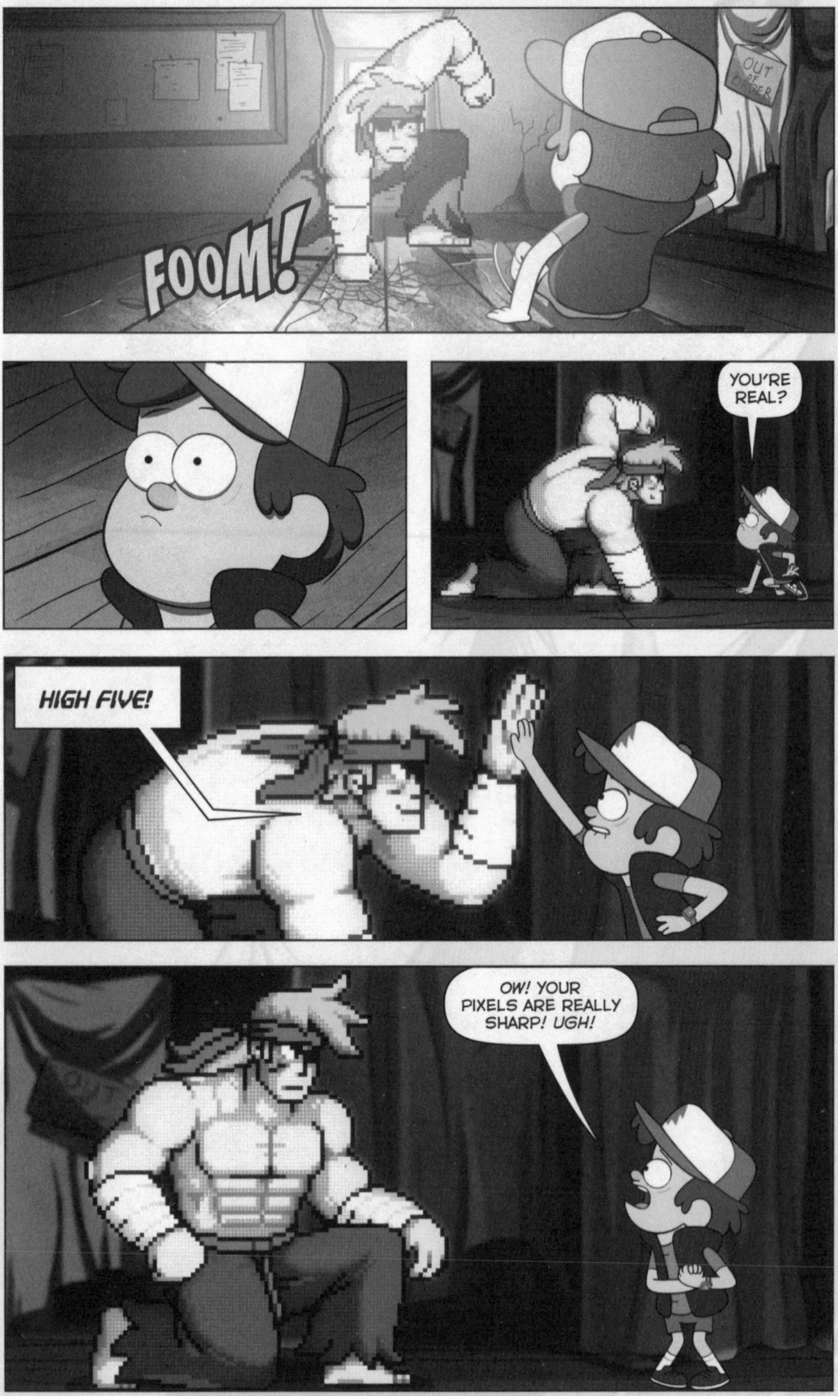
FOOM!
OUT OF ORDER
YOU'RE REAL?
HIGH FIVE!
OW! YOUR PIXELS ARE REALLY SHARP! UGH!

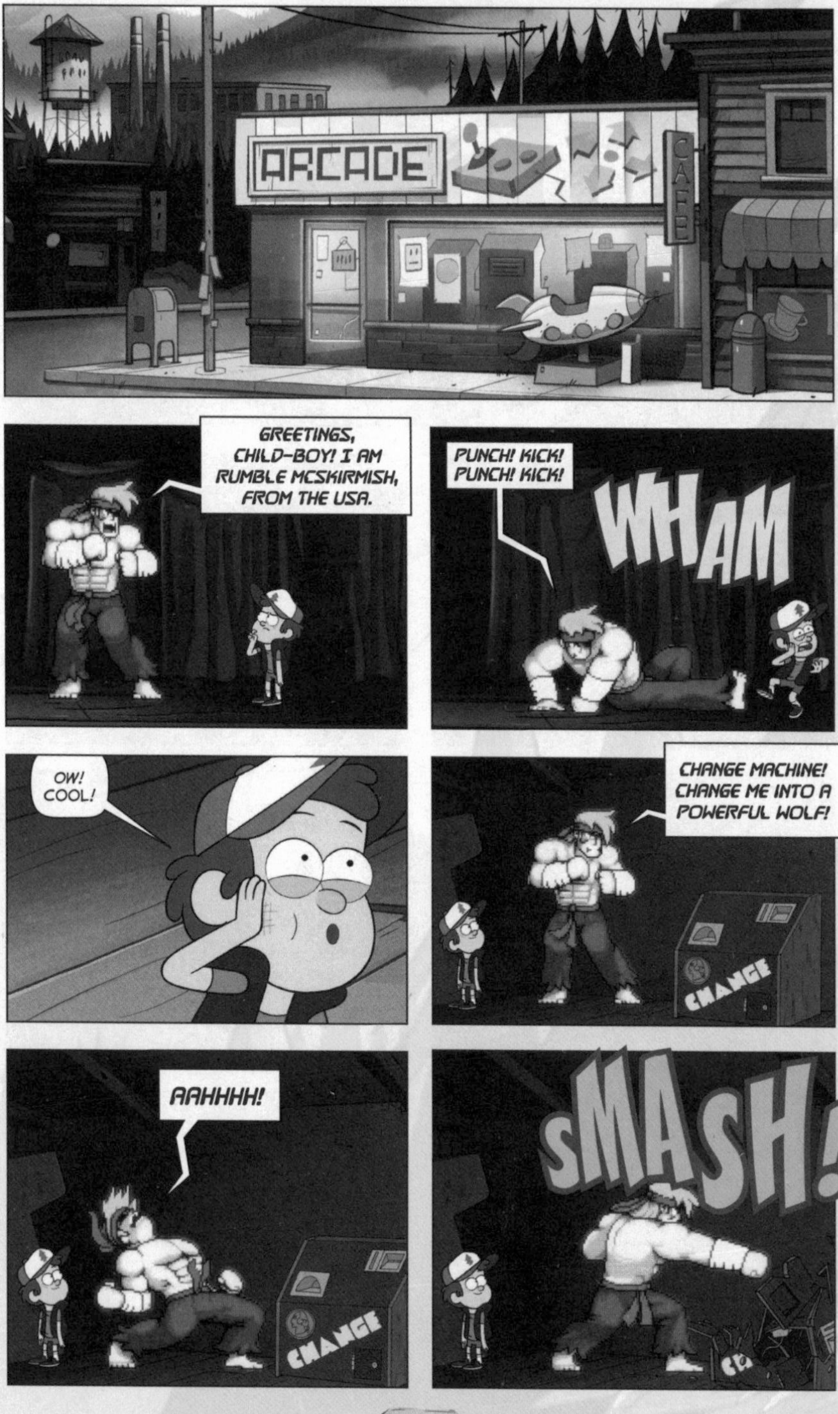
ARCADE
CAFE
GREETINGS, CHILD-BOY! I AM RUMBLE MCSKIRMISH, FROM THE USA.
PUNCH! KICK! PUNCH! KICK!
WHAM
OW! COOL!
CHANGE MACHINE! CHANGE ME INTO A POWERFUL WOLF!
CHANGE
AAHHHH!
CHANGE
SMASH!

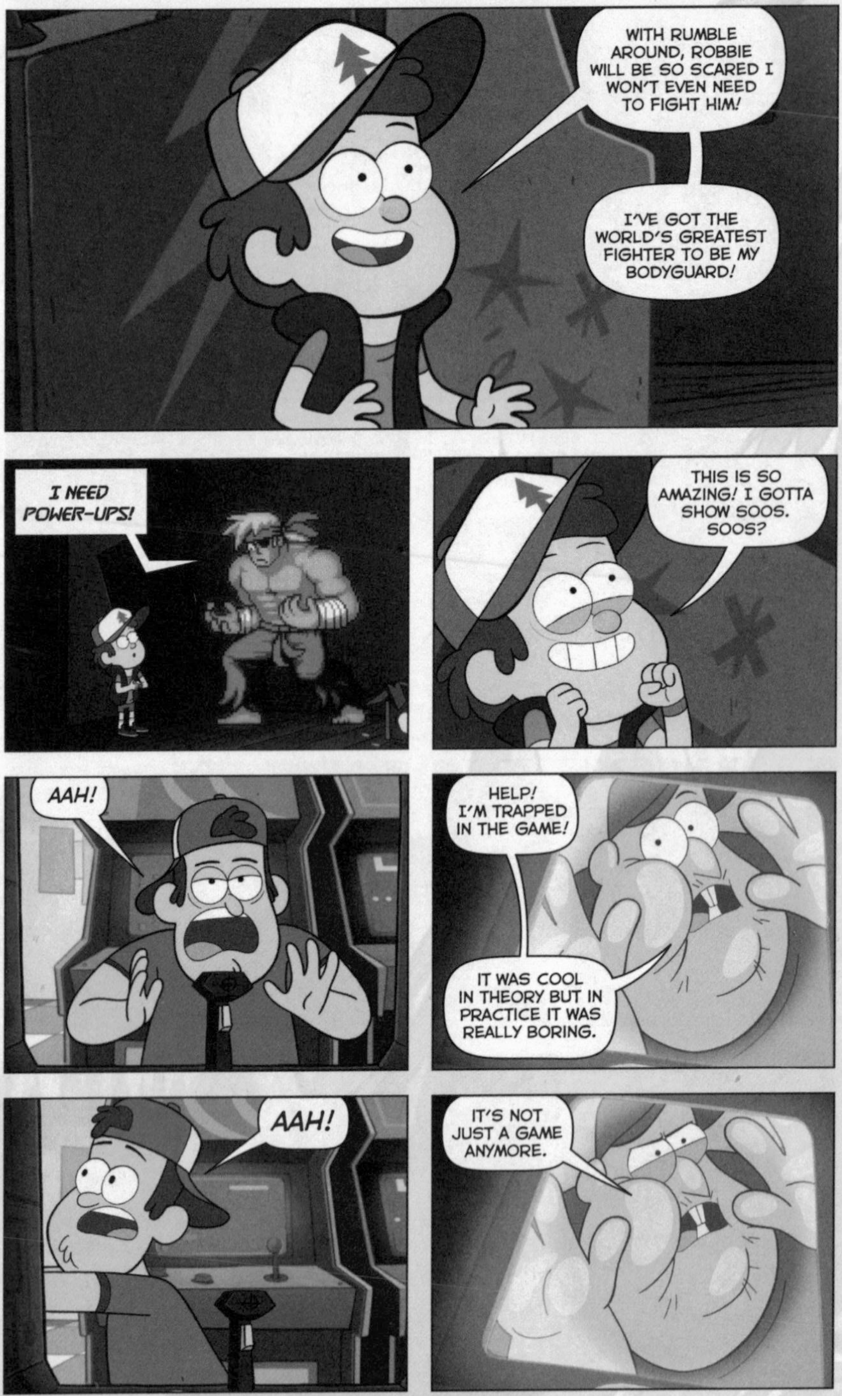
WITH RUMBLE AROUND, ROBBIE WILL BE SO SCARED I WON'T EVEN NEED TO FIGHT HIM!
I'VE GOT THE WORLD'S GREATEST FIGHTER TO BE MY BODYGUARD!
I NEED POWER-UPS!
THIS IS SO AMAZING! I GOTTA SHOW SOOS. SOOS?
AAH!
HELP! I'M TRAPPED IN THE GAME!
IT WAS COOL IN THEORY BUT IN PRACTICE IT WAS REALLY BORING.
AAH!
IT'S NOT JUST A GAME ANYMORE.

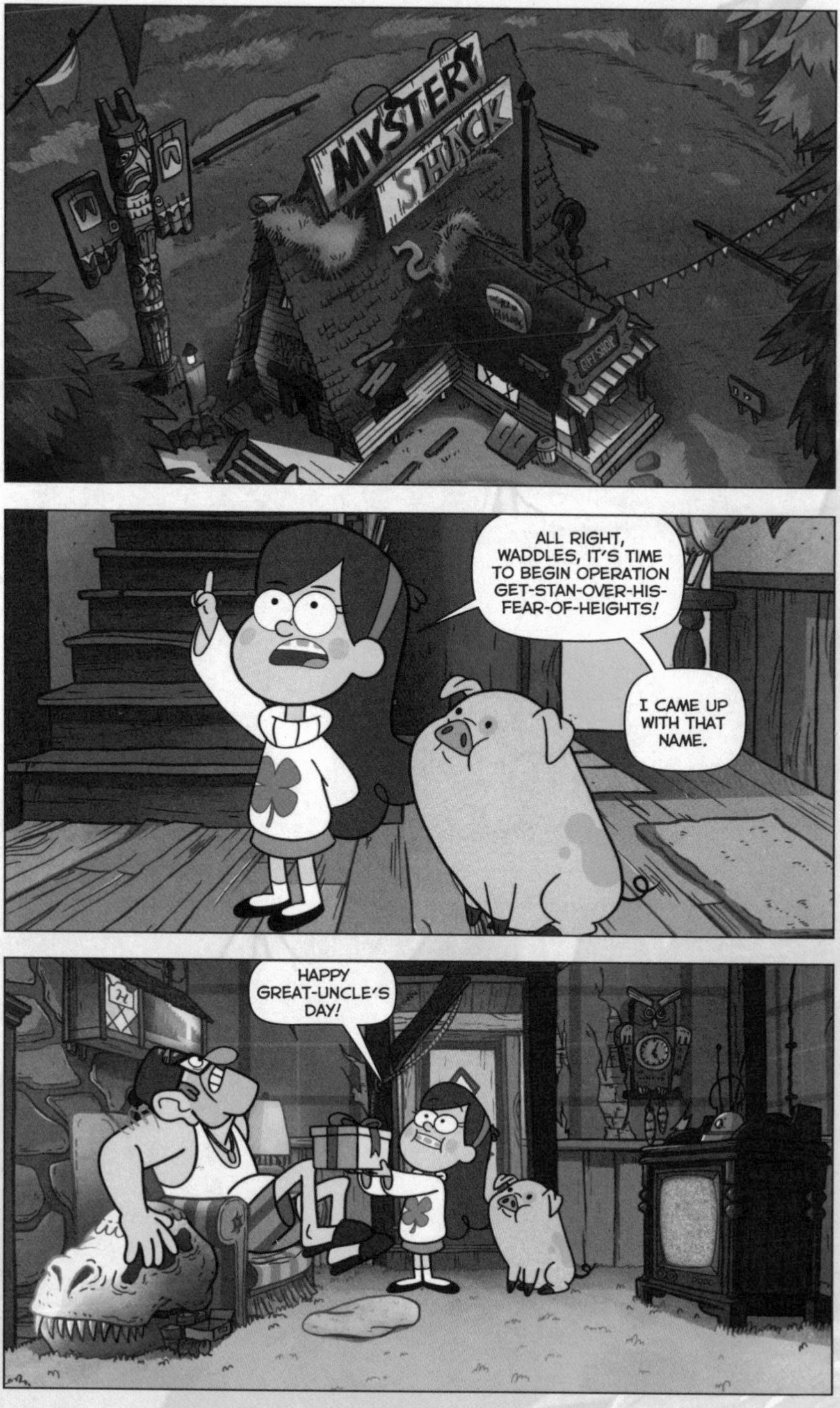
MYSTERY
SHACK
ALL RIGHT, WADDLES, IT'S TIME TO BEGIN OPERATION GET-STAN-OVER-HIS-FEAR-OF-HEIGHTS!
I CAME UP WITH THAT NAME.
HAPPY GREAT-UNCLE'S DAY!

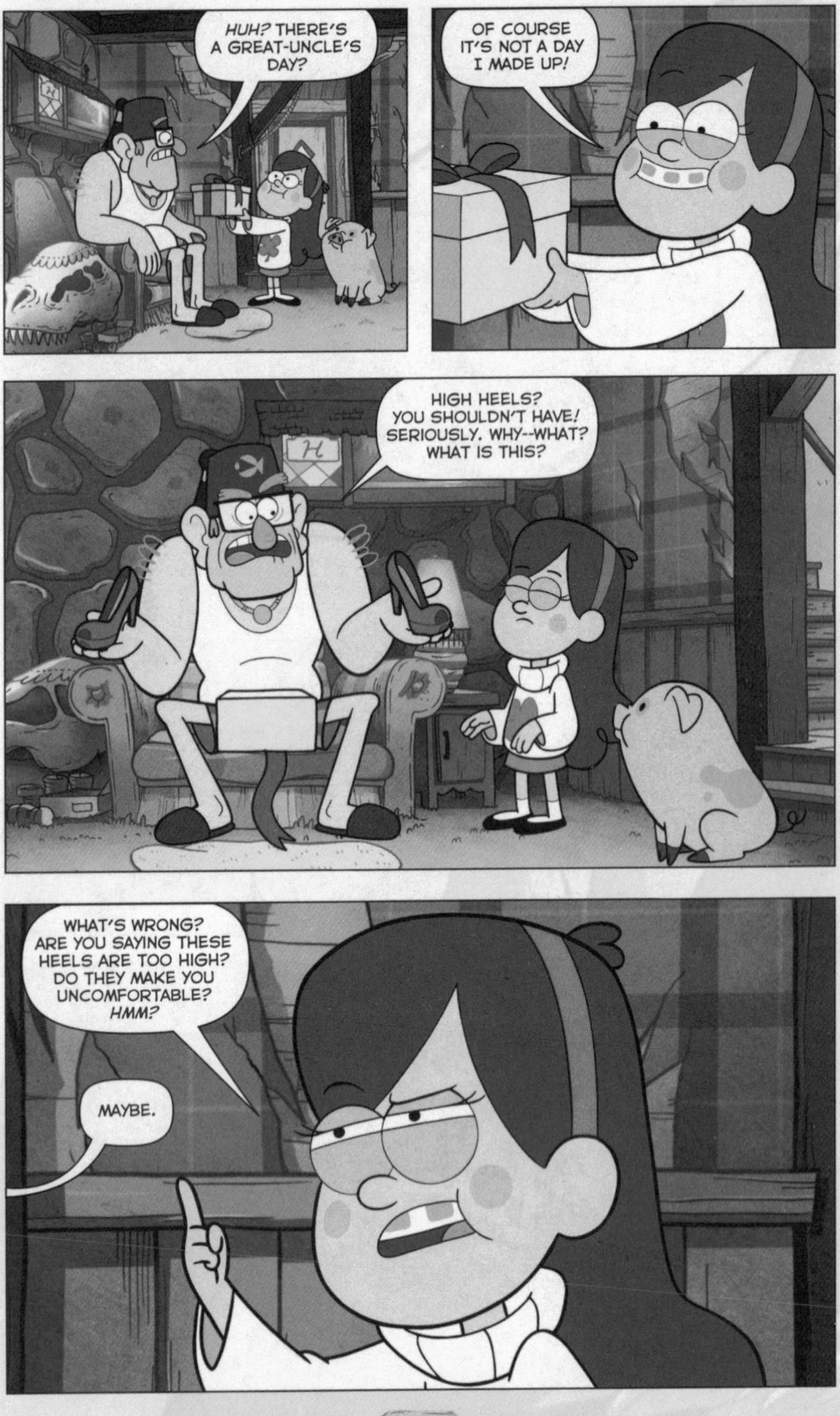
HUH? THERE'S A GREAT-UNCLE'S DAY?
OF COURSE IT'S NOT A DAY I MADE UP!
HIGH HEELS? YOU SHOULDN'T HAVE! SERIOUSLY. WHY--WHAT? WHAT IS THIS?
WHAT'S WRONG? ARE YOU SAYING THESE HEELS ARE TOO HIGH? DO THEY MAKE YOU UNCOMFORTABLE? HMM?
MAYBE.

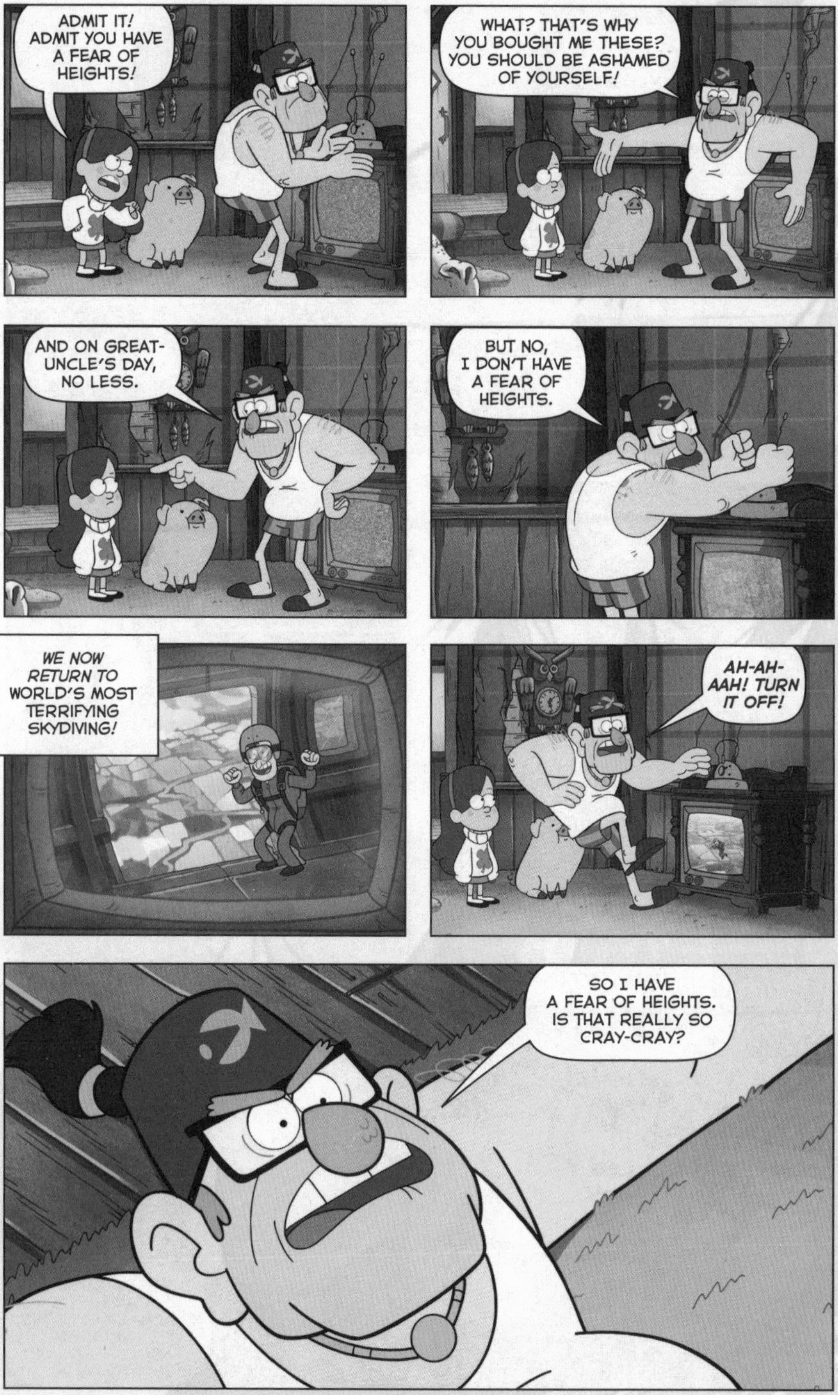
ADMIT IT! ADMIT YOU HAVE A FEAR OF HEIGHTS!
WHAT? THAT'S WHY YOU BOUGHT ME THESE? YOU SHOULD BE ASHAMED OF YOURSELF!
AND ON GREAT-UNCLE'S DAY, NO LESS.
BUT NO, I DON'T HAVE A FEAR OF HEIGHTS.
WE NOW RETURN TO WORLD'S MOST TERRIFYING SKYDIVING!
AH-AH-AAH! TURN IT OFF!
SO I HAVE A FEAR OF HEIGHTS. IS THAT REALLY SO CRAY-CRAY?

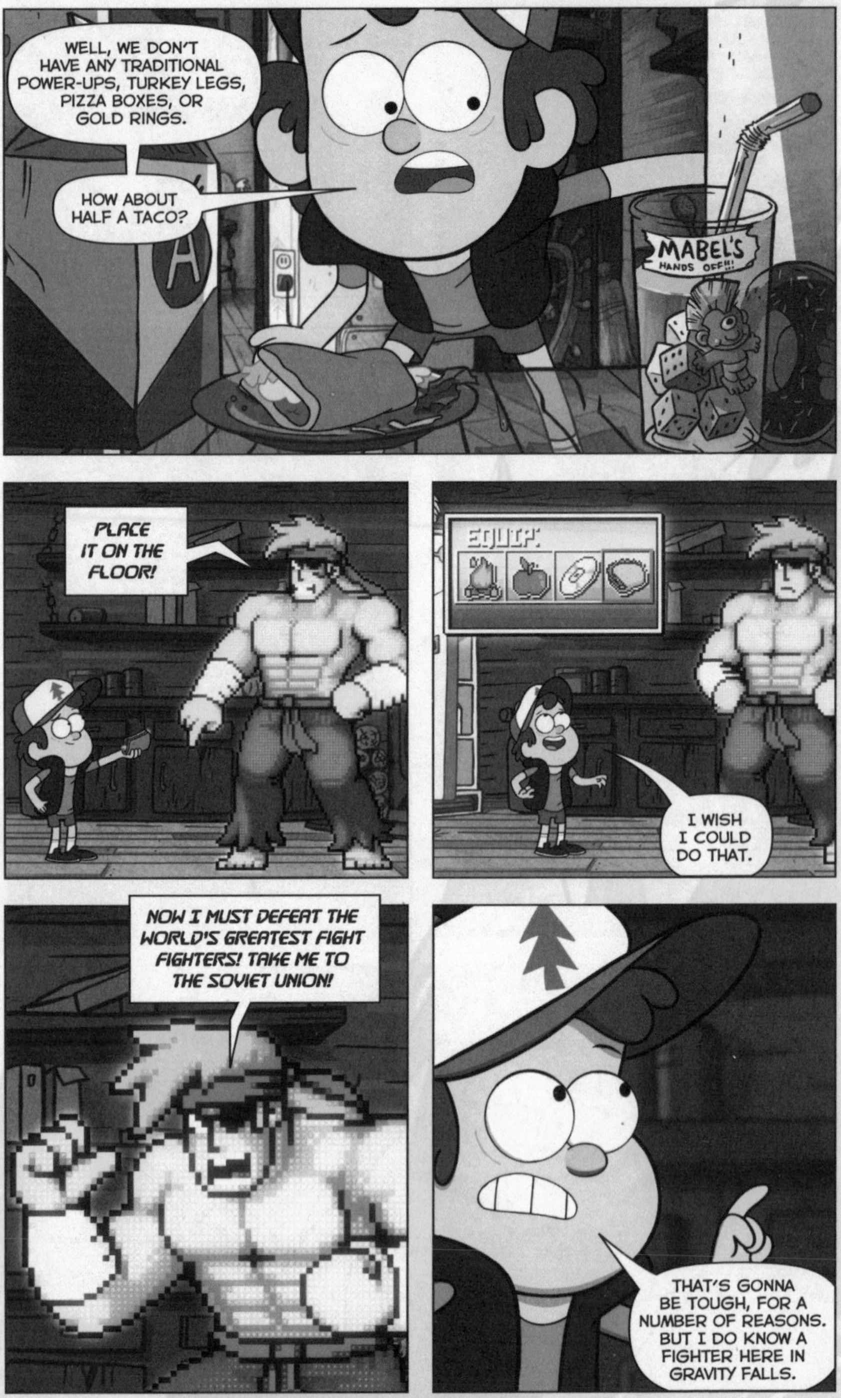
WELL, WE DON'T HAVE ANY TRADITIONAL POWER-UPS, TURKEY LEGS, PIZZA BOXES, OR GOLD RINGS.
HOW ABOUT HALF A TACO?
MABEL'S HANDS OFF!!!
PLACE IT ON THE FLOOR!
EQUIP:
I WISH I COULD DO THAT.
NOW I MUST DEFEAT THE WORLD'S GREATEST FIGHT FIGHTERS! TAKE ME TO THE SOVIET UNION!
THAT'S GONNA BE TOUGH, FOR A NUMBER OF REASONS. BUT I DO KNOW A FIGHTER HERE IN GRAVITY FALLS.

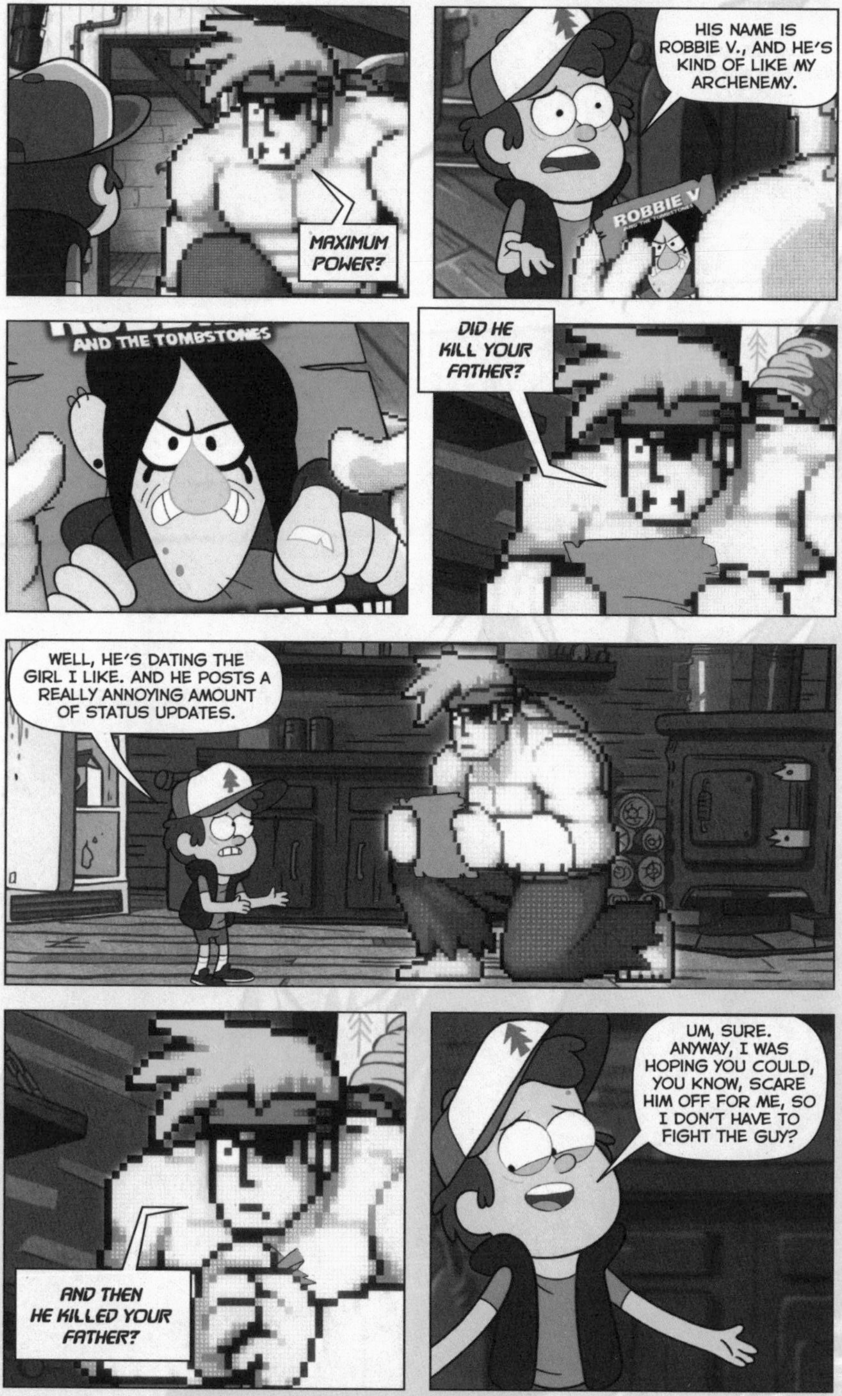
MAXIMUM POWER?
HIS NAME IS ROBBIE V., AND HE'S KIND OF LIKE MY ARCHENEMY.
ROBBIE V
AND THE TOMBSTONES
DID HE KILL YOUR FATHER?
WELL, HE'S DATING THE GIRL I LIKE. AND HE POSTS A REALLY ANNOYING AMOUNT OF STATUS UPDATES.
AND THEN HE KILLED YOUR FATHER?
UM, SURE. ANYWAY, I WAS HOPING YOU COULD, YOU KNOW, SCARE HIM OFF FOR ME, SO I DON'T HAVE TO FIGHT THE GUY?

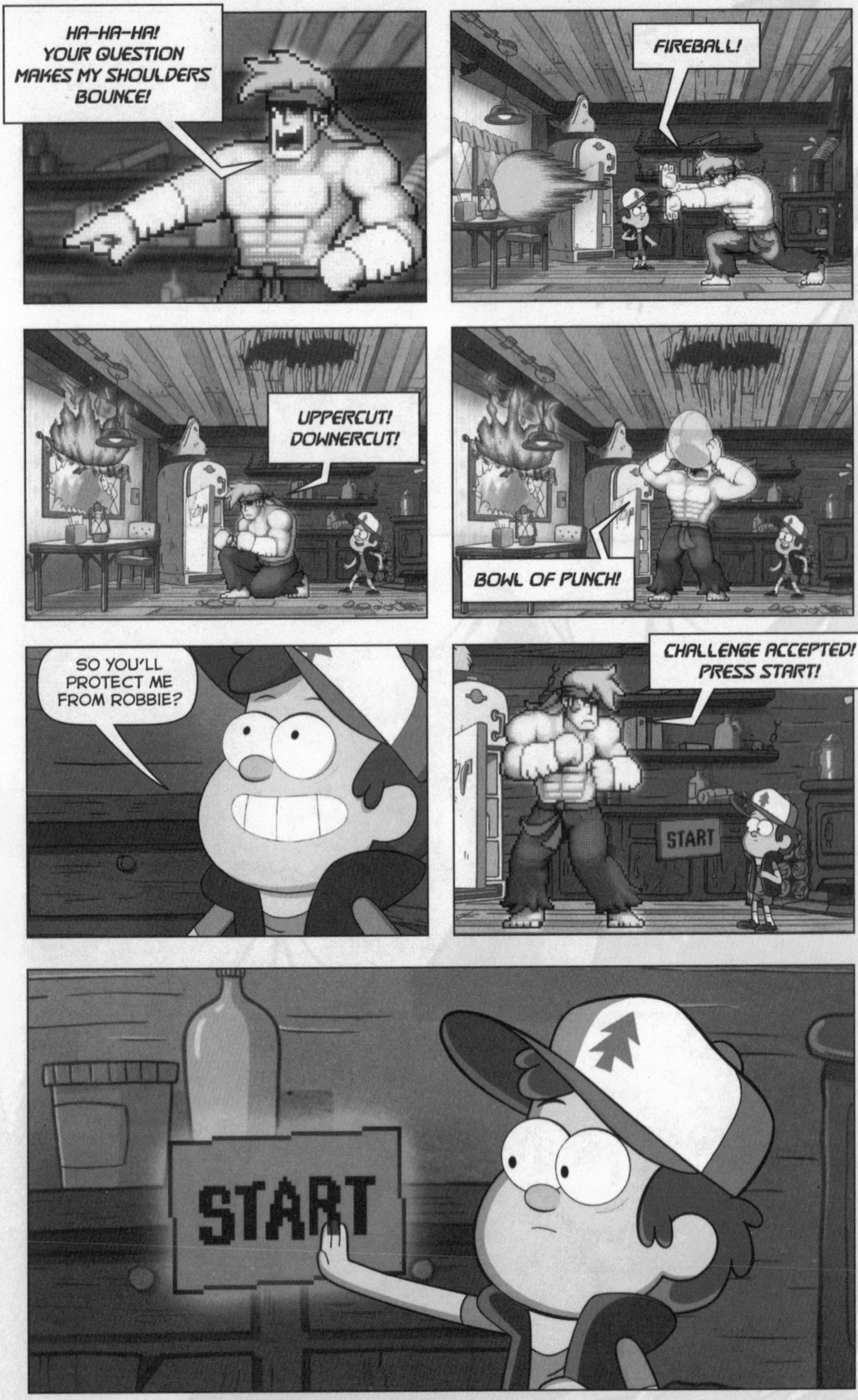
HA-HA-HA! YOUR QUESTION MAKES MY SHOULDERS BOUNCE!
FIREBALL!
UPPERCUT! DOWNERCUT!
BOWL OF PUNCH!
SO YOU'LL PROTECT ME FROM ROBBIE?
CHALLENGE ACCEPTED! PRESS START!
START
START

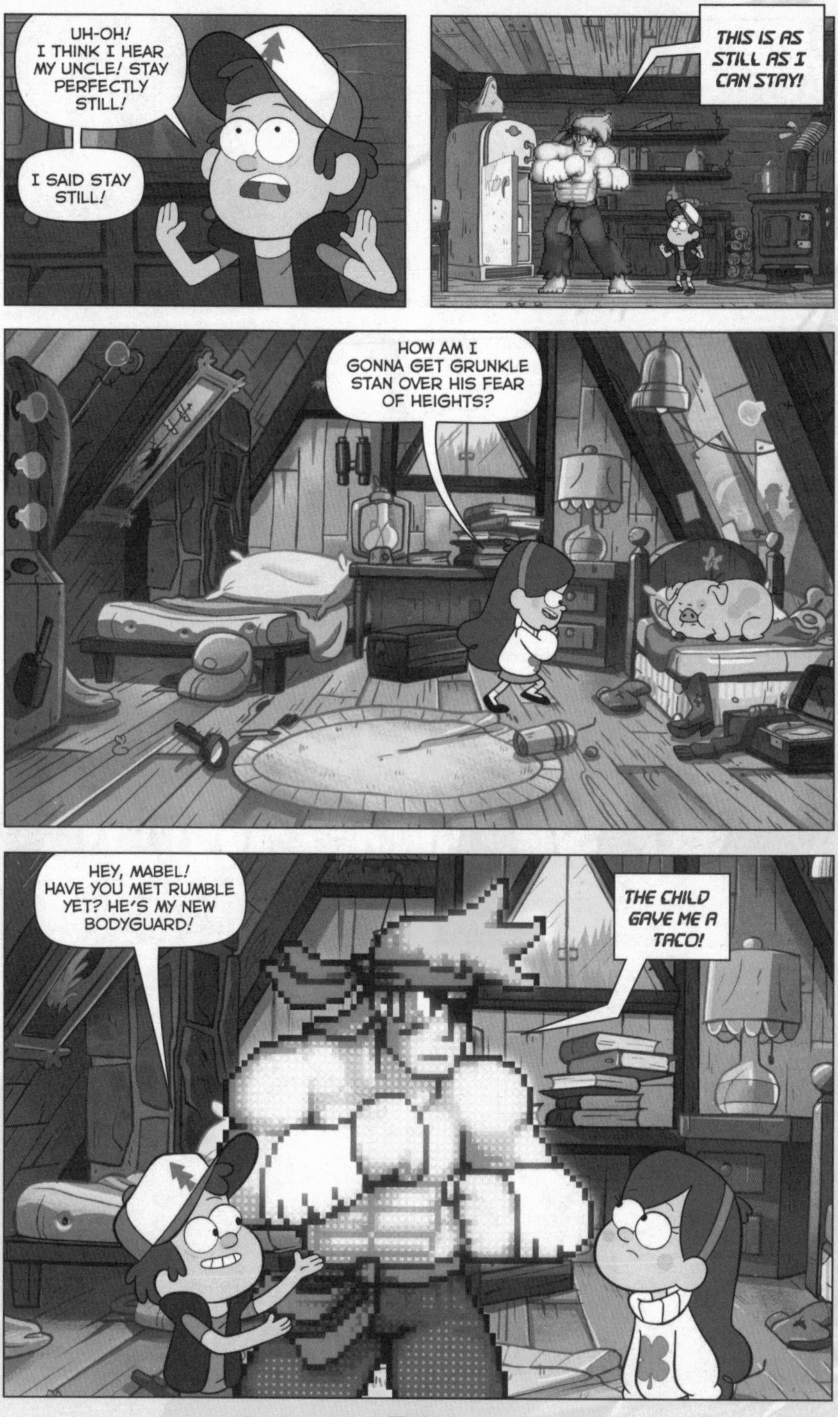
UH-OH! I THINK I HEAR MY UNCLE! STAY PERFECTLY STILL!
I SAID STAY STILL!
THIS IS AS STILL AS I CAN STAY!
HOW AM I GONNA GET GRUNKLE STAN OVER HIS FEAR OF HEIGHTS?
HEY, MABEL! HAVE YOU MET RUMBLE YET? HE'S MY NEW BODYGUARD!
THE CHILD GAVE ME A TACO!

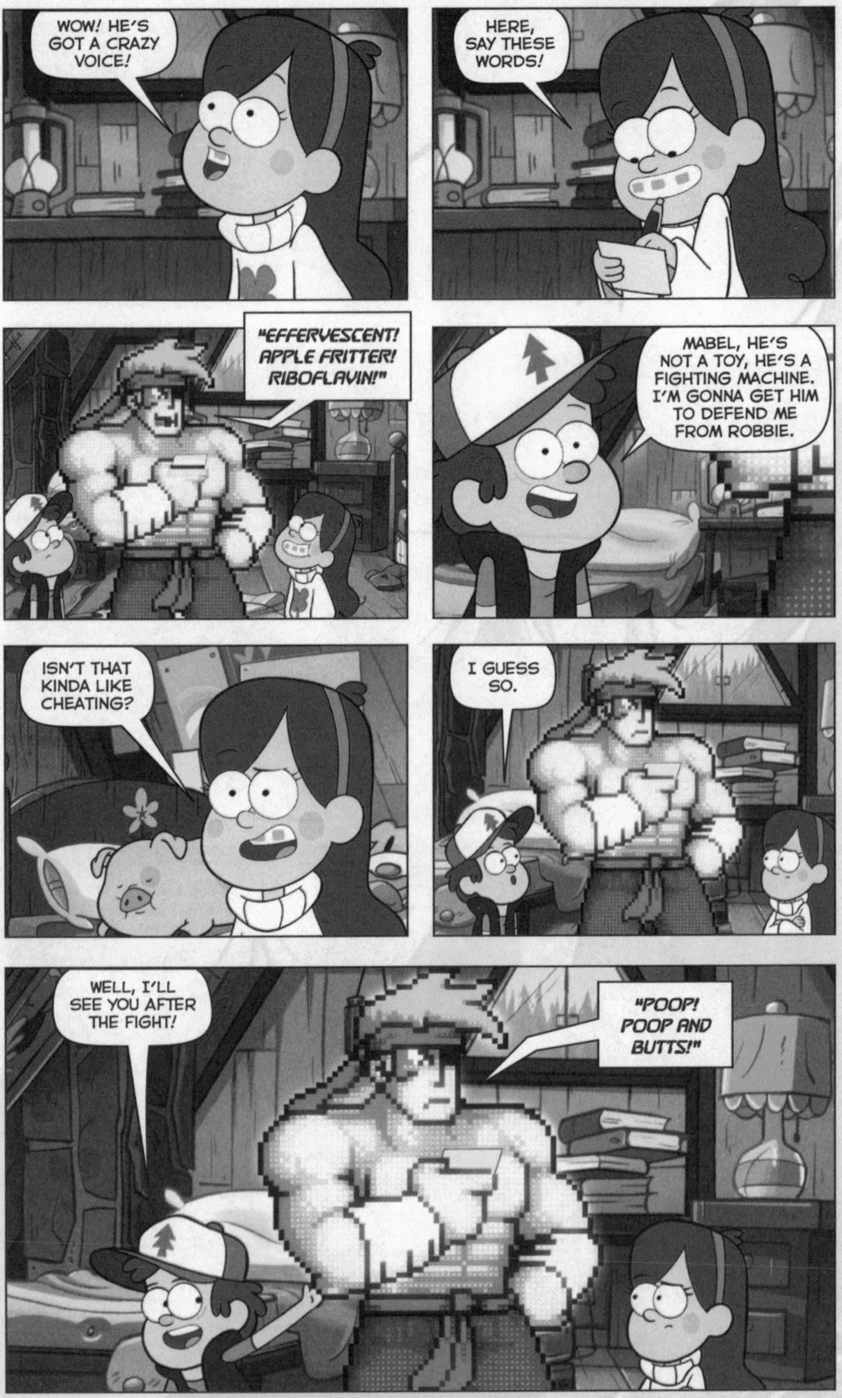
WOW! HE'S GOT A CRAZY VOICE!
HERE, SAY THESE WORDS!
"EFFERVESCENT! APPLE FRITTER! RIBOFLAVIN!"
MABEL, HE'S NOT A TOY, HE'S A FIGHTING MACHINE. I'M GONNA GET HIM TO DEFEND ME FROM ROBBIE.
ISN'T THAT KINDA LIKE CHEATING?
I GUESS SO.
WELL, I'LL SEE YOU AFTER THE FIGHT!
"POOP! POOP AND BUTTS!"

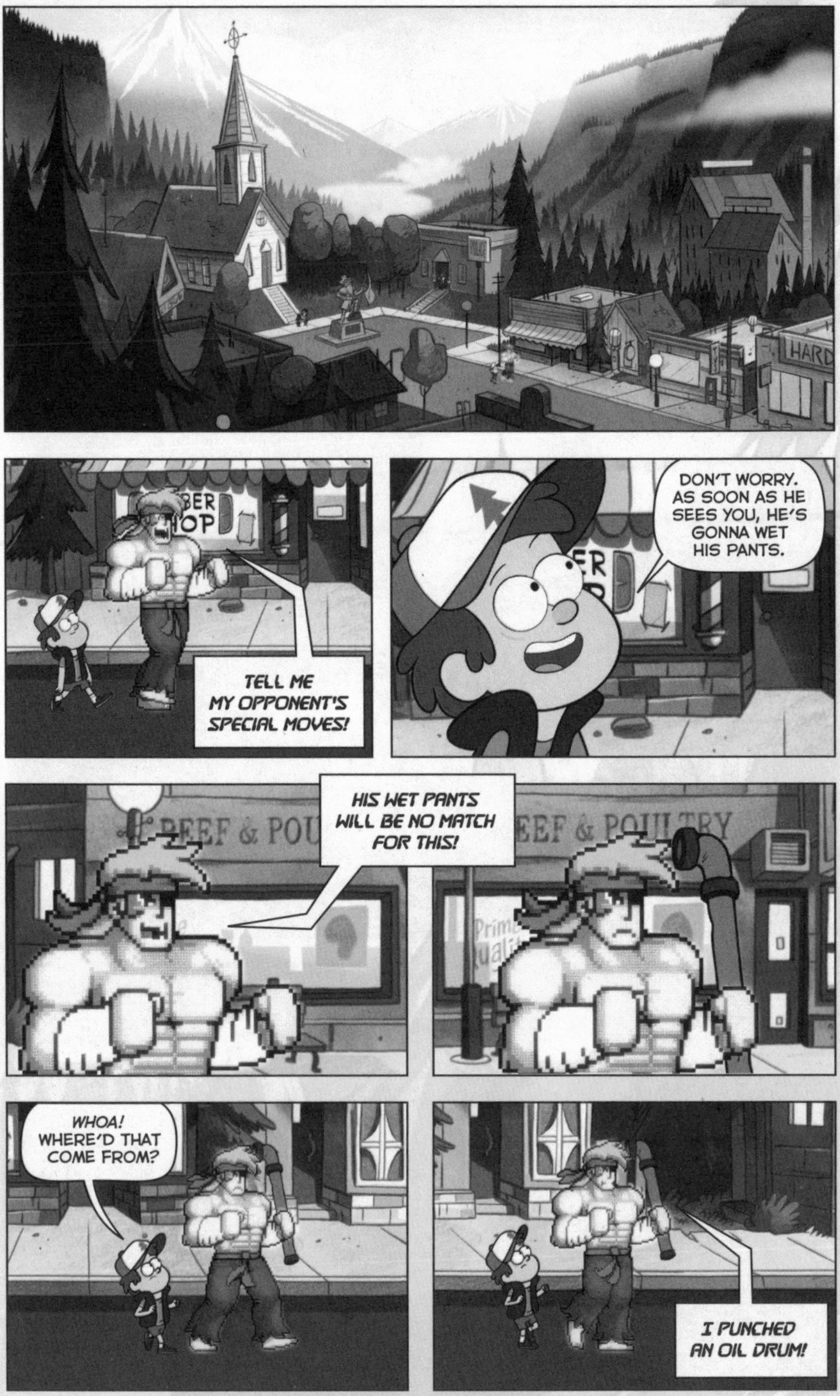
TELL ME MY OPPONENT'S SPECIAL MOVES!
DON'T WORRY. AS SOON AS HE SEES YOU, HE'S GONNA WET HIS PANTS.
HIS WET PANTS WILL BE NO MATCH FOR THIS!
WHOA! WHERE'D THAT COME FROM?
I PUNCHED AN OIL DRUM!

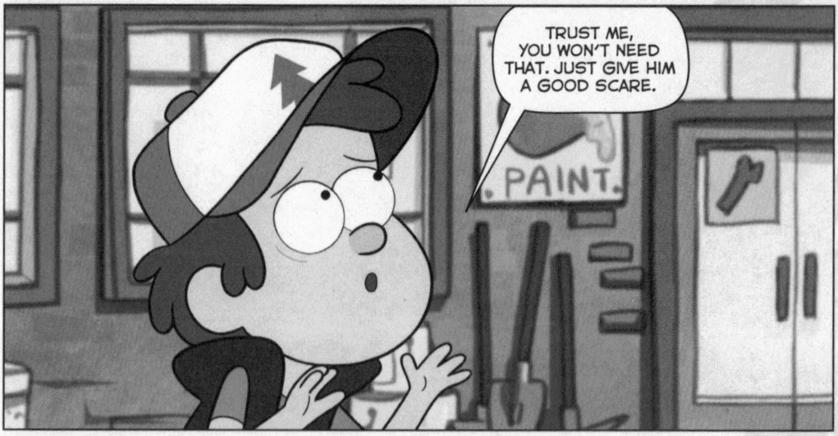
TRUST ME, YOU WON'T NEED THAT. JUST GIVE HIM A GOOD SCARE.
PAINT.

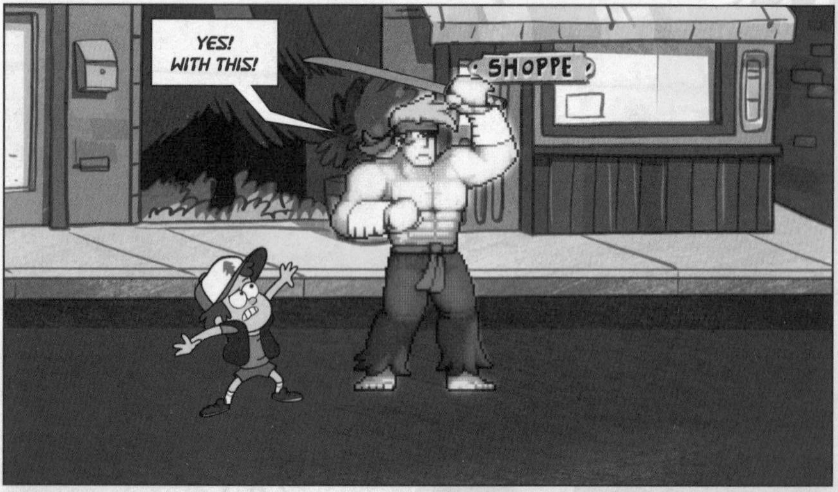
YES! WITH THIS!
SHOPPE

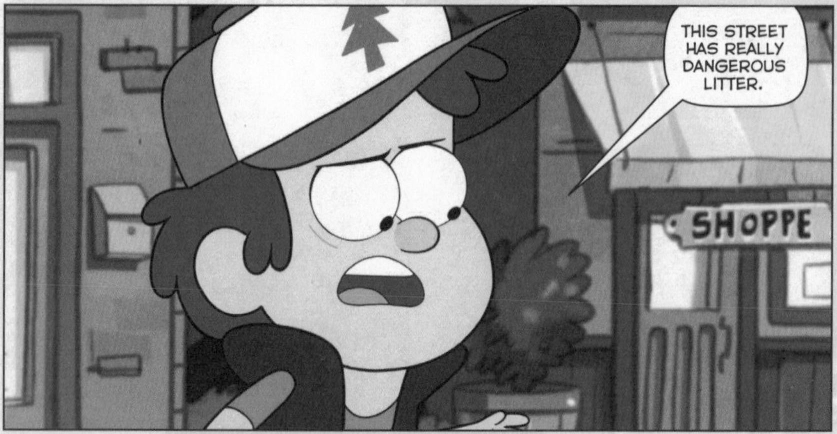
THIS STREET HAS REALLY DANGEROUS LITTER.
SHOPPE

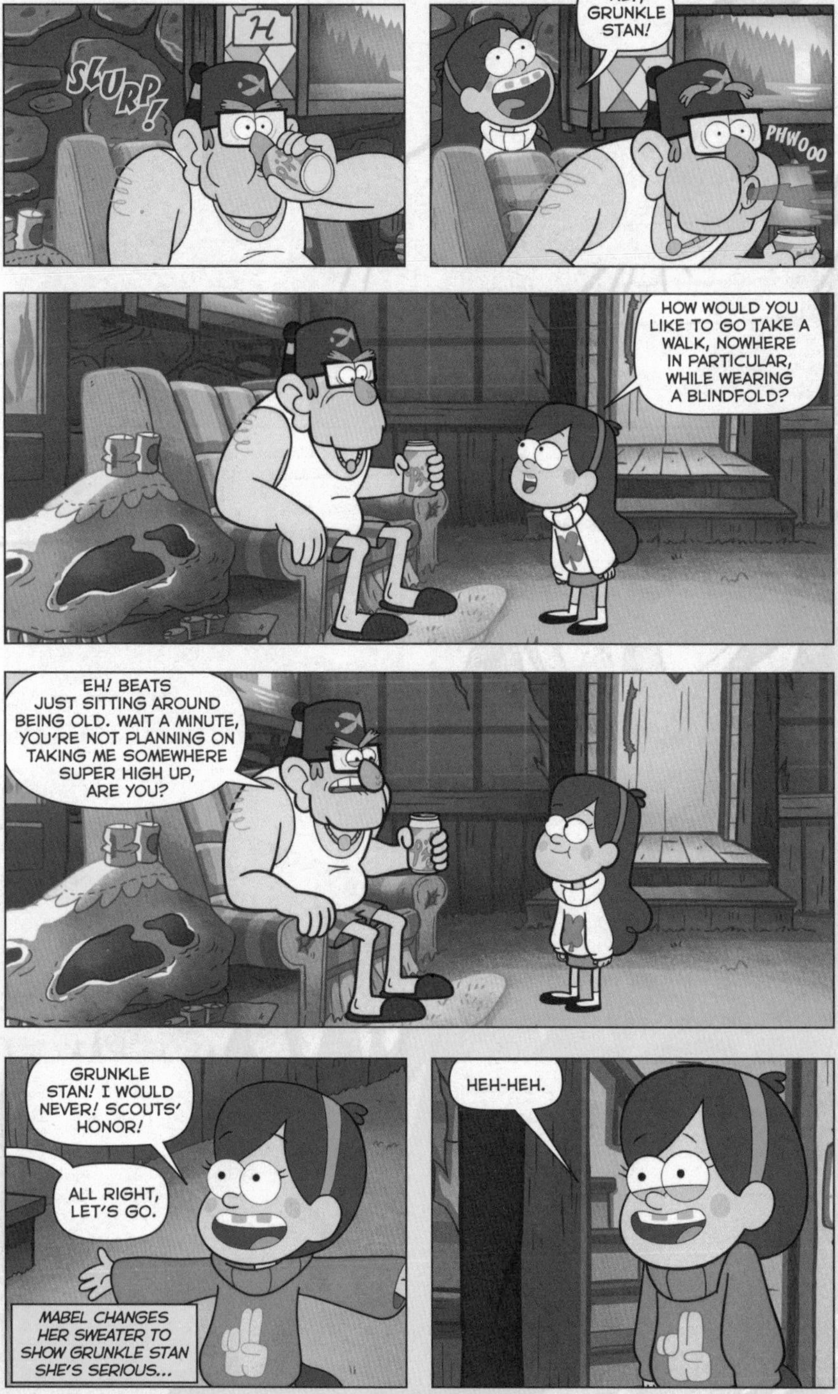
SLURP!
HEY, GRUNKLE STAN!
PHWOOO
HOW WOULD YOU LIKE TO GO TAKE A WALK, NOWHERE IN PARTICULAR, WHILE WEARING A BLINDFOLD?
EH! BEATS JUST SITTING AROUND BEING OLD. WAIT A MINUTE, YOU'RE NOT PLANNING ON TAKING ME SOMEWHERE SUPER HIGH UP, ARE YOU?
GRUNKLE STAN! I WOULD NEVER! SCOUTS' HONOR!
ALL RIGHT, LET'S GO.
MABEL CHANGES HER SWEATER TO SHOW GRUNKLE STAN SHE'S SERIOUS...
HEH-HEH.

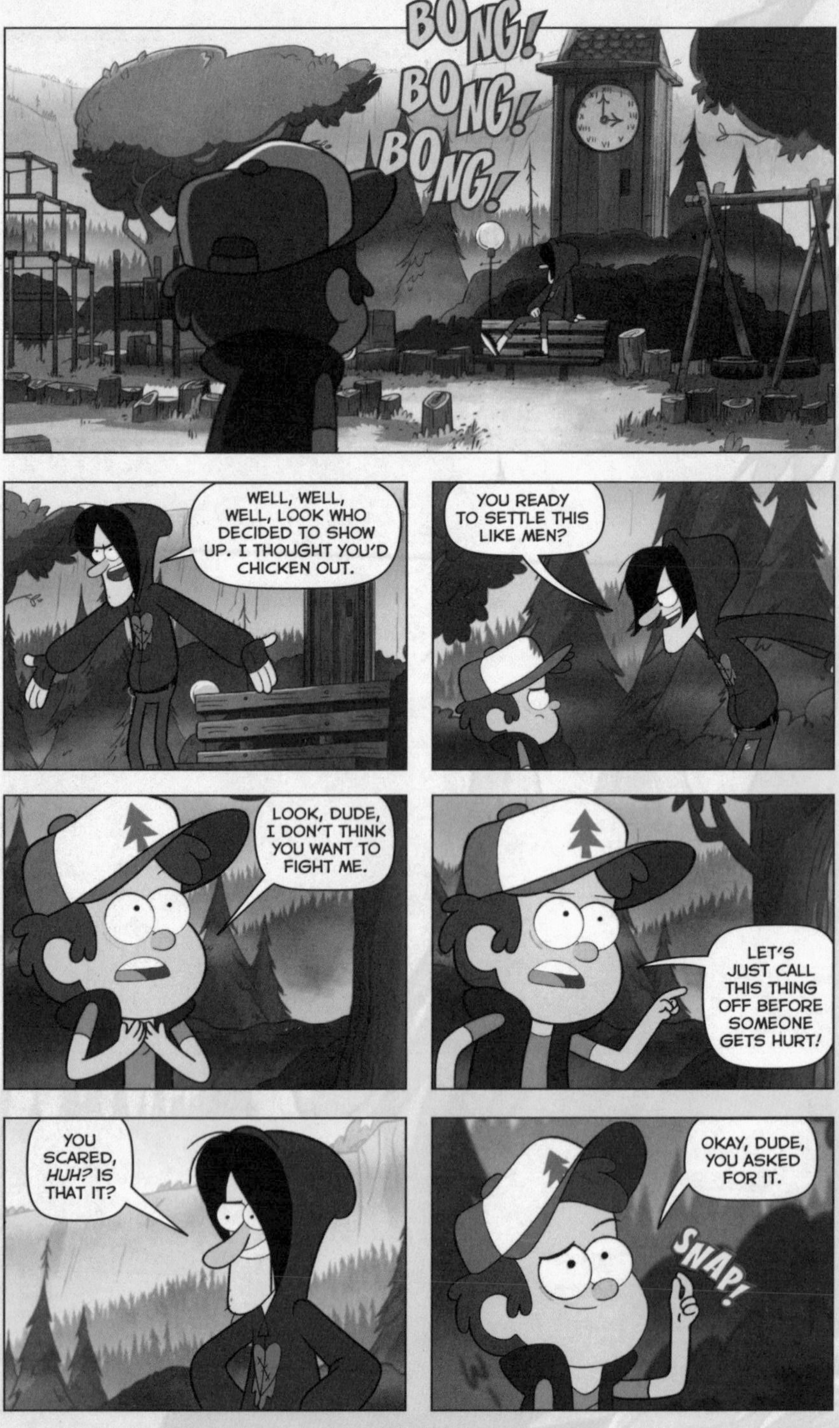
BONG! BONG! BONG!
WELL, WELL, WELL, LOOK WHO DECIDED TO SHOW UP. I THOUGHT YOU'D CHICKEN OUT.
YOU READY TO SETTLE THIS LIKE MEN?
LOOK, DUDE, I DON'T THINK YOU WANT TO FIGHT ME.
LET'S JUST CALL THIS THING OFF BEFORE SOMEONE GETS HURT!
YOU SCARED, *HUH?* IS THAT IT?
OKAY, DUDE, YOU ASKED FOR IT.
SNAP!

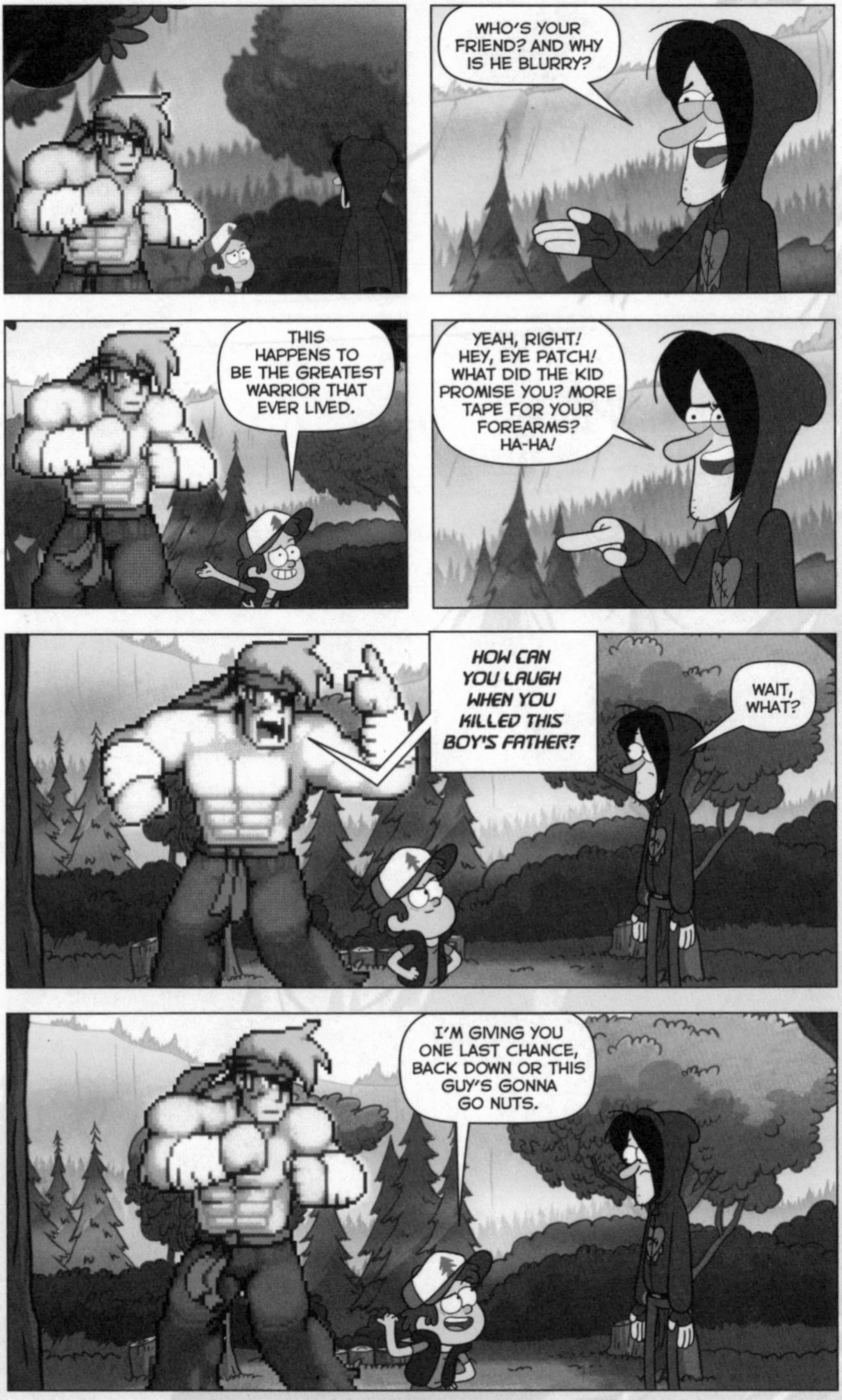
WHO'S YOUR FRIEND? AND WHY IS HE BLURRY?
THIS HAPPENS TO BE THE GREATEST WARRIOR THAT EVER LIVED.
YEAH, RIGHT! HEY, EYE PATCH! WHAT DID THE KID PROMISE YOU? MORE TAPE FOR YOUR FOREARMS? HA-HA!
HOW CAN YOU LAUGH WHEN YOU KILLED THIS BOY'S FATHER?
WAIT, WHAT?
I'M GIVING YOU ONE LAST CHANCE, BACK DOWN OR THIS GUY'S GONNA GO NUTS.

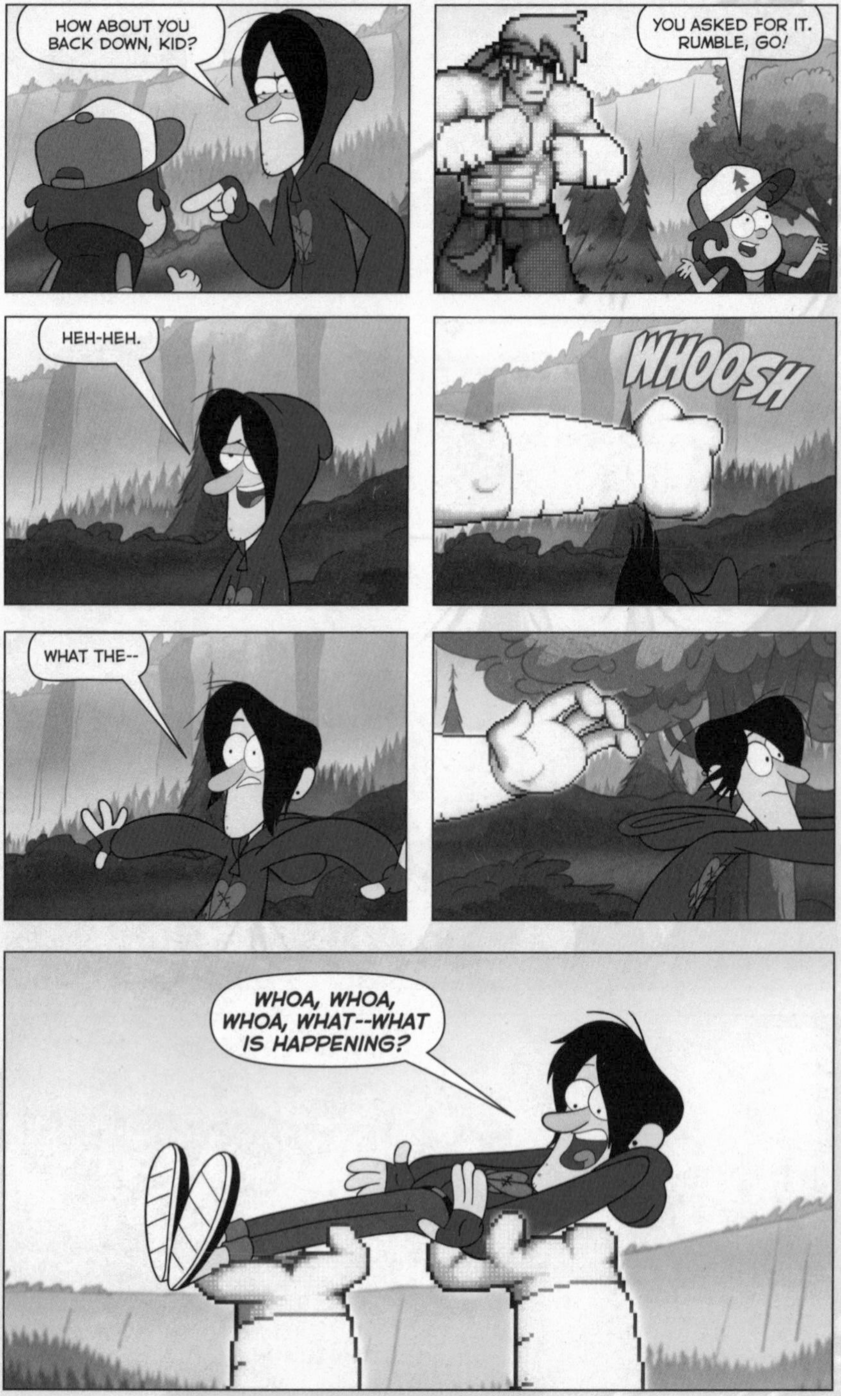
HOW ABOUT YOU BACK DOWN, KID?
YOU ASKED FOR IT. RUMBLE, GO!
HEH-HEH.
WHOOSH
WHAT THE--
WHOA, WHOA, WHOA, WHAT--WHAT IS HAPPENING?

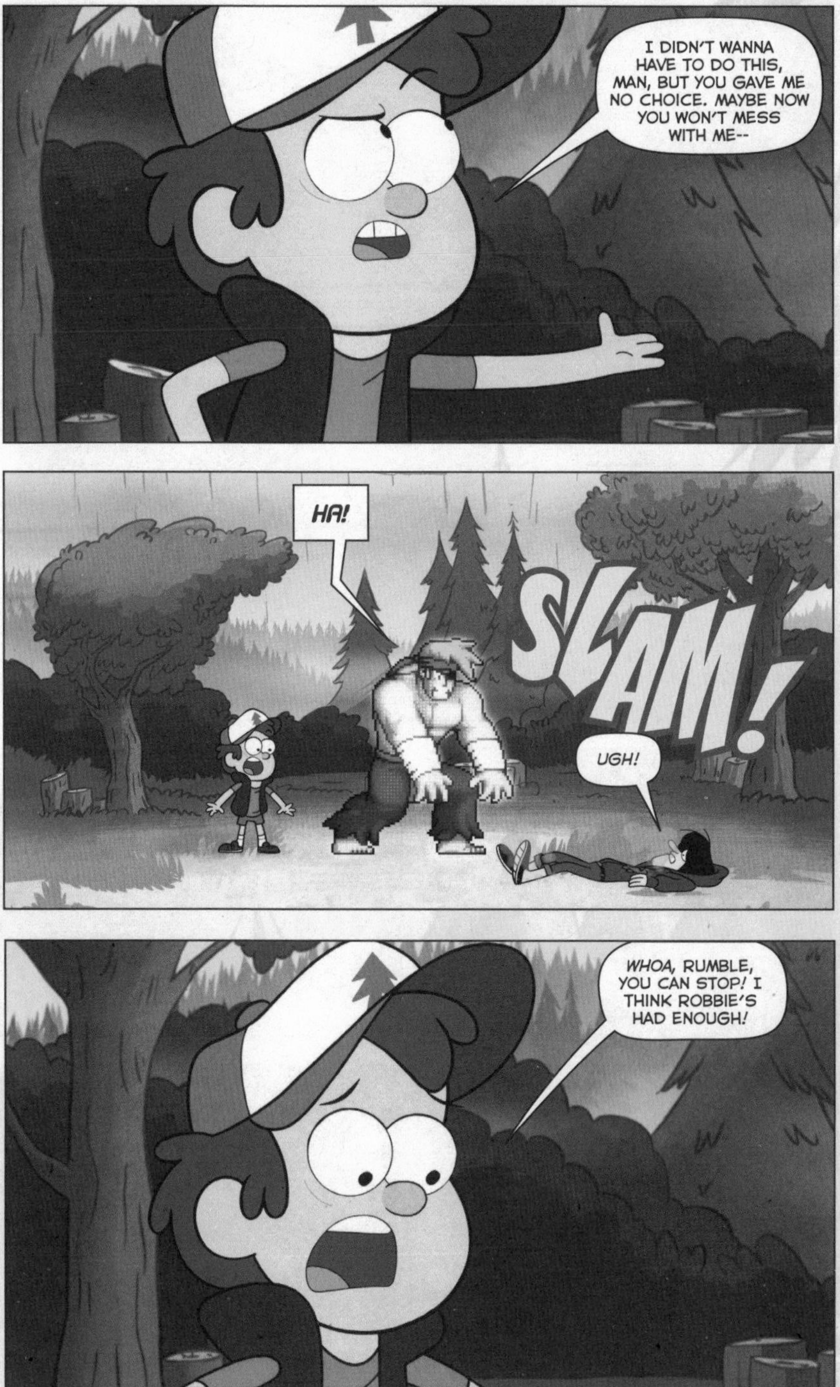
I DIDN'T WANNA HAVE TO DO THIS, MAN, BUT YOU GAVE ME NO CHOICE. MAYBE NOW YOU WON'T MESS WITH ME--
HA!
SLAM!
UGH!
WHOA, RUMBLE, YOU CAN STOP! I THINK ROBBIE'S HAD ENOUGH!

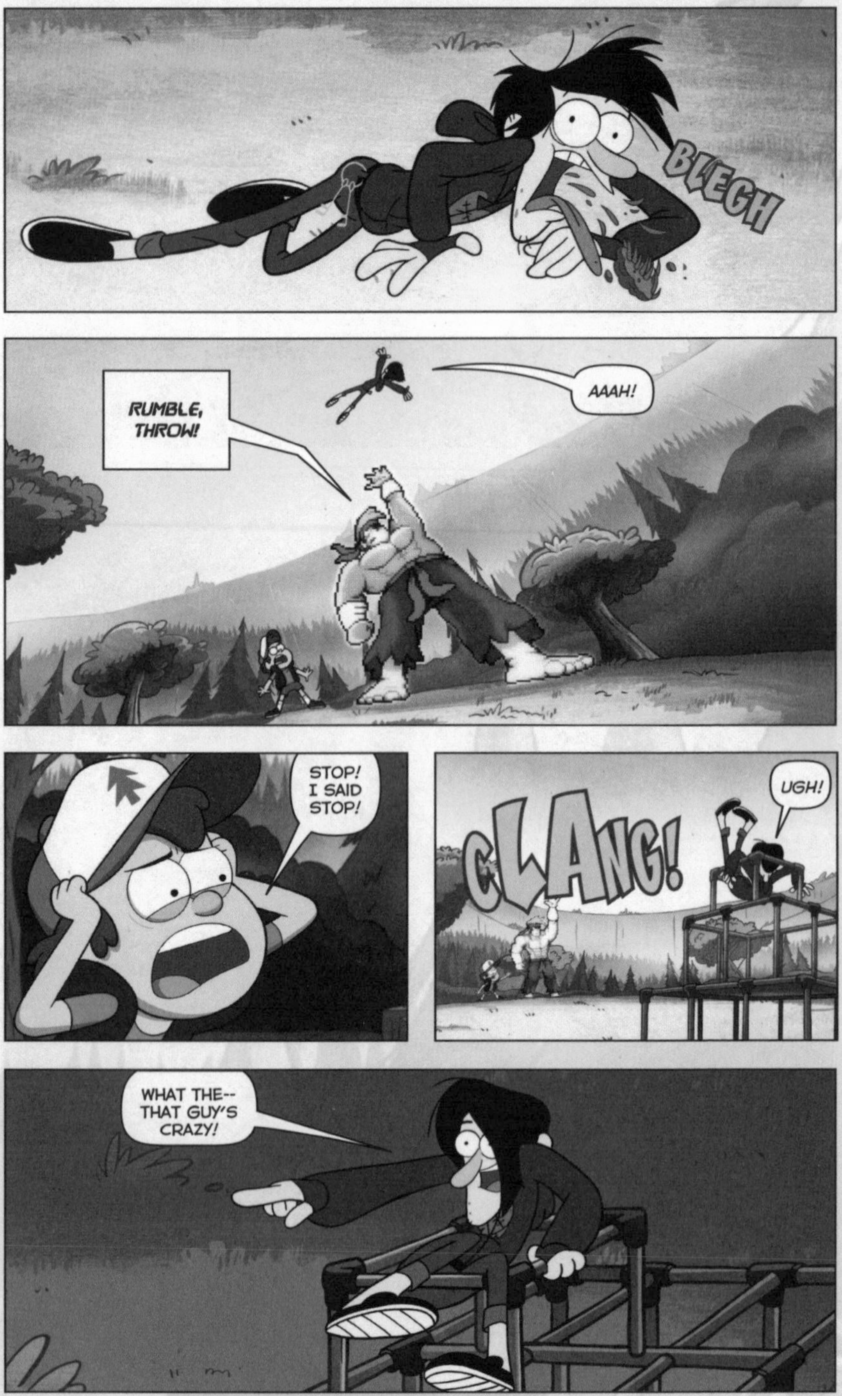
BLEGH
RUMBLE, THROW!
AAAH!
STOP! I SAID STOP!
CLANG!
UGH!
WHAT THE-- THAT GUY'S CRAZY!

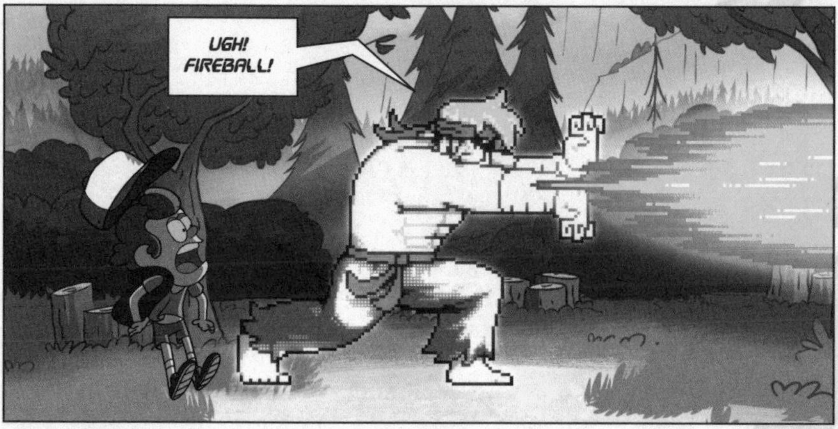
UGH! FIREBALL!

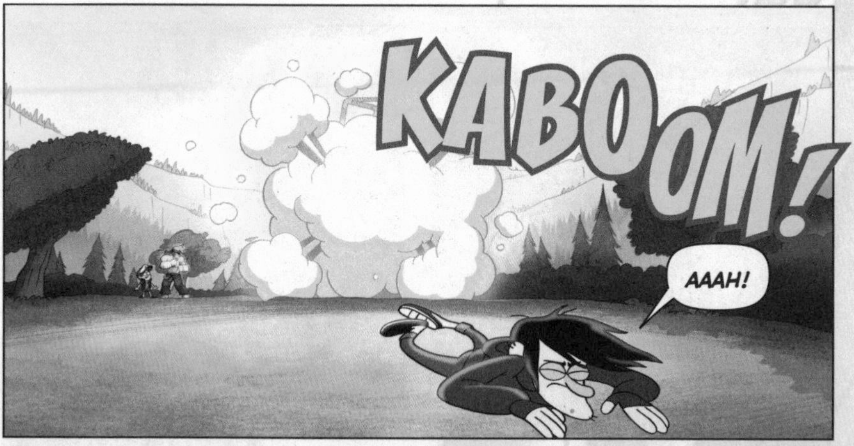
KABOOM!
AAAH!

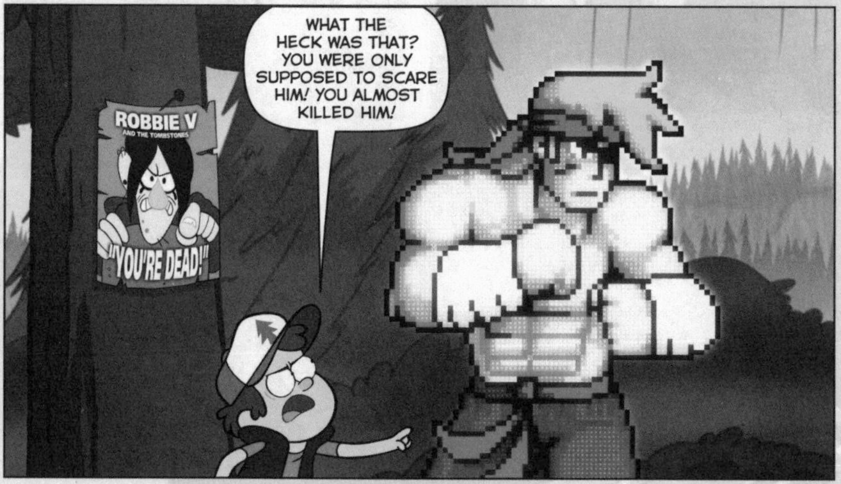
ROBBIE V
AND THE TOMBSTONES
"YOU'RE DEAD!"
WHAT THE HECK WAS THAT? YOU WERE ONLY SUPPOSED TO SCARE HIM! YOU ALMOST KILLED HIM!

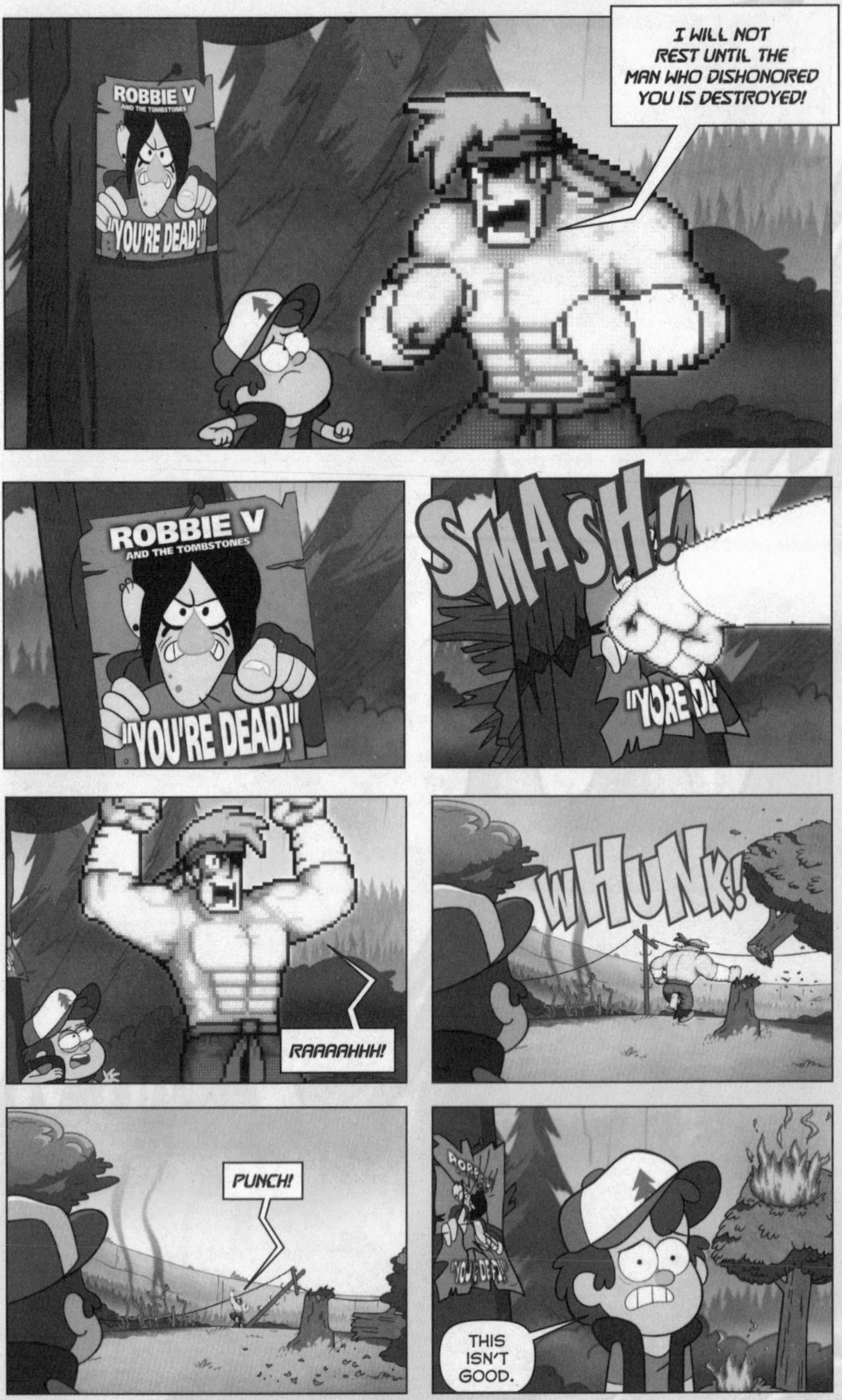

ROBBIE V
AND THE TOMBSTONES
"YOU'RE DEAD!"
I WILL NOT REST UNTIL THE MAN WHO DISHONORED YOU IS DESTROYED!
ROBBIE V
AND THE TOMBSTONES
"YOU'RE DEAD!"
SMASH!
RAAAAHHH!
WHUNK!
PUNCH!
THIS ISN'T GOOD.

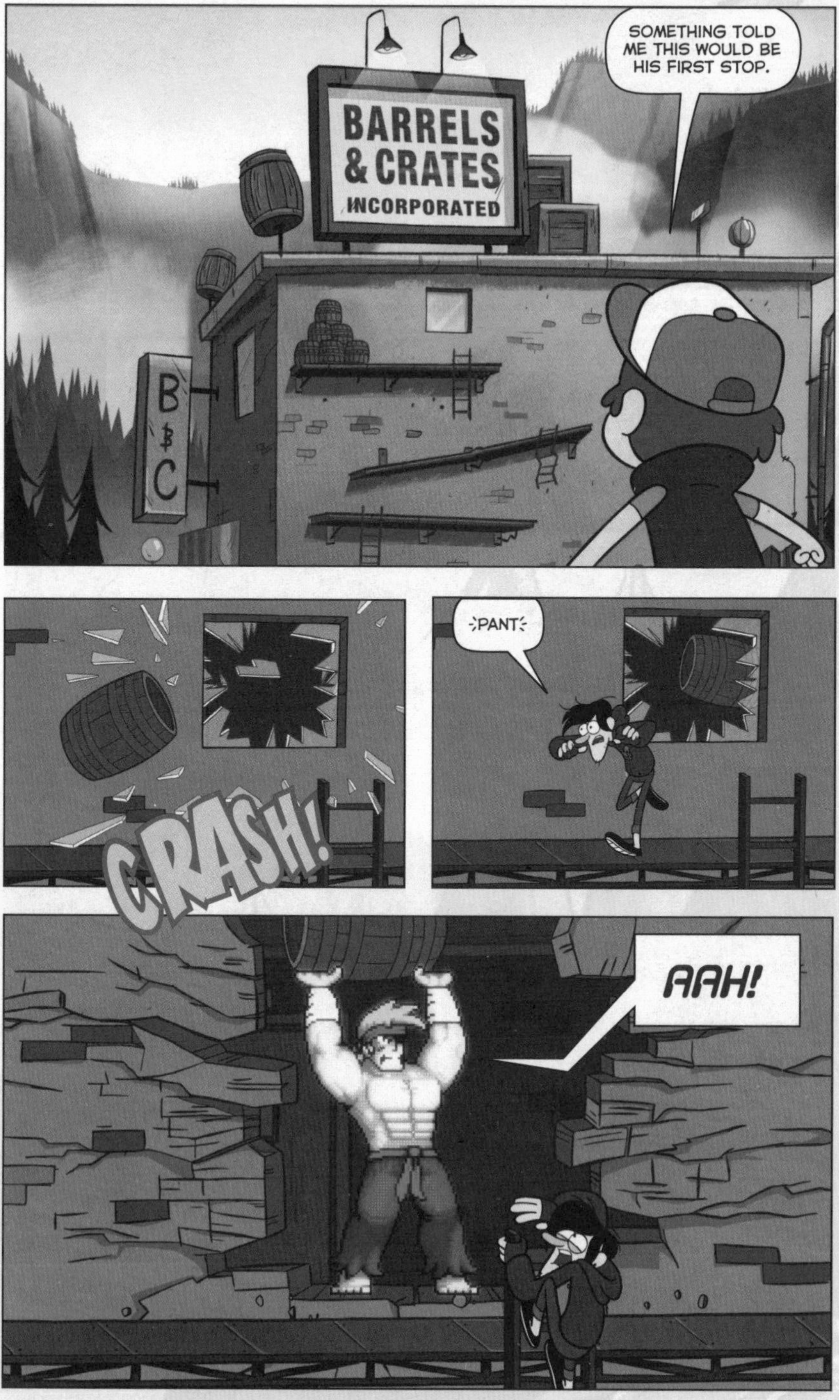
SOMETHING TOLD ME THIS WOULD BE HIS FIRST STOP.
BARRELS & CRATES INCORPORATED
B & C
CRASH!
PANT
AAH!

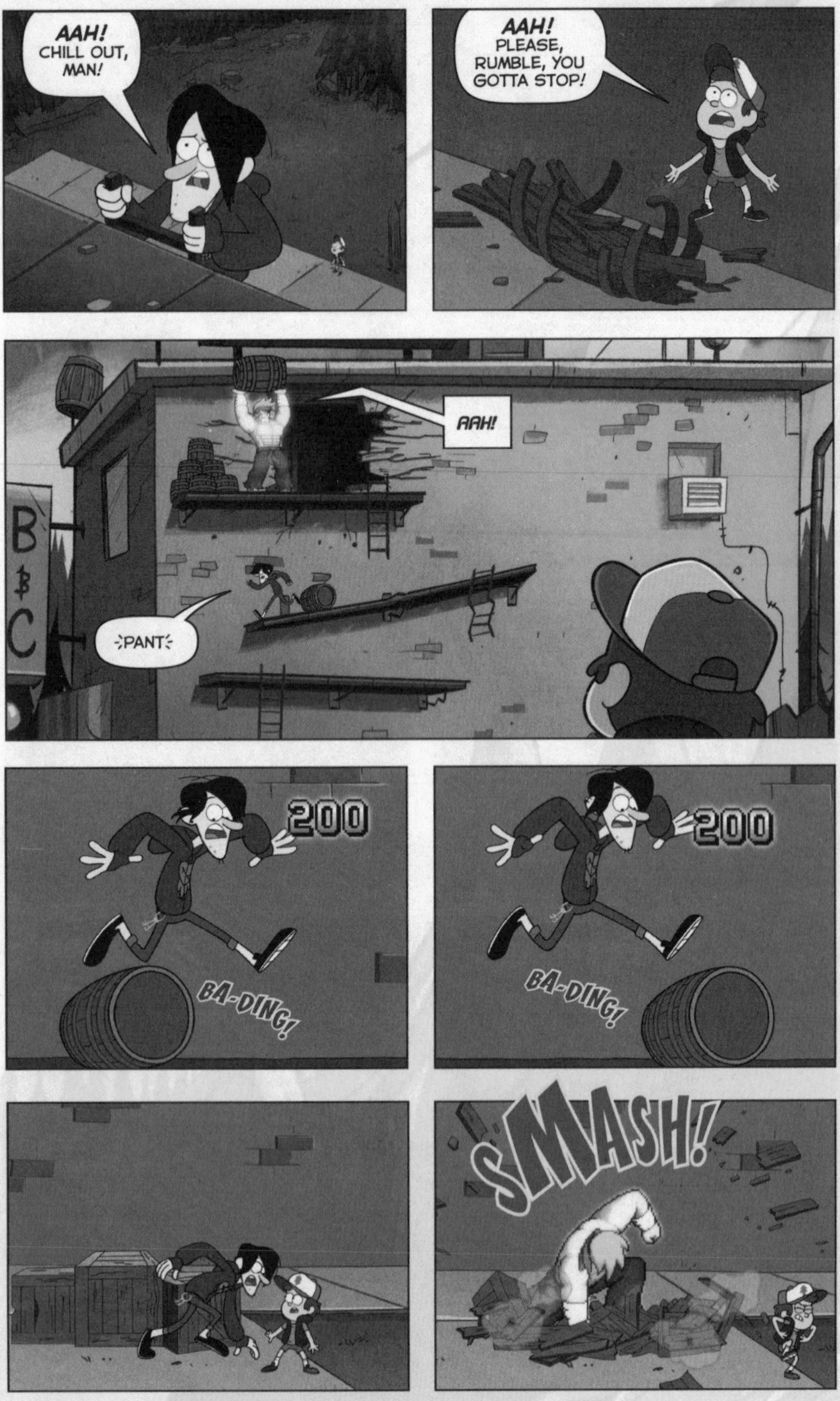
AAH! CHILL OUT, MAN!
AAH! PLEASE, RUMBLE, YOU GOTTA STOP!
AAH!
PANT
200
BA-DING!
200
BA-DING!
SMASH!

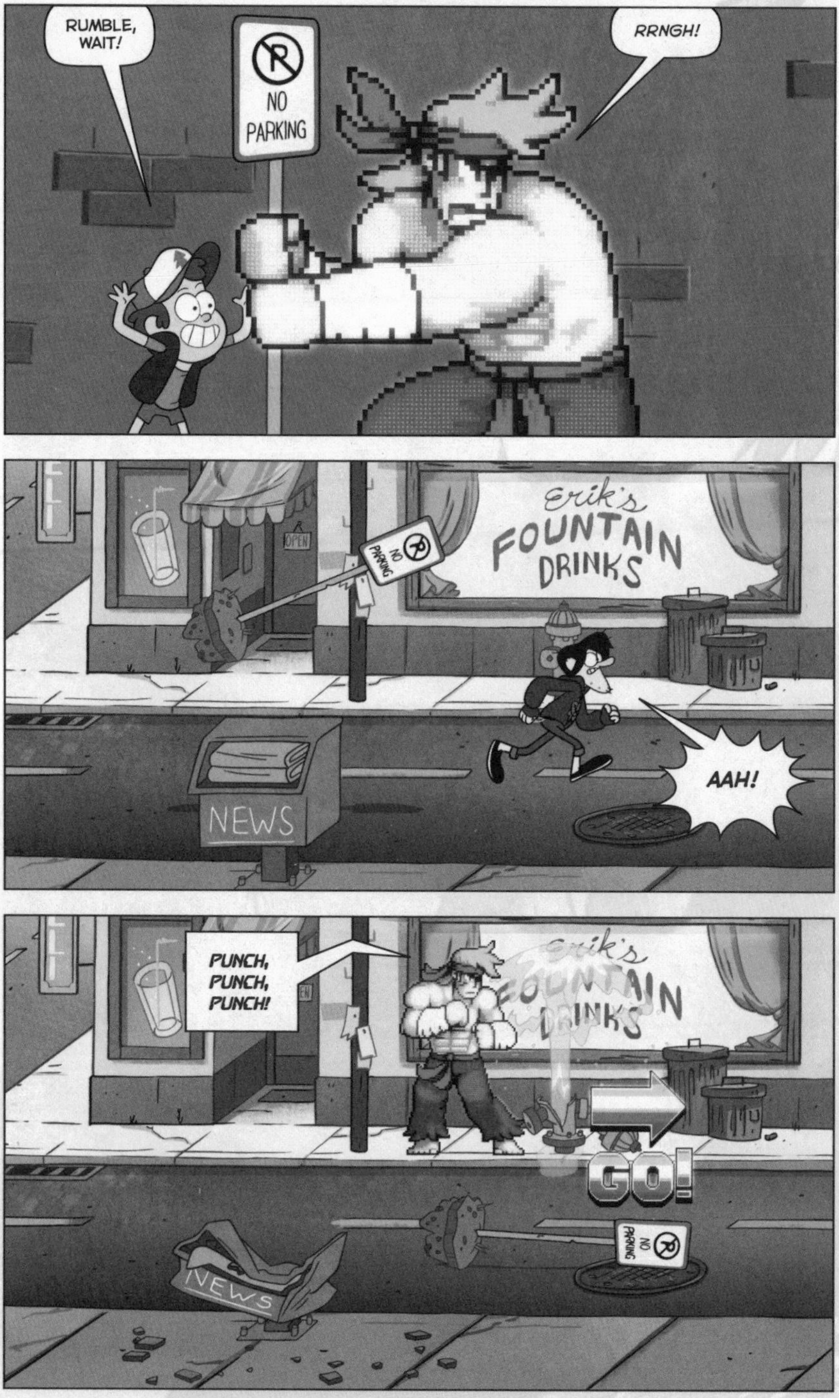
RUMBLE, WAIT!
NO PARKING
RRNGH!
Erik's FOUNTAIN DRINKS
OPEN
NO PARKING
AAH!
NEWS
PUNCH, PUNCH, PUNCH!
Erik's FOUNTAIN DRINKS
GO!
NO PARKING
NEWS

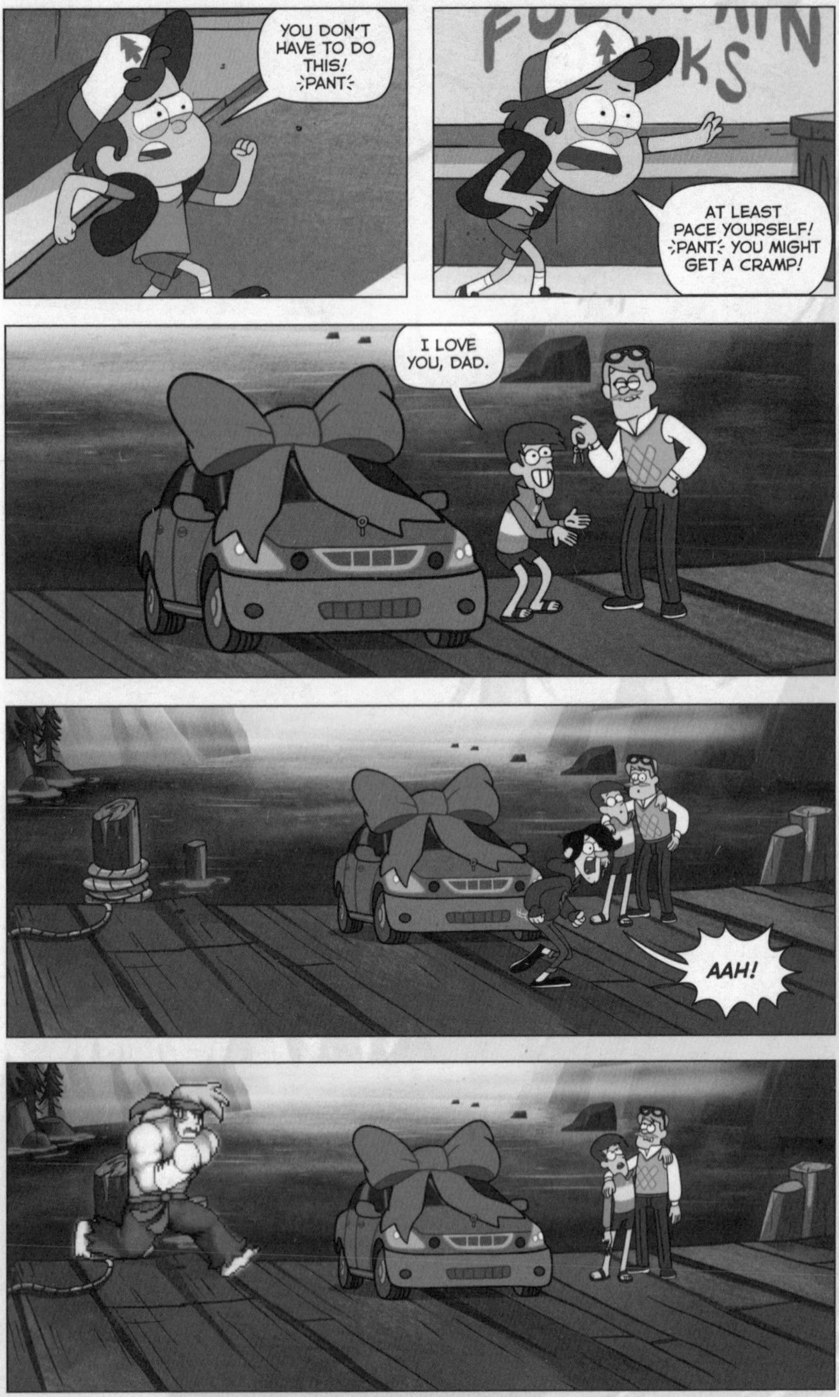
YOU DON'T HAVE TO DO THIS! PANT
AT LEAST PACE YOURSELF! PANT YOU MIGHT GET A CRAMP!
I LOVE YOU, DAD.
AAH!

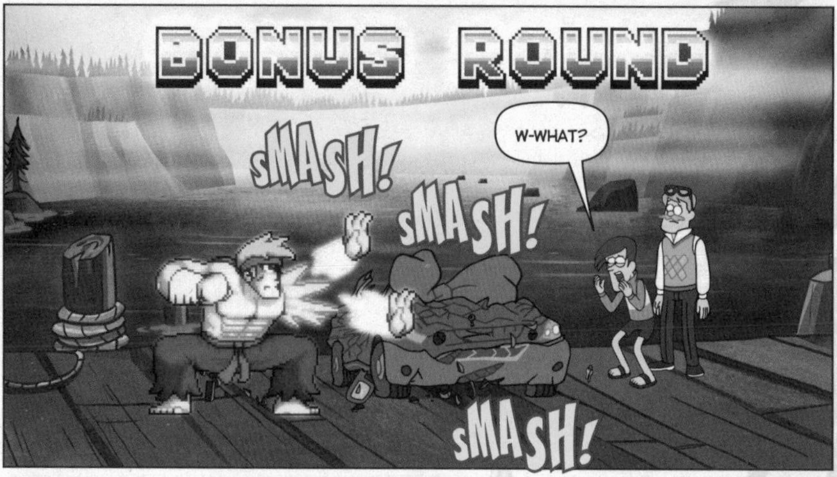
BONUS ROUND
SMASH!
SMASH!
W-WHAT?
SMASH!

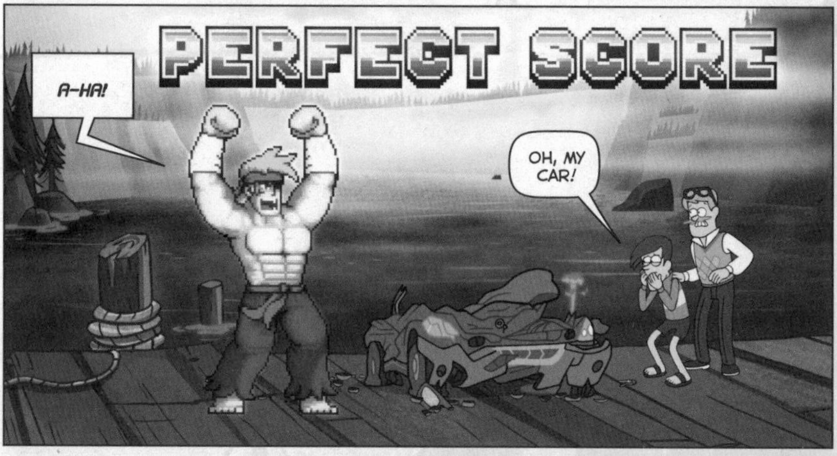
PERFECT SCORE
A-HA!
OH, MY CAR!

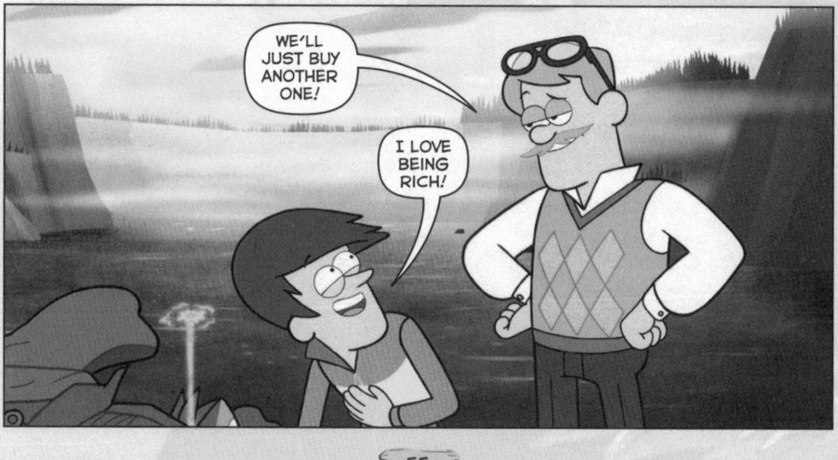
WE'LL JUST BUY ANOTHER ONE!
I LOVE BEING RICH!

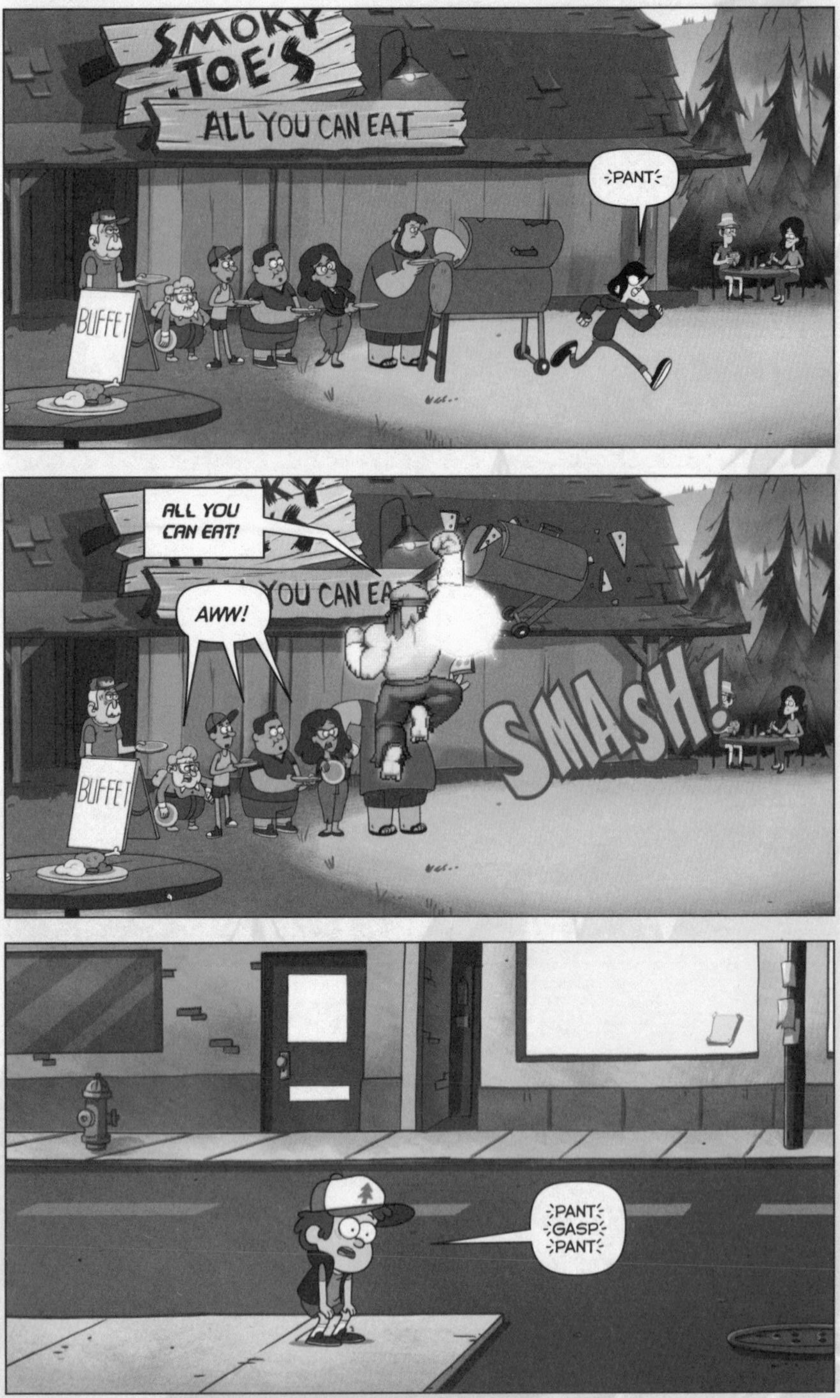
SMOKY TOE'S
ALL YOU CAN EAT
BUFFET
PANT
ALL YOU CAN EAT!
AWW!
SMASH!
PANT
GASP
PANT

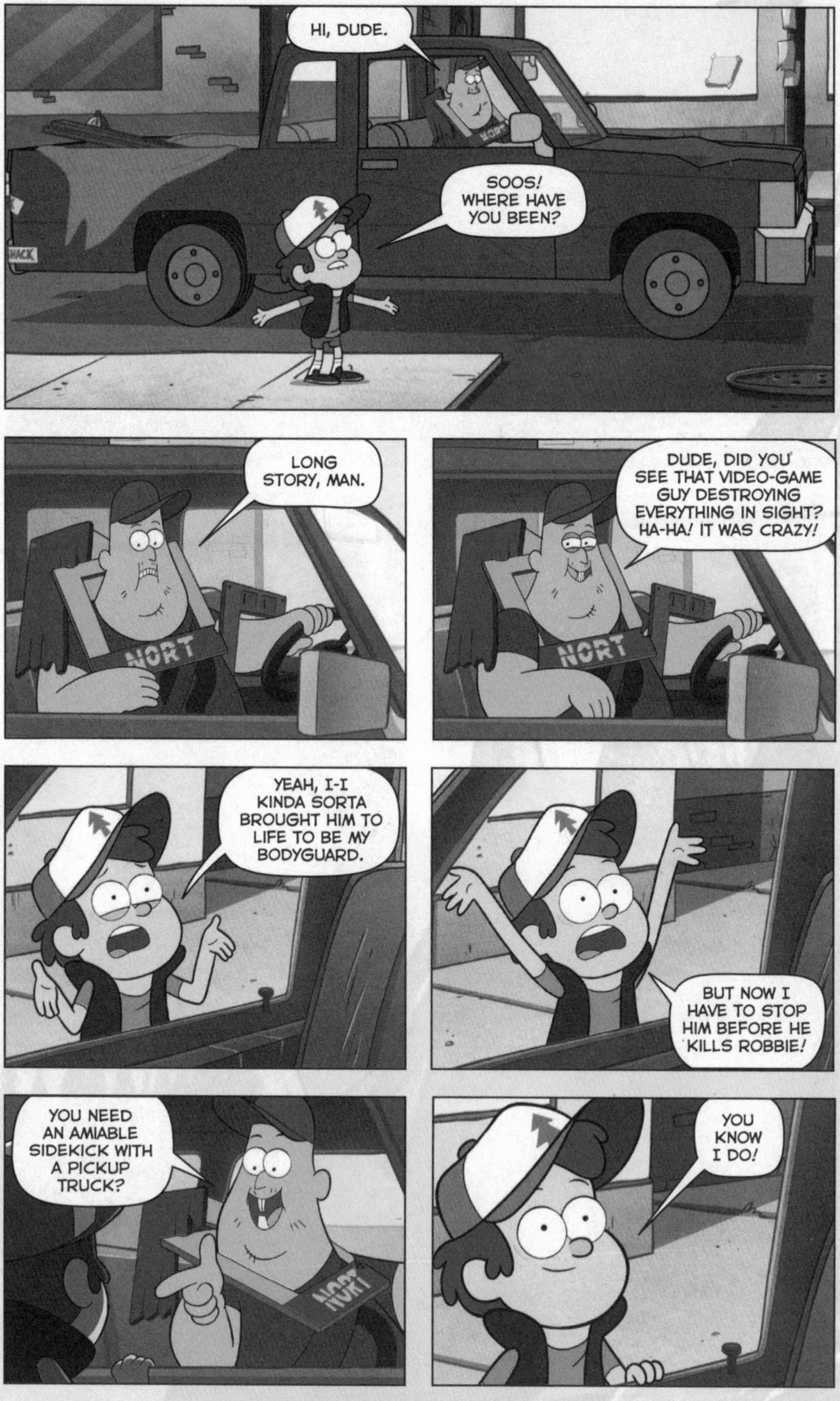
HI, DUDE.
SOOS! WHERE HAVE YOU BEEN?
LONG STORY, MAN.
DUDE, DID YOU SEE THAT VIDEO-GAME GUY DESTROYING EVERYTHING IN SIGHT? HA-HA! IT WAS CRAZY!
YEAH, I-I KINDA SORTA BROUGHT HIM TO LIFE TO BE MY BODYGUARD.
BUT NOW I HAVE TO STOP HIM BEFORE HE KILLS ROBBIE!
YOU NEED AN AMIABLE SIDEKICK WITH A PICKUP TRUCK?
YOU KNOW I DO!

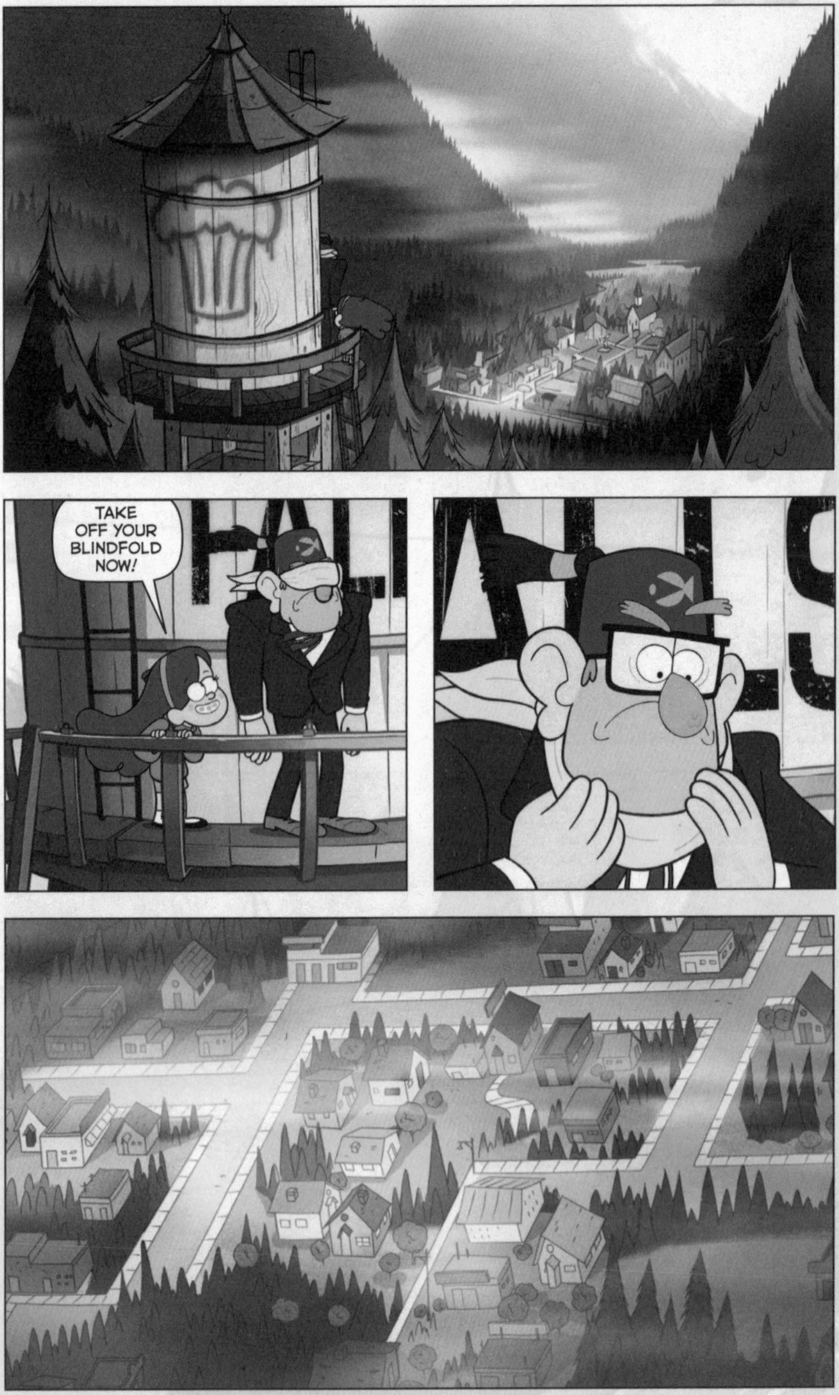
TAKE OFF YOUR BLINDFOLD NOW!

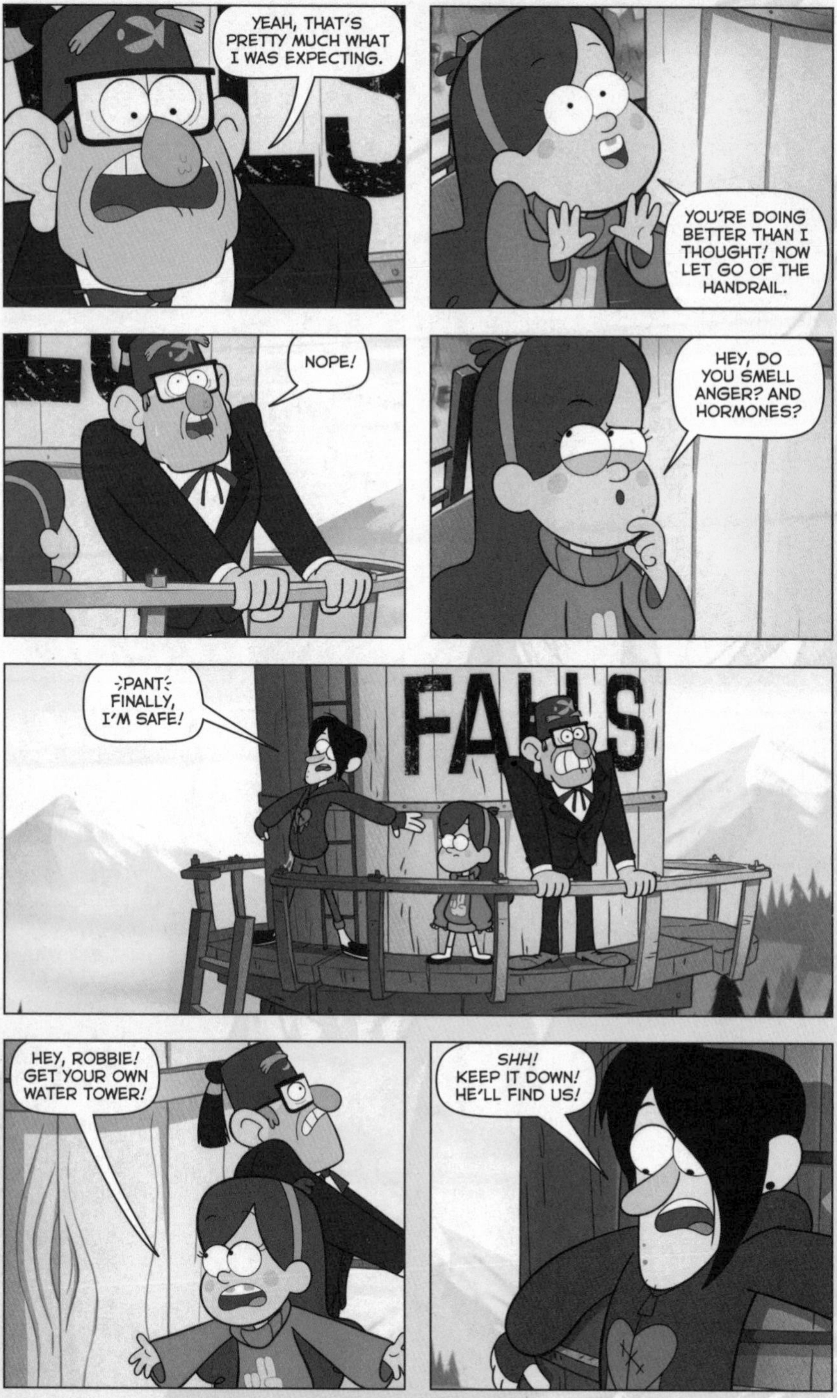
YEAH, THAT'S PRETTY MUCH WHAT I WAS EXPECTING.
YOU'RE DOING BETTER THAN I THOUGHT! NOW LET GO OF THE HANDRAIL.
NOPE!
HEY, DO YOU SMELL ANGER? AND HORMONES?
FALLS
PANT FINALLY, I'M SAFE!
HEY, ROBBIE! GET YOUR OWN WATER TOWER!
SHH! KEEP IT DOWN! HE'LL FIND US!

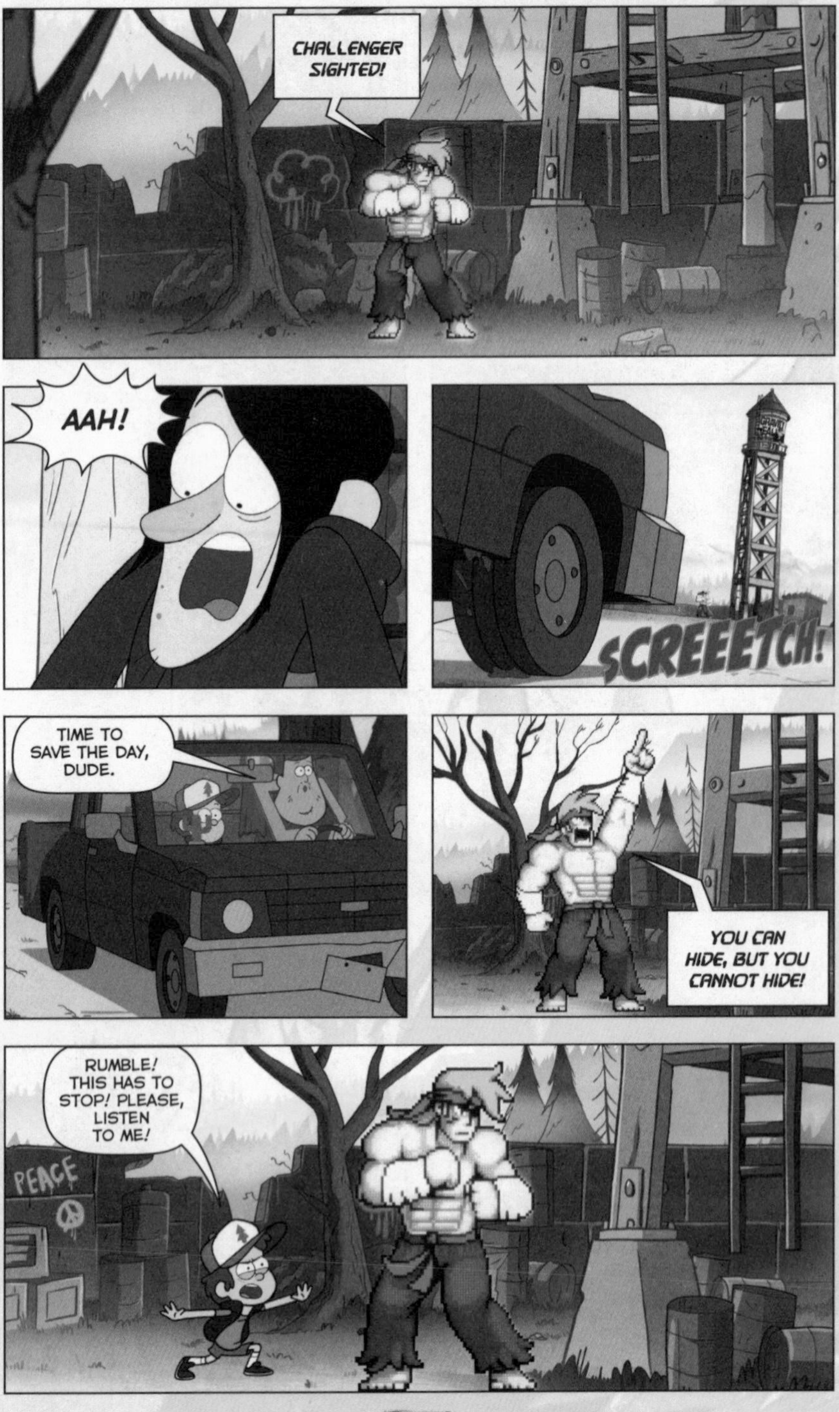
CHALLENGER SIGHTED!
AAH!
SCREEETCH!
TIME TO SAVE THE DAY, DUDE.
YOU CAN HIDE, BUT YOU CANNOT HIDE!
RUMBLE! THIS HAS TO STOP! PLEASE, LISTEN TO ME!
PEACE

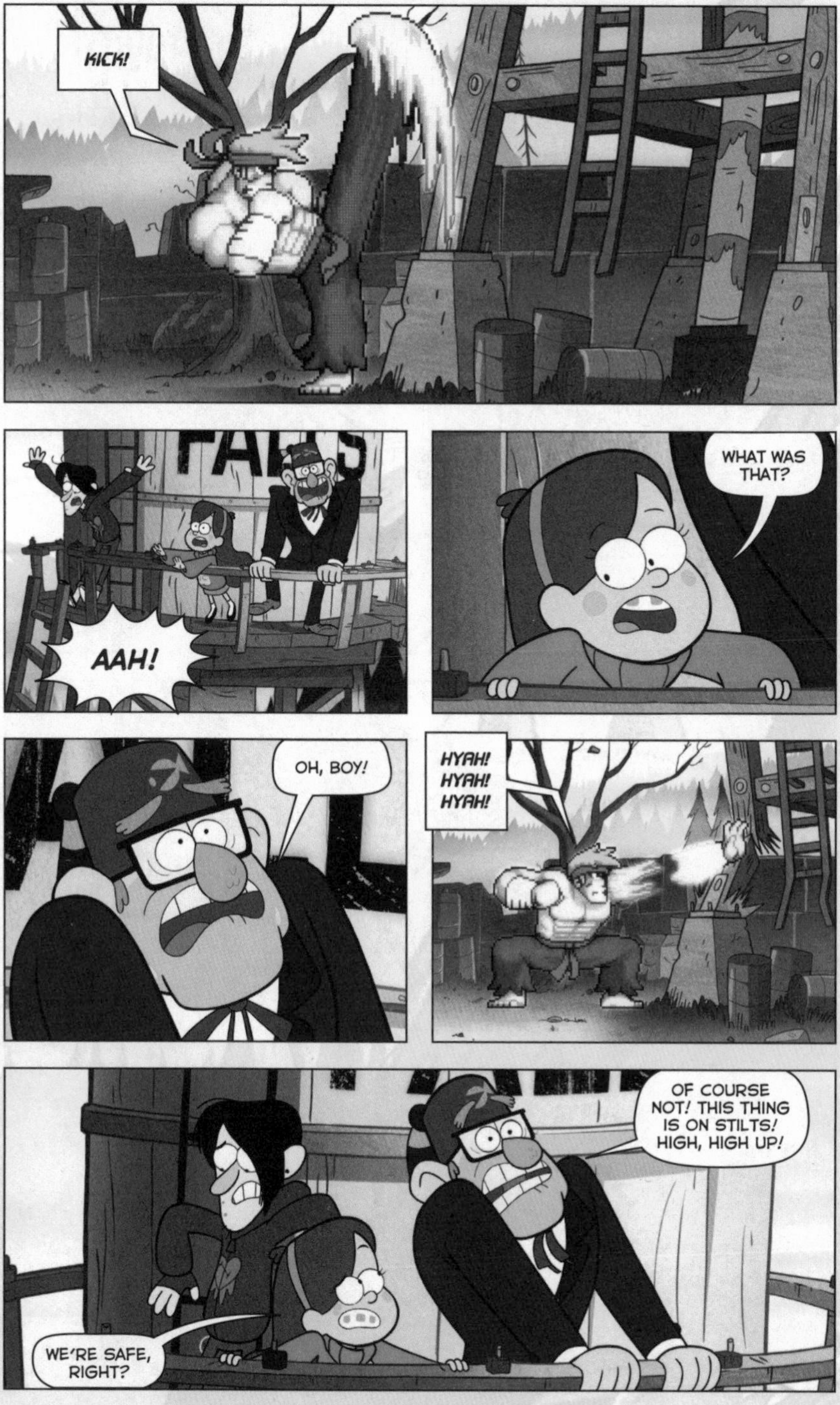
KICK!
AAH!
WHAT WAS THAT?
OH, BOY!
HYAH! HYAH! HYAH!
OF COURSE NOT! THIS THING IS ON STILTS! HIGH, HIGH UP!
WE'RE SAFE, RIGHT?

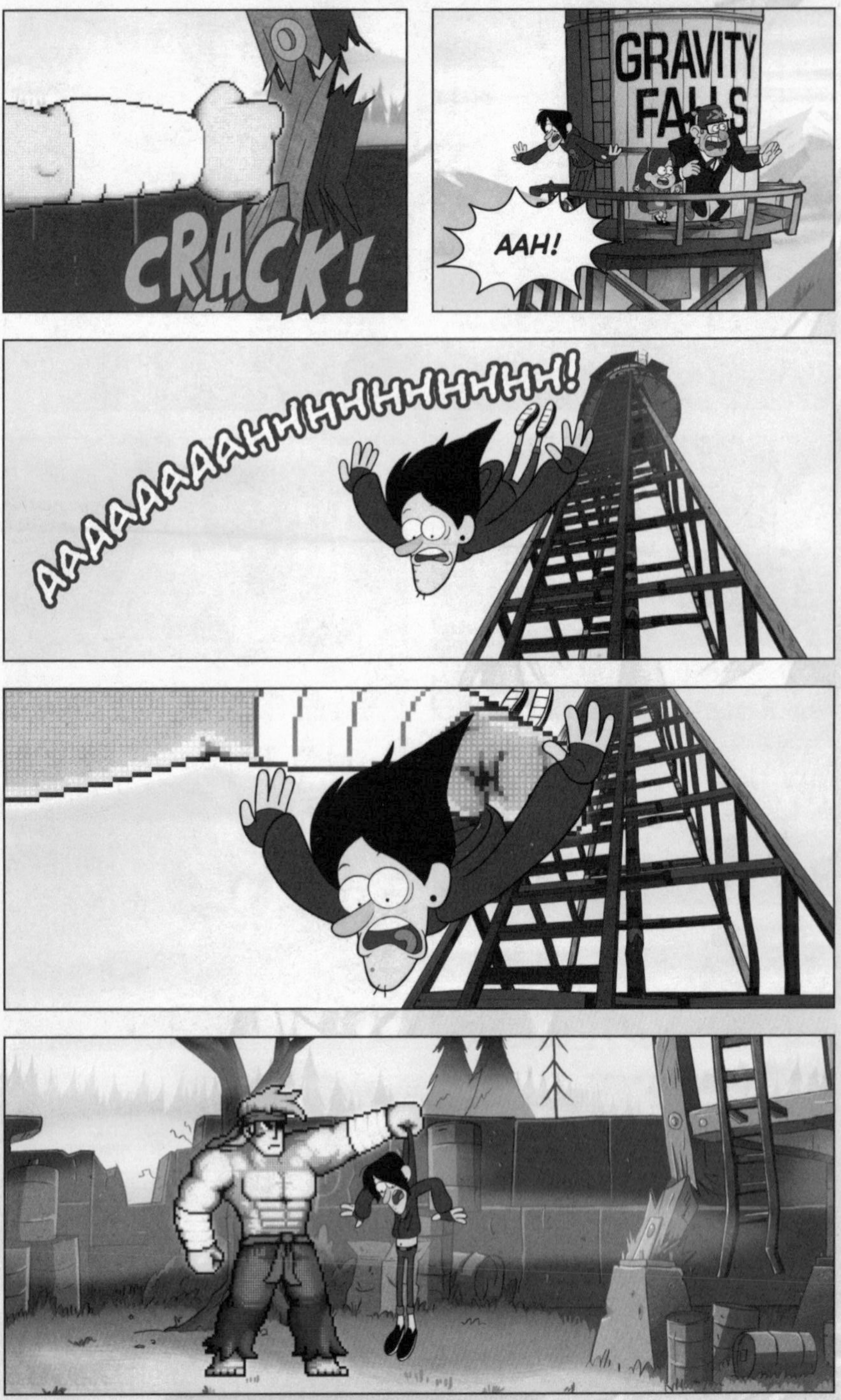
CRACK!
GRAVITY FALLS
AAH!
AAAAAAAAAHHHHHHHH!

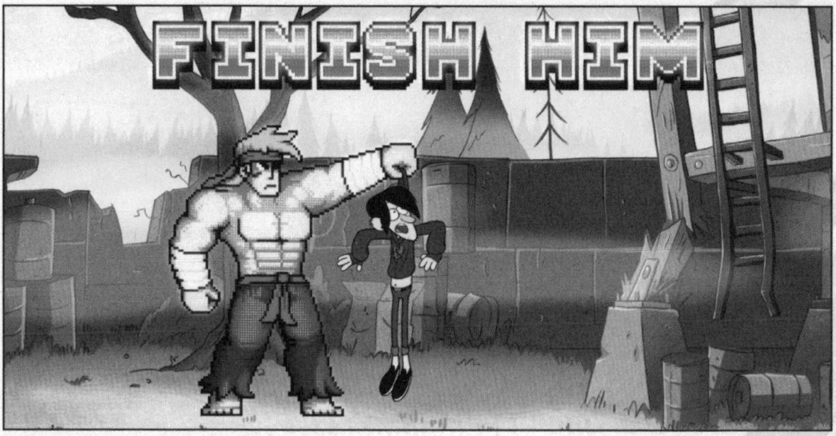
FINISH HIM

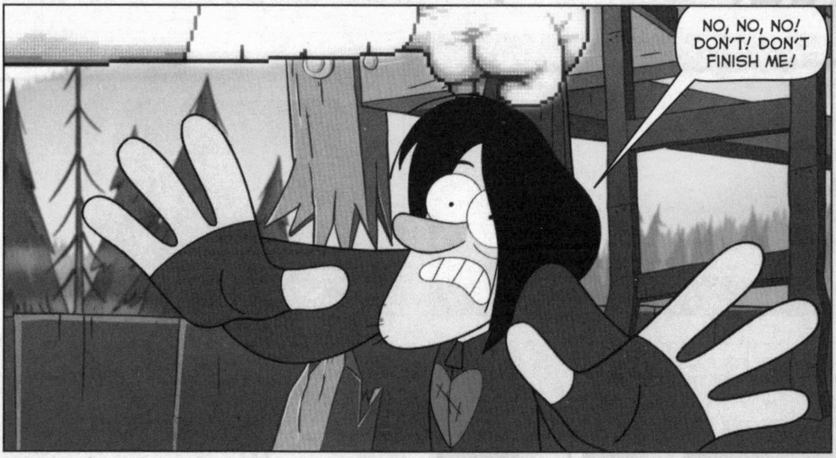
NO, NO, NO! DON'T! DON'T FINISH ME!

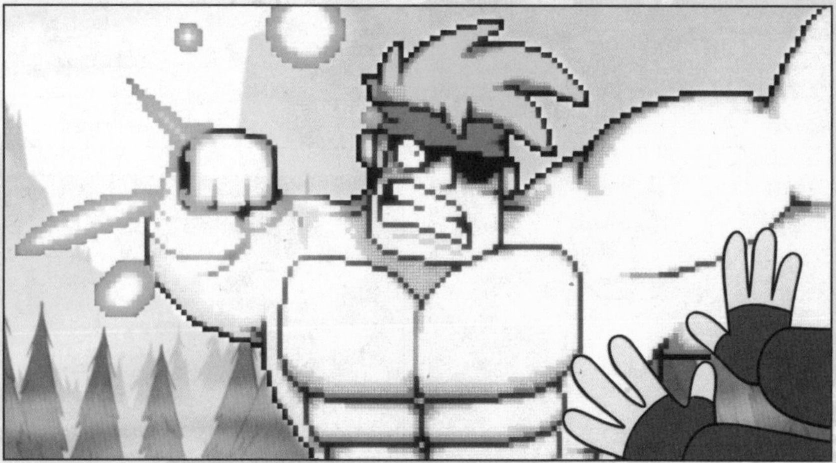

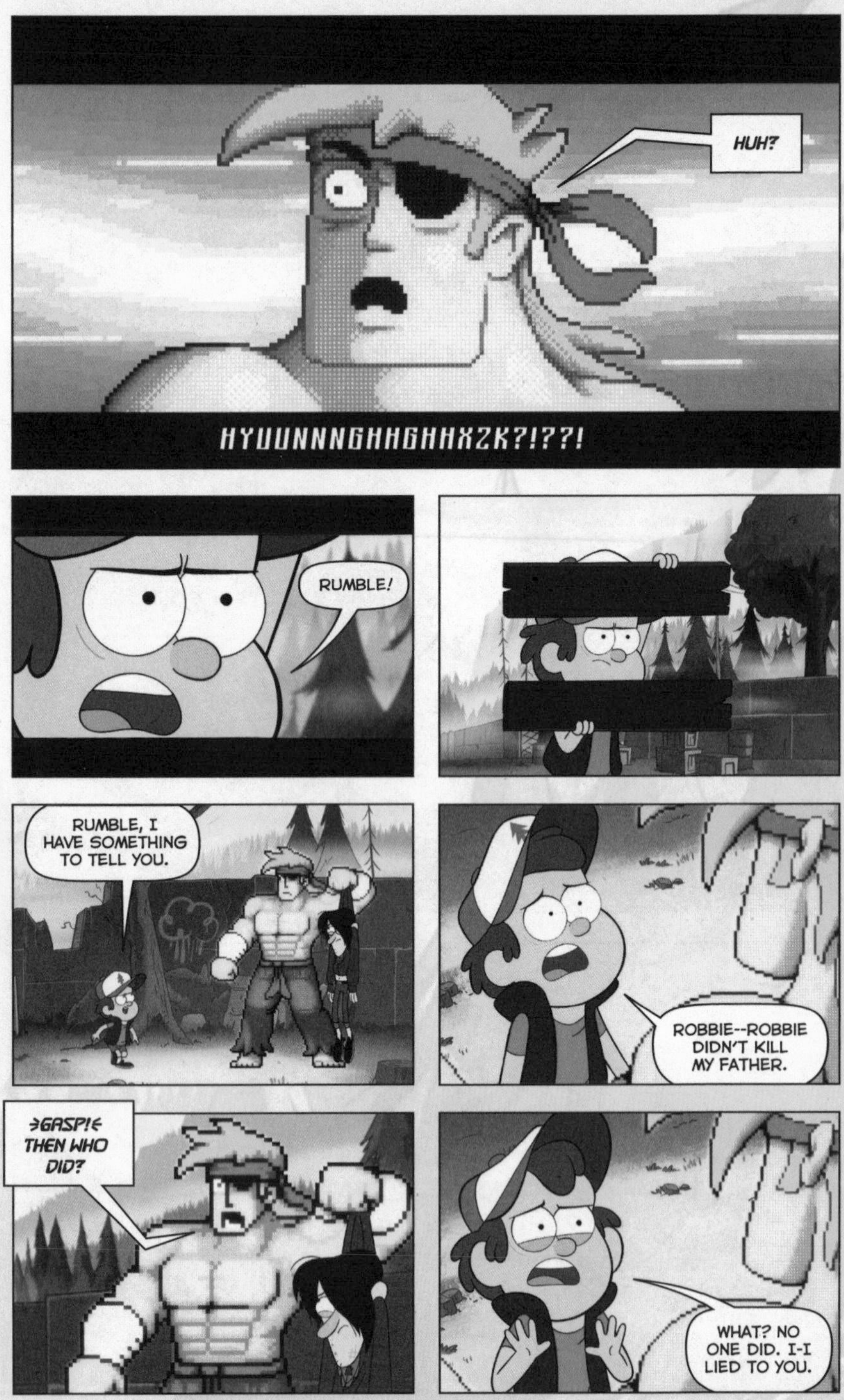
HUH?
HYUUNNNGHHGHHXZK?!??!
RUMBLE!
RUMBLE, I HAVE SOMETHING TO TELL YOU.
ROBBIE--ROBBIE DIDN'T KILL MY FATHER.
GASP! THEN WHO DID?
WHAT? NO ONE DID. I-I LIED TO YOU.

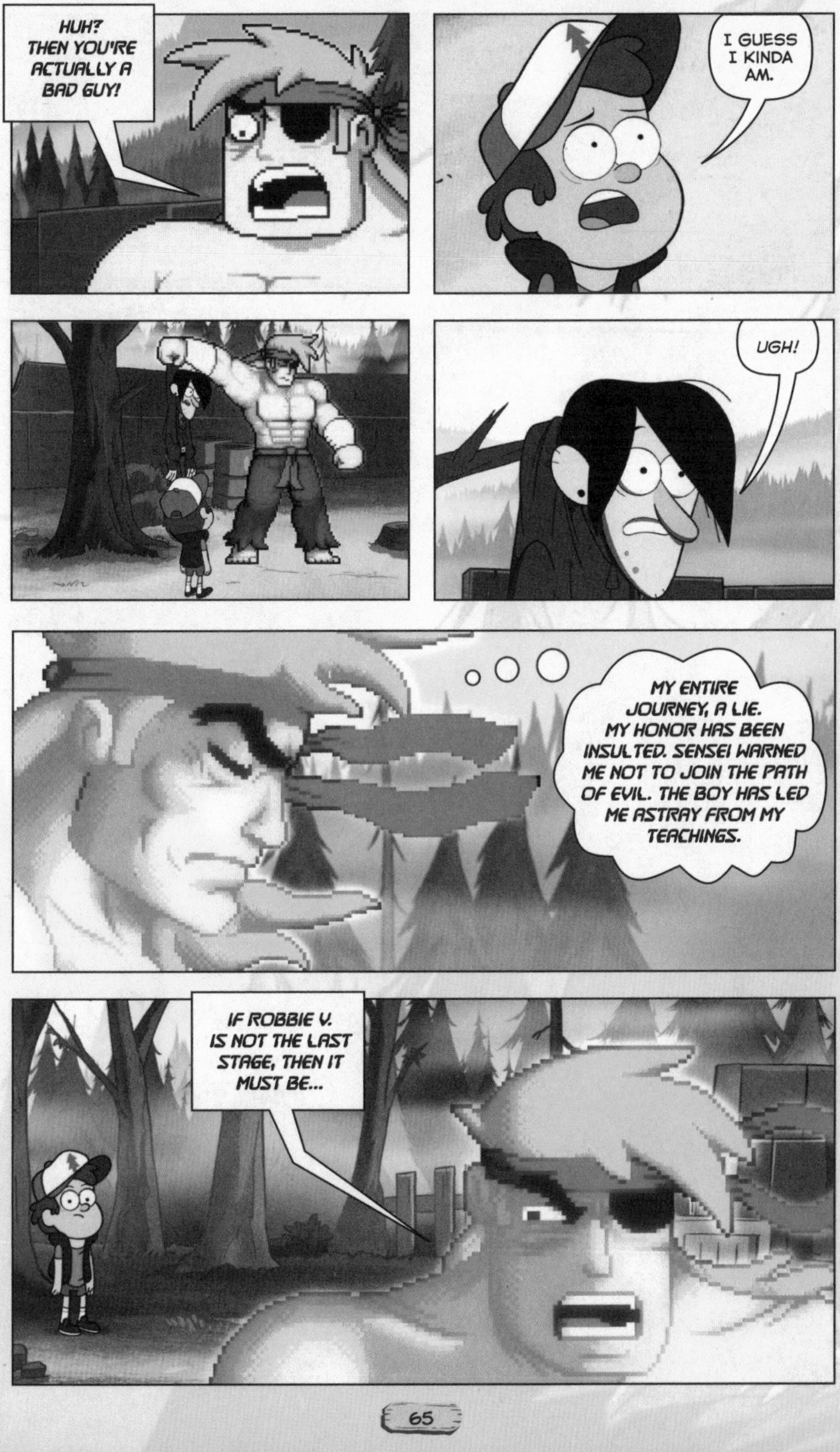
HUH? THEN YOU'RE ACTUALLY A BAD GUY!
I GUESS I KINDA AM.
UGH!
MY ENTIRE JOURNEY, A LIE. MY HONOR HAS BEEN INSULTED. SENSEI WARNED ME NOT TO JOIN THE PATH OF EVIL. THE BOY HAS LED ME ASTRAY FROM MY TEACHINGS.
IF ROBBIE V. IS NOT THE LAST STAGE, THEN IT MUST BE...

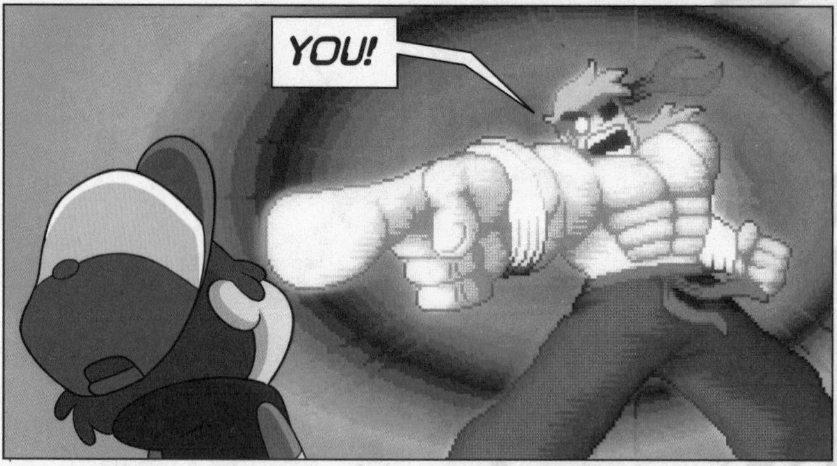
YOU!

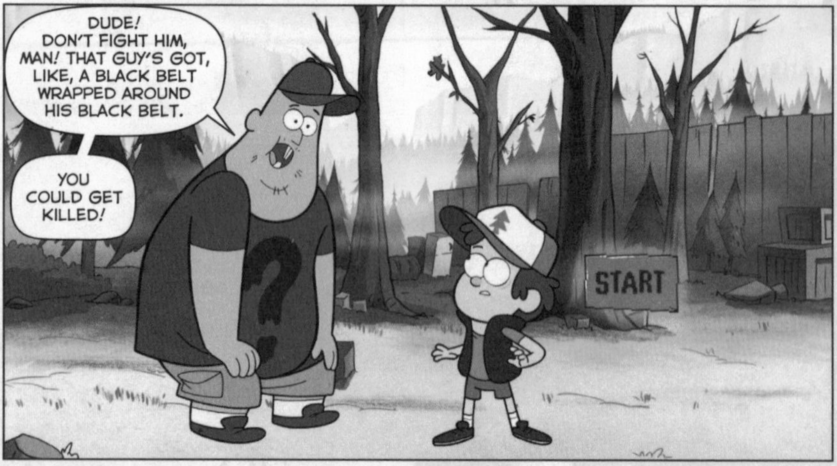
DUDE! DON'T FIGHT HIM, MAN! THAT GUY'S GOT, LIKE, A BLACK BELT WRAPPED AROUND HIS BLACK BELT.
YOU COULD GET KILLED!
START

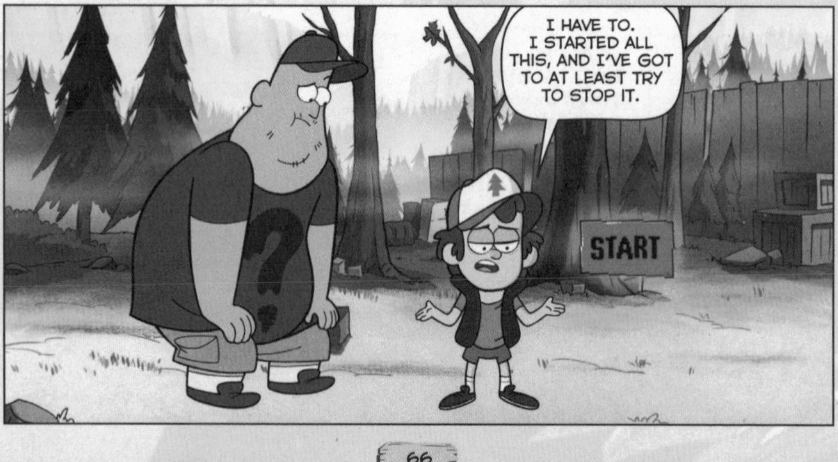
I HAVE TO. I STARTED ALL THIS, AND I'VE GOT TO AT LEAST TRY TO STOP IT.
START

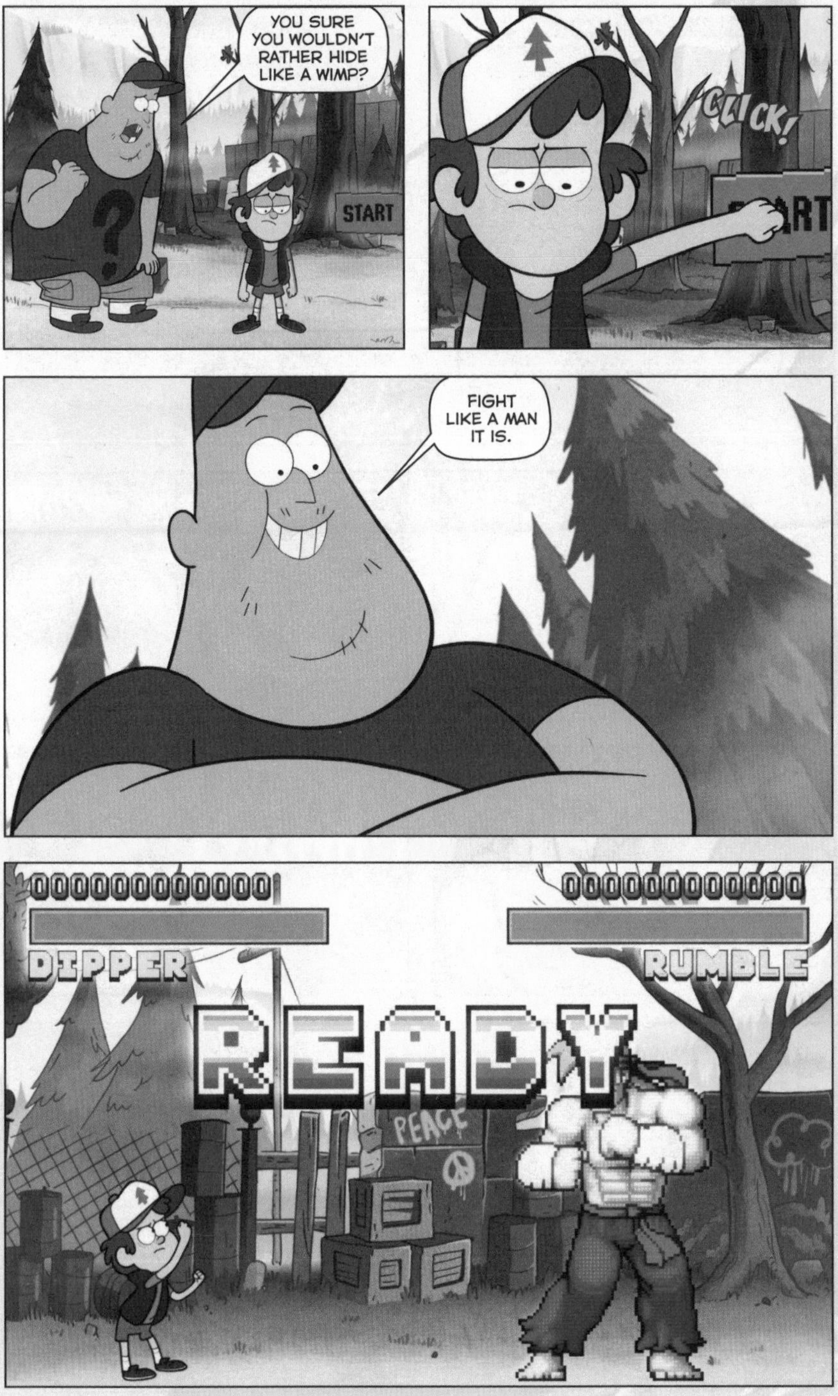
YOU SURE YOU WOULDN'T RATHER HIDE LIKE A WIMP?
START
CLICK!
FIGHT LIKE A MAN IT IS.
0000000000000
0000000000000
DIPPER
RUMBLE
READY
PEACE

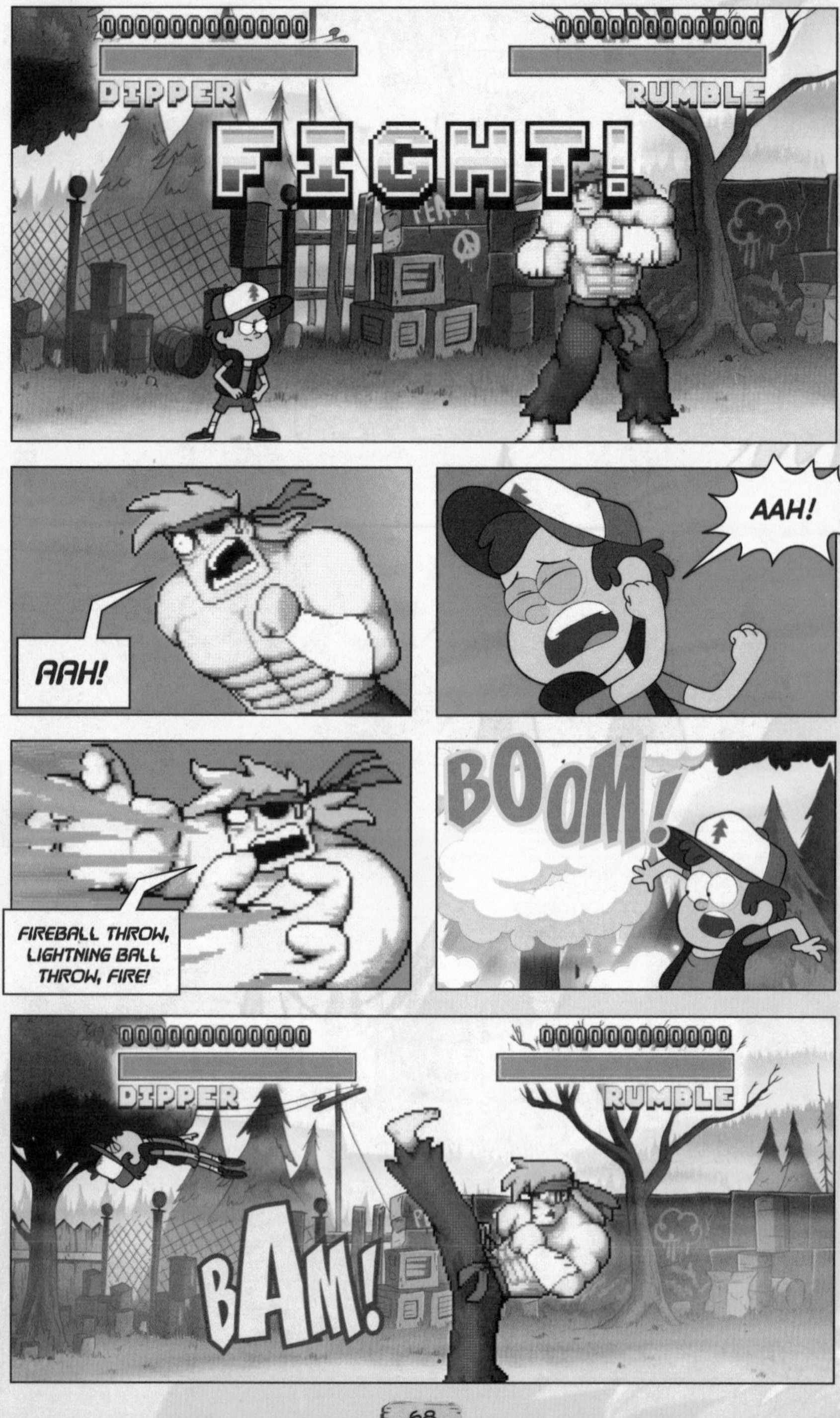
DIPPER
RUMBLE
FIGHT!
AAH!
AAH!
FIREBALL THROW, LIGHTNING BALL THROW, FIRE!
BOOOM!
DIPPER
RUMBLE
BAM!

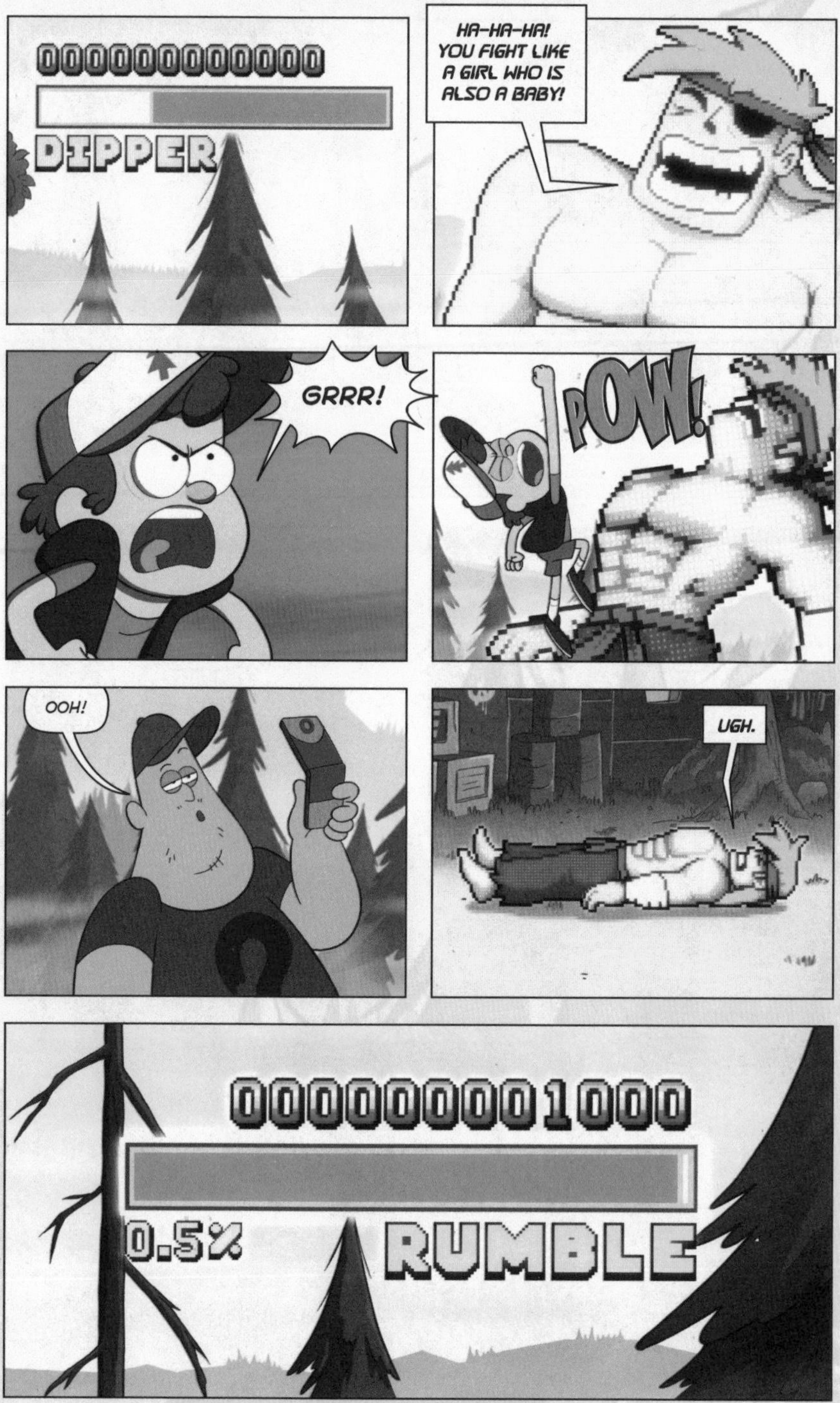
0000000000000
DIPPER
HA-HA-HA! YOU FIGHT LIKE A GIRL WHO IS ALSO A BABY!
GRRR!
POW!
OOH!
UGH.
0000000001000
0.5%
RUMBLE

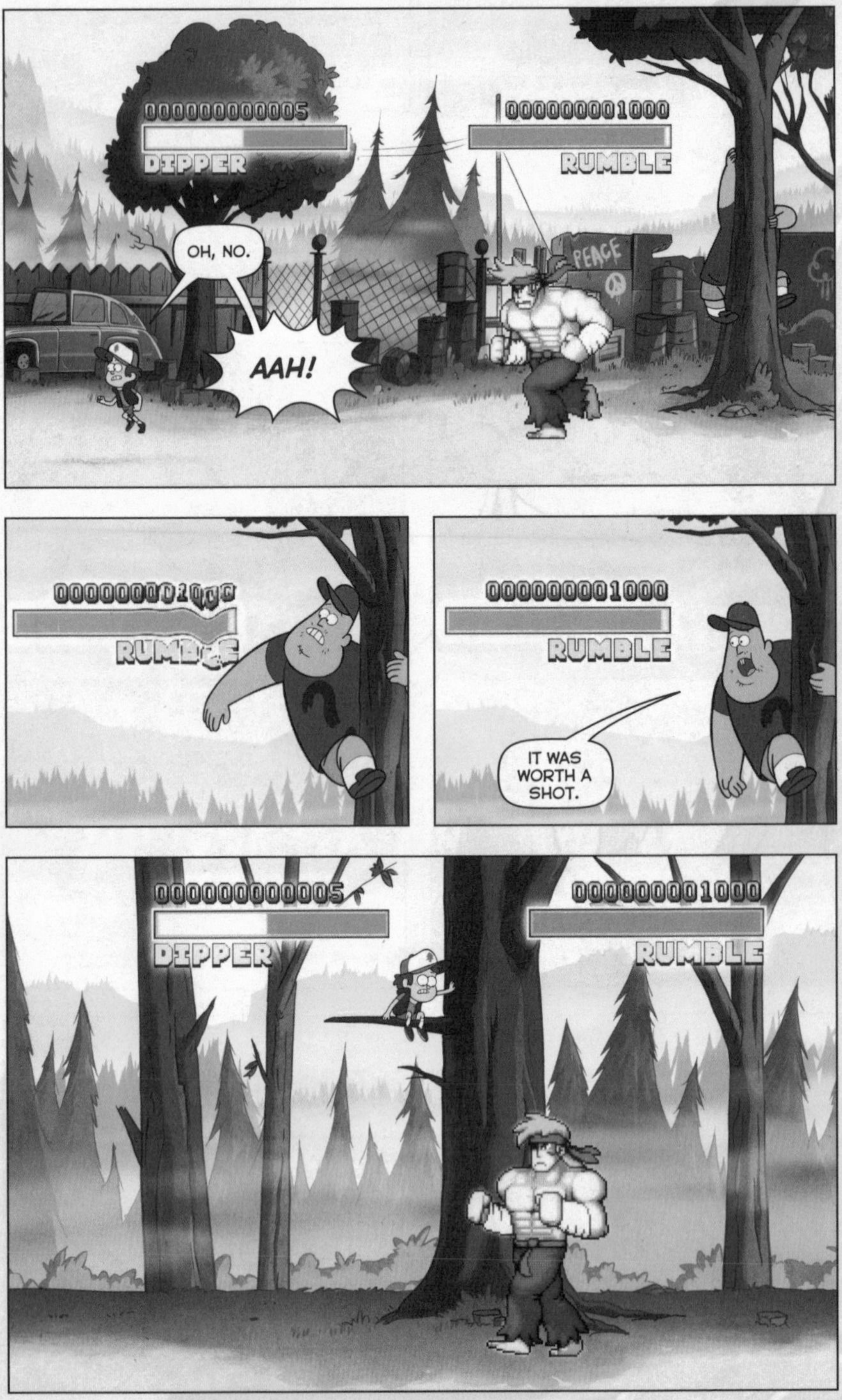
000000000005
DIPPER
000000001000
RUMBLE
PEACE
OH, NO.
AAH!
000000001000
RUMBLE
IT WAS WORTH A SHOT.
000000000005
DIPPER
000000001000
RUMBLE

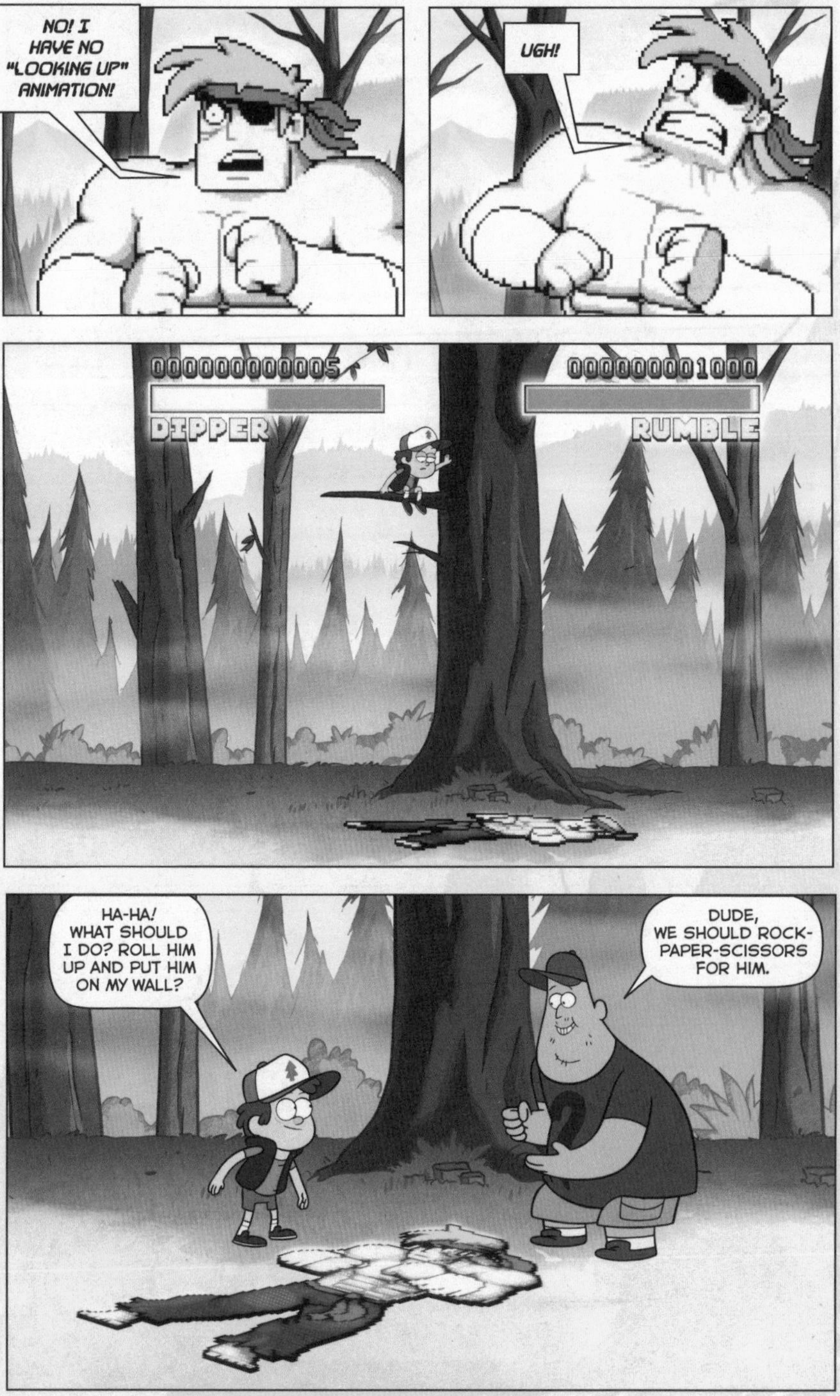
NO! I HAVE NO "LOOKING UP" ANIMATION!
UGH!
000000000005
000000001000
DIPPER
RUMBLE
HA-HA! WHAT SHOULD I DO? ROLL HIM UP AND PUT HIM ON MY WALL?
DUDE, WE SHOULD ROCK-PAPER-SCISSORS FOR HIM.

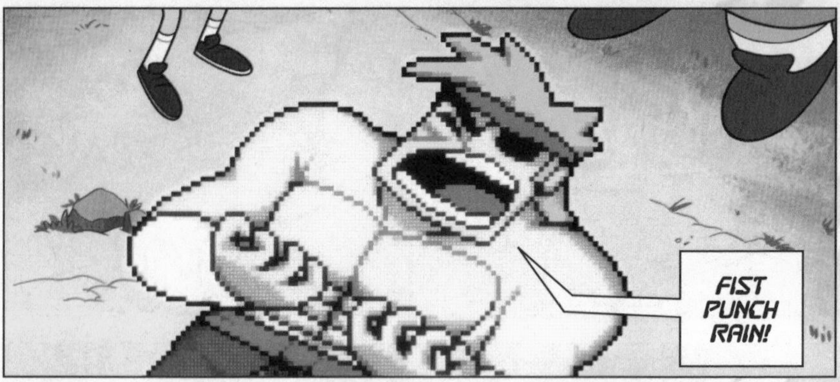
FIST PUNCH RAIN!

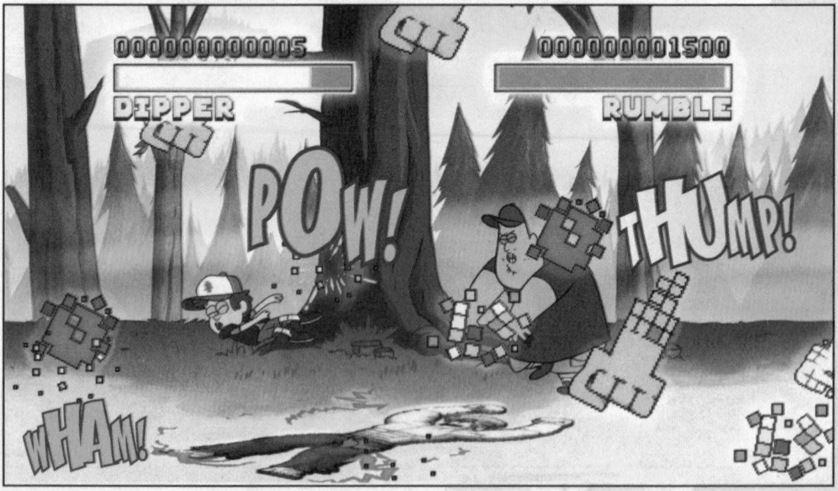
000000000005
DIPPER
000000001500
RUMBLE
POW!
THUMP!
WHAM!

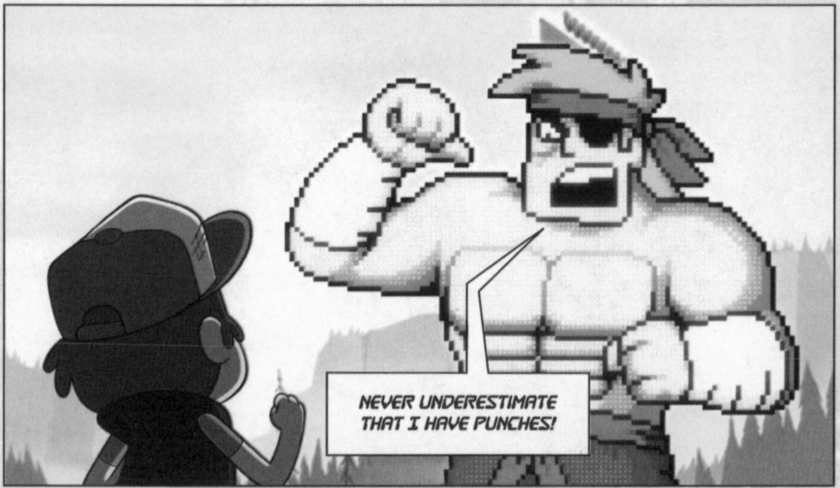
NEVER UNDERESTIMATE THAT I HAVE PUNCHES!

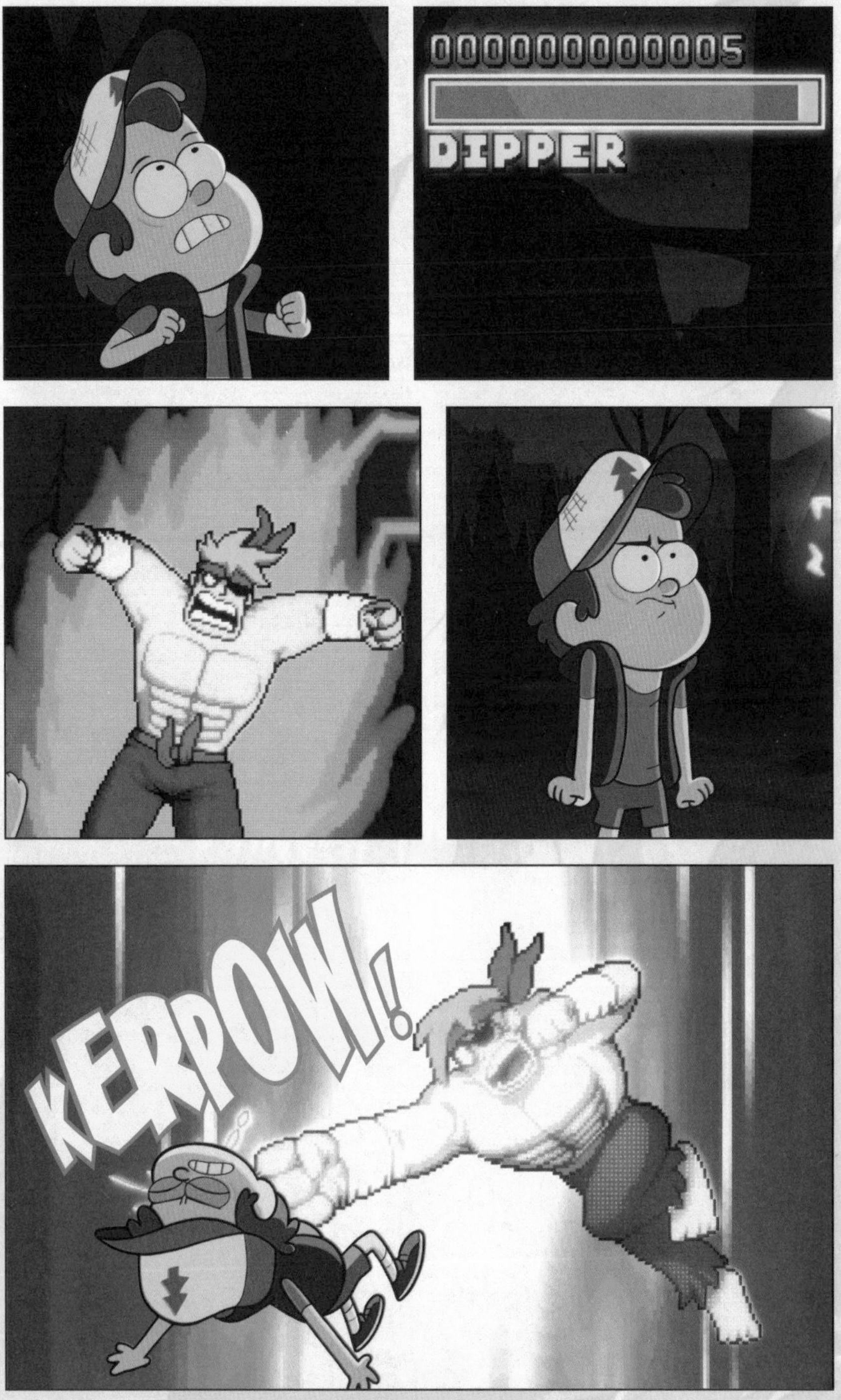
000000000005
DIPPER
KERPOW!

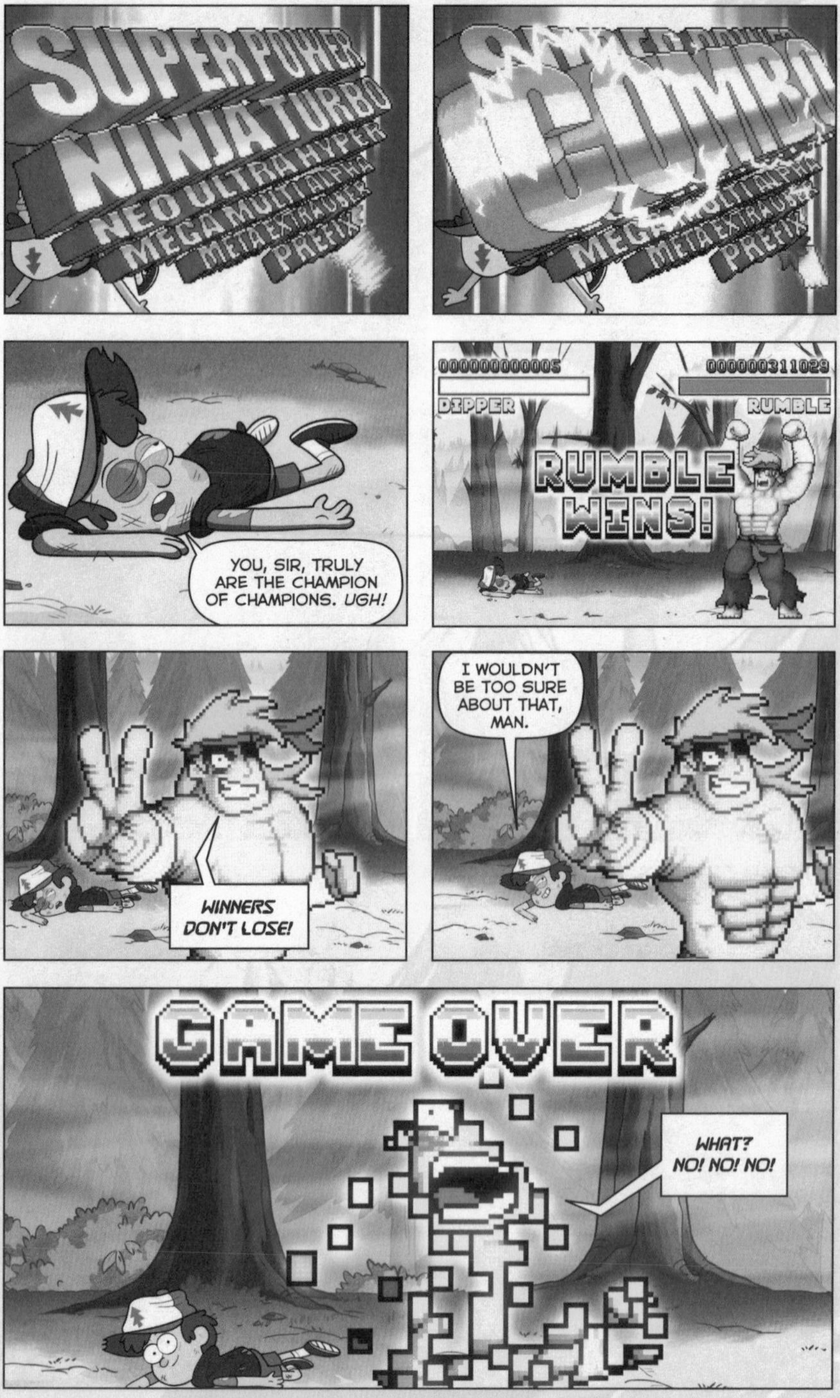
SUPERPOWER
NINJA TURBO
NEO ULTRA HYPER
MEGA MULTI ALPHA
META EXTRA UBER
PREFIX
COMBO
MEGA MULTI ALPHA
META EXTRA UBER
PREFIX
YOU, SIR, TRULY ARE THE CHAMPION OF CHAMPIONS. *UGH!*
000000000005
DIPPER
000000311029
RUMBLE
RUMBLE WINS!
WINNERS DON'T LOSE!
I WOULDN'T BE TOO SURE ABOUT THAT, MAN.
GAME OVER
WHAT? NO! NO! NO!

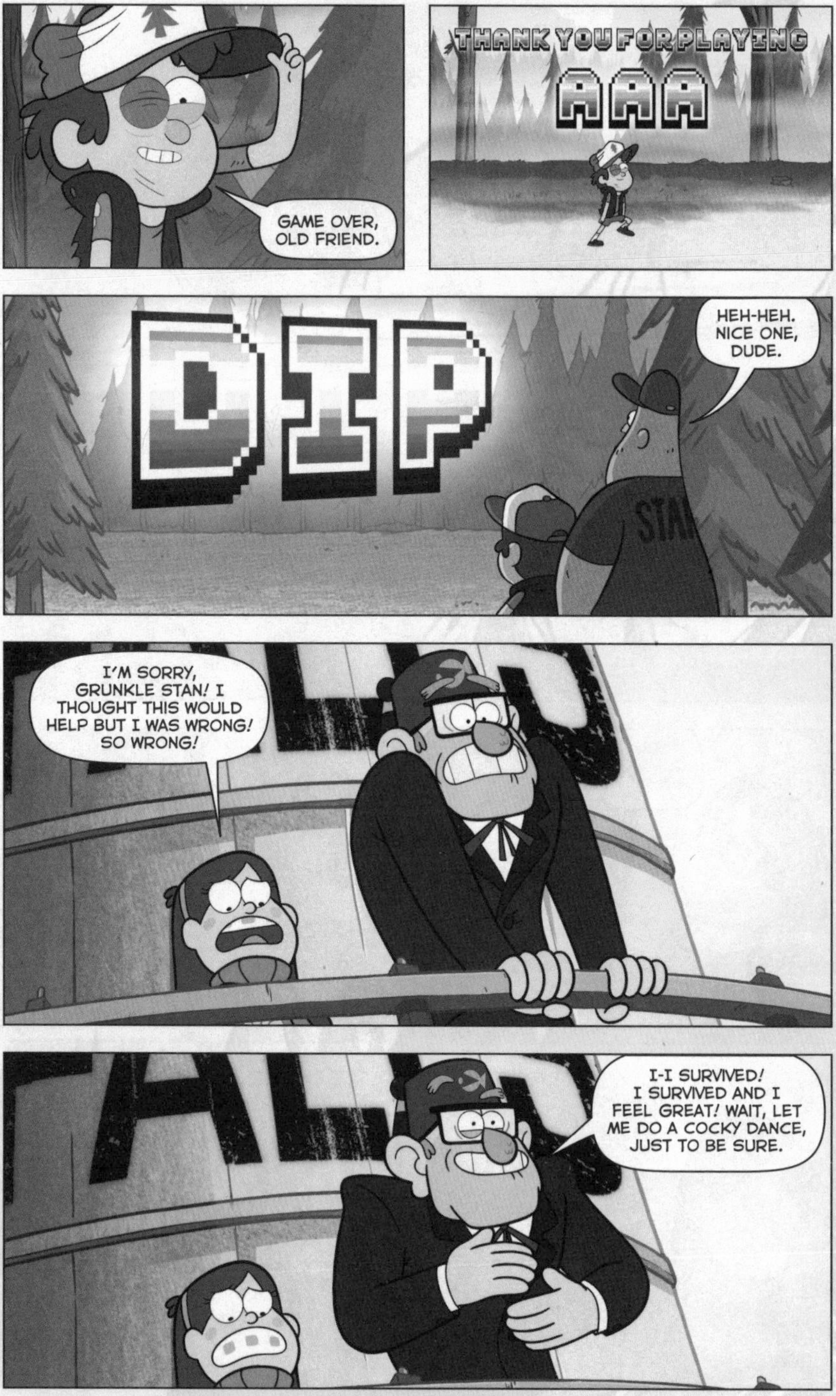
GAME OVER, OLD FRIEND.
THANK YOU FOR PLAYING
AAA
DIP
HEH-HEH. NICE ONE, DUDE.
STAN
I'M SORRY, GRUNKLE STAN! I THOUGHT THIS WOULD HELP BUT I WAS WRONG! SO WRONG!
I-I SURVIVED! I SURVIVED AND I FEEL GREAT! WAIT, LET ME DO A COCKY DANCE, JUST TO BE SURE.

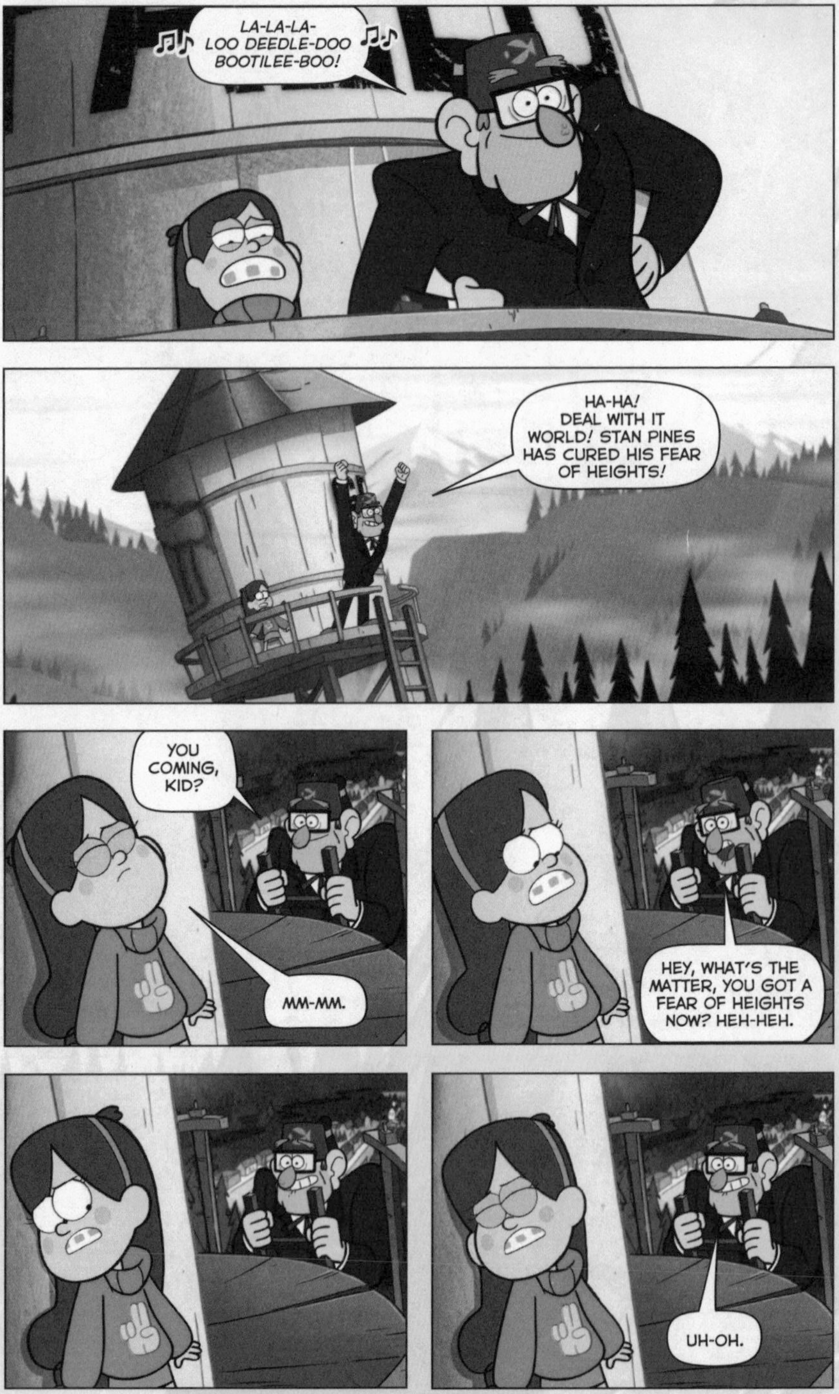
LA-LA-LA-
LOO DEEDLE-DOO
BOOTILEE-BOO!
HA-HA!
DEAL WITH IT
WORLD! STAN PINES
HAS CURED HIS FEAR
OF HEIGHTS!
YOU
COMING,
KID?
MM-MM.
HEY, WHAT'S THE
MATTER, YOU GOT A
FEAR OF HEIGHTS
NOW? HEH-HEH.
UH-OH.

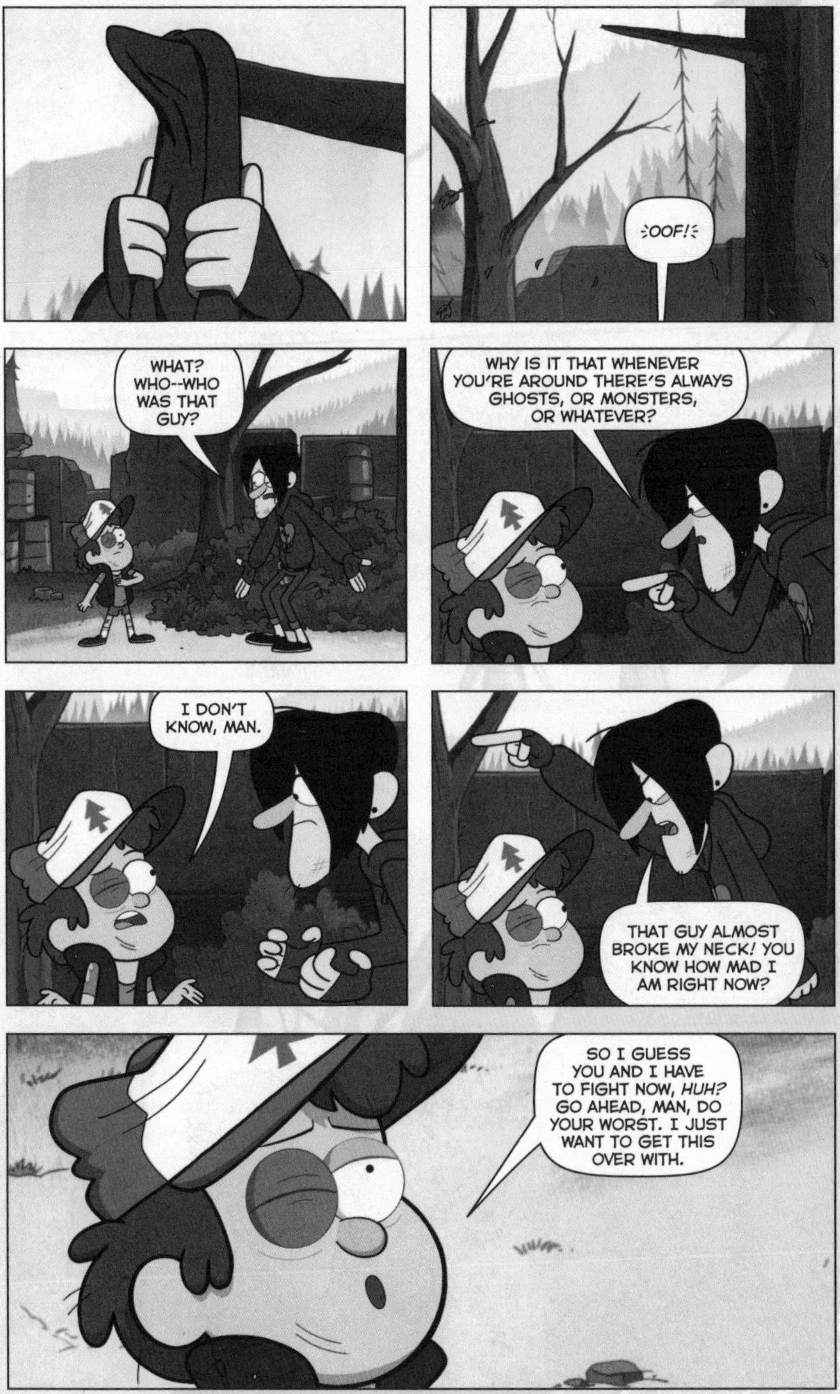
OOF!
WHAT? WHO--WHO WAS THAT GUY?
WHY IS IT THAT WHENEVER YOU'RE AROUND THERE'S ALWAYS GHOSTS, OR MONSTERS, OR WHATEVER?
I DON'T KNOW, MAN.
THAT GUY ALMOST BROKE MY NECK! YOU KNOW HOW MAD I AM RIGHT NOW?
SO I GUESS YOU AND I HAVE TO FIGHT NOW, HUH? GO AHEAD, MAN, DO YOUR WORST. I JUST WANT TO GET THIS OVER WITH.

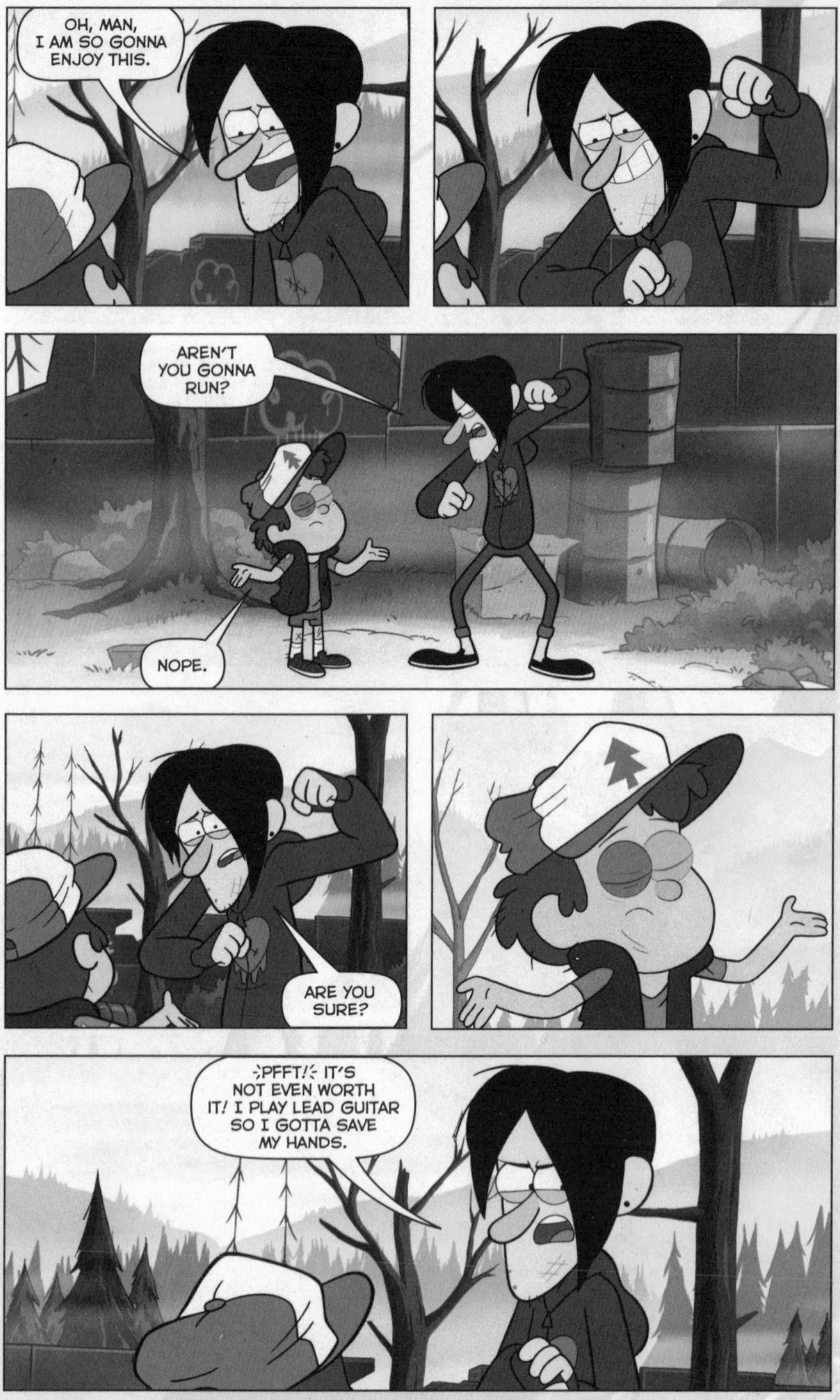
OH, MAN, I AM SO GONNA ENJOY THIS.
AREN'T YOU GONNA RUN?
NOPE.
ARE YOU SURE?
-PFFT!- IT'S NOT EVEN WORTH IT! I PLAY LEAD GUITAR SO I GOTTA SAVE MY HANDS.

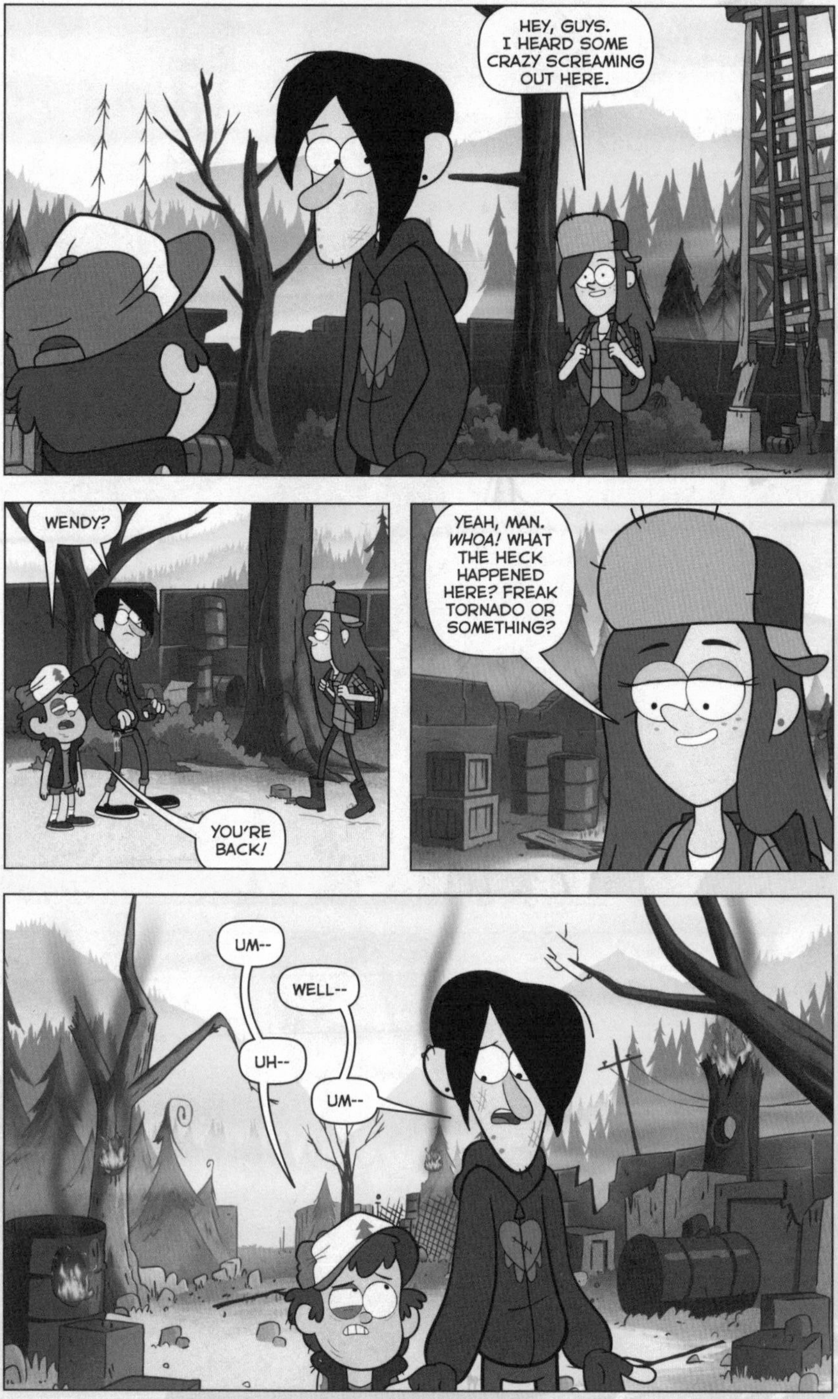
HEY, GUYS. I HEARD SOME CRAZY SCREAMING OUT HERE.
WENDY?
YOU'RE BACK!
YEAH, MAN. *WHOA!* WHAT THE HECK HAPPENED HERE? FREAK TORNADO OR SOMETHING?
UM--
WELL--
UH--
UM--

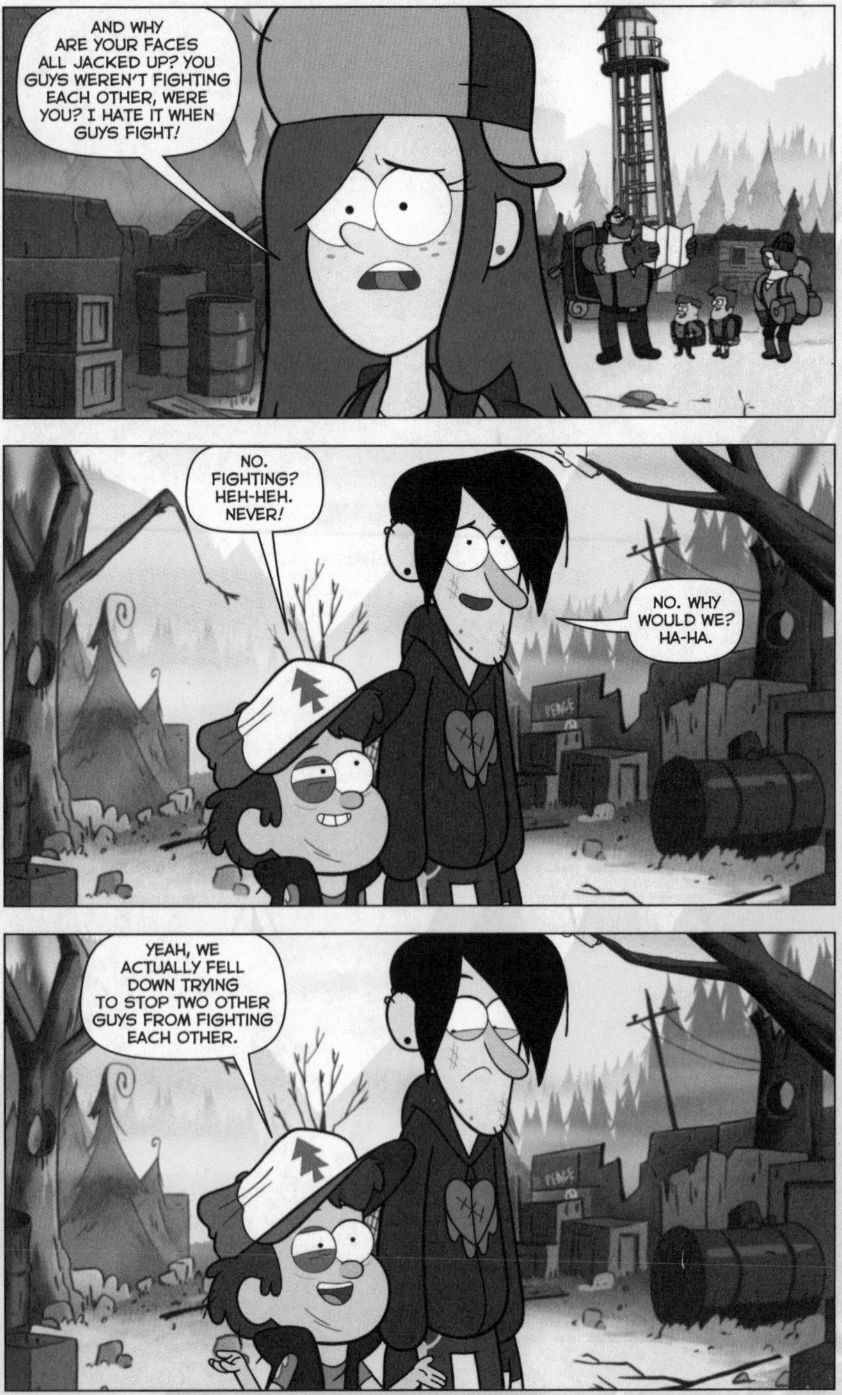
AND WHY ARE YOUR FACES ALL JACKED UP? YOU GUYS WEREN'T FIGHTING EACH OTHER, WERE YOU? I HATE IT WHEN GUYS FIGHT!
NO. FIGHTING? HEH-HEH. NEVER!
NO. WHY WOULD WE? HA-HA.
YEAH, WE ACTUALLY FELL DOWN TRYING TO STOP TWO OTHER GUYS FROM FIGHTING EACH OTHER.

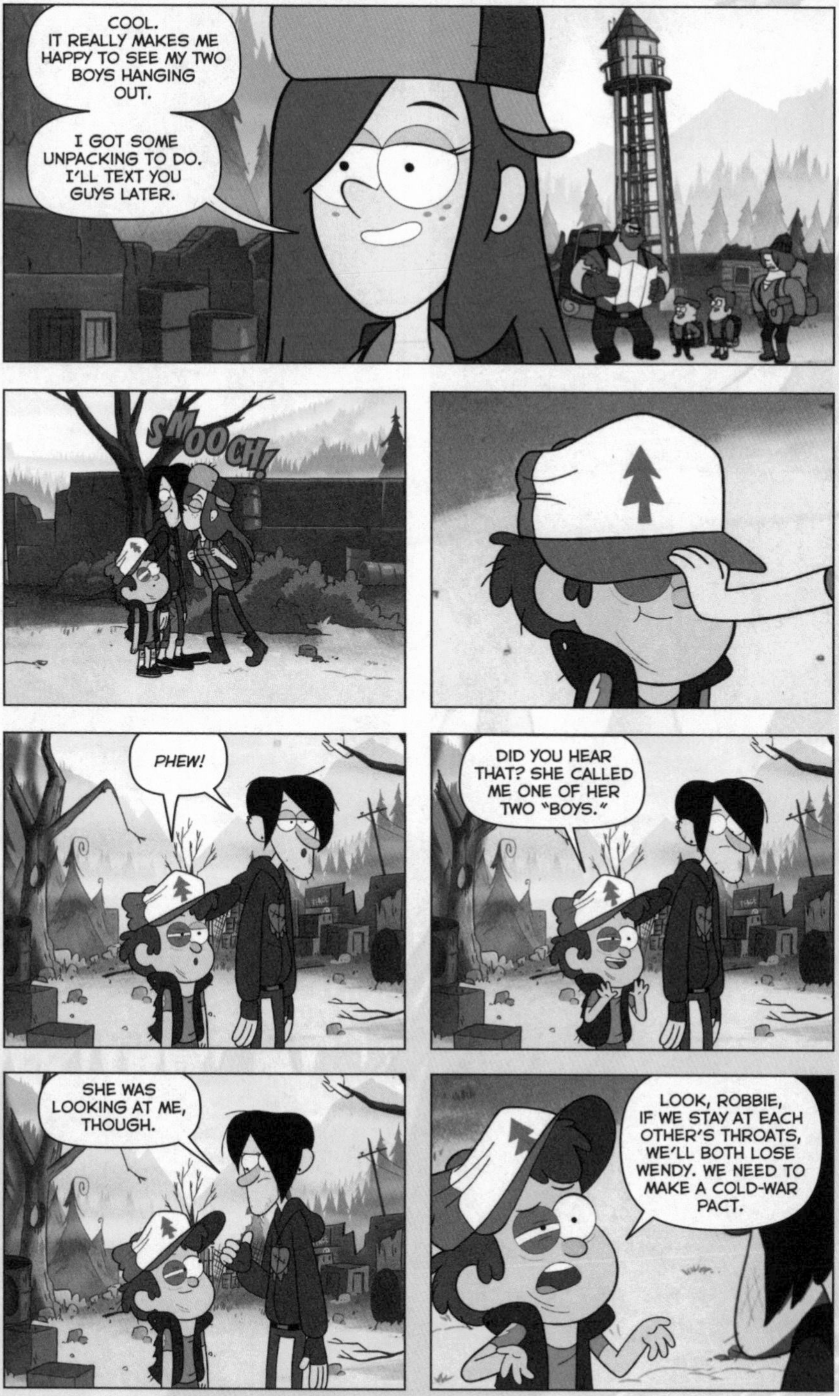
COOL. IT REALLY MAKES ME HAPPY TO SEE MY TWO BOYS HANGING OUT.
I GOT SOME UNPACKING TO DO. I'LL TEXT YOU GUYS LATER.
SMOOCH!
PHEW!
DID YOU HEAR THAT? SHE CALLED ME ONE OF HER TWO "BOYS."
SHE WAS LOOKING AT ME, THOUGH.
LOOK, ROBBIE, IF WE STAY AT EACH OTHER'S THROATS, WE'LL BOTH LOSE WENDY. WE NEED TO MAKE A COLD-WAR PACT.

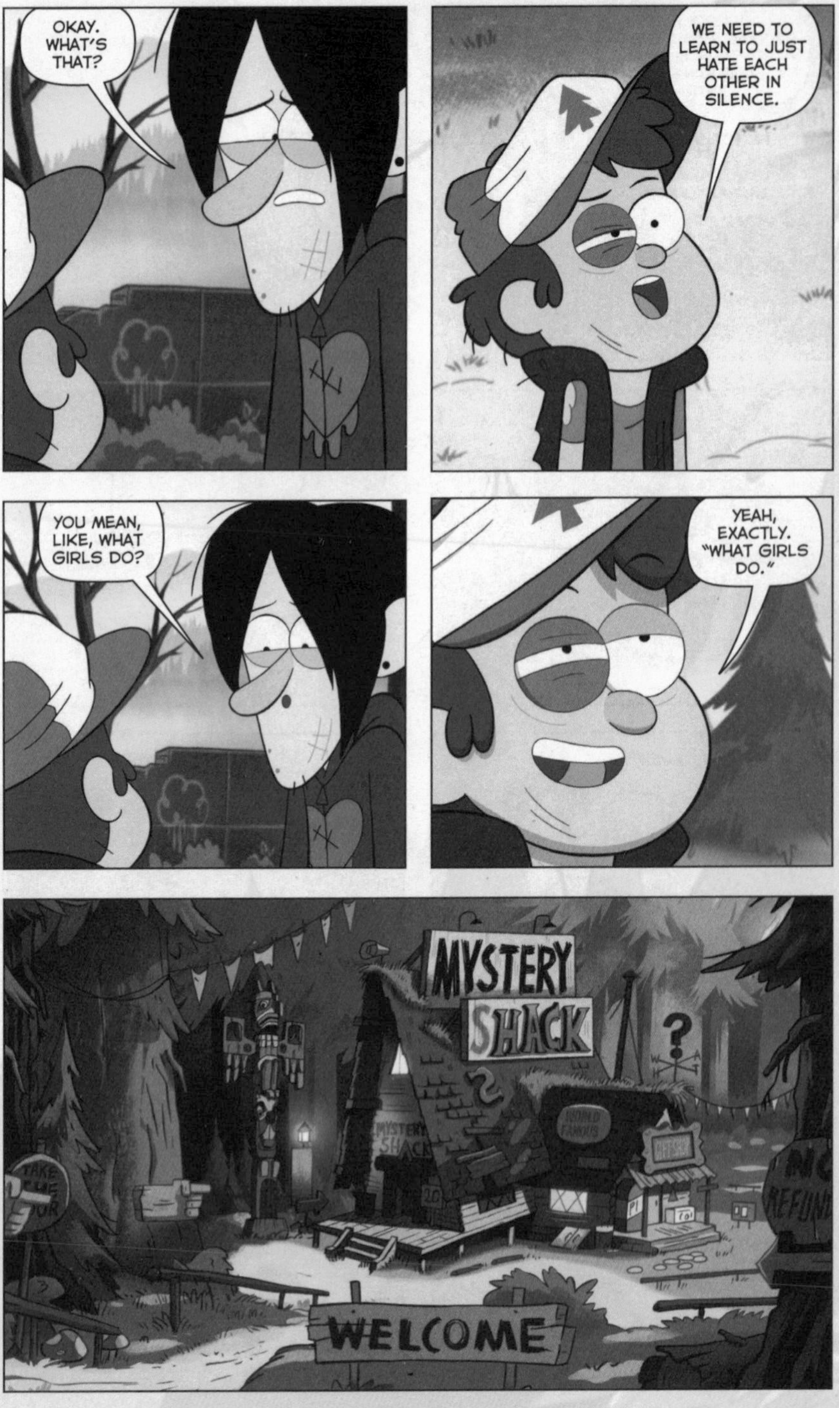
OKAY. WHAT'S THAT?
WE NEED TO LEARN TO JUST HATE EACH OTHER IN SILENCE.
YOU MEAN, LIKE, WHAT GIRLS DO?
YEAH, EXACTLY. "WHAT GIRLS DO."
MYSTERY SHACK
WELCOME

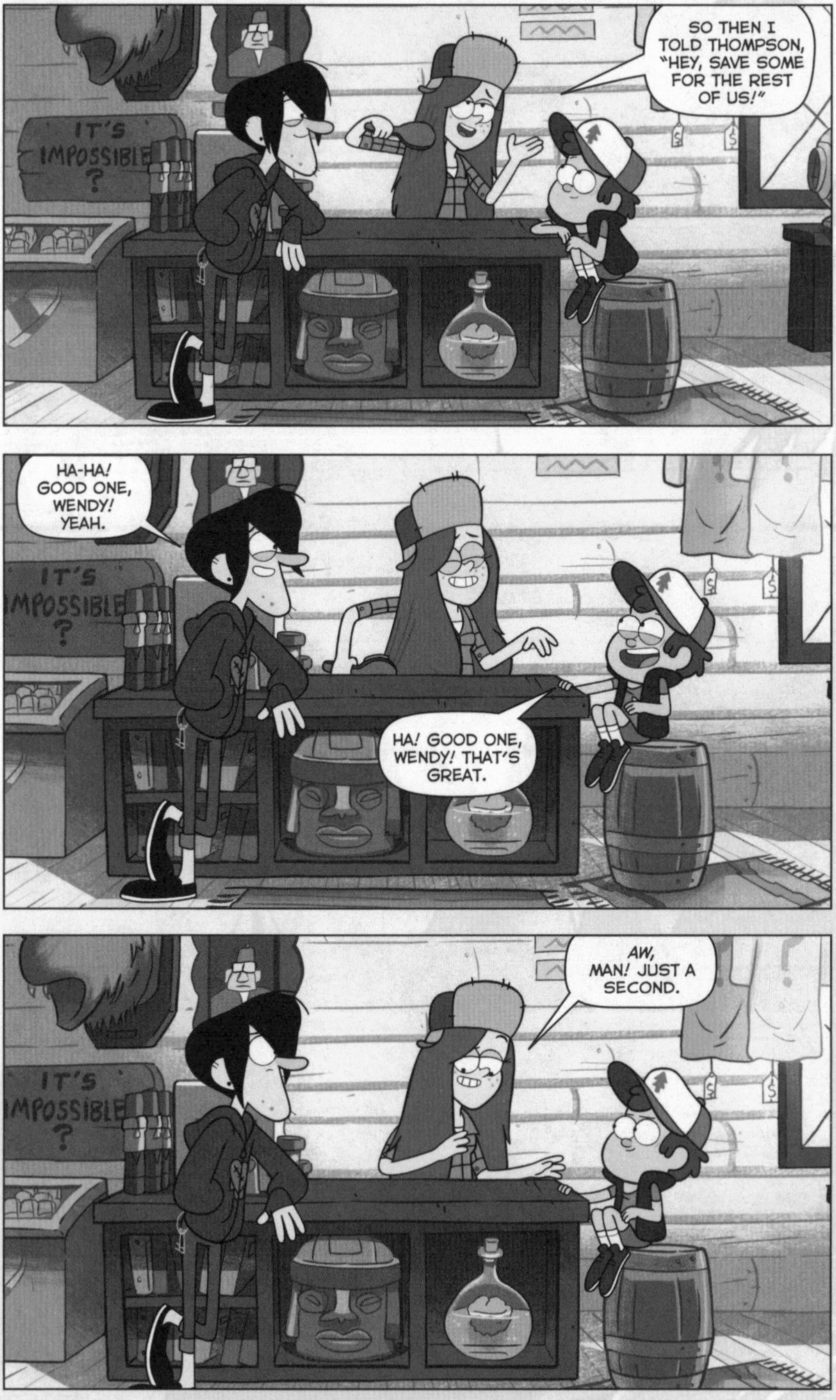
IT'S IMPOSSIBLE ?
SO THEN I TOLD THOMPSON, "HEY, SAVE SOME FOR THE REST OF US!"
HA-HA! GOOD ONE, WENDY! YEAH.
HA! GOOD ONE, WENDY! THAT'S GREAT.
AW, MAN! JUST A SECOND.

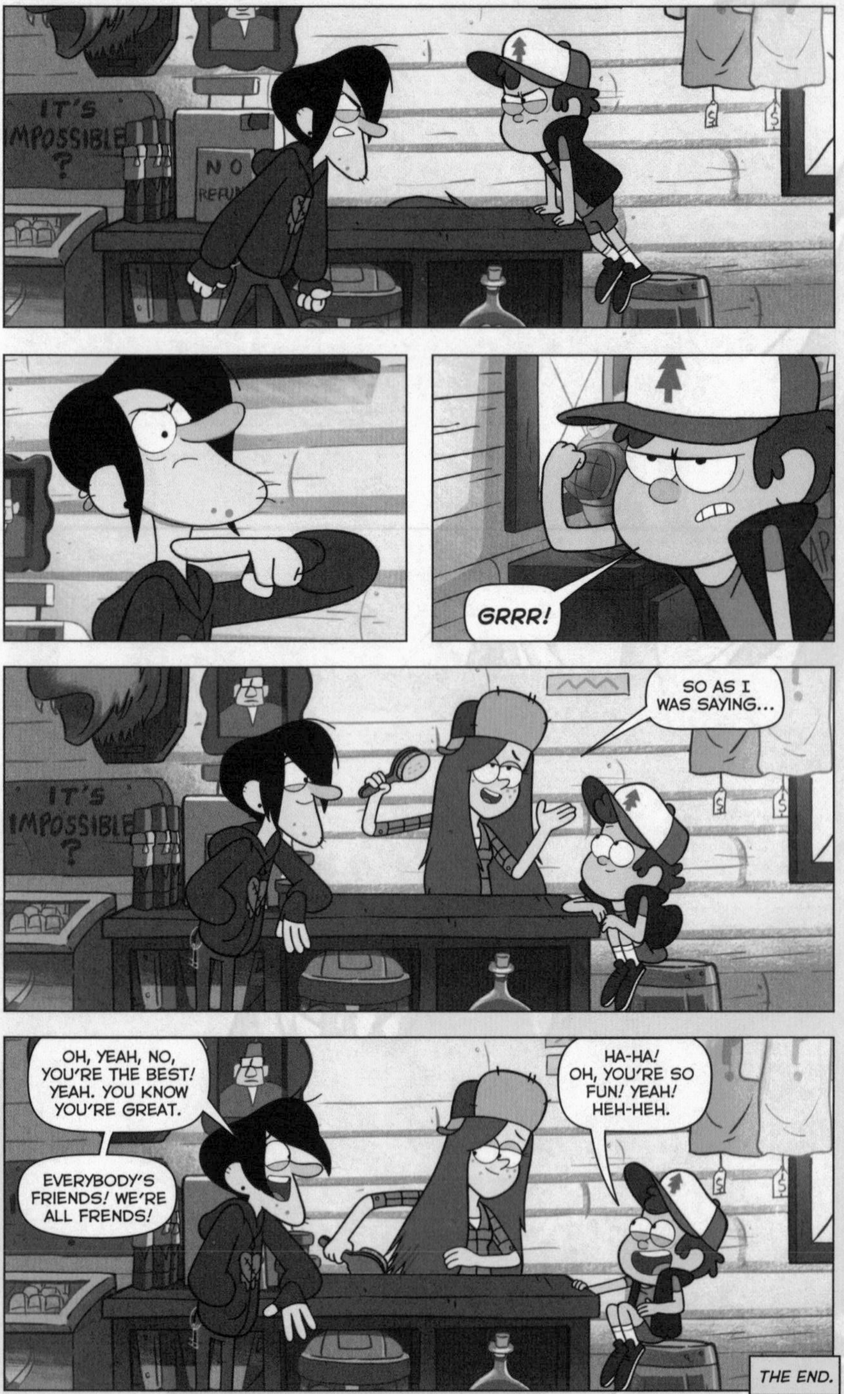
IT'S IMPOSSIBLE?
NO REFUN
GRRR!
SO AS I WAS SAYING...
OH, YEAH, NO, YOU'RE THE BEST! YEAH. YOU KNOW YOU'RE GREAT.
EVERYBODY'S FRIENDS! WE'RE ALL FRENDS!
HA-HA! OH, YOU'RE SO FUN! YEAH! HEH-HEH.
THE END.

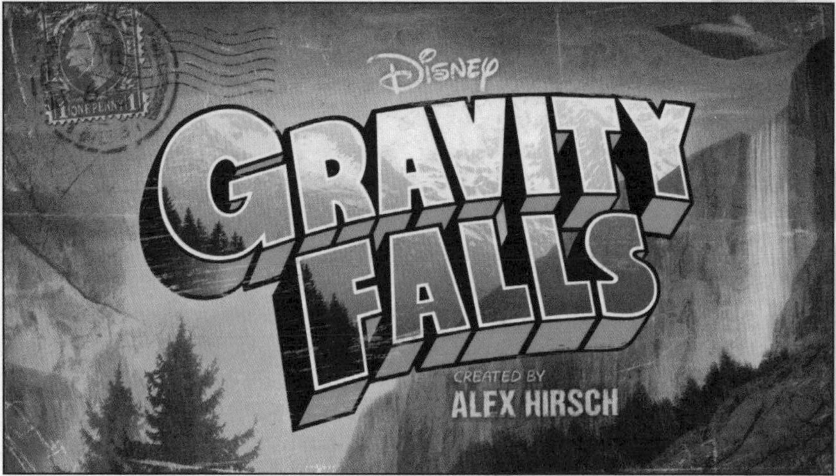
DISNEY
GRAVITY FALLS
CREATED BY
ALEX HIRSCH

LITTLE DIPPER
EPISODE 11

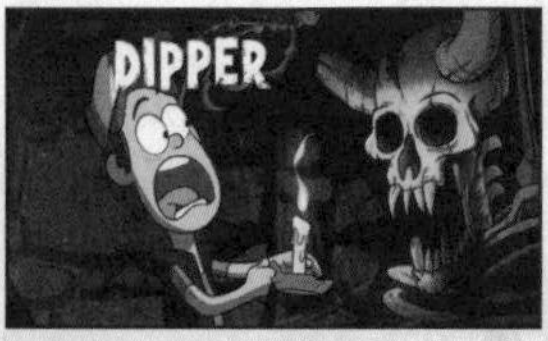
DIPPER
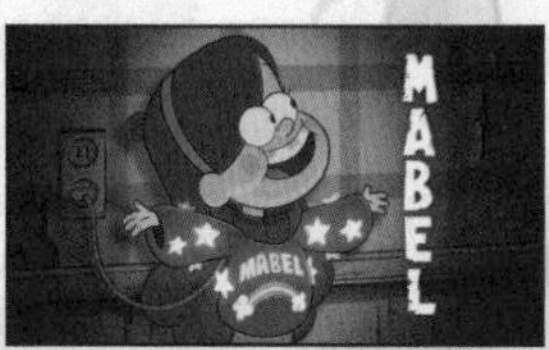
MABEL
MABEL
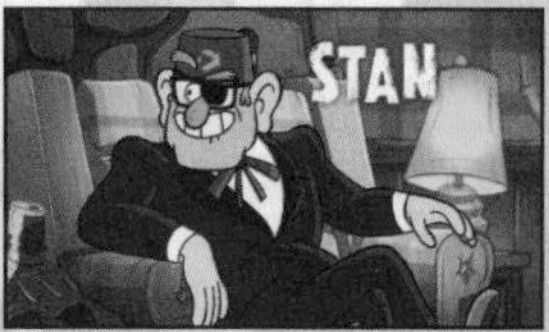
STAN

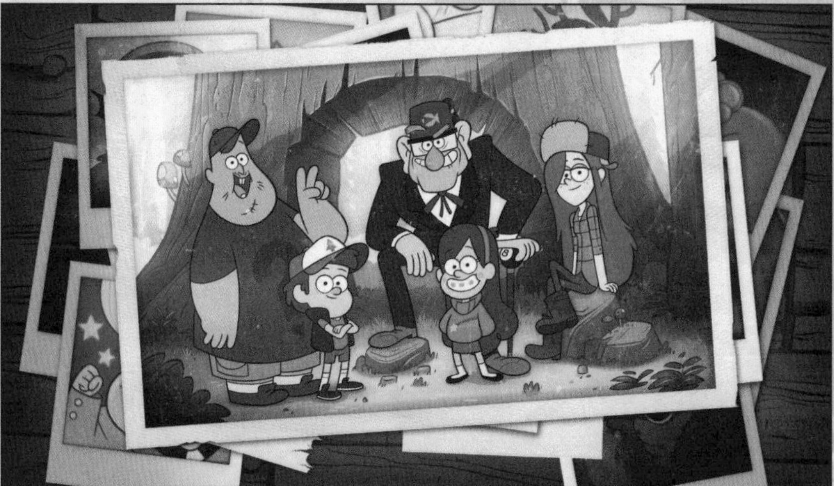

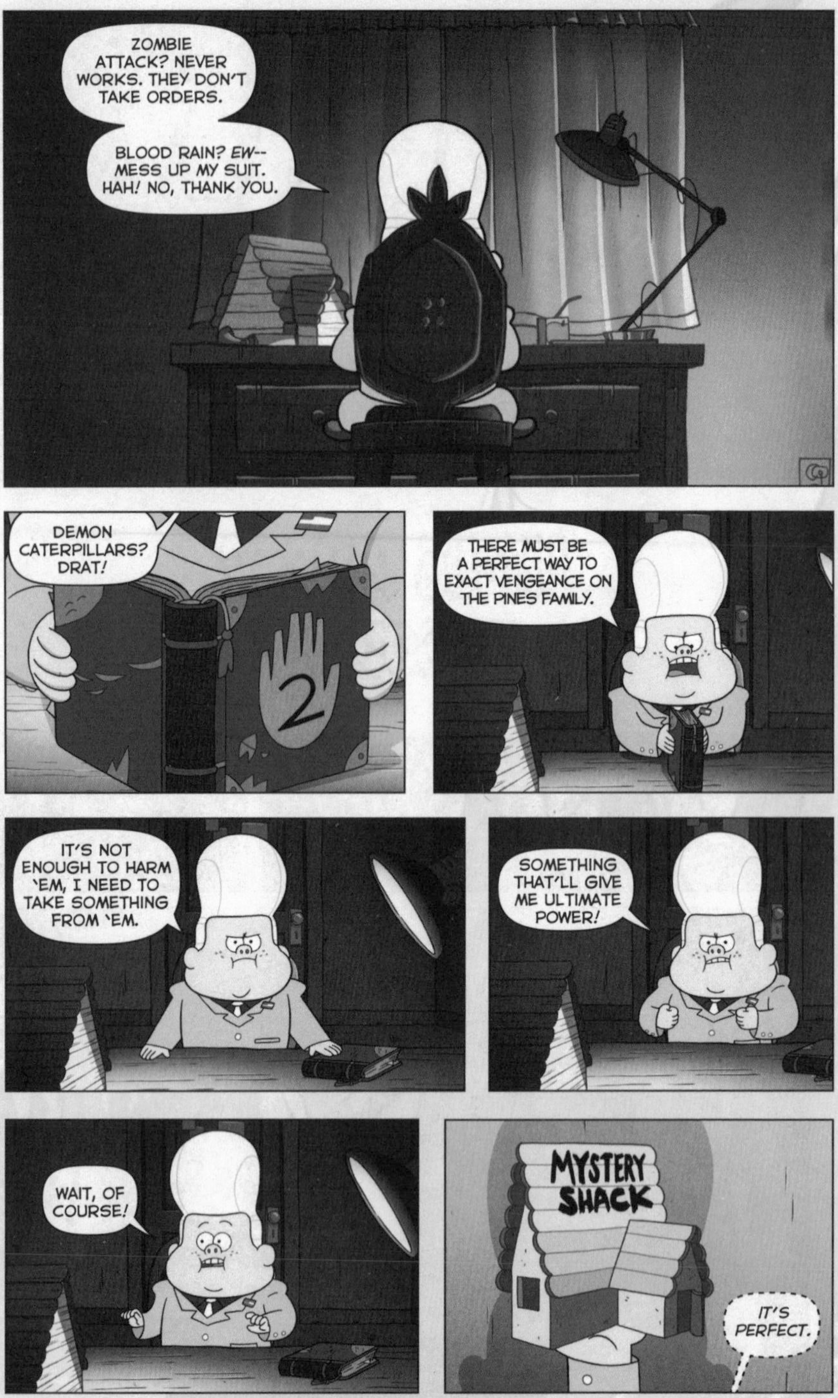
ZOMBIE ATTACK? NEVER WORKS. THEY DON'T TAKE ORDERS.
BLOOD RAIN? *EW*-- MESS UP MY SUIT. HAH! NO, THANK YOU.
DEMON CATERPILLARS? DRAT!
THERE MUST BE A PERFECT WAY TO EXACT VENGEANCE ON THE PINES FAMILY.
IT'S NOT ENOUGH TO HARM 'EM, I NEED TO TAKE SOMETHING FROM 'EM.
SOMETHING THAT'LL GIVE ME ULTIMATE POWER!
WAIT, OF COURSE!
MYSTERY SHACK
IT'S PERFECT.

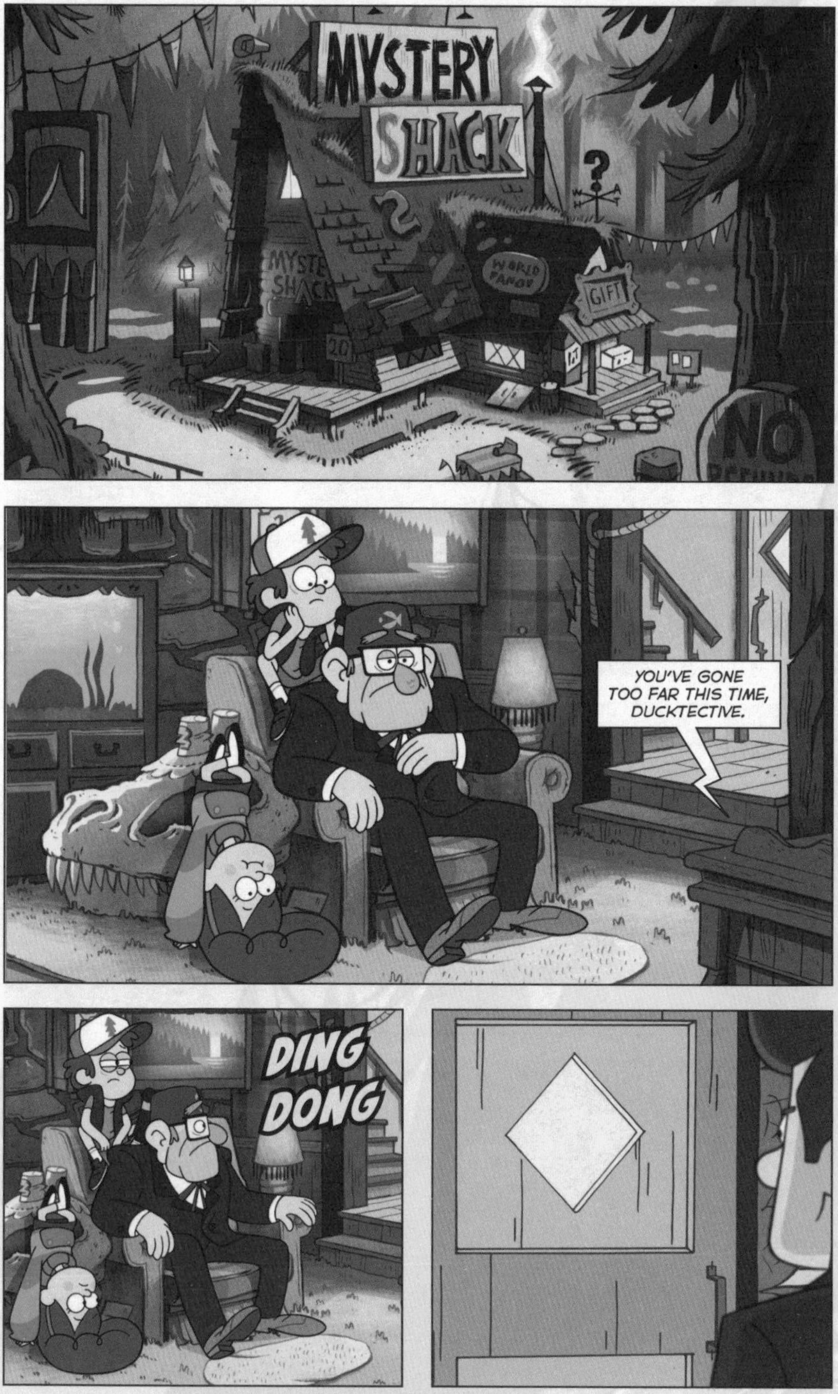
MYSTERY
SHACK
GIFT
NO
YOU'VE GONE TOO FAR THIS TIME, DUCKTECTIVE.
DING DONG

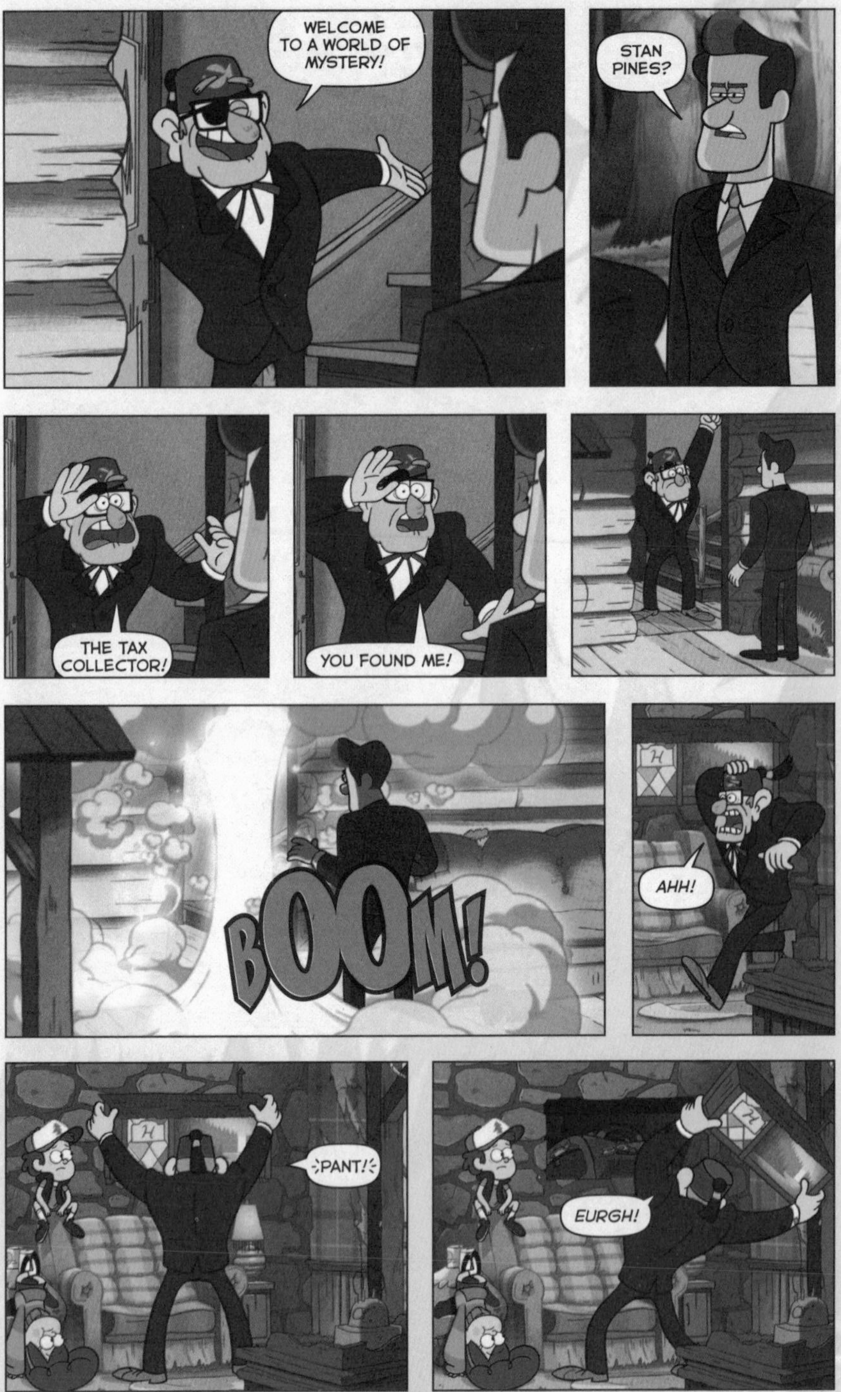
WELCOME TO A WORLD OF MYSTERY!
STAN PINES?
THE TAX COLLECTOR!
YOU FOUND ME!
BOOM!
AHH!
PANT!
EURGH!

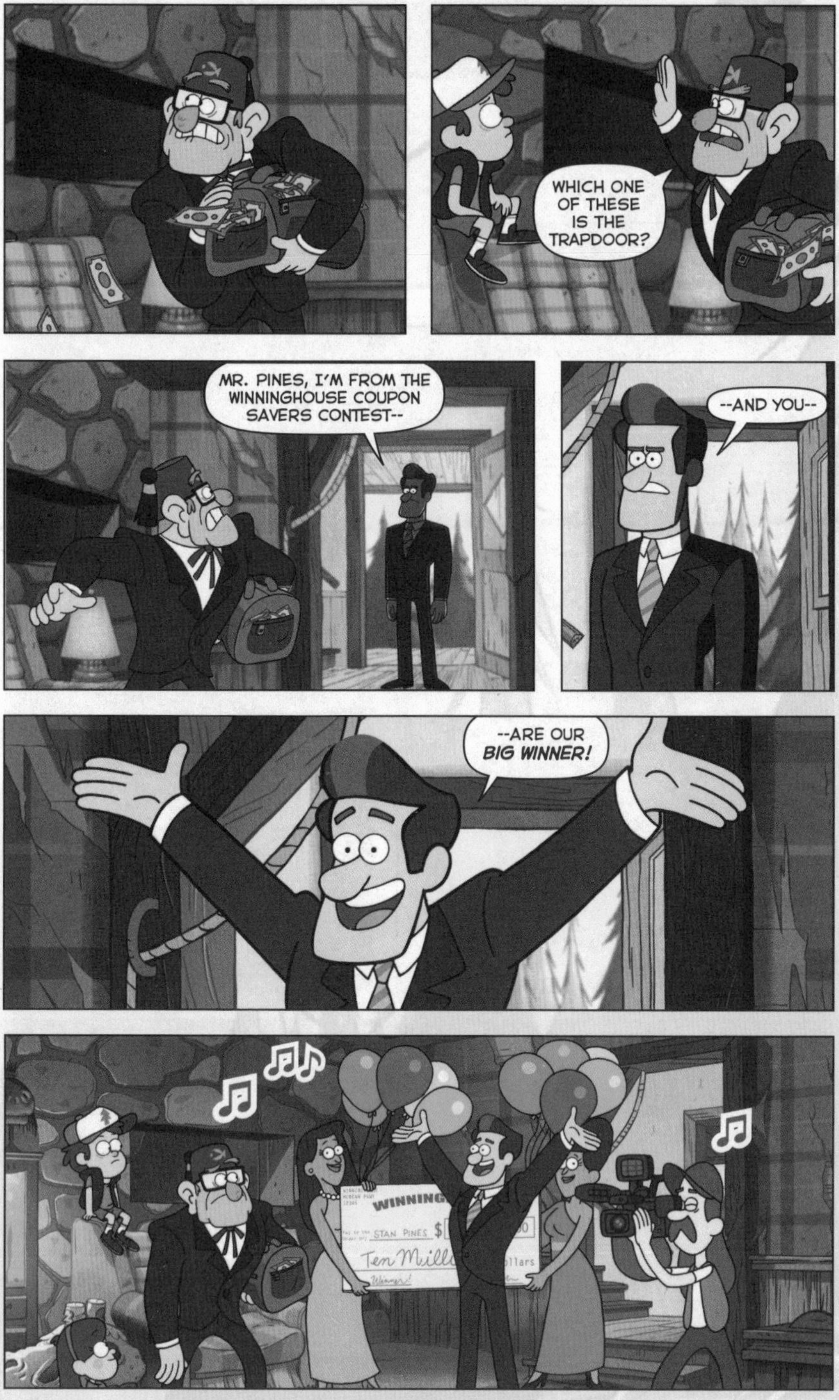
WHICH ONE OF THESE IS THE TRAPDOOR?
MR. PINES, I'M FROM THE WINNINGHOUSE COUPON SAVERS CONTEST--
--AND YOU--
--ARE OUR *BIG WINNER!*
WINNING
STAN PINES
Ten Milli
llars

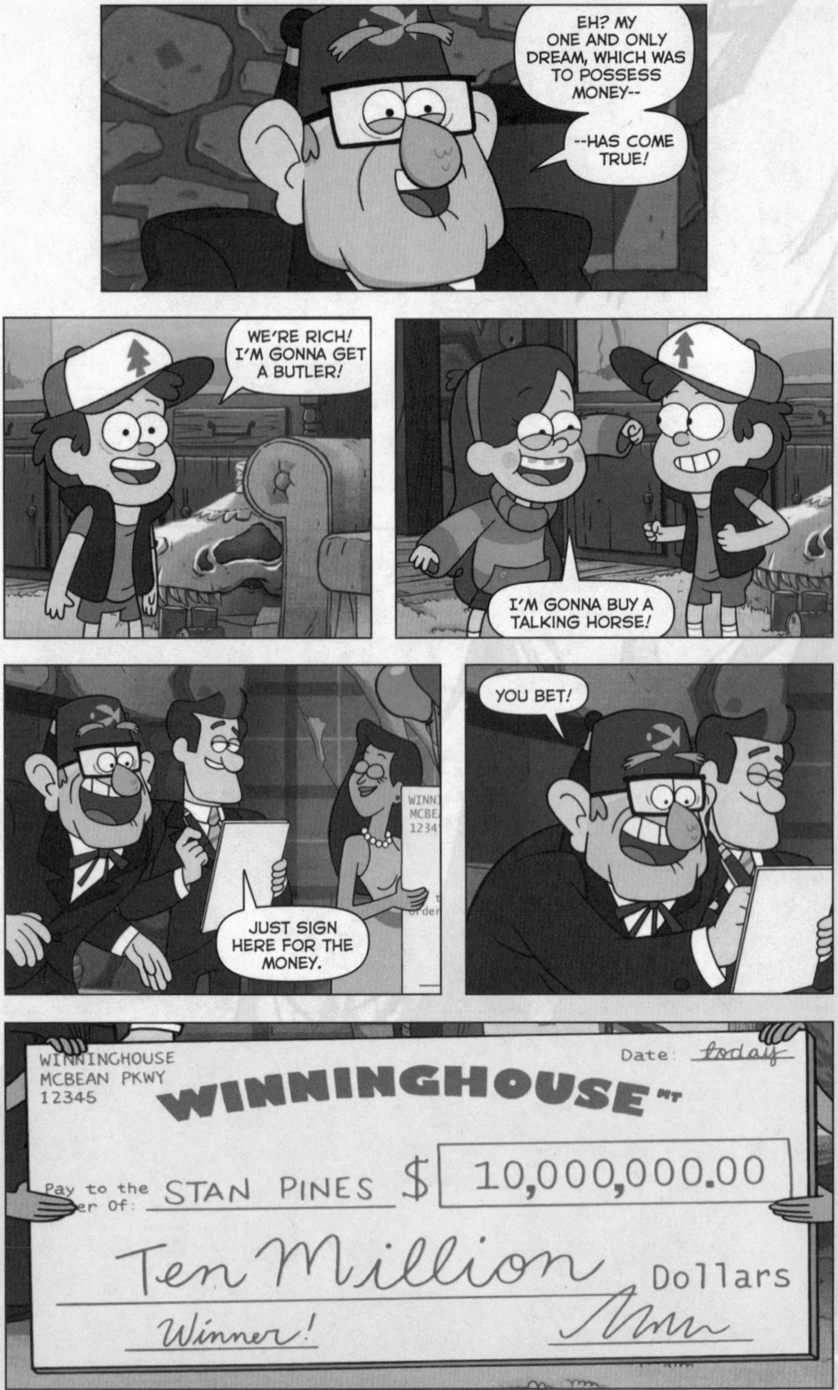
EH? MY ONE AND ONLY DREAM, WHICH WAS TO POSSESS MONEY--
--HAS COME TRUE!
WE'RE RICH! I'M GONNA GET A BUTLER!
I'M GONNA BUY A TALKING HORSE!
JUST SIGN HERE FOR THE MONEY.
YOU BET!
WINNINGHOUSE
MCBEAN PKWY
12345
Date: today
WINNINGHOUSE
Pay to the Order Of: STAN PINES
$ 10,000,000.00
Ten Million Dollars
Winner!

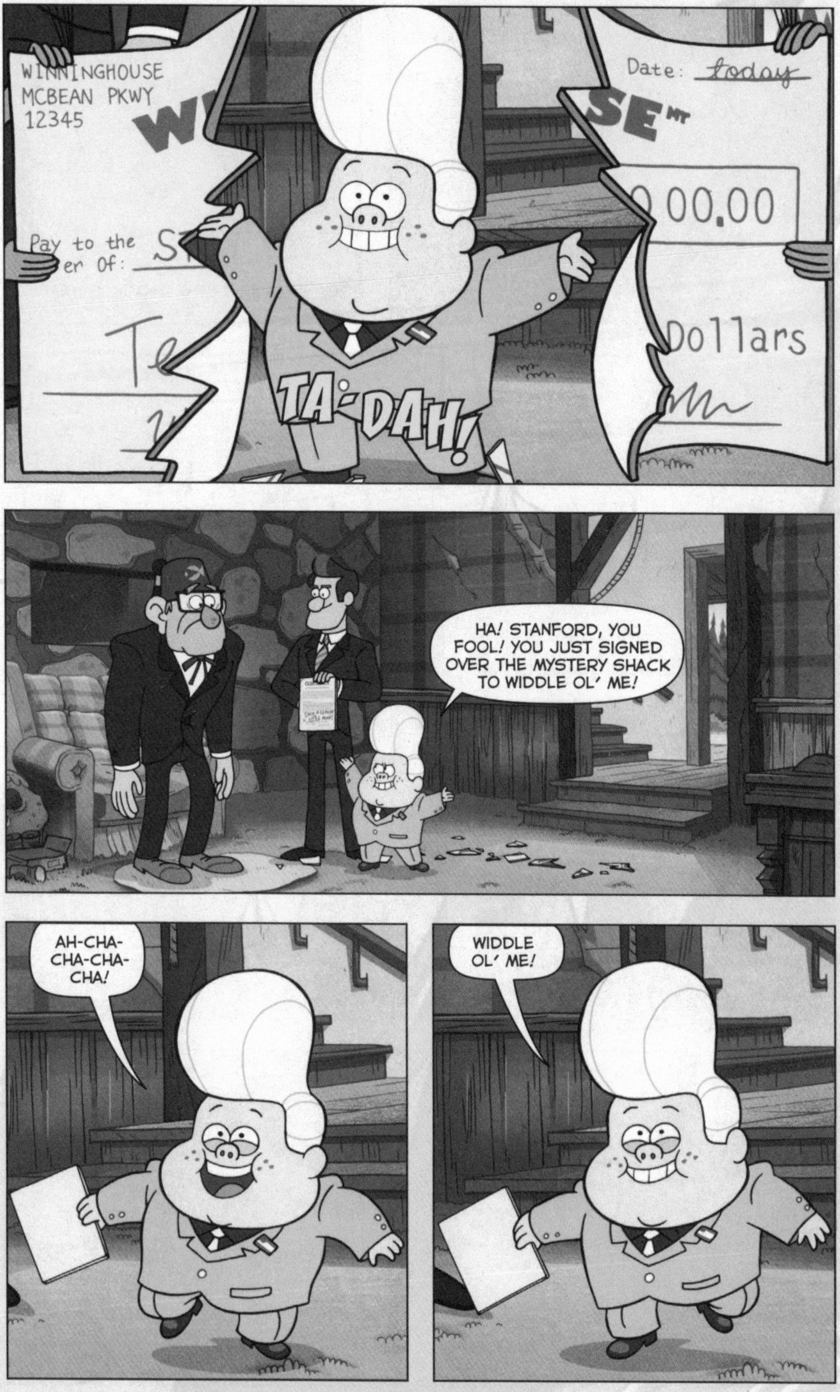
WINNINGHOUSE
MCBEAN PKWY
12345
Date: today
Pay to the
er Of:
Dollars
TA-DAH!
HA! STANFORD, YOU FOOL! YOU JUST SIGNED OVER THE MYSTERY SHACK TO WIDDLE OL' ME!
AH-CHA-CHA-CHA-CHA!
WIDDLE OL' ME!

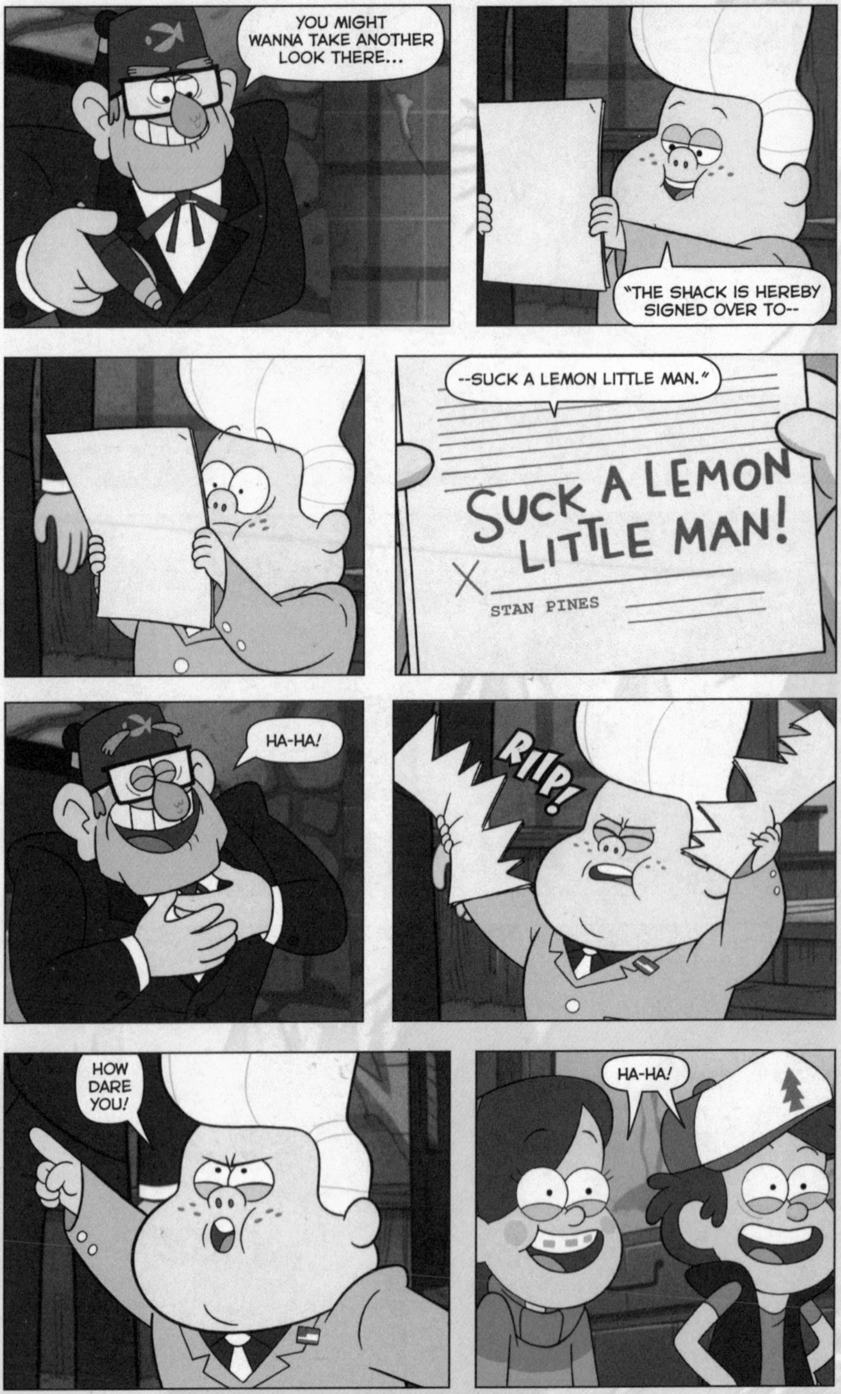
YOU MIGHT WANNA TAKE ANOTHER LOOK THERE...
"THE SHACK IS HEREBY SIGNED OVER TO--
--SUCK A LEMON LITTLE MAN."
SUCK A LEMON LITTLE MAN!
STAN PINES
HA-HA!
RIIP!
HOW DARE YOU!
HA-HA!

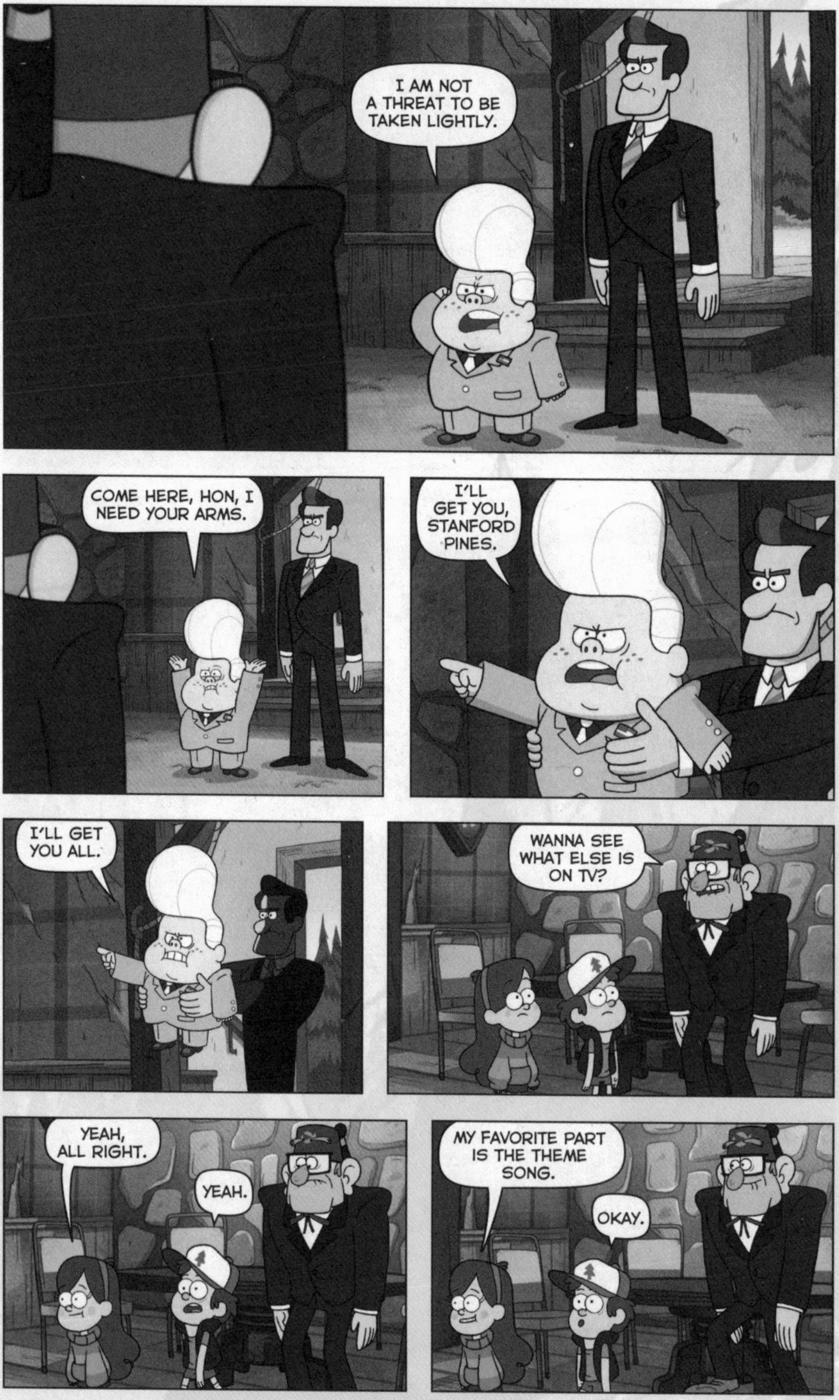
I AM NOT A THREAT TO BE TAKEN LIGHTLY.
COME HERE, HON, I NEED YOUR ARMS.
I'LL GET YOU, STANFORD PINES.
I'LL GET YOU ALL.
WANNA SEE WHAT ELSE IS ON TV?
YEAH, ALL RIGHT.
YEAH.
MY FAVORITE PART IS THE THEME SONG.
OKAY.

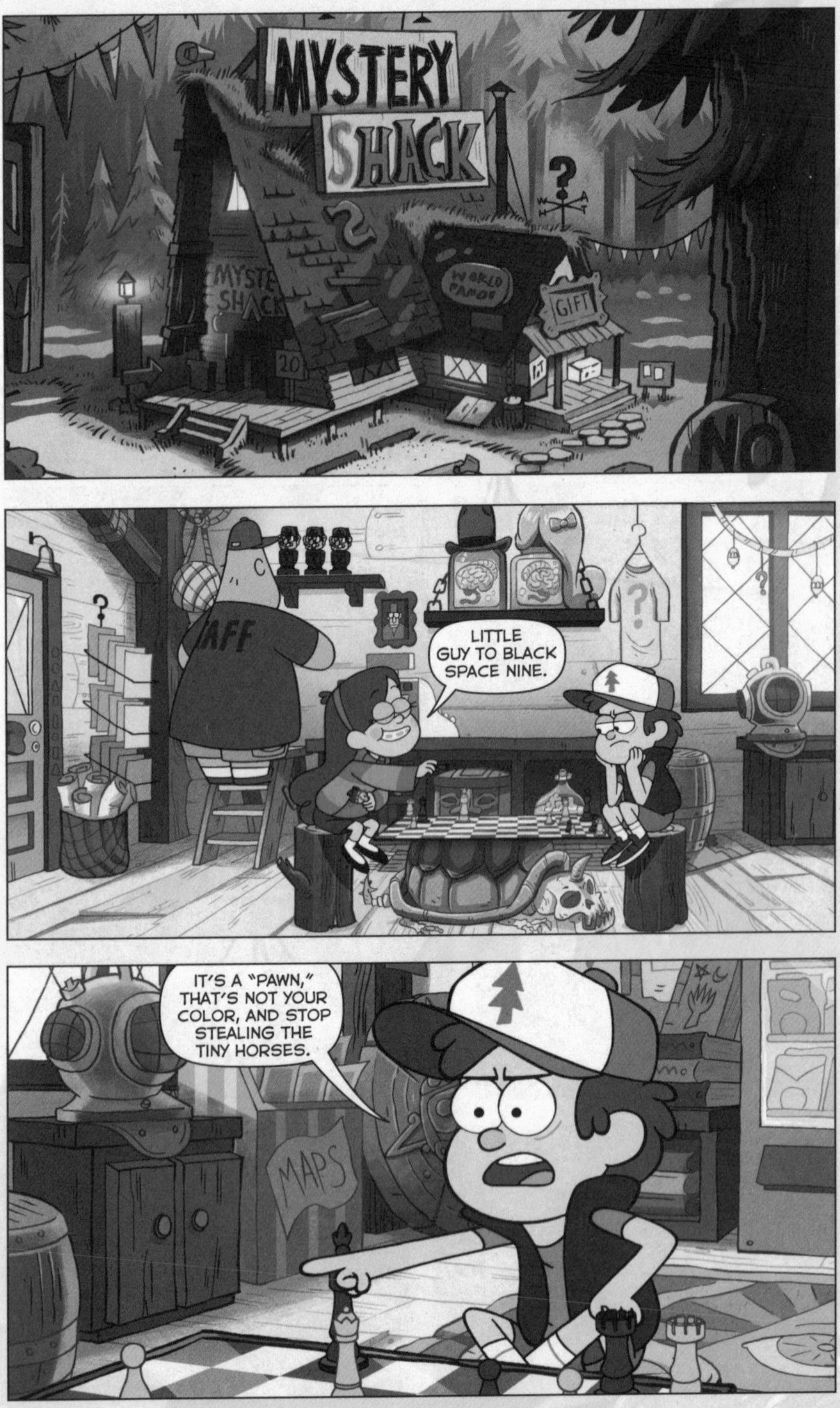
MYSTERY SHACK
GIFT
NO
LITTLE GUY TO BLACK SPACE NINE.
IT'S A "PAWN," THAT'S NOT YOUR COLOR, AND STOP STEALING THE TINY HORSES.
MAPS

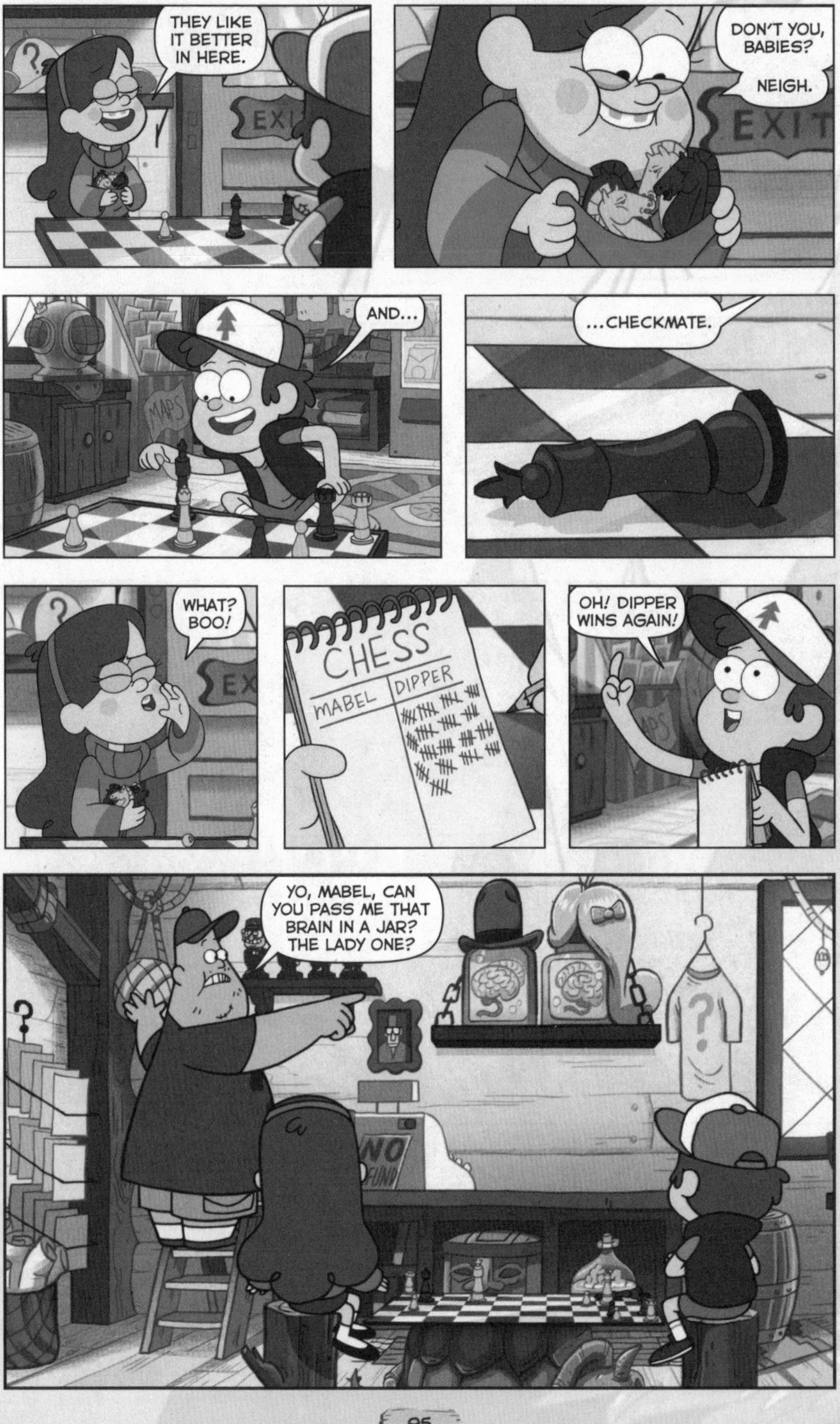
THEY LIKE IT BETTER IN HERE.
EXI
DON'T YOU, BABIES?
NEIGH.
EXIT
AND...
MAPS
...CHECKMATE.
WHAT? BOO!
CHESS
MABEL
DIPPER
OH! DIPPER WINS AGAIN!
YO, MABEL, CAN YOU PASS ME THAT BRAIN IN A JAR? THE LADY ONE?
NO

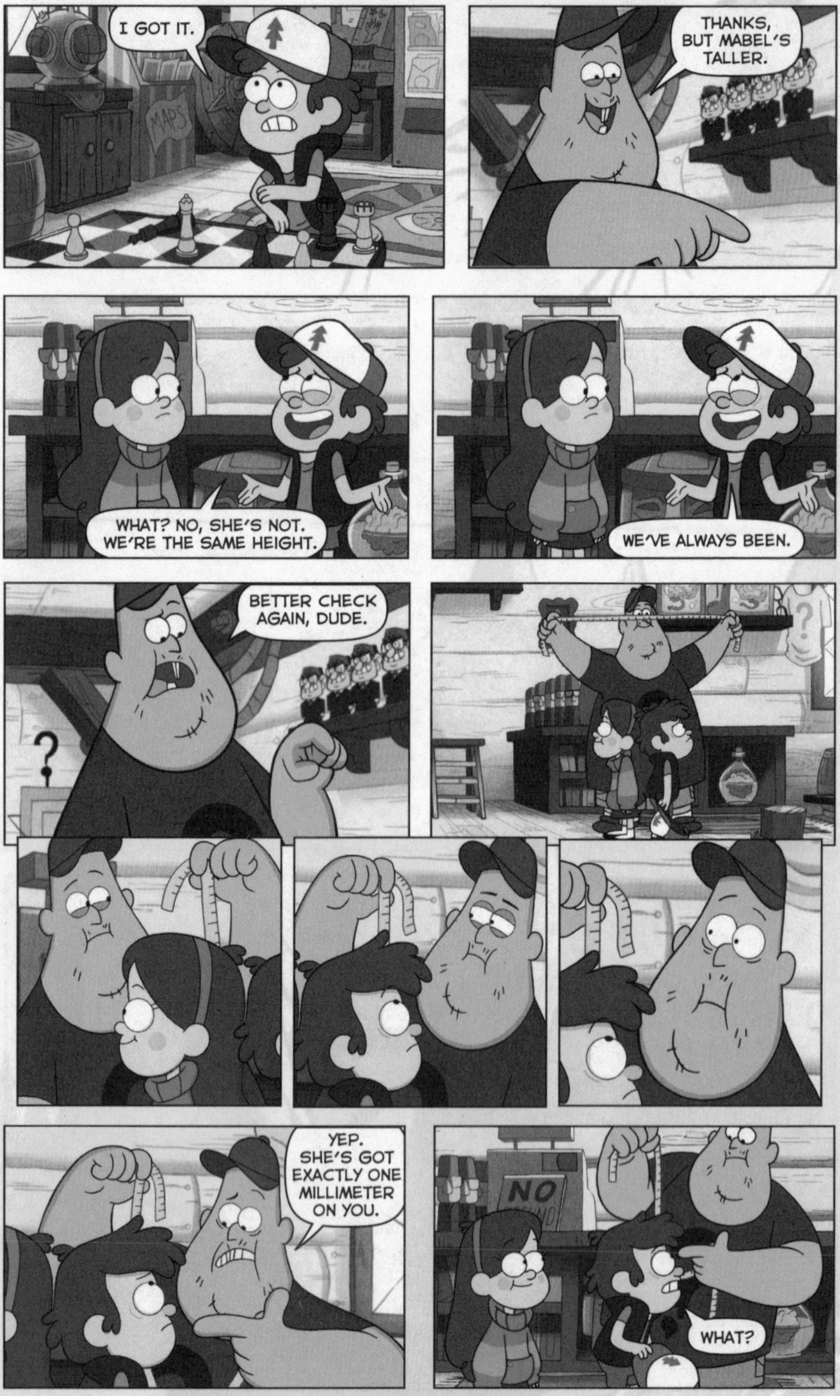
I GOT IT.
THANKS, BUT MABEL'S TALLER.
WHAT? NO, SHE'S NOT. WE'RE THE SAME HEIGHT.
WE'VE ALWAYS BEEN.
BETTER CHECK AGAIN, DUDE.
YEP. SHE'S GOT EXACTLY ONE MILLIMETER ON YOU.
NO
WHAT?

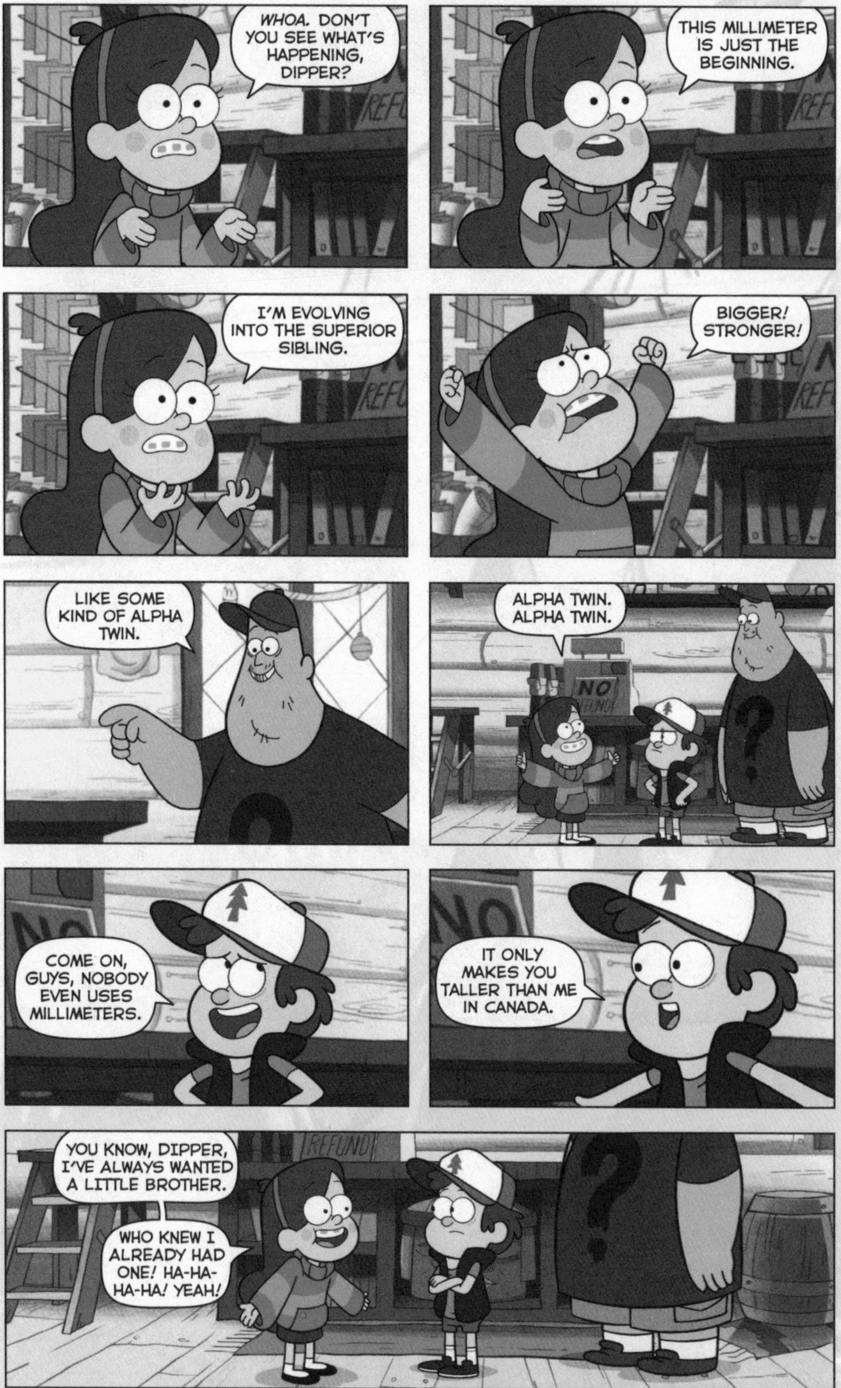
WHOA. DON'T YOU SEE WHAT'S HAPPENING, DIPPER?
THIS MILLIMETER IS JUST THE BEGINNING.
I'M EVOLVING INTO THE SUPERIOR SIBLING.
BIGGER! STRONGER!
LIKE SOME KIND OF ALPHA TWIN.
ALPHA TWIN. ALPHA TWIN.
NO
COME ON, GUYS, NOBODY EVEN USES MILLIMETERS.
IT ONLY MAKES YOU TALLER THAN ME IN CANADA.
YOU KNOW, DIPPER, I'VE ALWAYS WANTED A LITTLE BROTHER.
WHO KNEW I ALREADY HAD ONE! HA-HA-HA-HA! YEAH!

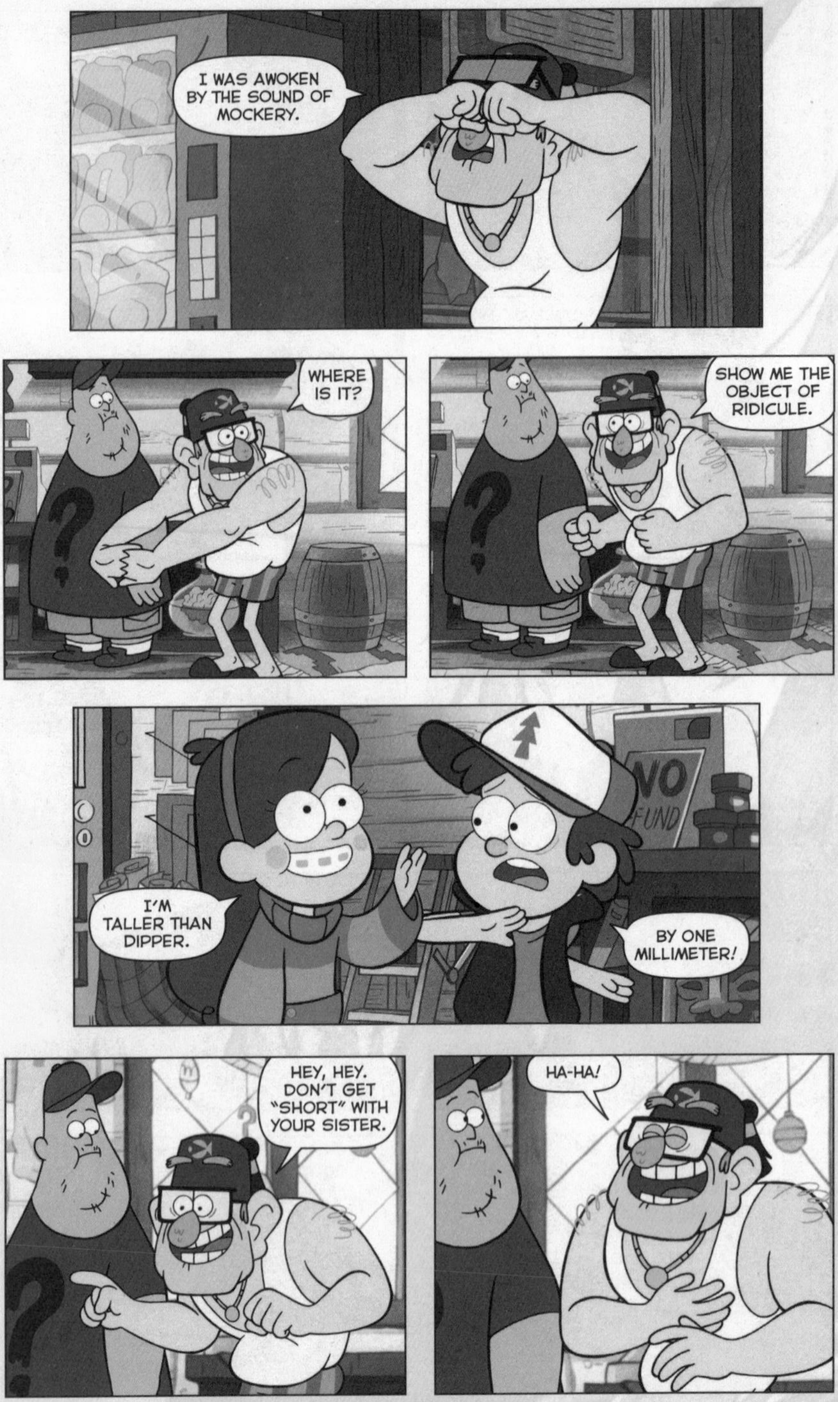
I WAS AWOKEN BY THE SOUND OF MOCKERY.
WHERE IS IT?
SHOW ME THE OBJECT OF RIDICULE.
I'M TALLER THAN DIPPER.
BY ONE MILLIMETER!
NO FUND
HEY, HEY. DON'T GET "SHORT" WITH YOUR SISTER.
HA-HA!

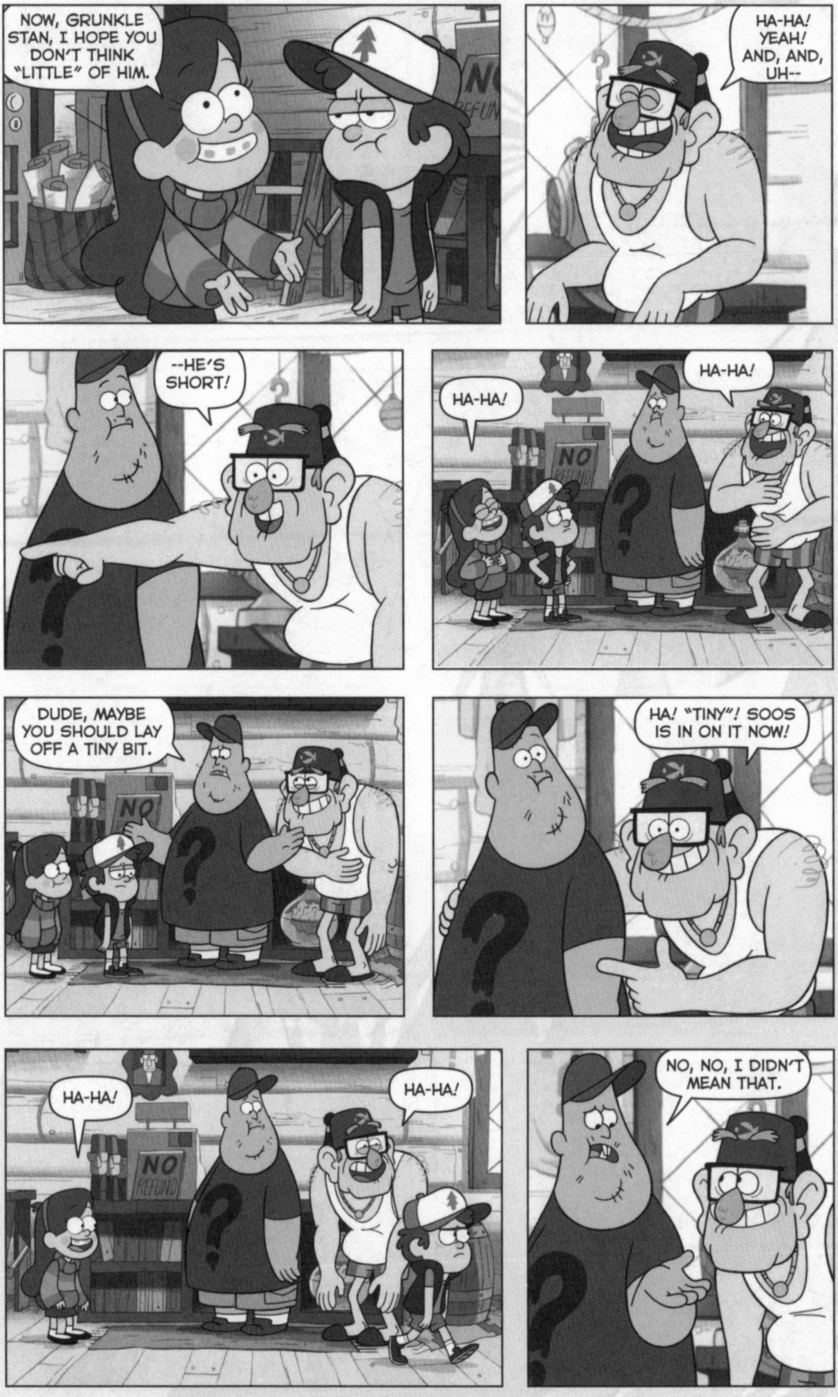
NOW, GRUNKLE STAN, I HOPE YOU DON'T THINK "LITTLE" OF HIM.
HA-HA! YEAH! AND, AND, UH--
--HE'S SHORT!
HA-HA!
HA-HA!
NO REFUND
DUDE, MAYBE YOU SHOULD LAY OFF A TINY BIT.
HA! "TINY"! SOOS IS IN ON IT NOW!
HA-HA!
HA-HA!
NO REFUND
NO, NO, I DIDN'T MEAN THAT.

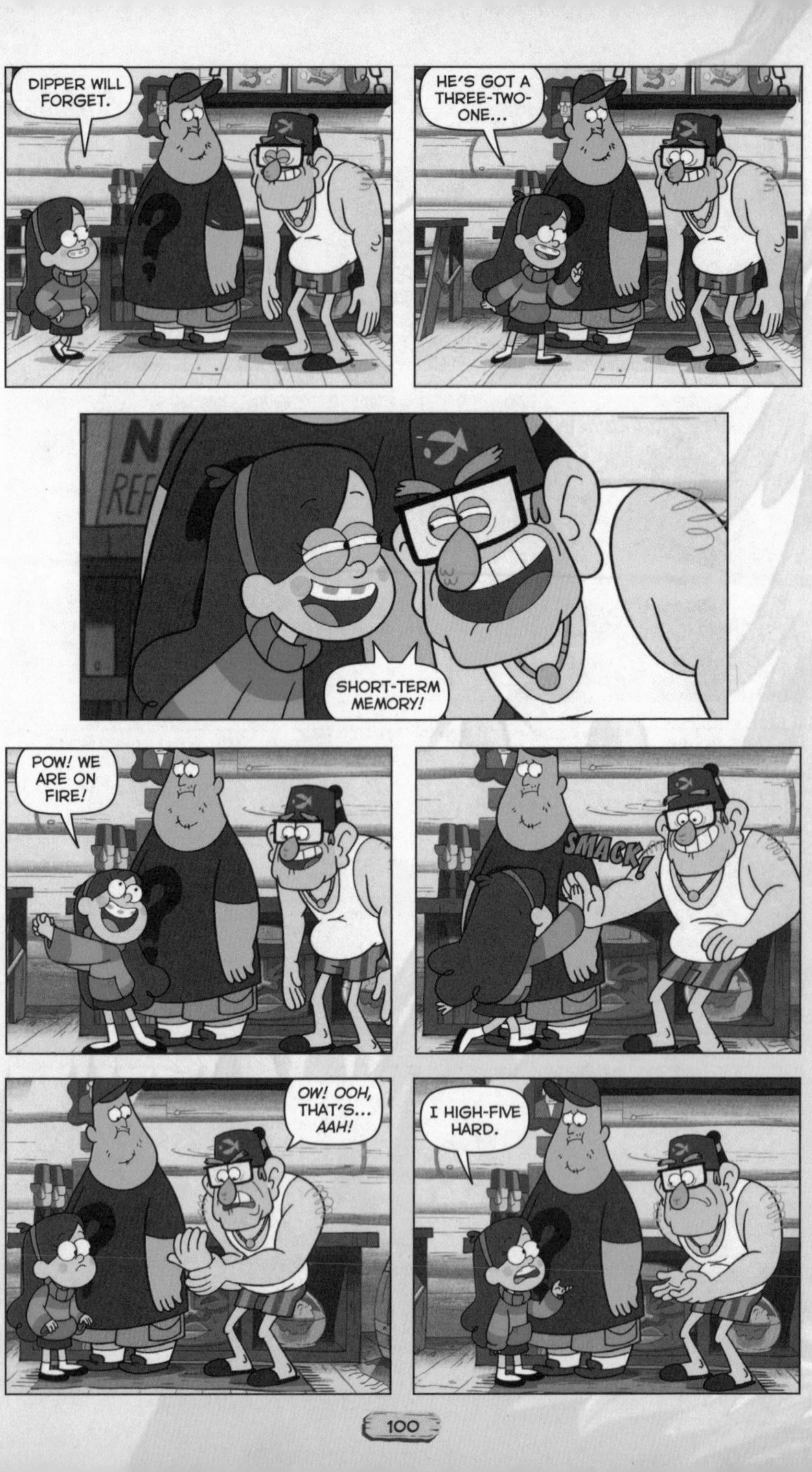
DIPPER WILL FORGET.
HE'S GOT A THREE-TWO-ONE...
SHORT-TERM MEMORY!
POW! WE ARE ON FIRE!
SMACK!
OW! OOH, THAT'S... AAH!
I HIGH-FIVE HARD.

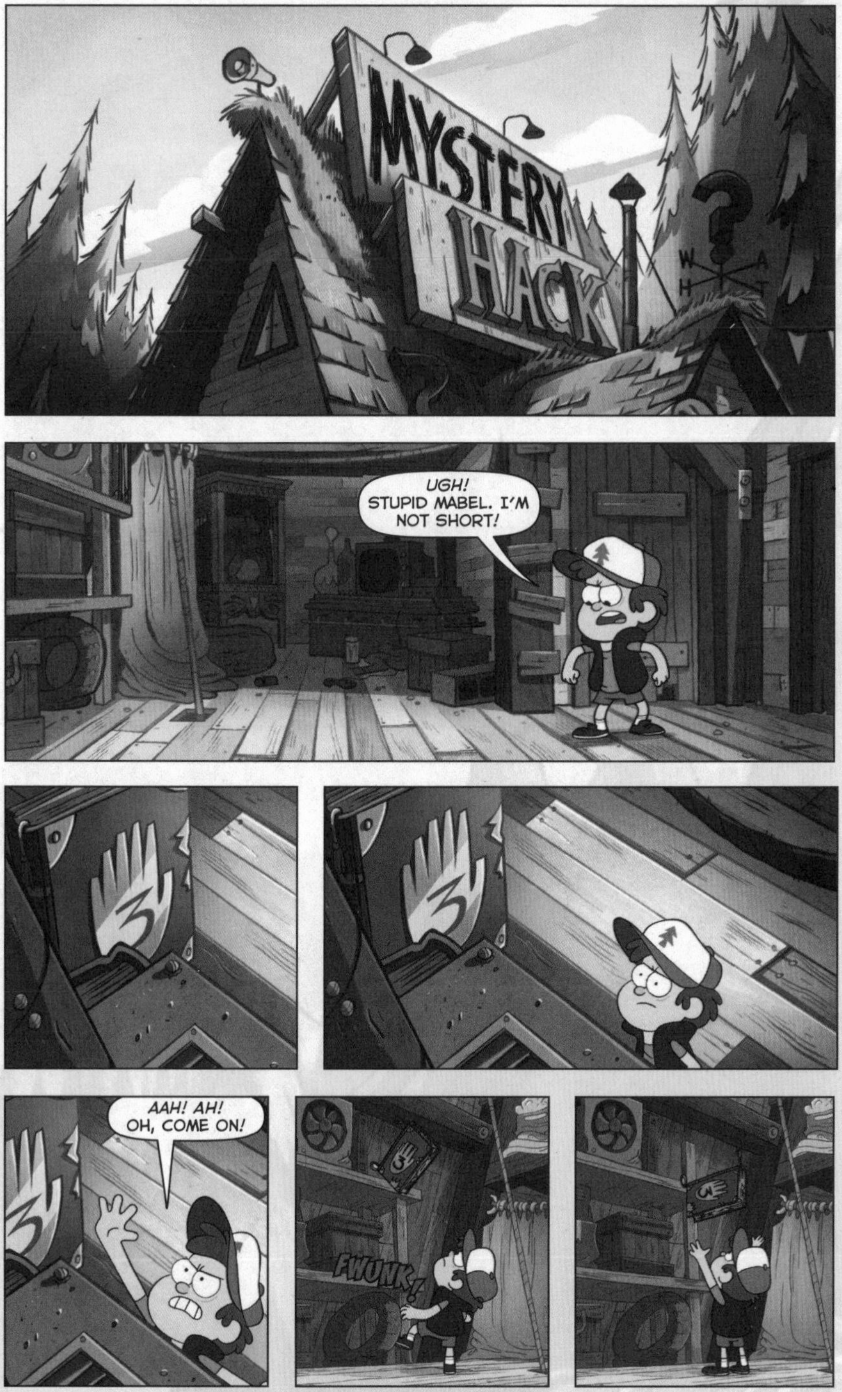
MYSTERY
HACK
W
H
A
T
UGH!
STUPID MABEL. I'M
NOT SHORT!
AAH! AH!
OH, COME ON!
FWUNK!

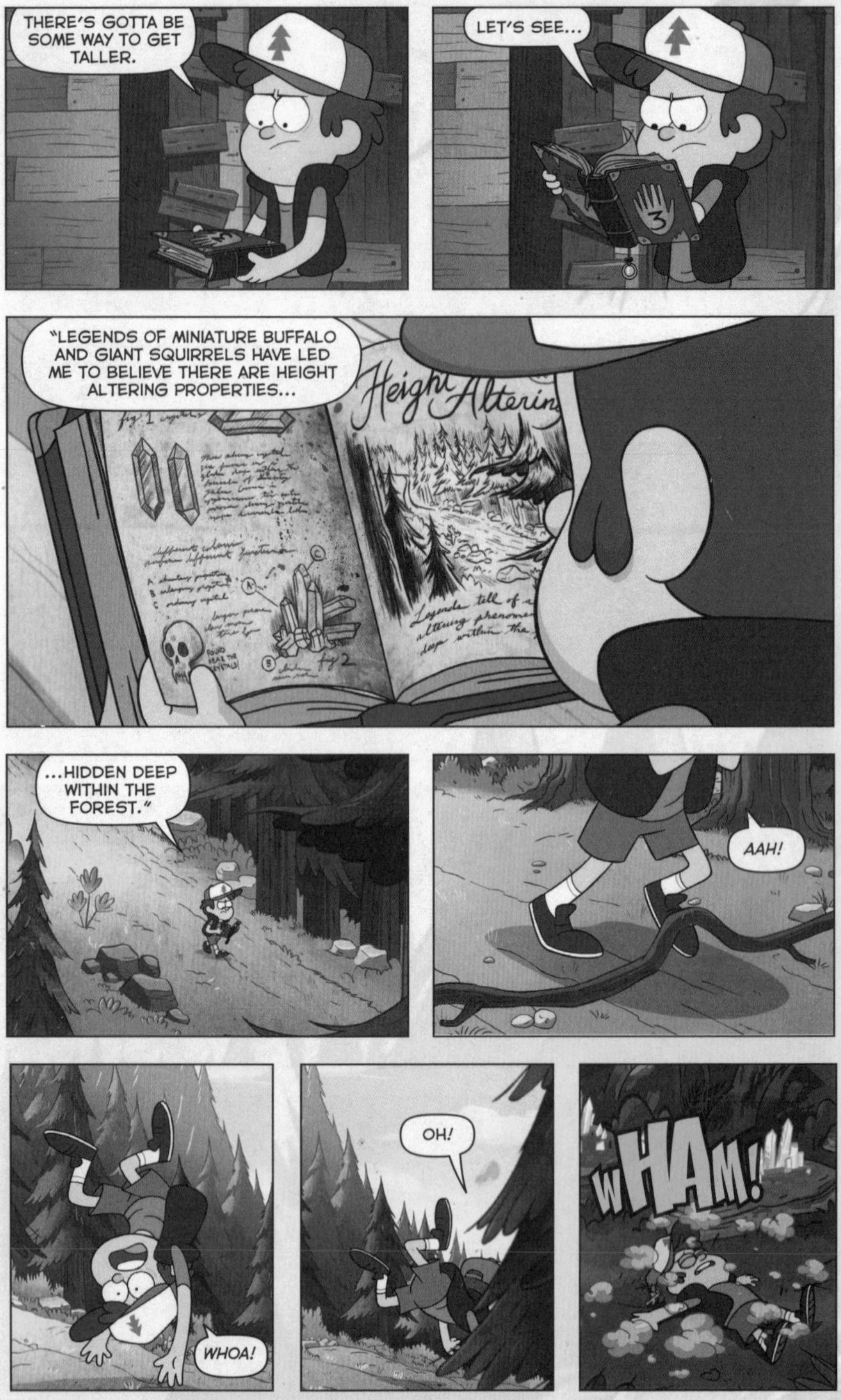
THERE'S GOTTA BE SOME WAY TO GET TALLER.
LET'S SEE...
"LEGENDS OF MINIATURE BUFFALO AND GIANT SQUIRRELS HAVE LED ME TO BELIEVE THERE ARE HEIGHT ALTERING PROPERTIES...
...HIDDEN DEEP WITHIN THE FOREST."
AAH!
WHOA!
OH!
WHAM!

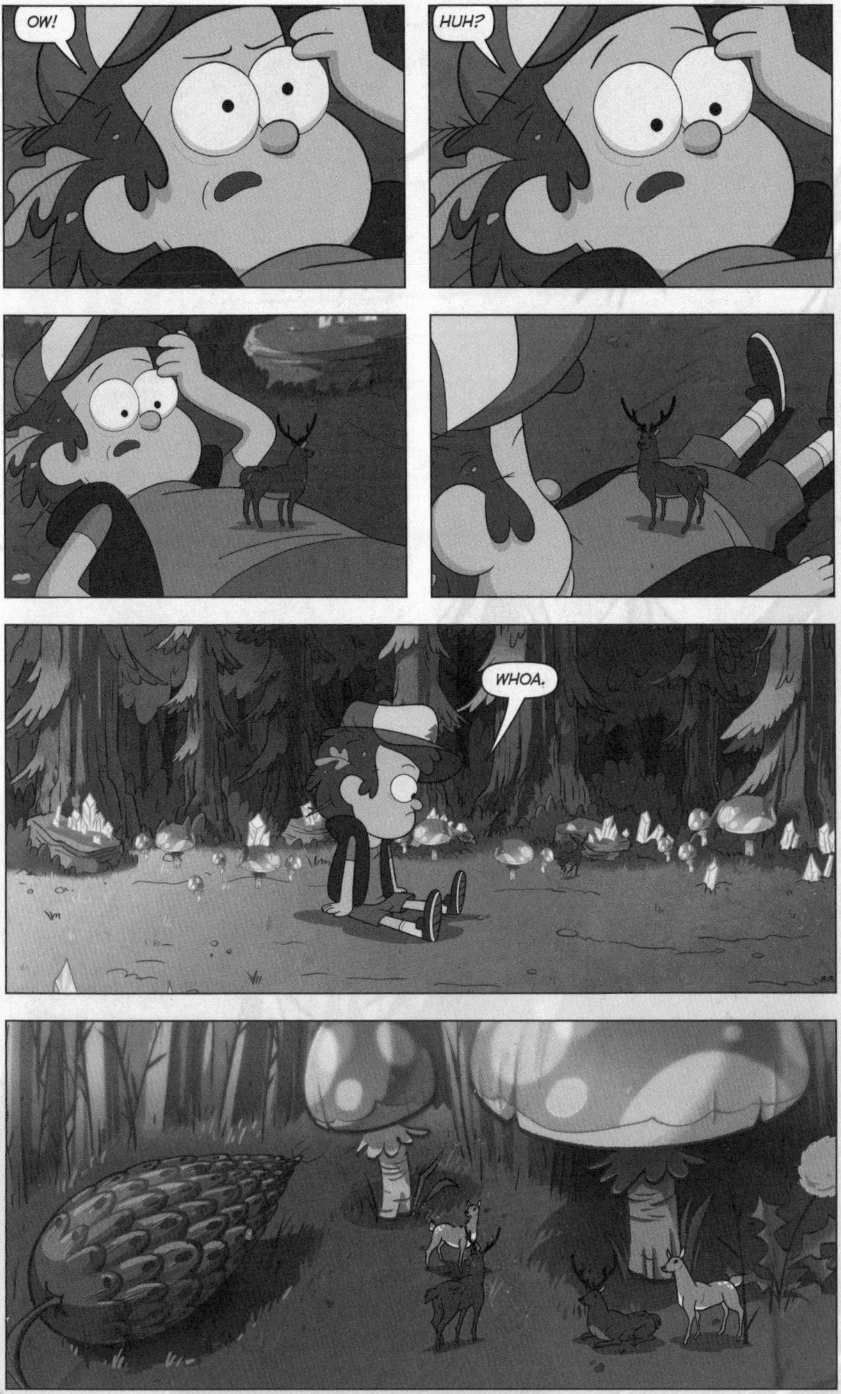
OW!
HUH?
WHOA.

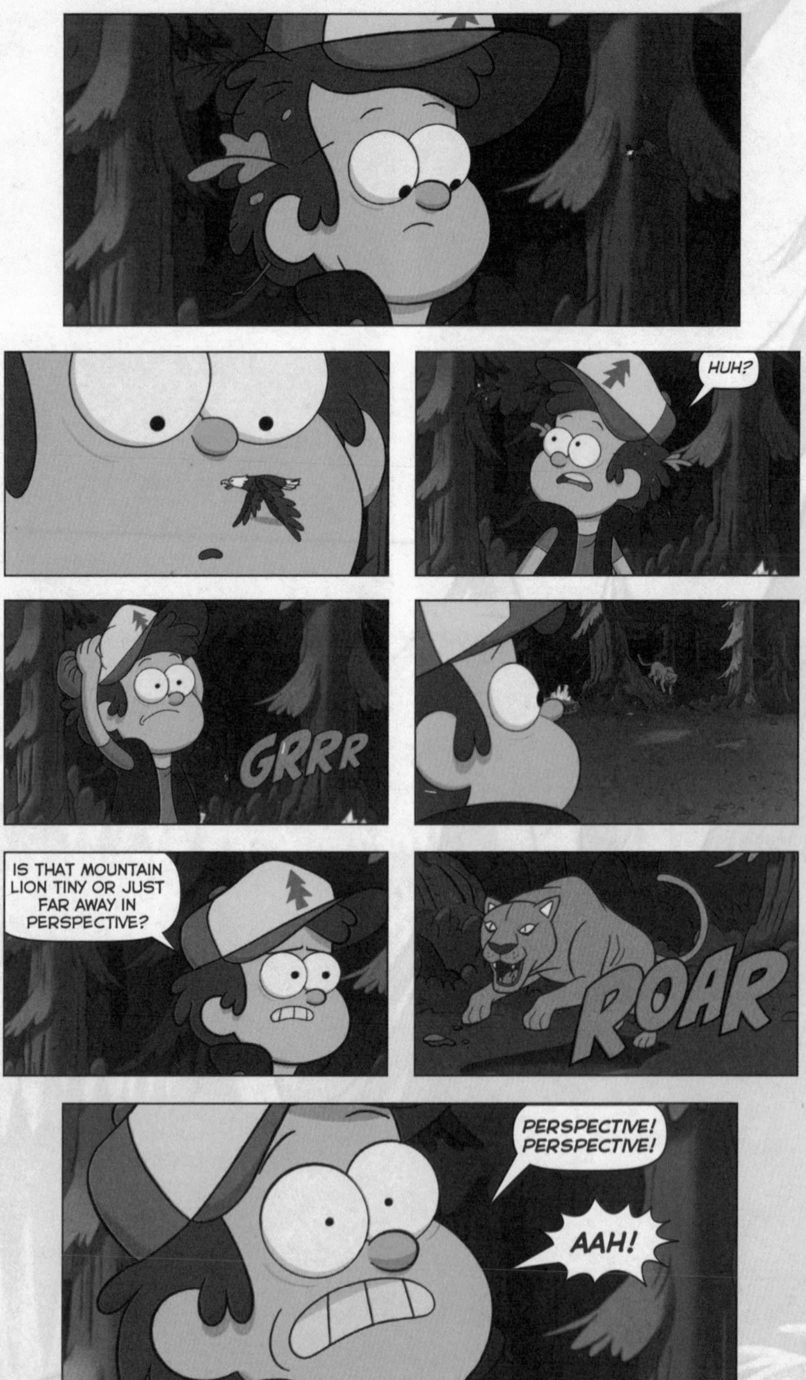
HUH?
GRRR
IS THAT MOUNTAIN LION TINY OR JUST FAR AWAY IN PERSPECTIVE?
ROAR
PERSPECTIVE! PERSPECTIVE!
AAH!

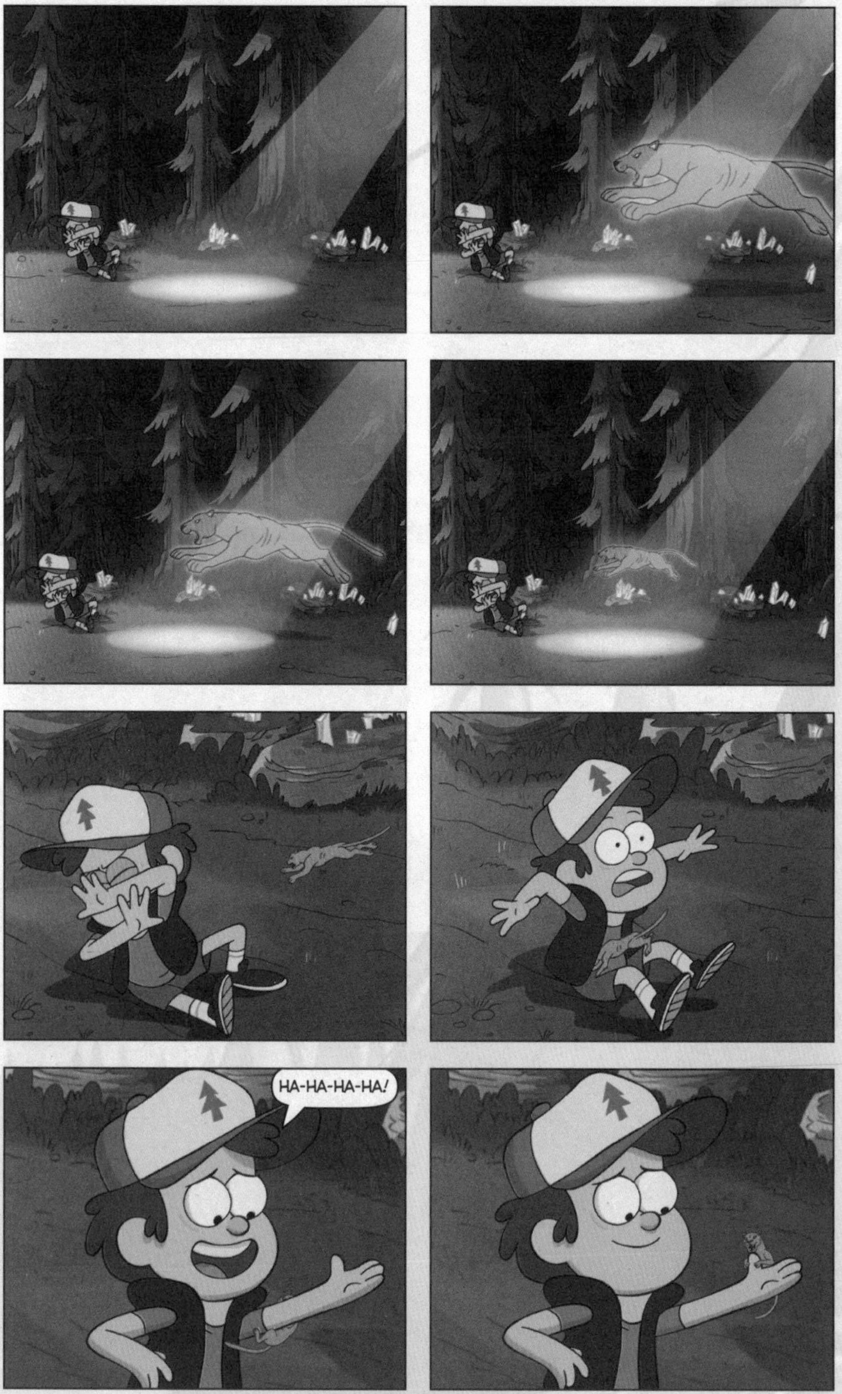
HA-HA-HA-HA!

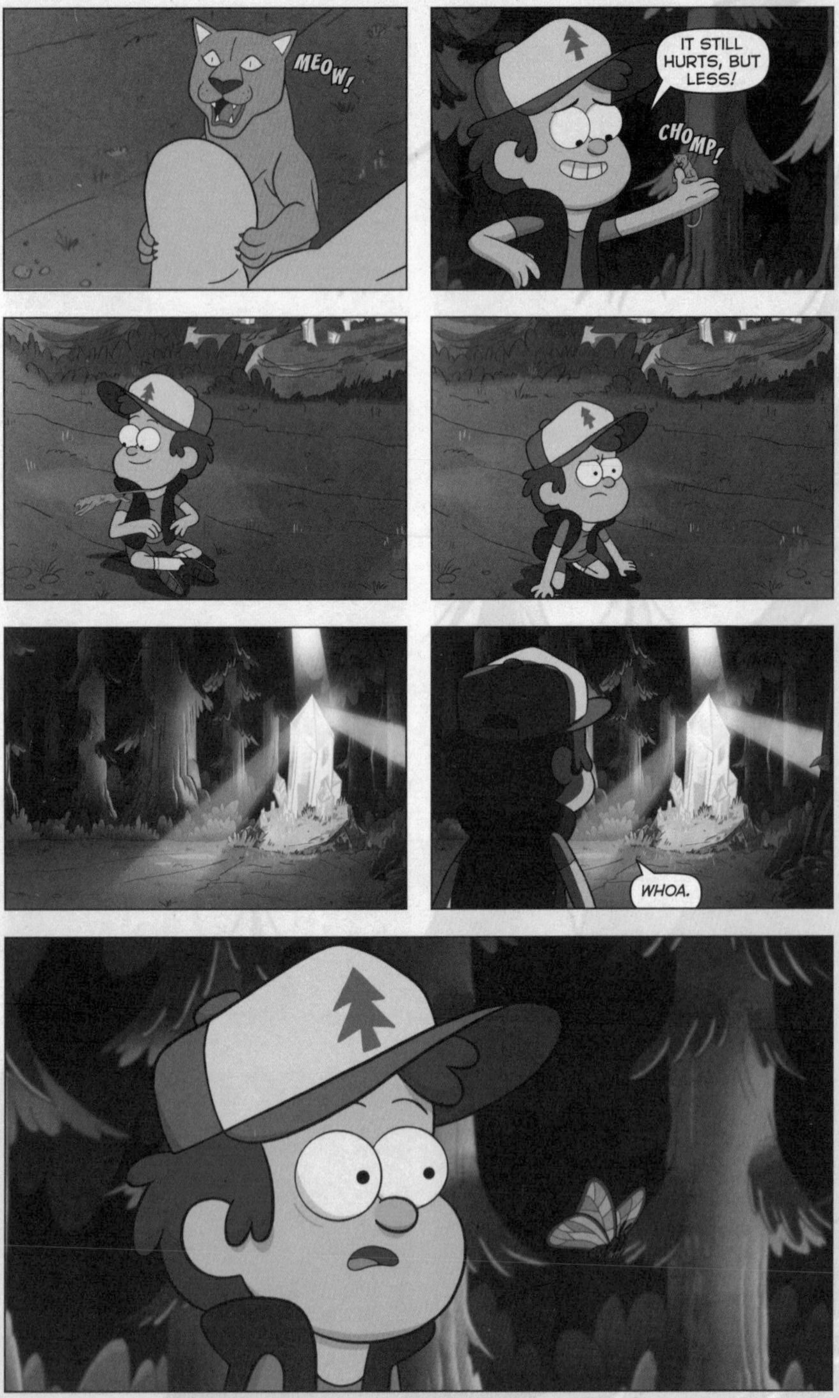
MEOW!
IT STILL HURTS, BUT LESS!
CHOMP!
WHOA.

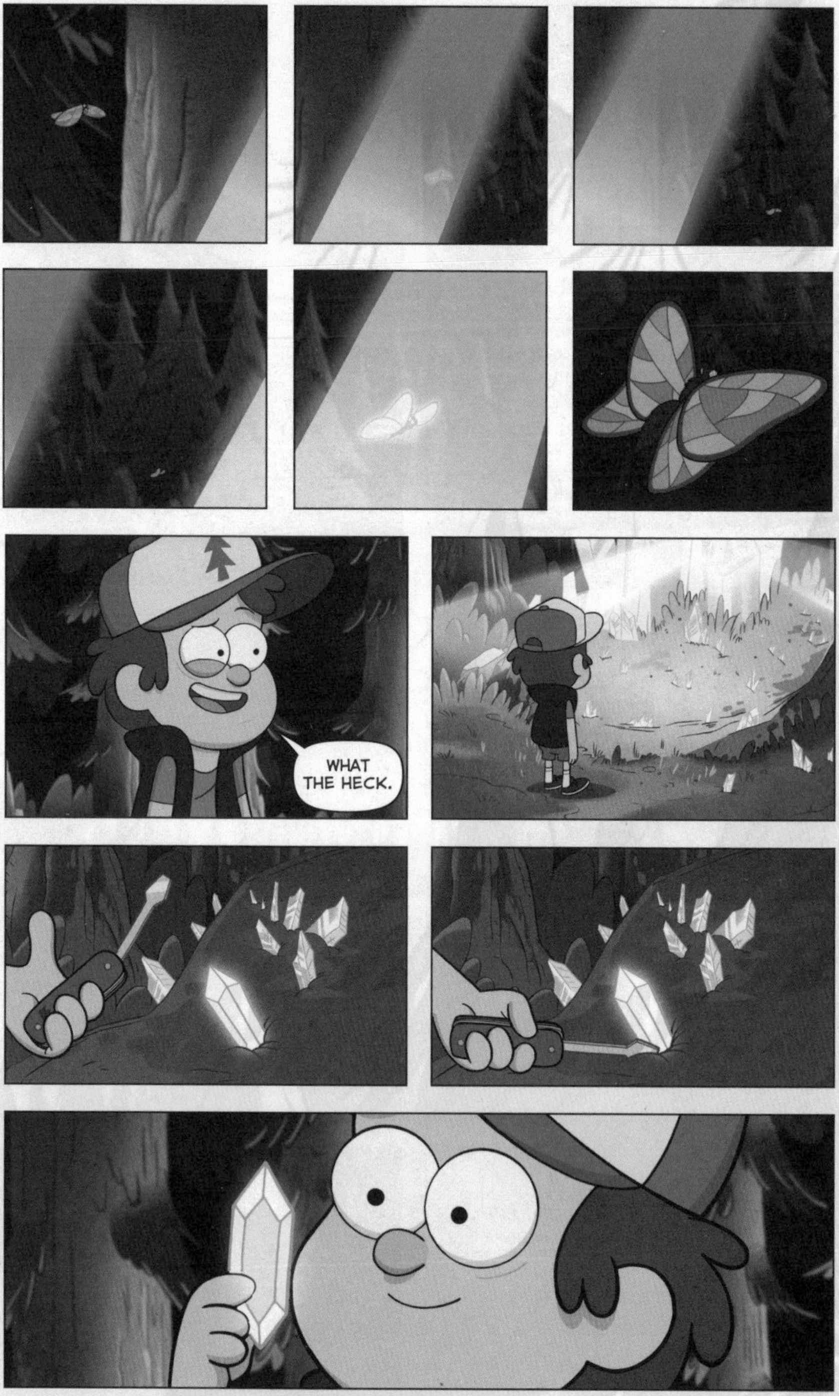
WHAT THE HECK.

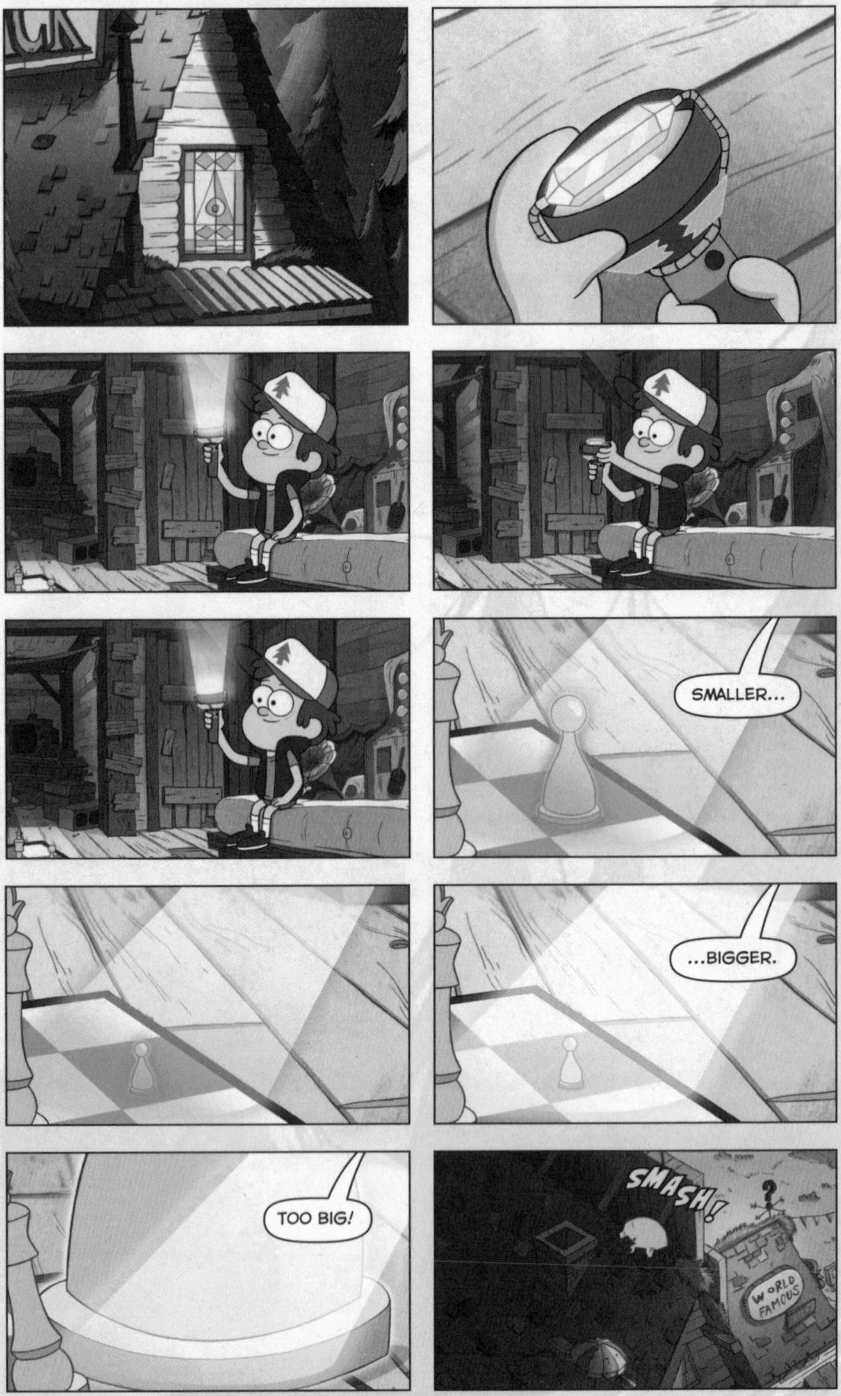
SMALLER...
...BIGGER.
TOO BIG!
SMASH!
WORLD FAMOUS

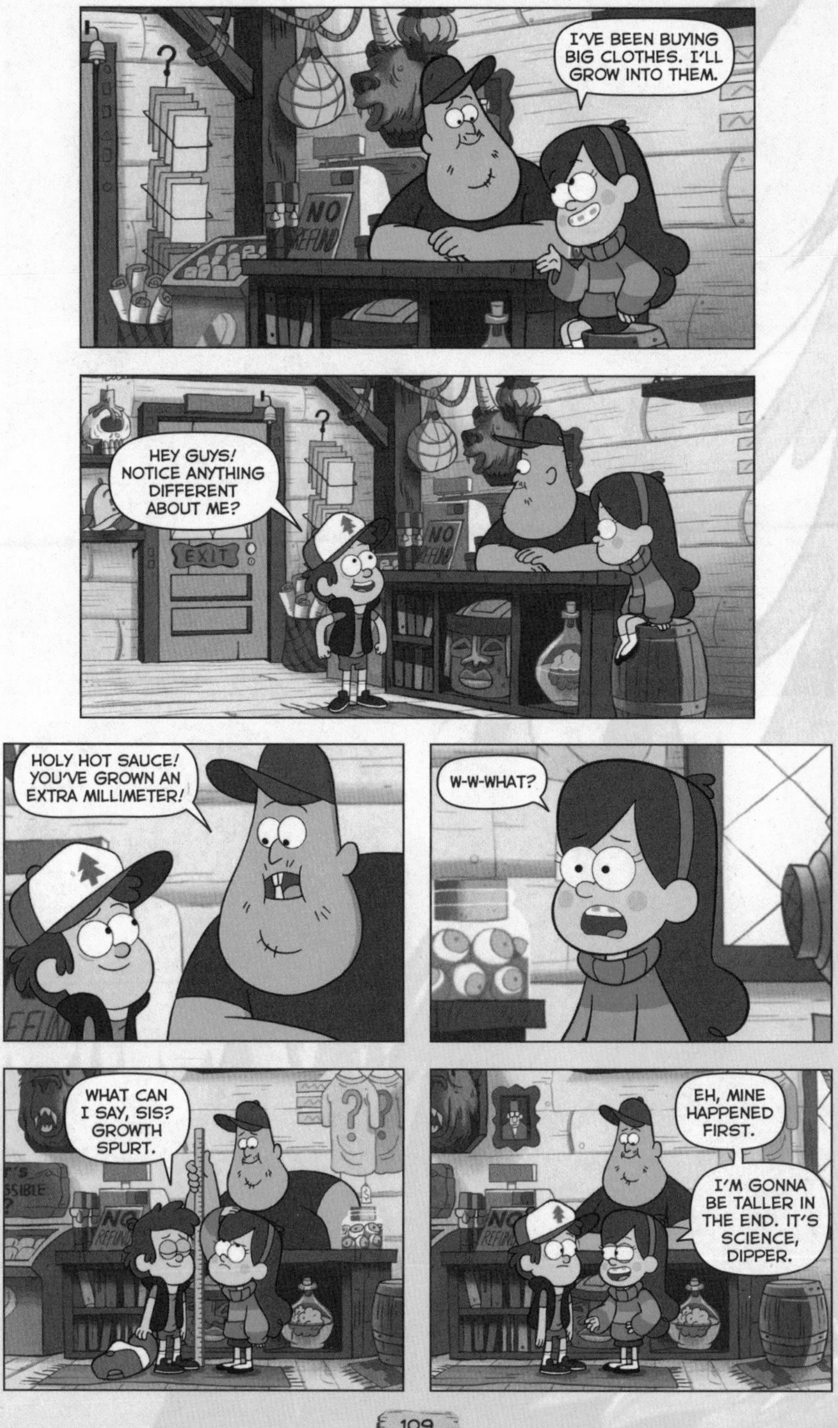

I'VE BEEN BUYING BIG CLOTHES. I'LL GROW INTO THEM.
NO REFUND
HEY GUYS! NOTICE ANYTHING DIFFERENT ABOUT ME?
EXIT
NO REFUND
HOLY HOT SAUCE! YOU'VE GROWN AN EXTRA MILLIMETER!
W-W-WHAT?
WHAT CAN I SAY, SIS? GROWTH SPURT.
NO REFUND
EH, MINE HAPPENED FIRST.
I'M GONNA BE TALLER IN THE END. IT'S SCIENCE, DIPPER.

WHAT? BUT, WE'RE THE SAME HEIGHT NOW.

ALPHA TWIN! ALPHA TWIN!

OH, YEAH? SOMETHING TELLS ME I'VE GOT ANOTHER GROWTH SPURT COMING ON RIGHT NOW.

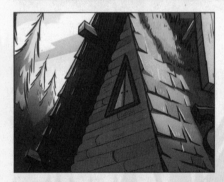

SHIIING

GIVE IT UP, DIPPER!

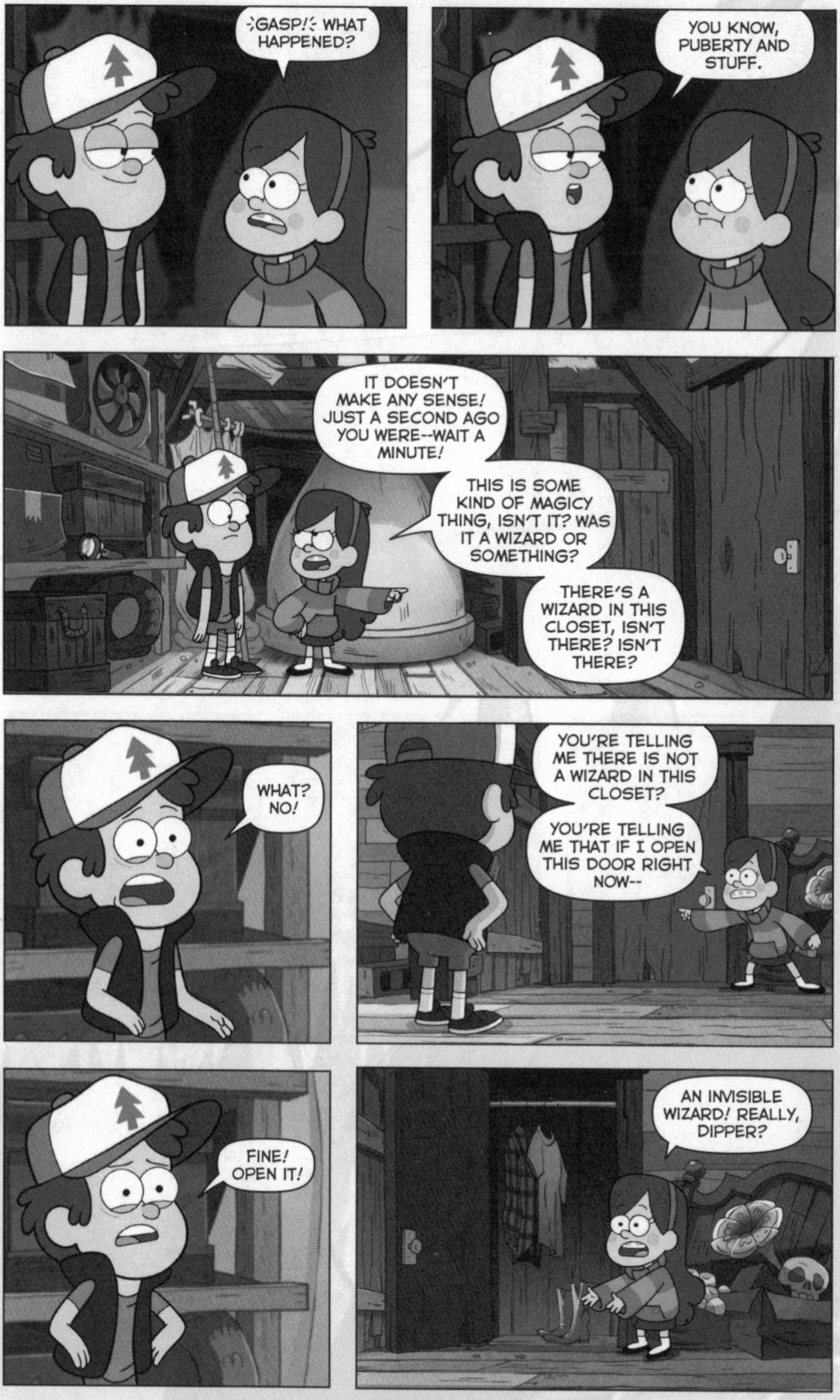

-GASP!- WHAT HAPPENED?
YOU KNOW, PUBERTY AND STUFF.
IT DOESN'T MAKE ANY SENSE! JUST A SECOND AGO YOU WERE--WAIT A MINUTE!
THIS IS SOME KIND OF MAGICY THING, ISN'T IT? WAS IT A WIZARD OR SOMETHING?
THERE'S A WIZARD IN THIS CLOSET, ISN'T THERE? ISN'T THERE?
WHAT? NO!
YOU'RE TELLING ME THERE IS NOT A WIZARD IN THIS CLOSET?
YOU'RE TELLING ME THAT IF I OPEN THIS DOOR RIGHT NOW--
FINE! OPEN IT!
AN INVISIBLE WIZARD! REALLY, DIPPER?

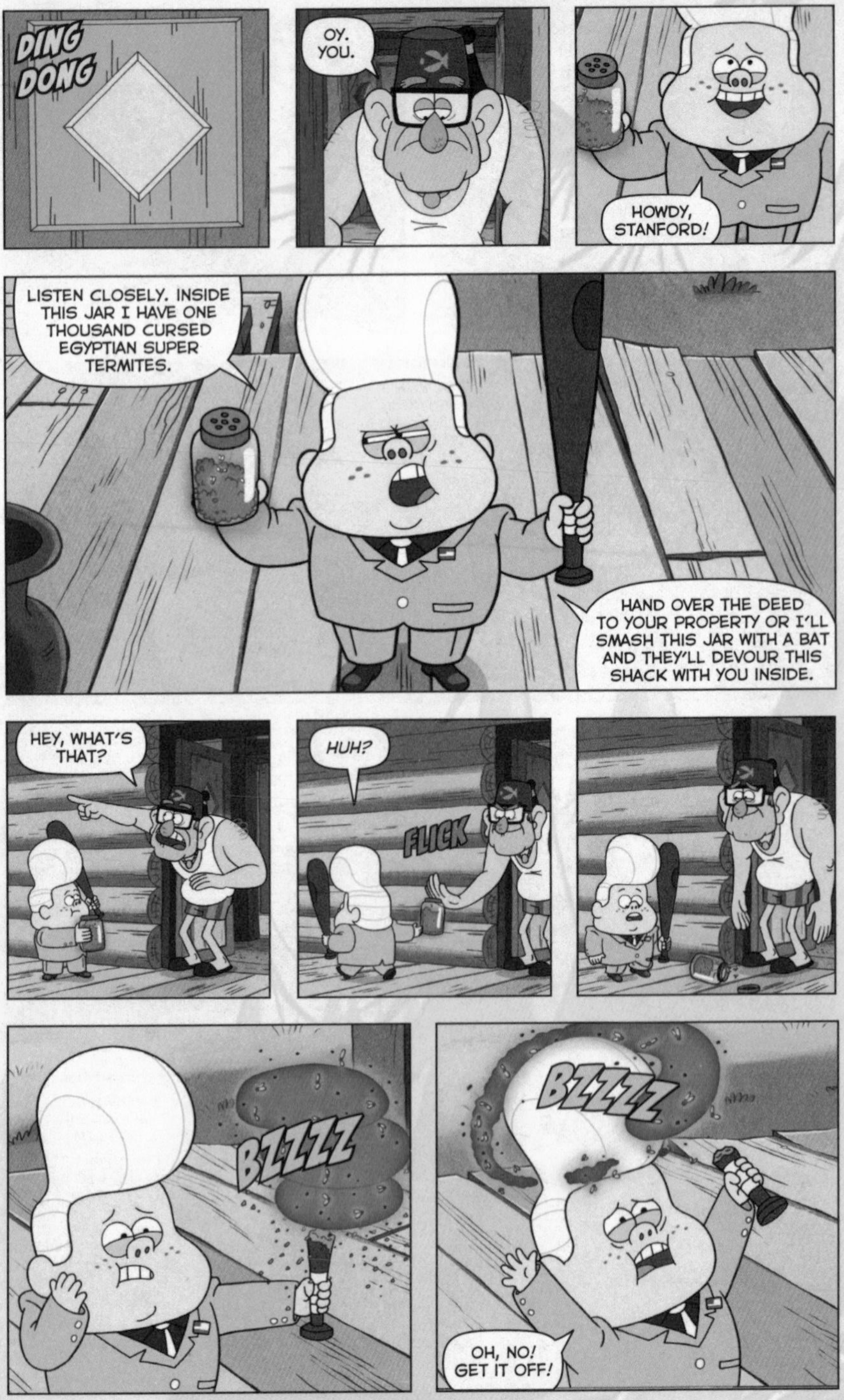
DING DONG
OY. YOU.
HOWDY, STANFORD!
LISTEN CLOSELY. INSIDE THIS JAR I HAVE ONE THOUSAND CURSED EGYPTIAN SUPER TERMITES.
HAND OVER THE DEED TO YOUR PROPERTY OR I'LL SMASH THIS JAR WITH A BAT AND THEY'LL DEVOUR THIS SHACK WITH YOU INSIDE.
HEY, WHAT'S THAT?
HUH?
FLICK
BZZZZ
BZZZZ
OH, NO! GET IT OFF!

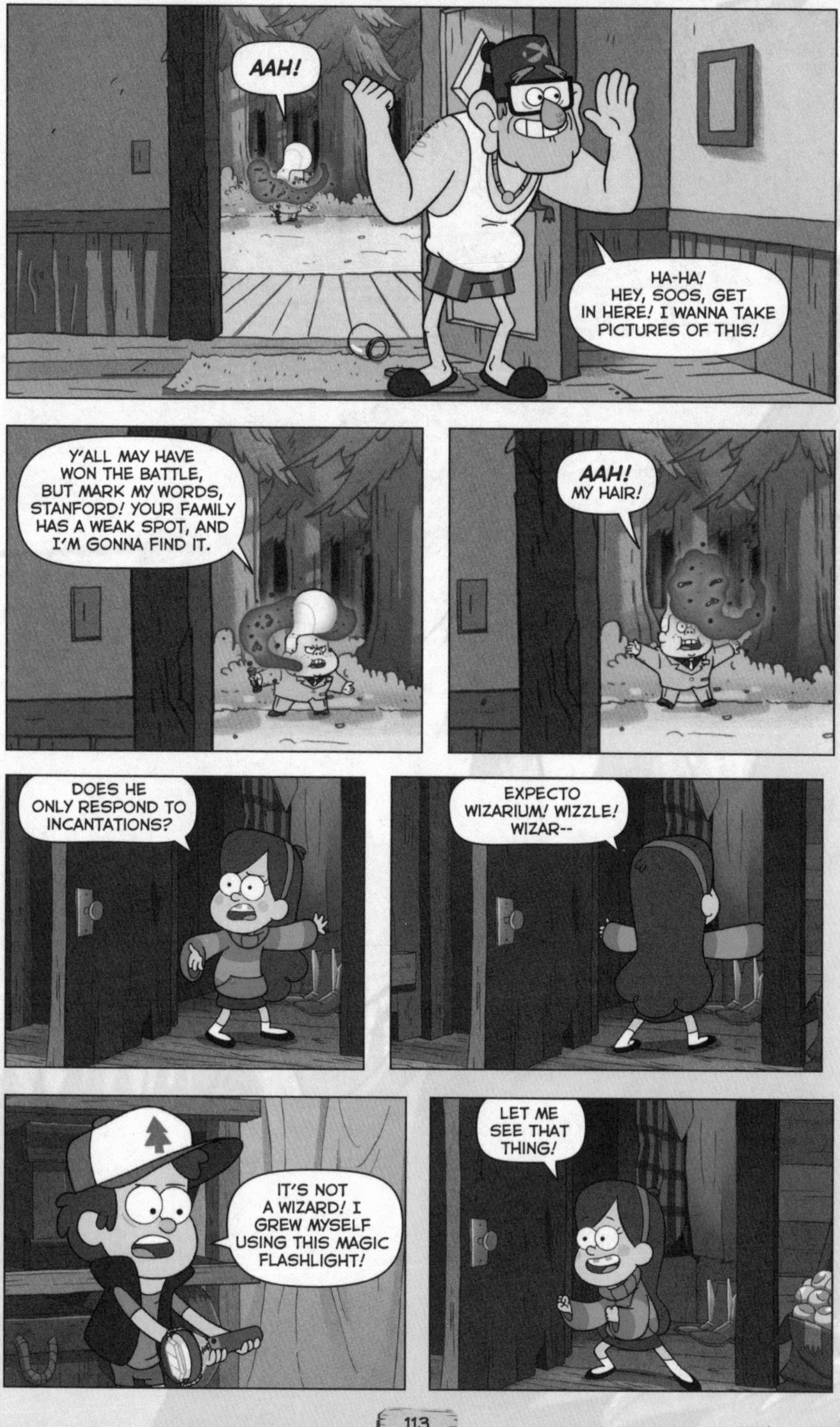
AAH!
HA-HA! HEY, SOOS, GET IN HERE! I WANNA TAKE PICTURES OF THIS!
Y'ALL MAY HAVE WON THE BATTLE, BUT MARK MY WORDS, STANFORD! YOUR FAMILY HAS A WEAK SPOT, AND I'M GONNA FIND IT.
AAH! MY HAIR!
DOES HE ONLY RESPOND TO INCANTATIONS?
EXPECTO WIZARIUM! WIZZLE! WIZAR--
IT'S NOT A WIZARD! I GREW MYSELF USING THIS MAGIC FLASHLIGHT!
LET ME SEE THAT THING!

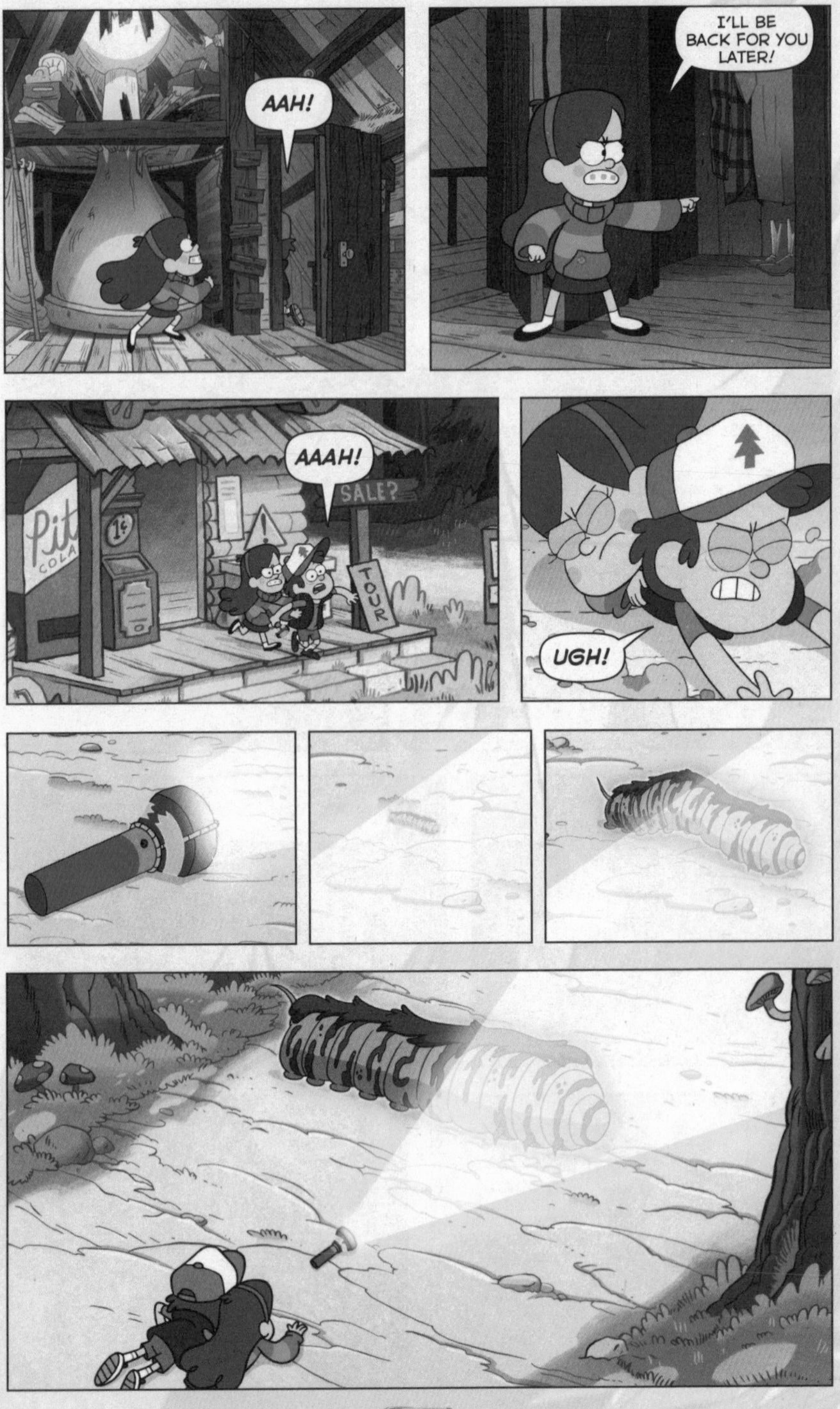
AAH!
I'LL BE BACK FOR YOU LATER!
AAAH!
SALE?
TOUR
Pit
COLA
1¢
UGH!

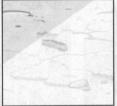

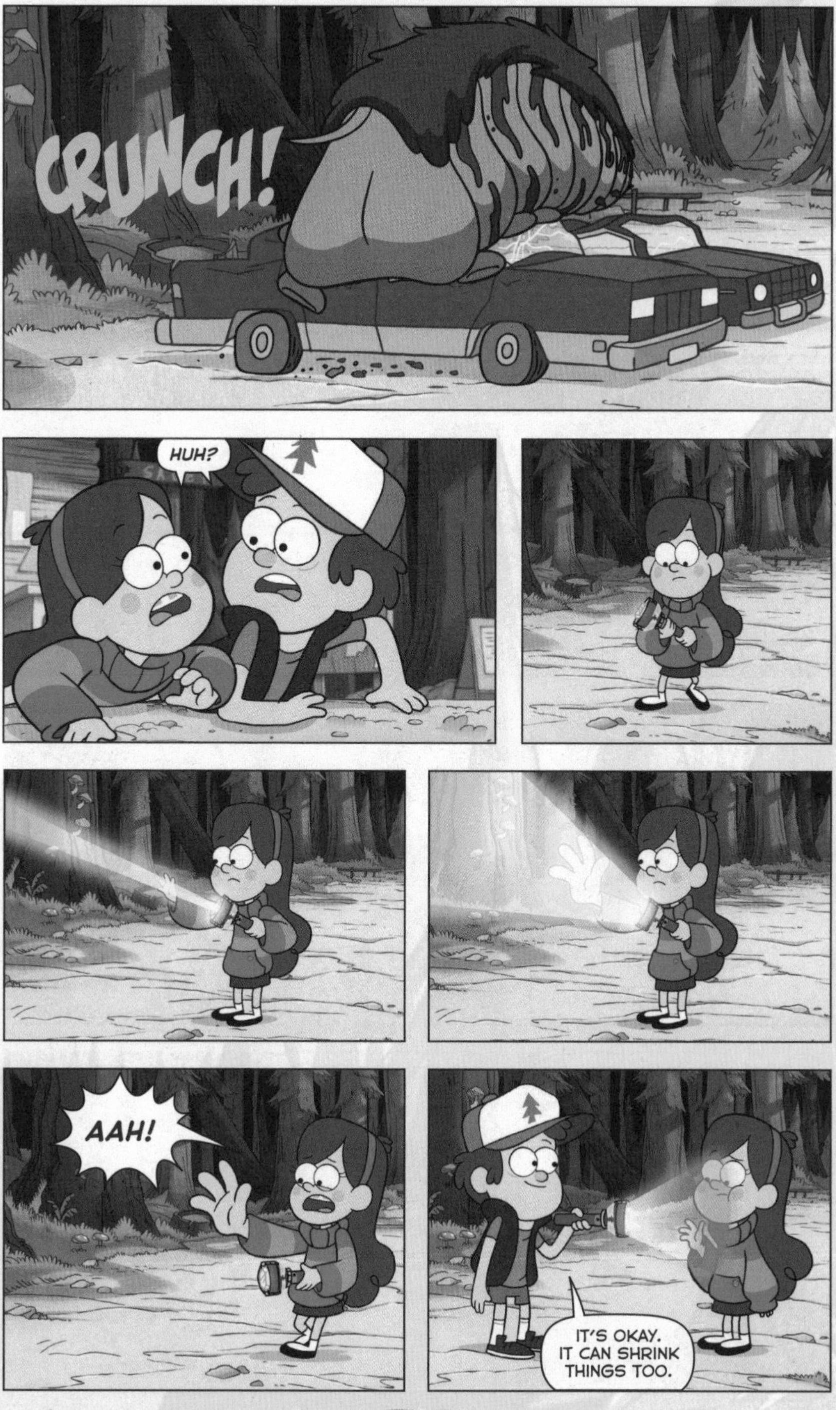
CRUNCH!
HUH?
AAH!
IT'S OKAY.
IT CAN SHRINK
THINGS TOO.

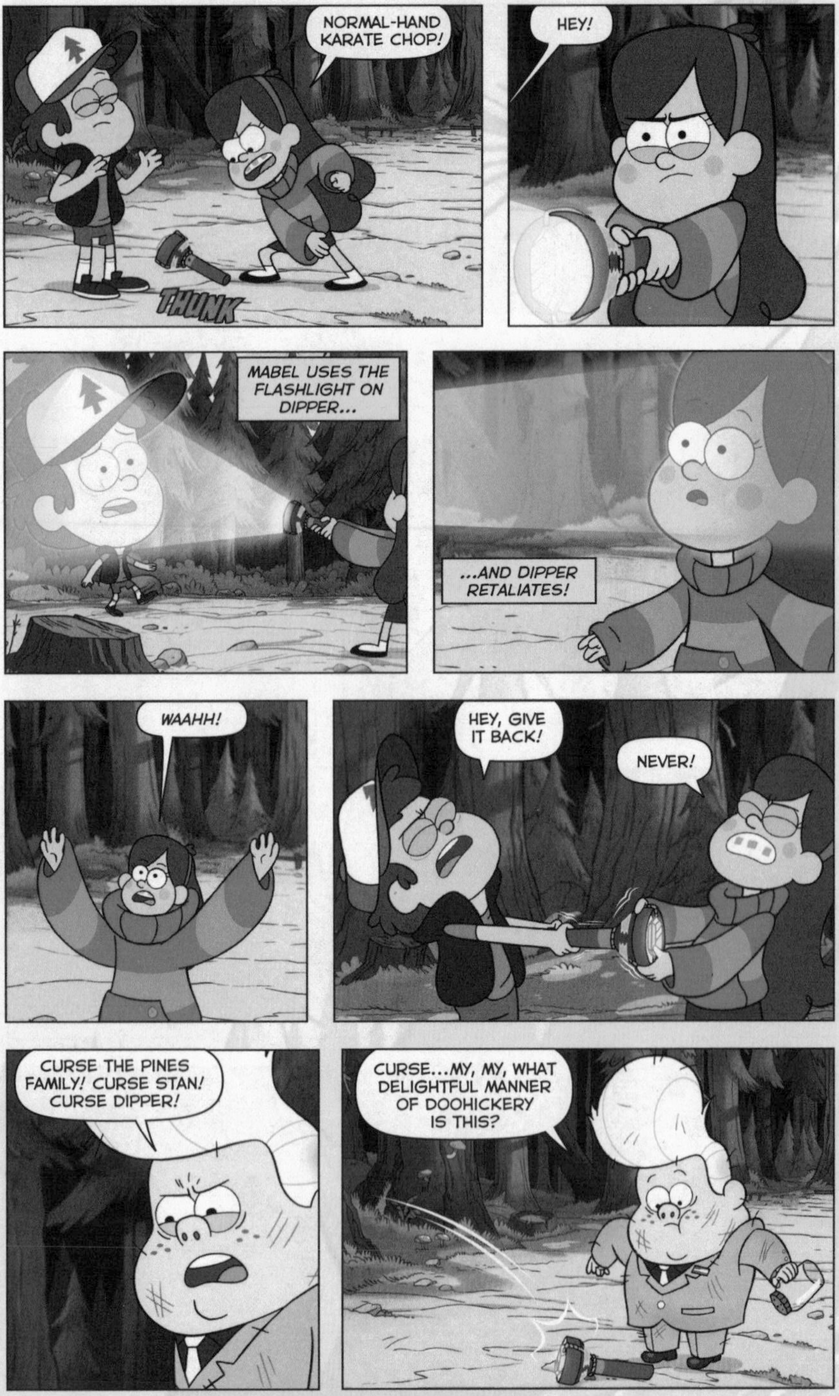
NORMAL-HAND KARATE CHOP!
THUNK
HEY!
MABEL USES THE FLASHLIGHT ON DIPPER...
...AND DIPPER RETALIATES!
WAAHH!
HEY, GIVE IT BACK!
NEVER!
CURSE THE PINES FAMILY! CURSE STAN! CURSE DIPPER!
CURSE...MY, MY, WHAT DELIGHTFUL MANNER OF DOOHICKERY IS THIS?

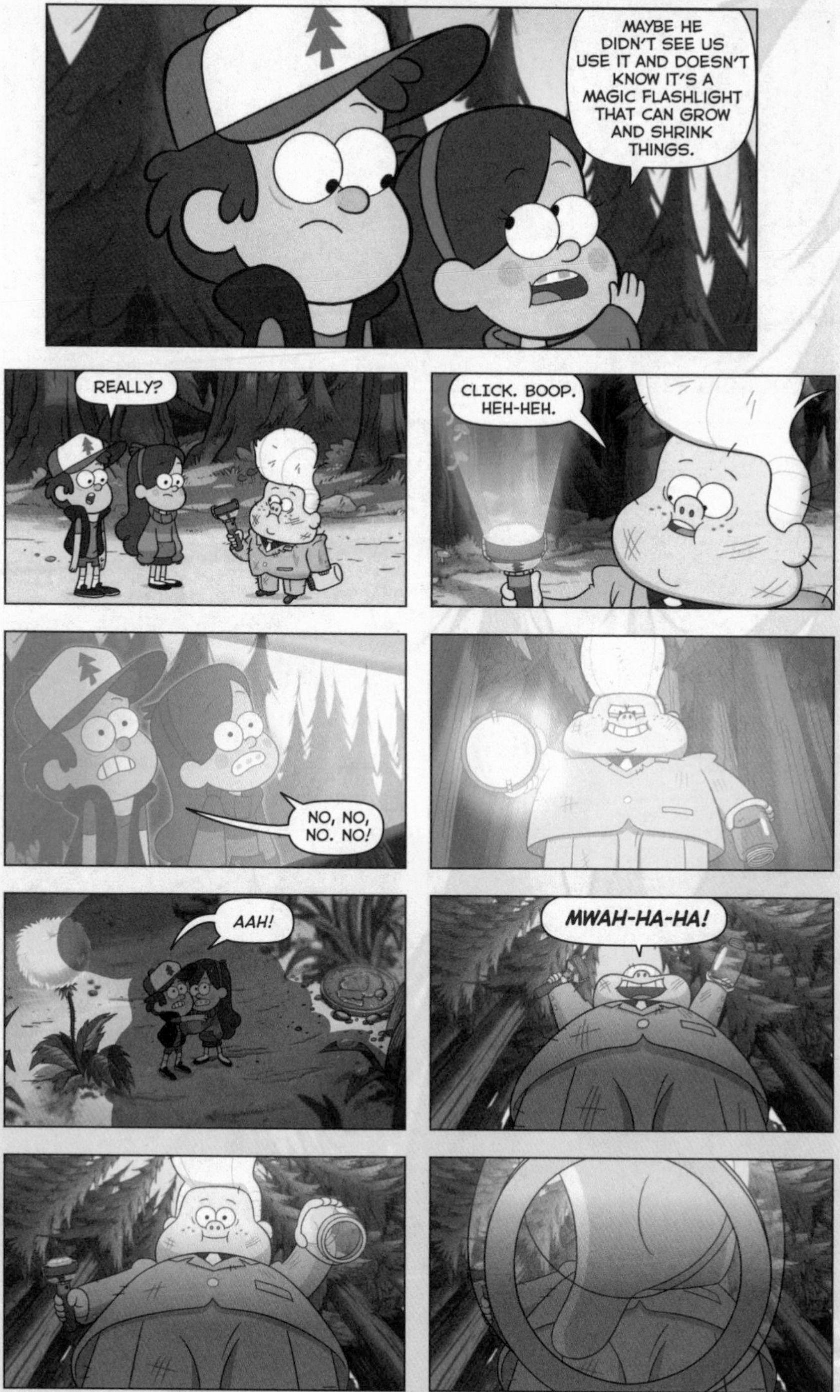
MAYBE HE DIDN'T SEE US USE IT AND DOESN'T KNOW IT'S A MAGIC FLASHLIGHT THAT CAN GROW AND SHRINK THINGS.
REALLY?
CLICK. BOOP. HEH-HEH.
NO, NO, NO. NO!
AAH!
MWAH-HA-HA!

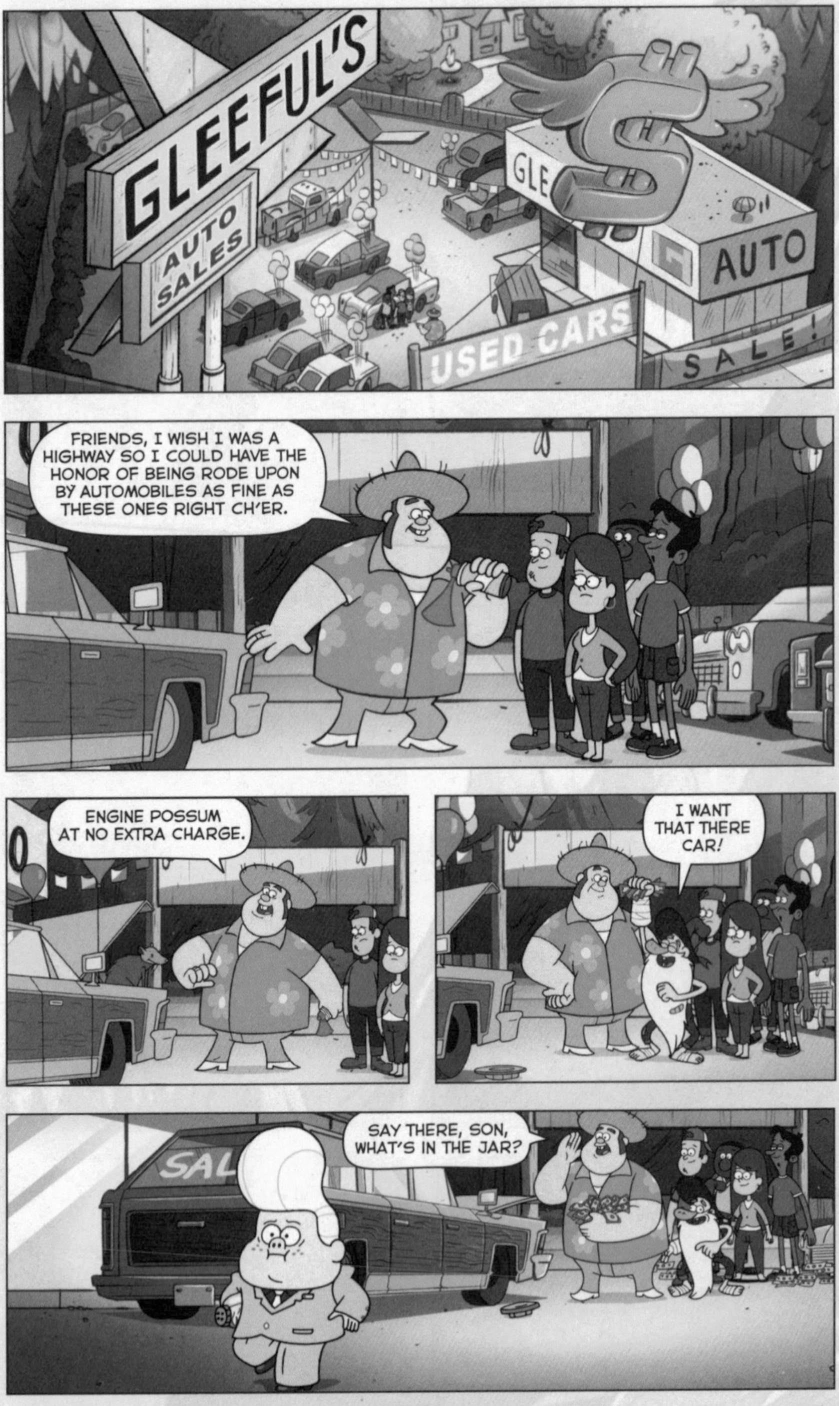
GLEEFUL'S
AUTO SALES
GLE
AUTO
USED CARS
SALE!
FRIENDS, I WISH I WAS A HIGHWAY SO I COULD HAVE THE HONOR OF BEING RODE UPON BY AUTOMOBILES AS FINE AS THESE ONES RIGHT CH'ER.
ENGINE POSSUM AT NO EXTRA CHARGE.
I WANT THAT THERE CAR!
SAY THERE, SON, WHAT'S IN THE JAR?

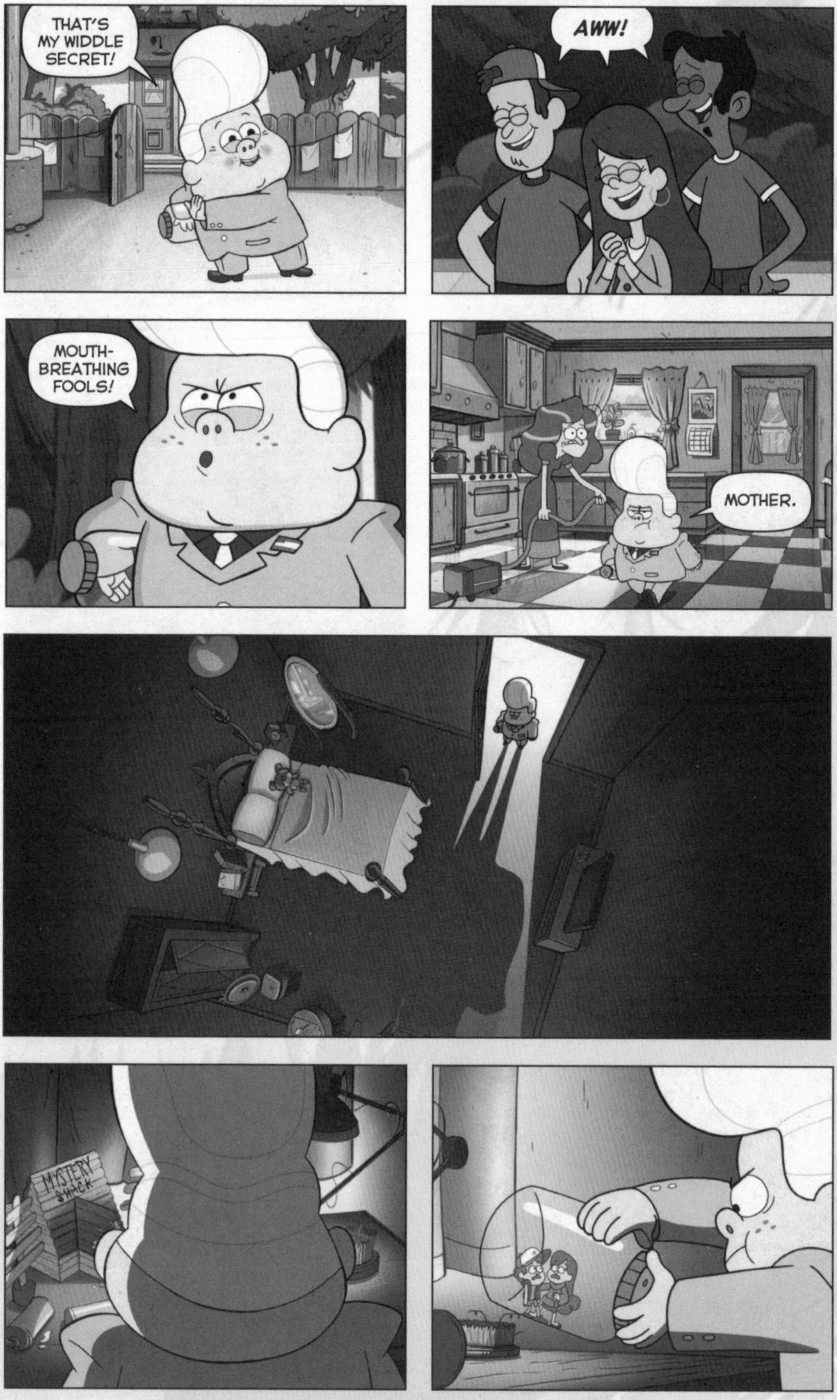
THAT'S MY WIDDLE SECRET!
AWW!
MOUTH-BREATHING FOOLS!
MOTHER.
MYSTERY SHACK

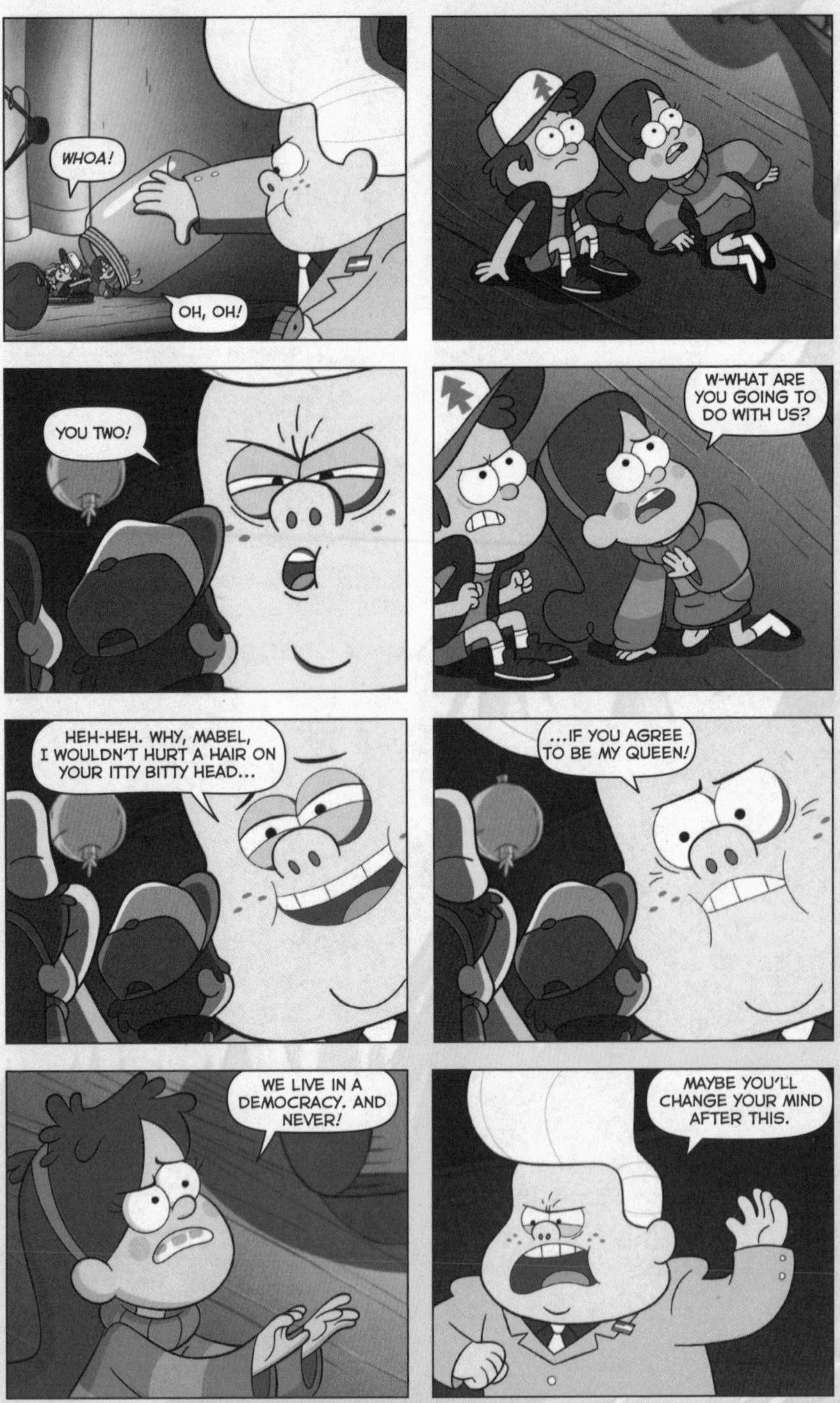
WHOA!
OH, OH!
YOU TWO!
W-WHAT ARE YOU GOING TO DO WITH US?
HEH-HEH. WHY, MABEL, I WOULDN'T HURT A HAIR ON YOUR ITTY BITTY HEAD...
...IF YOU AGREE TO BE MY QUEEN!
WE LIVE IN A DEMOCRACY. AND NEVER!
MAYBE YOU'LL CHANGE YOUR MIND AFTER THIS.

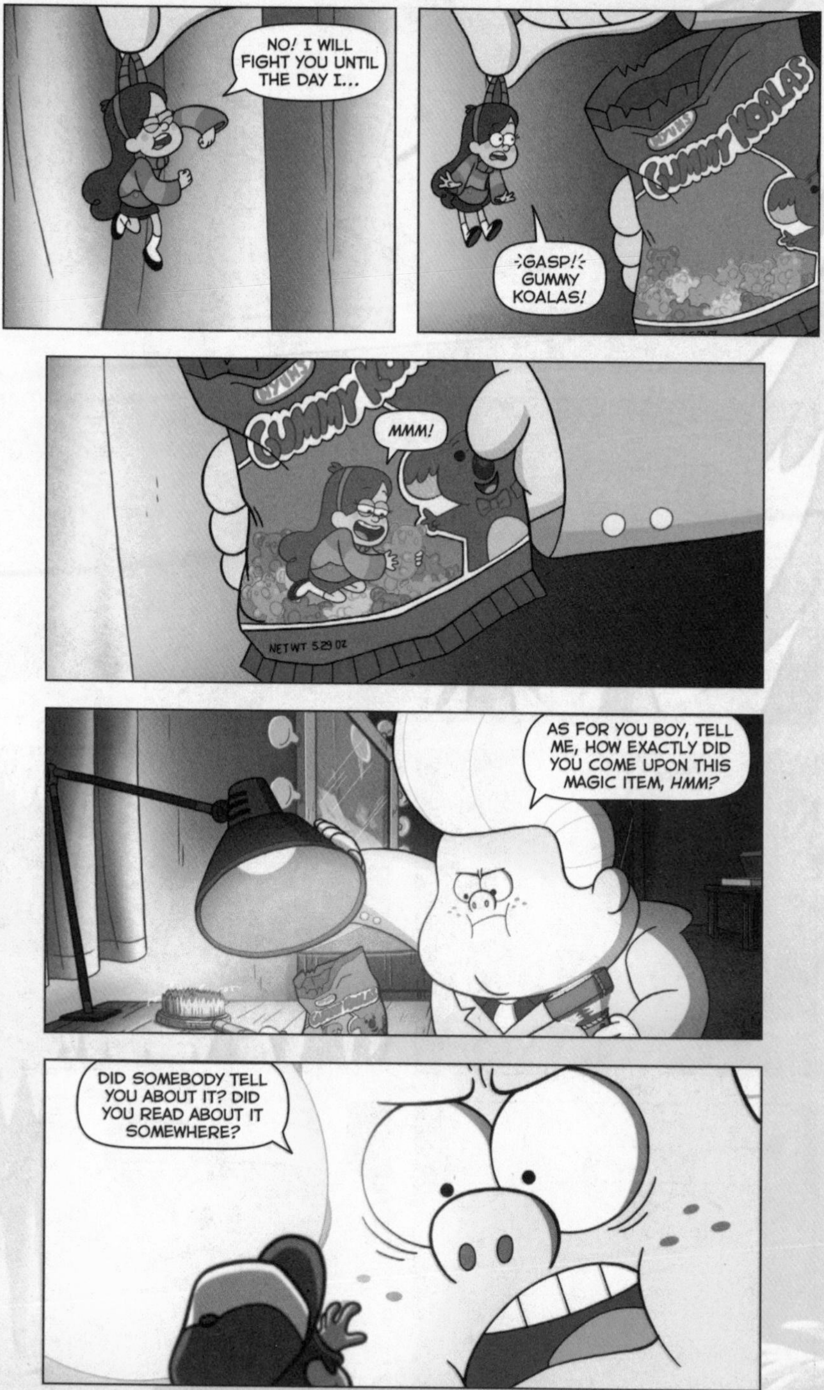
NO! I WILL FIGHT YOU UNTIL THE DAY I...
GUMMY KOALAS
NYUKS
GASP! GUMMY KOALAS!
MMM!
NET WT 5.29 OZ
AS FOR YOU BOY, TELL ME, HOW EXACTLY DID YOU COME UPON THIS MAGIC ITEM, HMM?
DID SOMEBODY TELL YOU ABOUT IT? DID YOU READ ABOUT IT SOMEWHERE?

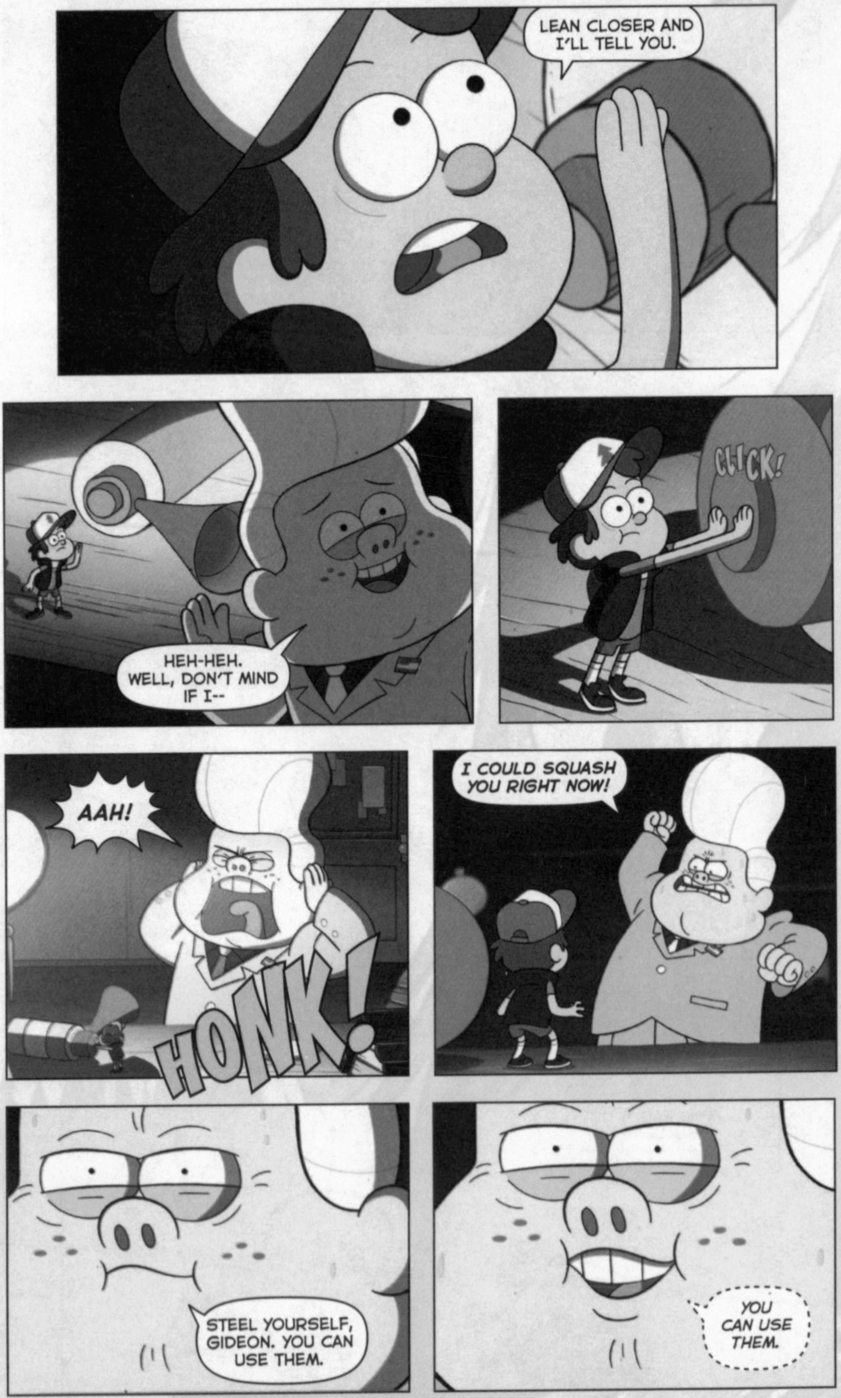
LEAN CLOSER AND I'LL TELL YOU.
HEH-HEH. WELL, DON'T MIND IF I--
CLICK!
AAH!
HONK!
I COULD SQUASH YOU RIGHT NOW!
STEEL YOURSELF, GIDEON. YOU CAN USE THEM.
YOU CAN USE THEM.

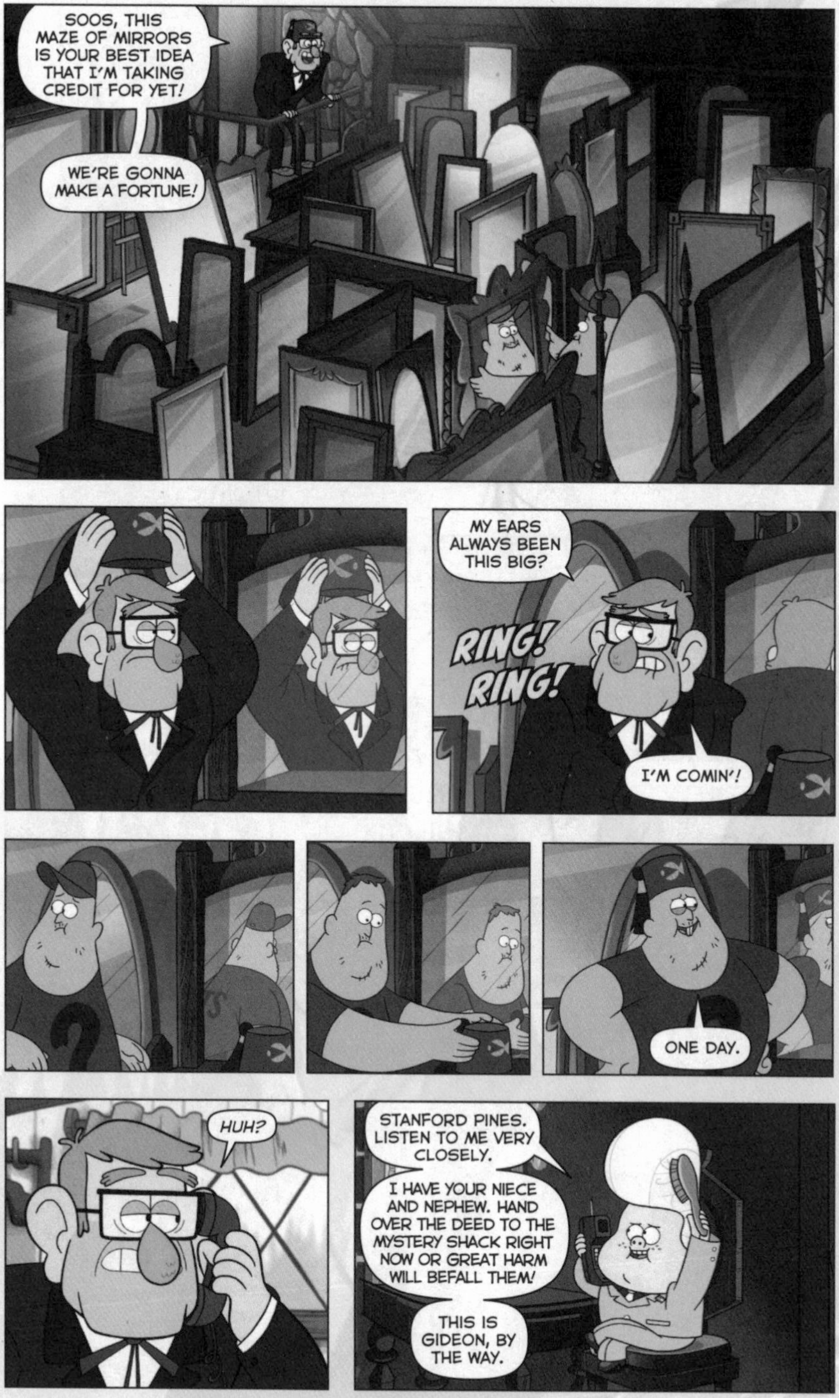
SOOS, THIS MAZE OF MIRRORS IS YOUR BEST IDEA THAT I'M TAKING CREDIT FOR YET!
WE'RE GONNA MAKE A FORTUNE!
MY EARS ALWAYS BEEN THIS BIG?
RING! RING!
I'M COMIN'!
ONE DAY.
HUH?
STANFORD PINES. LISTEN TO ME VERY CLOSELY.
I HAVE YOUR NIECE AND NEPHEW. HAND OVER THE DEED TO THE MYSTERY SHACK RIGHT NOW OR GREAT HARM WILL BEFALL THEM!
THIS IS GIDEON, BY THE WAY.

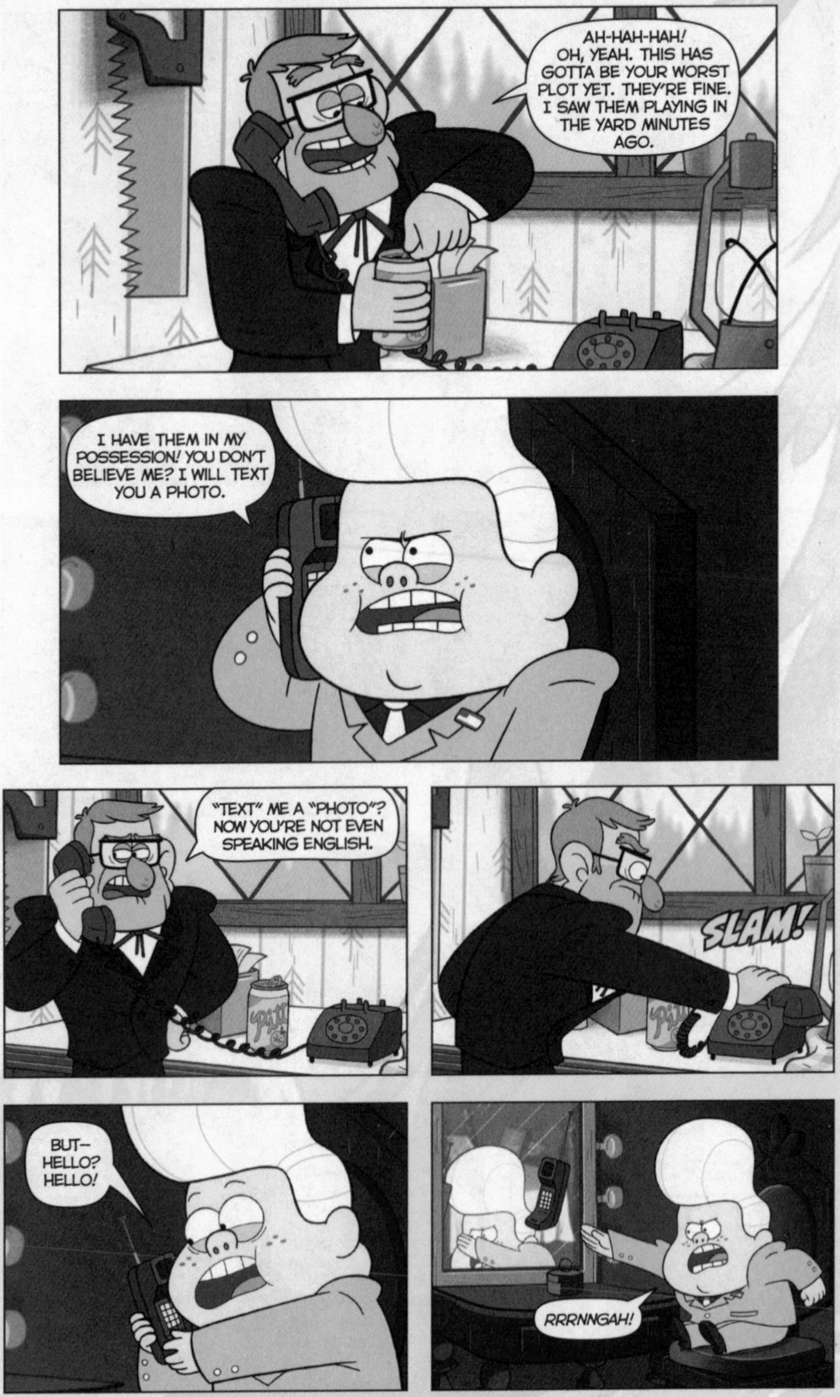
AH-HAH-HAH! OH, YEAH. THIS HAS GOTTA BE YOUR WORST PLOT YET. THEY'RE FINE. I SAW THEM PLAYING IN THE YARD MINUTES AGO.
I HAVE THEM IN MY POSSESSION! YOU DON'T BELIEVE ME? I WILL TEXT YOU A PHOTO.
"TEXT" ME A "PHOTO"? NOW YOU'RE NOT EVEN SPEAKING ENGLISH.
SLAM!
BUT— HELLO? HELLO!
RRRNNGAH!

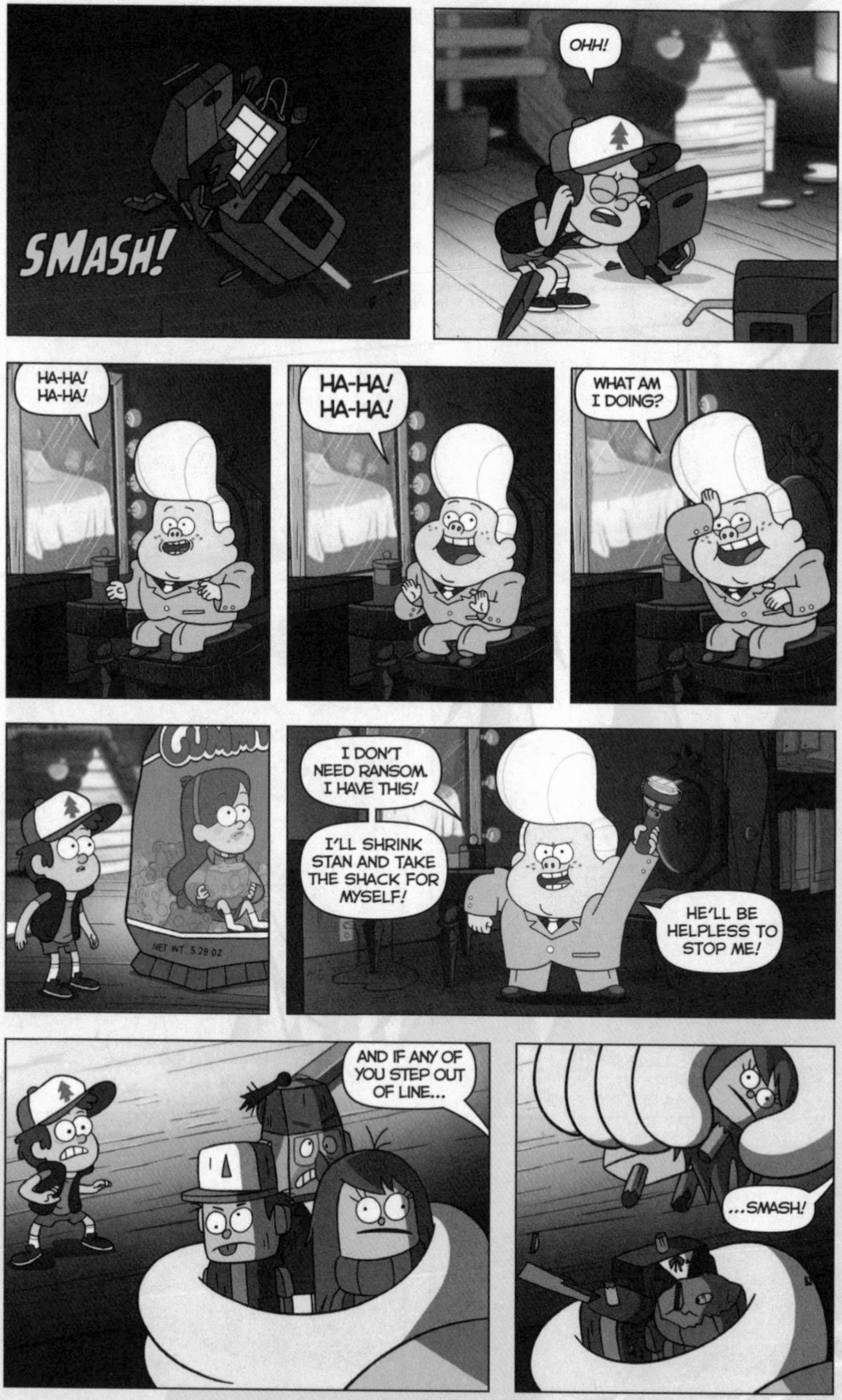
SMASH!
OHH!
HA-HA! HA-HA!
HA-HA! HA-HA!
WHAT AM I DOING?
NET WT. 5.29 OZ
I DON'T NEED RANSOM. I HAVE THIS!
I'LL SHRINK STAN AND TAKE THE SHACK FOR MYSELF!
HE'LL BE HELPLESS TO STOP ME!
AND IF ANY OF YOU STEP OUT OF LINE...
...SMASH!

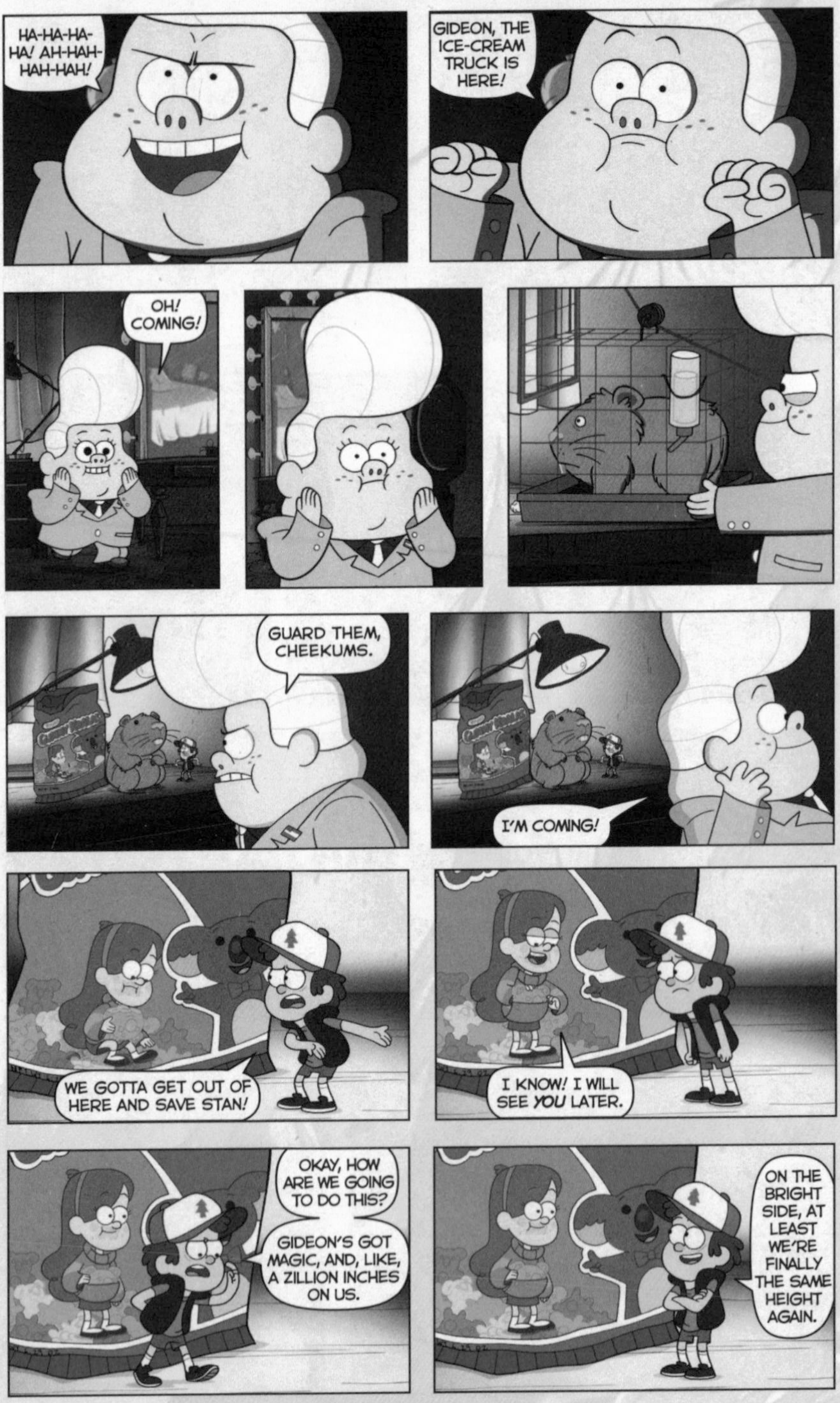
HA-HA-HA-HA! AH-HAH-HAH-HAH!
GIDEON, THE ICE-CREAM TRUCK IS HERE!
OH! COMING!
GUARD THEM, CHEEKUMS.
I'M COMING!
WE GOTTA GET OUT OF HERE AND SAVE STAN!
I KNOW! I WILL SEE *YOU* LATER.
OKAY, HOW ARE WE GOING TO DO THIS?
GIDEON'S GOT MAGIC, AND, LIKE, A ZILLION INCHES ON US.
ON THE BRIGHT SIDE, AT LEAST WE'RE FINALLY THE SAME HEIGHT AGAIN.

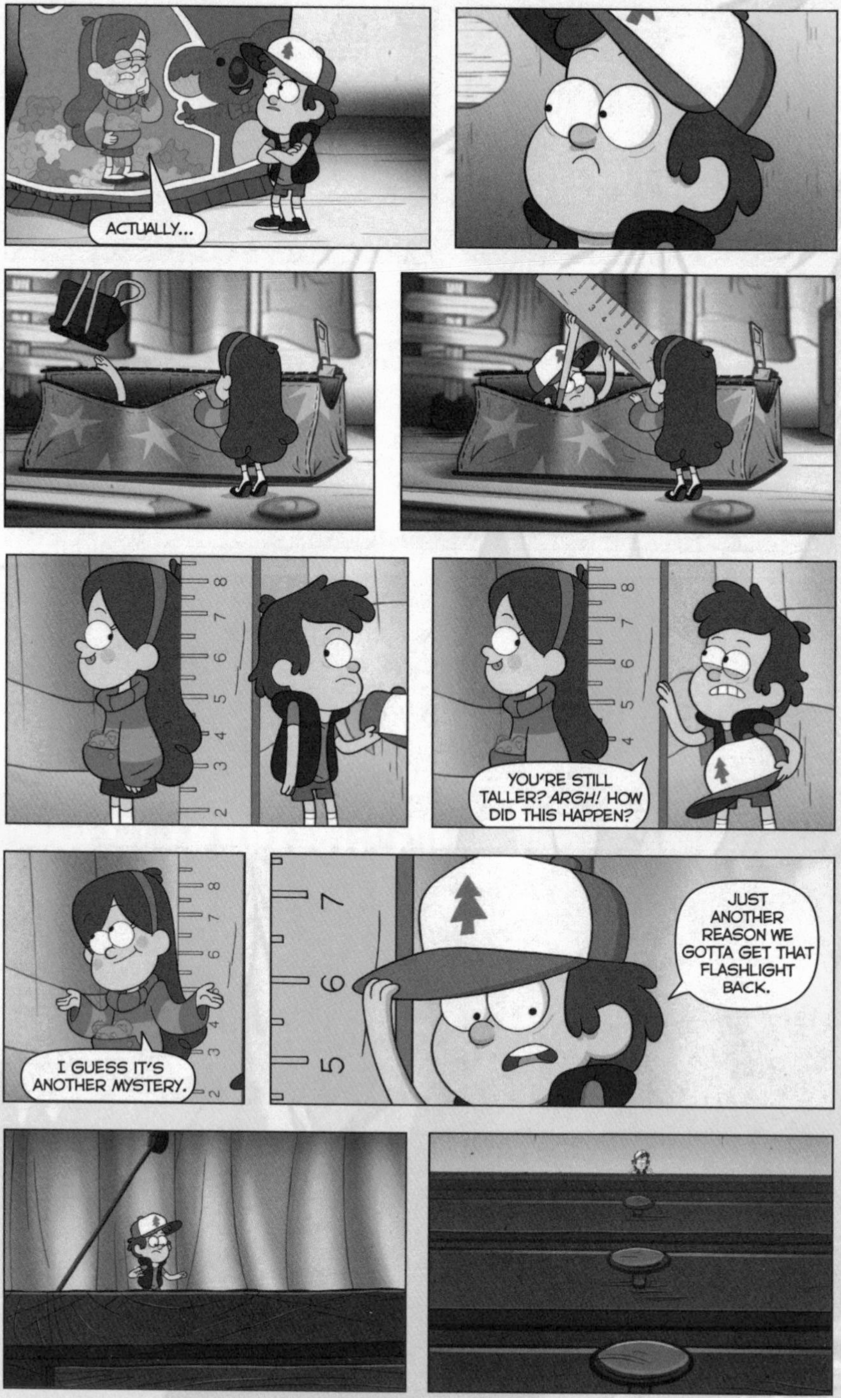
ACTUALLY...
YOU'RE STILL TALLER? *ARGH!* HOW DID THIS HAPPEN?
I GUESS IT'S ANOTHER MYSTERY.
JUST ANOTHER REASON WE GOTTA GET THAT FLASHLIGHT BACK.

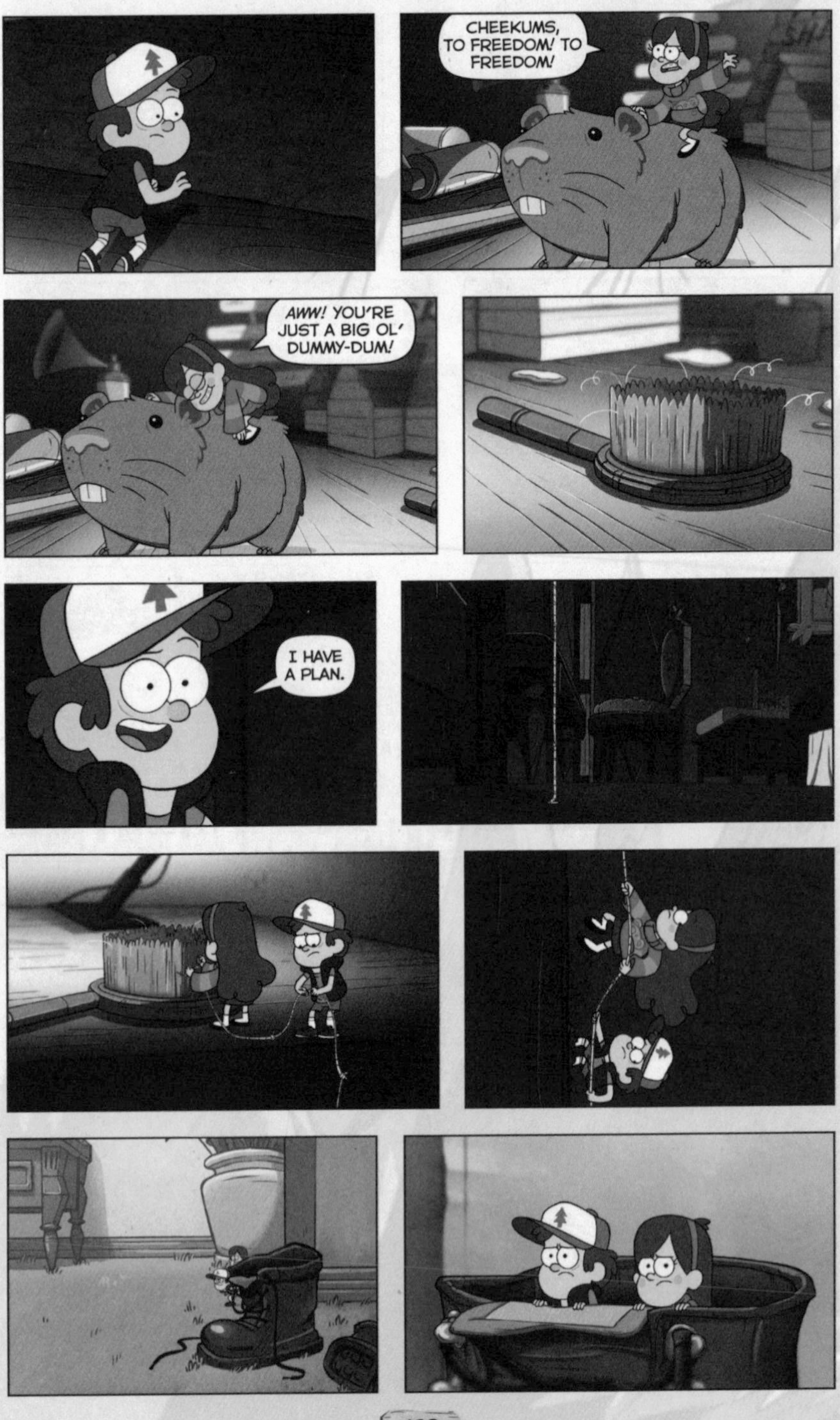
CHEEKUMS, TO FREEDOM! TO FREEDOM!
AWW! YOU'RE JUST A BIG OL' DUMMY-DUM!
I HAVE A PLAN.

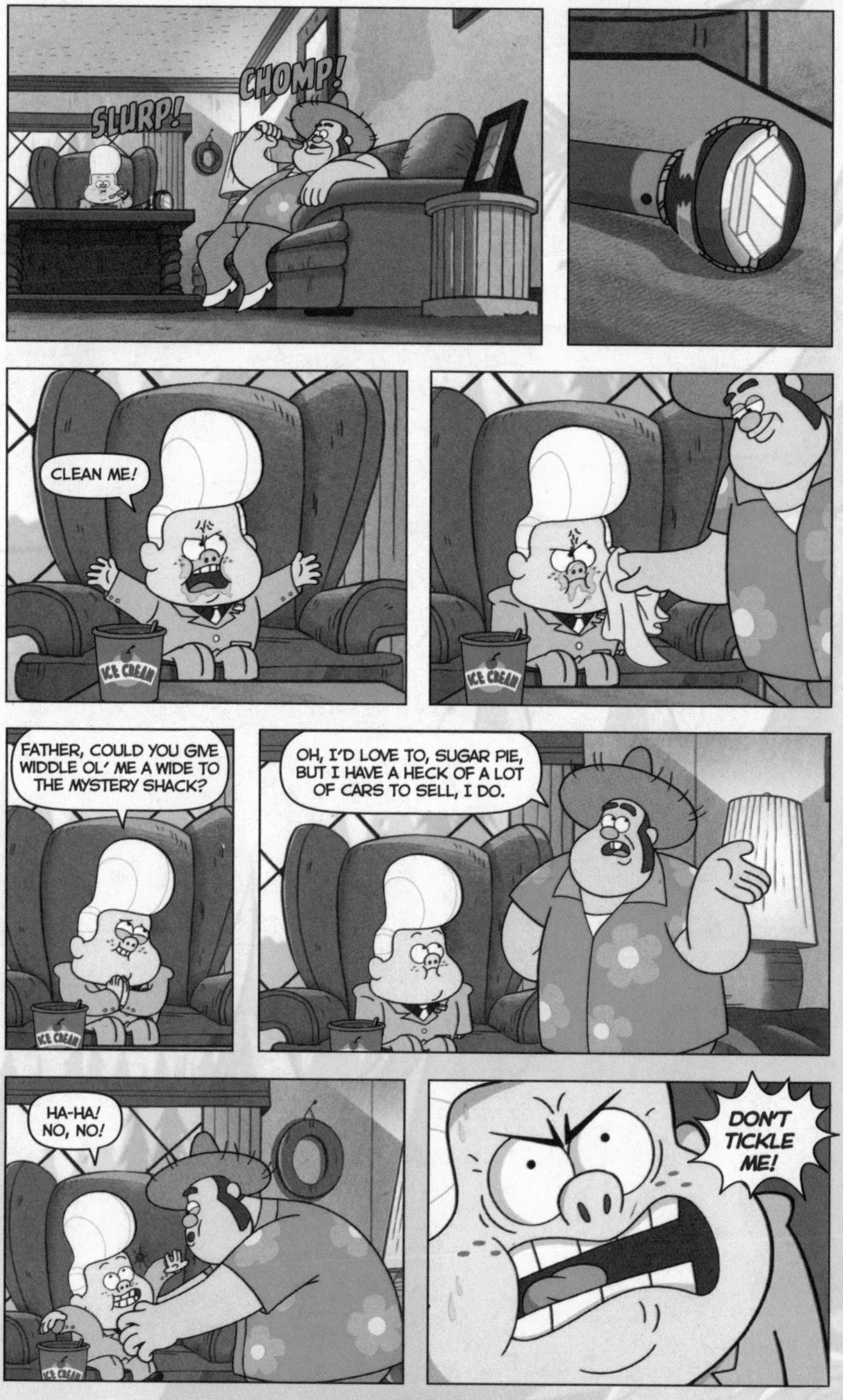
SLURP!
CHOMP!
CLEAN ME!
ICE CREAM
ICE CREAM
FATHER, COULD YOU GIVE WIDDLE OL' ME A WIDE TO THE MYSTERY SHACK?
ICE CREAM
OH, I'D LOVE TO, SUGAR PIE, BUT I HAVE A HECK OF A LOT OF CARS TO SELL, I DO.
HA-HA! NO, NO!
DON'T TICKLE ME!

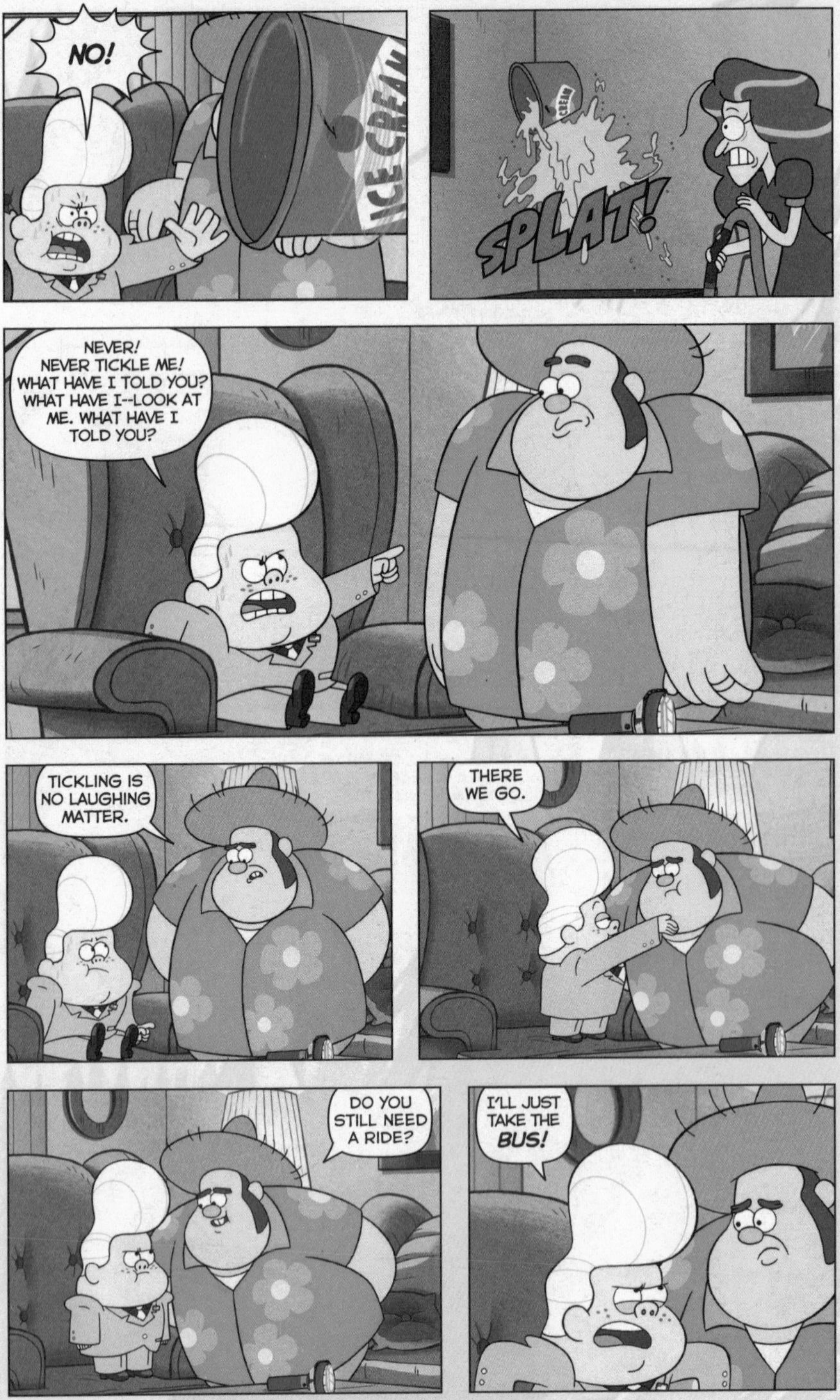
NO!
ICE CREAM
CREAM
SPLAT!
NEVER! NEVER TICKLE ME! WHAT HAVE I TOLD YOU? WHAT HAVE I--LOOK AT ME. WHAT HAVE I TOLD YOU?
TICKLING IS NO LAUGHING MATTER.
THERE WE GO.
DO YOU STILL NEED A RIDE?
I'LL JUST TAKE THE *BUS!*

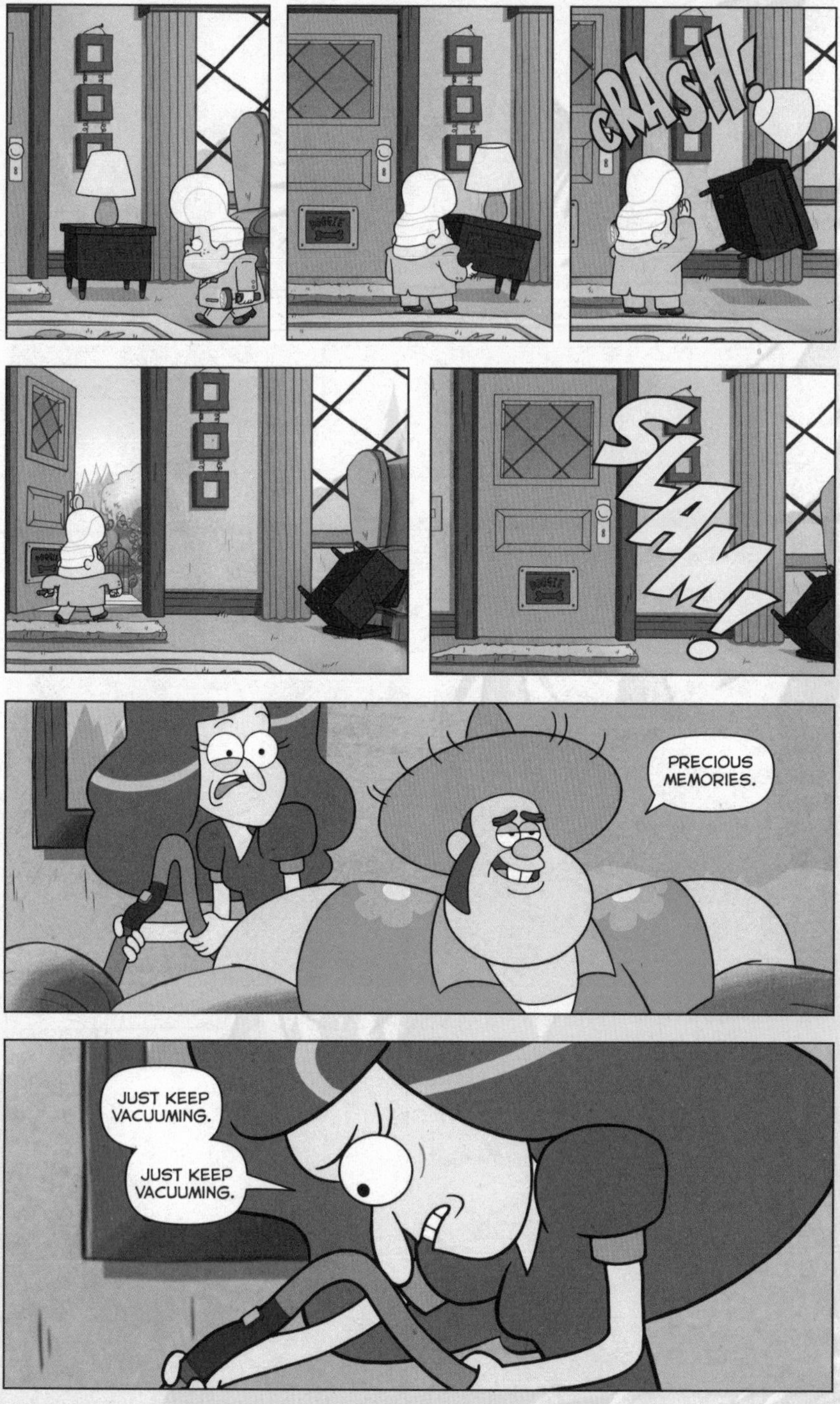
CRASH!
SLAM!
PRECIOUS MEMORIES.
JUST KEEP VACUUMING.
JUST KEEP VACUUMING.

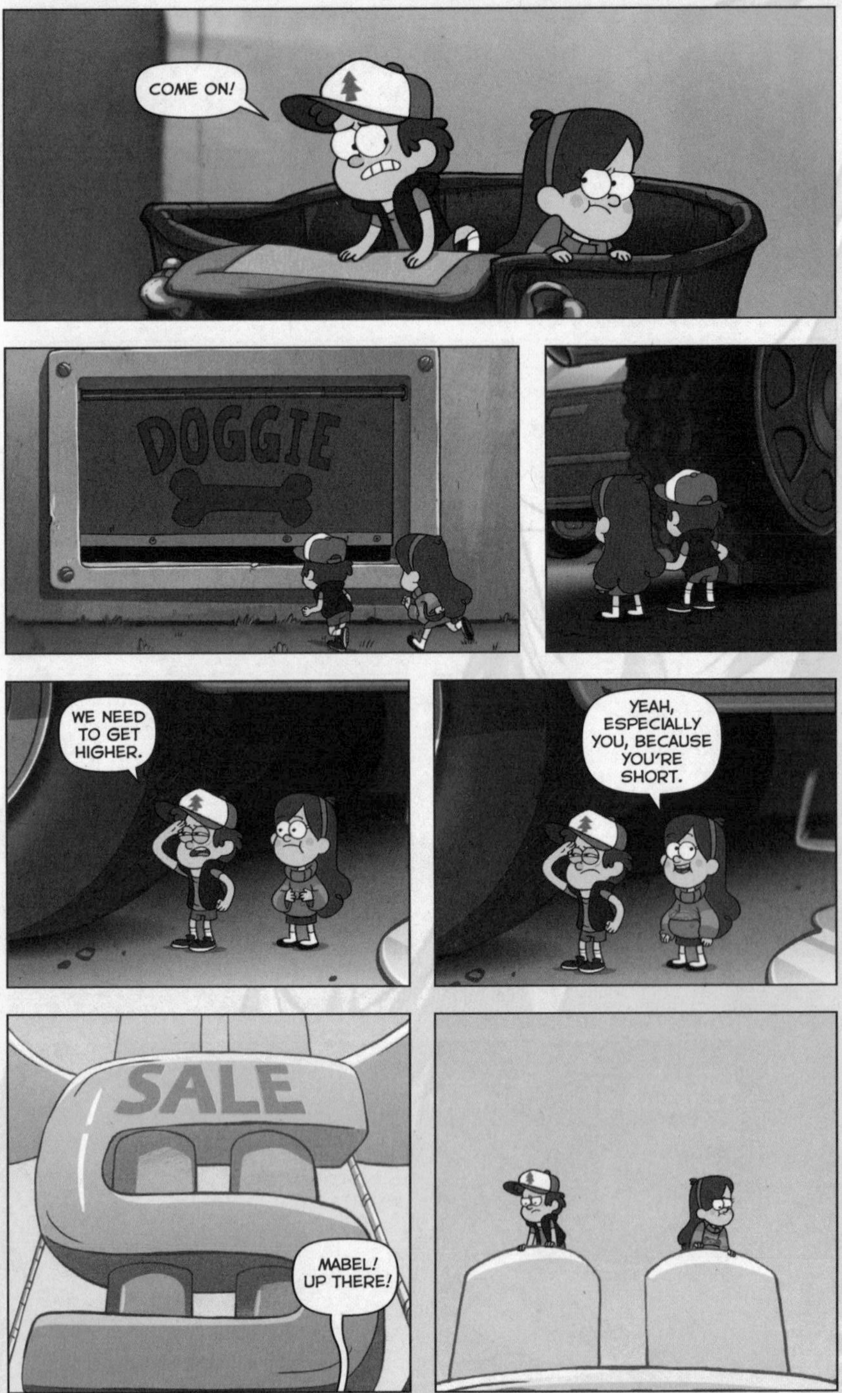
COME ON!
DOGGIE
WE NEED TO GET HIGHER.
YEAH, ESPECIALLY YOU, BECAUSE YOU'RE SHORT.
SALE
MABEL! UP THERE!

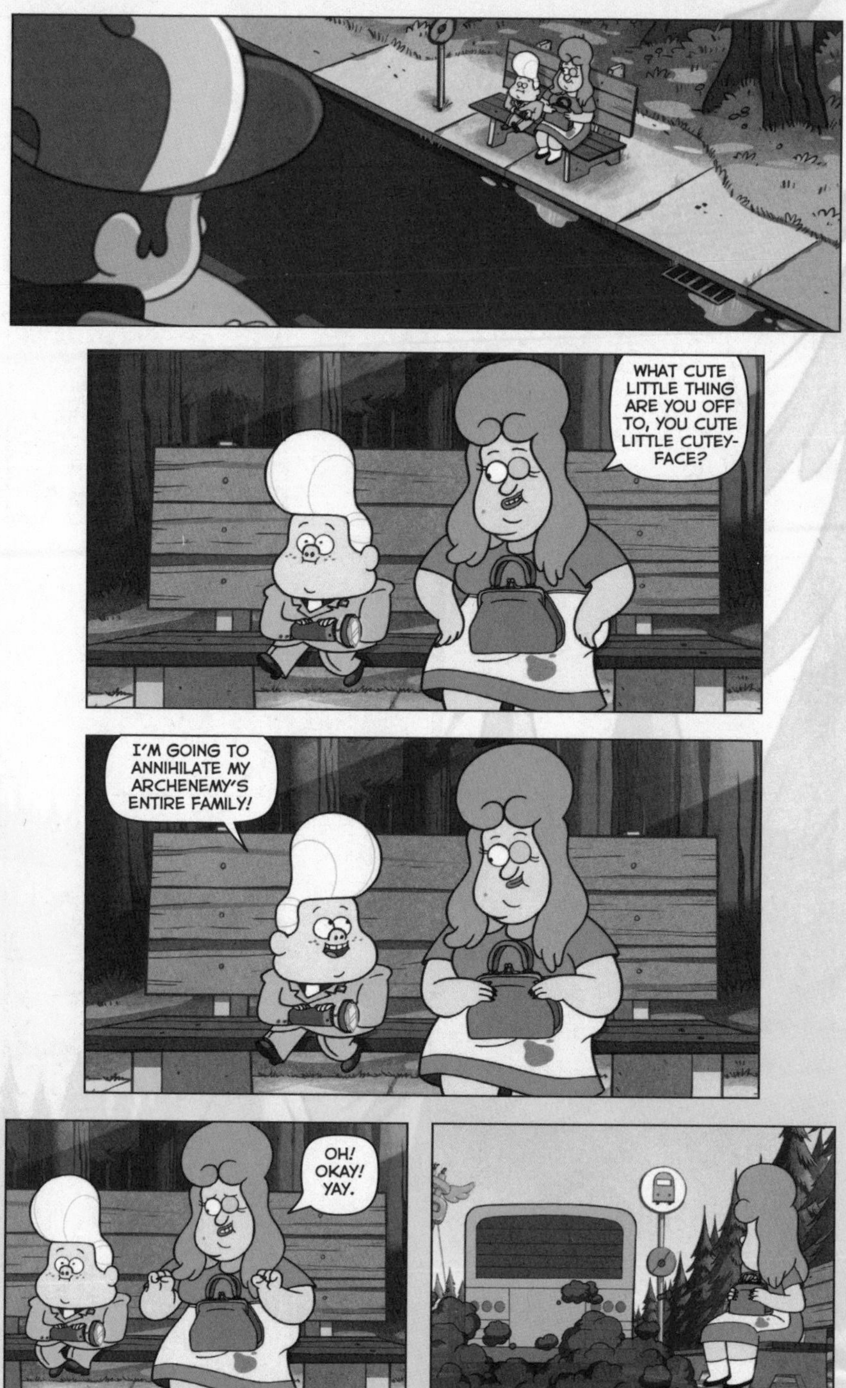
WHAT CUTE LITTLE THING ARE YOU OFF TO, YOU CUTE LITTLE CUTEY-FACE?
I'M GOING TO ANNIHILATE MY ARCHENEMY'S ENTIRE FAMILY!
OH! OKAY! YAY.

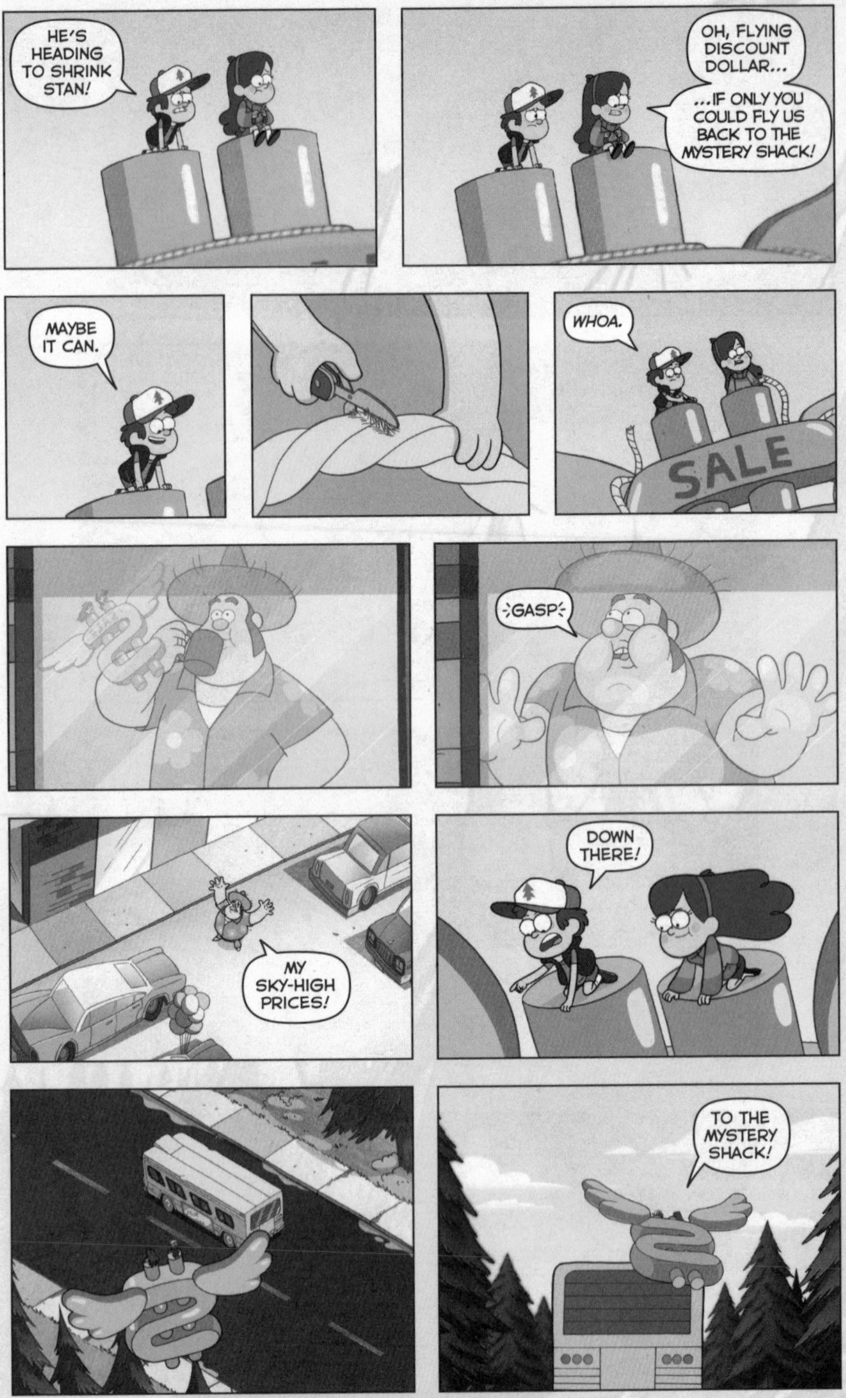
HE'S HEADING TO SHRINK STAN!
OH, FLYING DISCOUNT DOLLAR...
...IF ONLY YOU COULD FLY US BACK TO THE MYSTERY SHACK!
MAYBE IT CAN.
WHOA.
SALE
GASP
MY SKY-HIGH PRICES!
DOWN THERE!
TO THE MYSTERY SHACK!

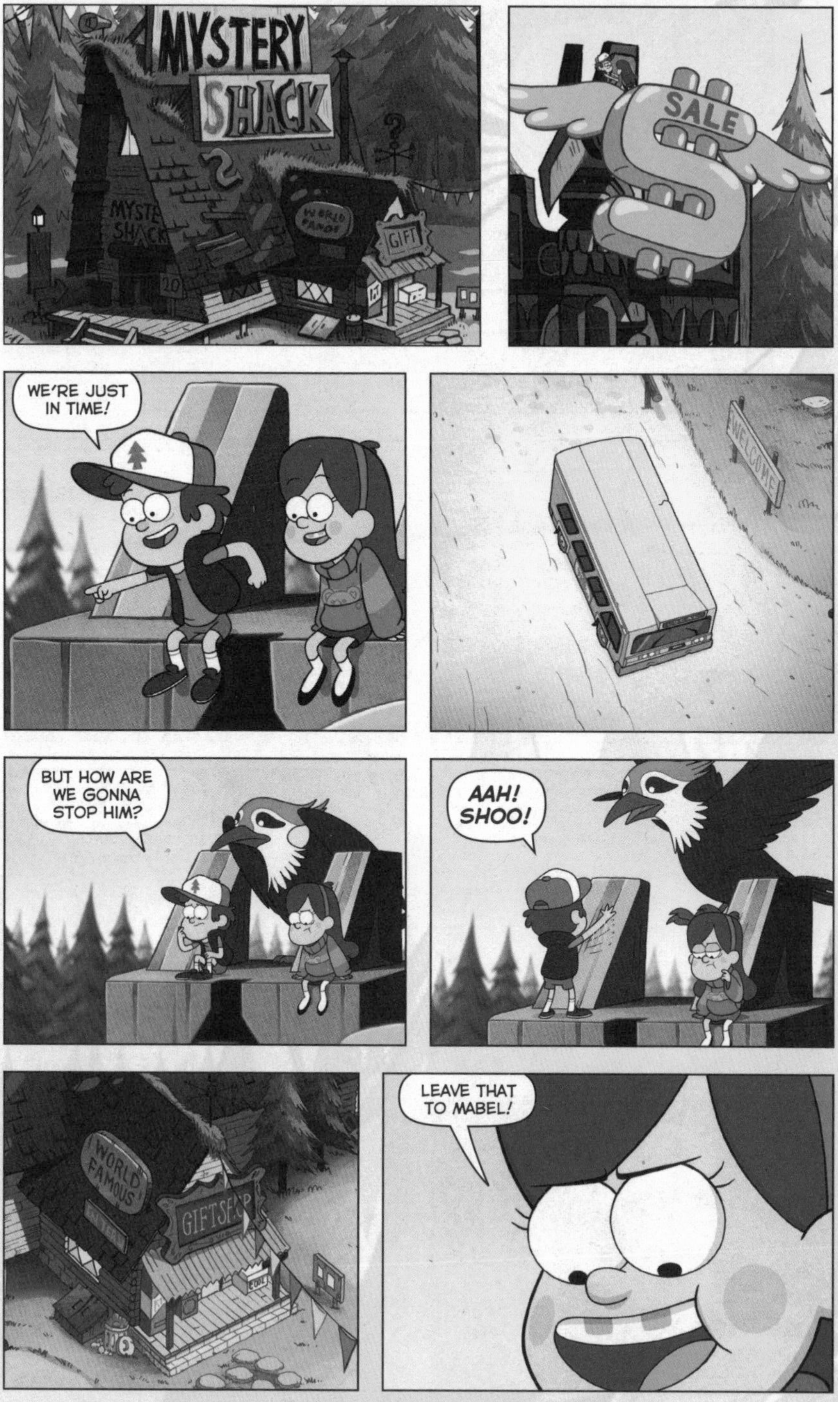
MYSTERY
SHACK
GIFT
SALE
WE'RE JUST IN TIME!
WELCOME
BUT HOW ARE WE GONNA STOP HIM?
AAH! SHOO!
WORLD FAMOUS
GIFT SHOP
LEAVE THAT TO MABEL!

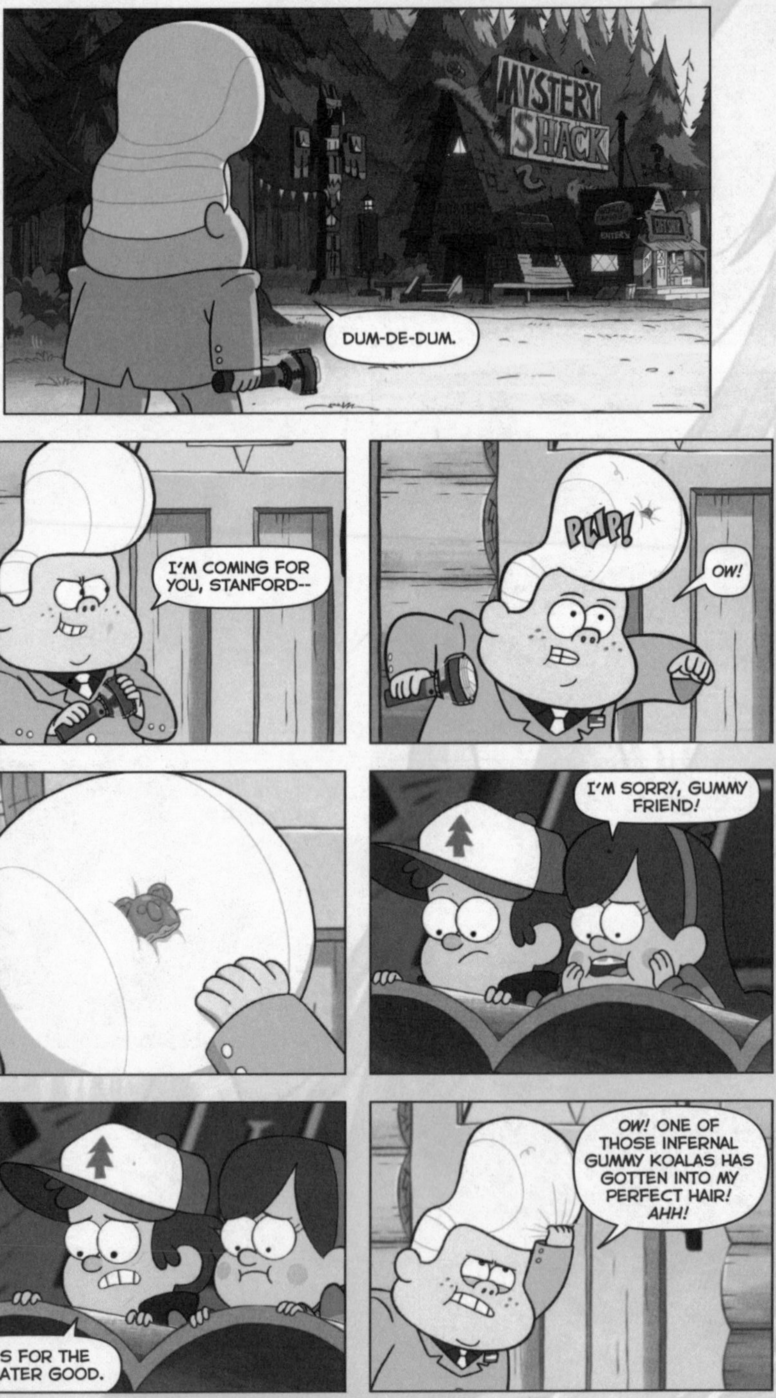
DUM-DE-DUM.
MYSTERY SHACK
I'M COMING FOR YOU, STANFORD--
PLIP!
OW!
I'M SORRY, GUMMY FRIEND!
IT'S FOR THE GREATER GOOD.
OW! ONE OF THOSE INFERNAL GUMMY KOALAS HAS GOTTEN INTO MY PERFECT HAIR! AHH!

AHH!

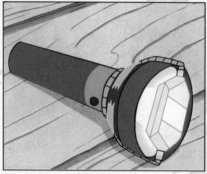

I CAN'T DEFEAT STAN LOOKING LIKE THIS!

Pitt COLA

☆HUMPH!☆

WHOO! WHOO-EE! HEH-HEH!

QUICK! GET IN FRONT AND I'LL REGROW YOU.

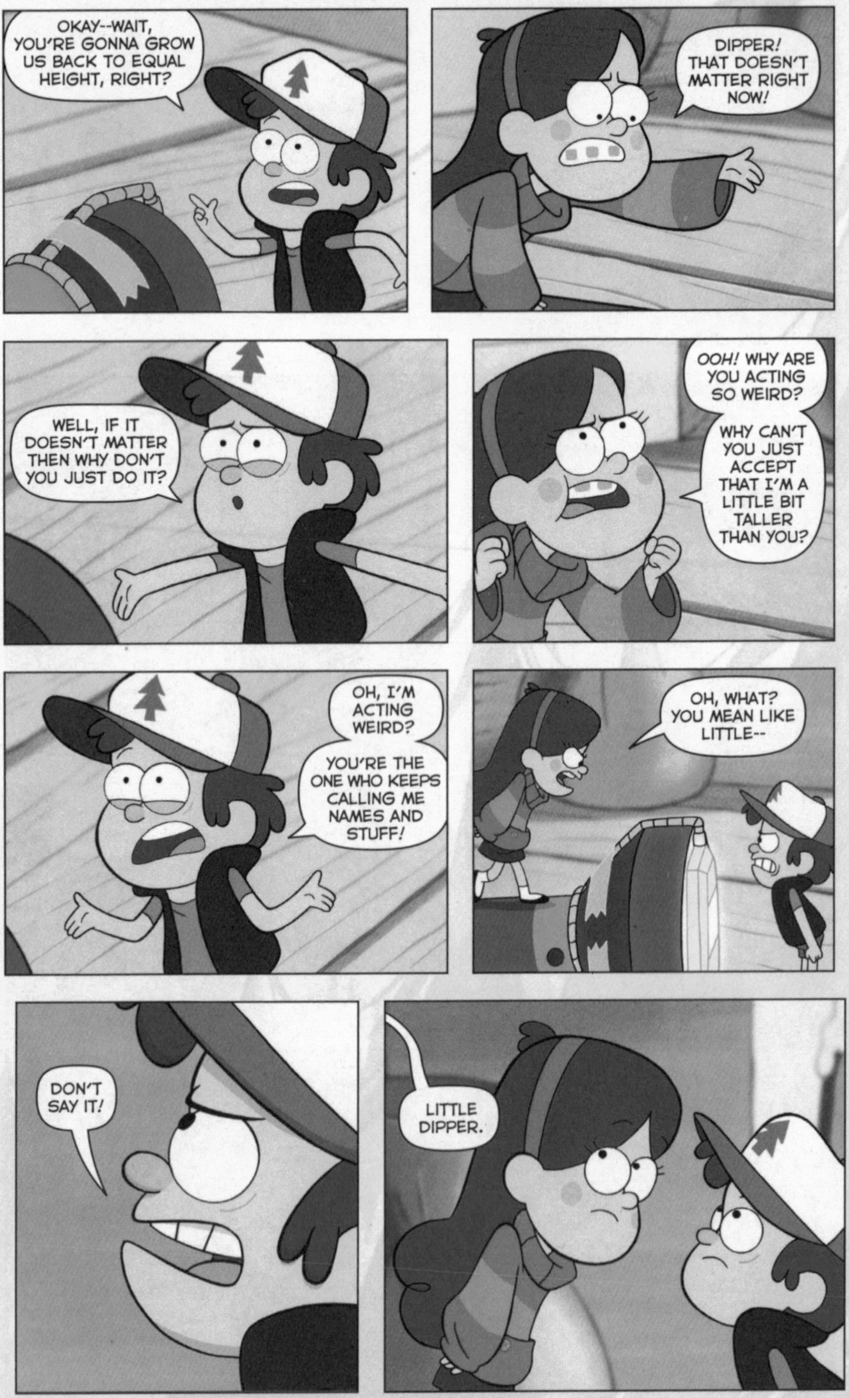
OKAY--WAIT, YOU'RE GONNA GROW US BACK TO EQUAL HEIGHT, RIGHT?
DIPPER! THAT DOESN'T MATTER RIGHT NOW!
WELL, IF IT DOESN'T MATTER THEN WHY DON'T YOU JUST DO IT?
OOH! WHY ARE YOU ACTING SO WEIRD?
WHY CAN'T YOU JUST ACCEPT THAT I'M A LITTLE BIT TALLER THAN YOU?
OH, I'M ACTING WEIRD?
YOU'RE THE ONE WHO KEEPS CALLING ME NAMES AND STUFF!
OH, WHAT? YOU MEAN LIKE LITTLE--
DON'T SAY IT!
LITTLE DIPPER.

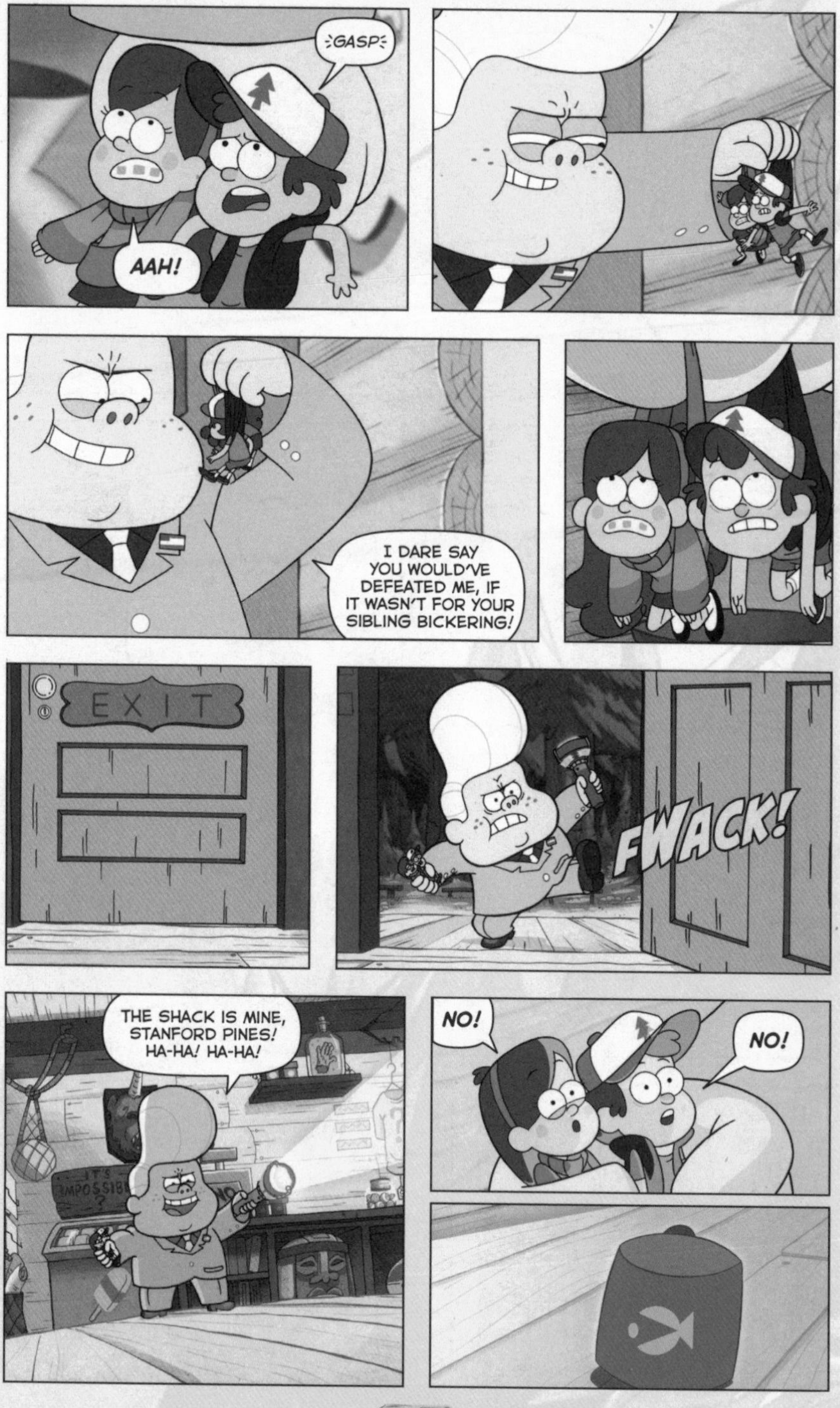
GASP
AAH!
I DARE SAY YOU WOULD'VE DEFEATED ME, IF IT WASN'T FOR YOUR SIBLING BICKERING!
EXIT
FWACK!
THE SHACK IS MINE, STANFORD PINES! HA-HA! HA-HA!
NO!
NO!

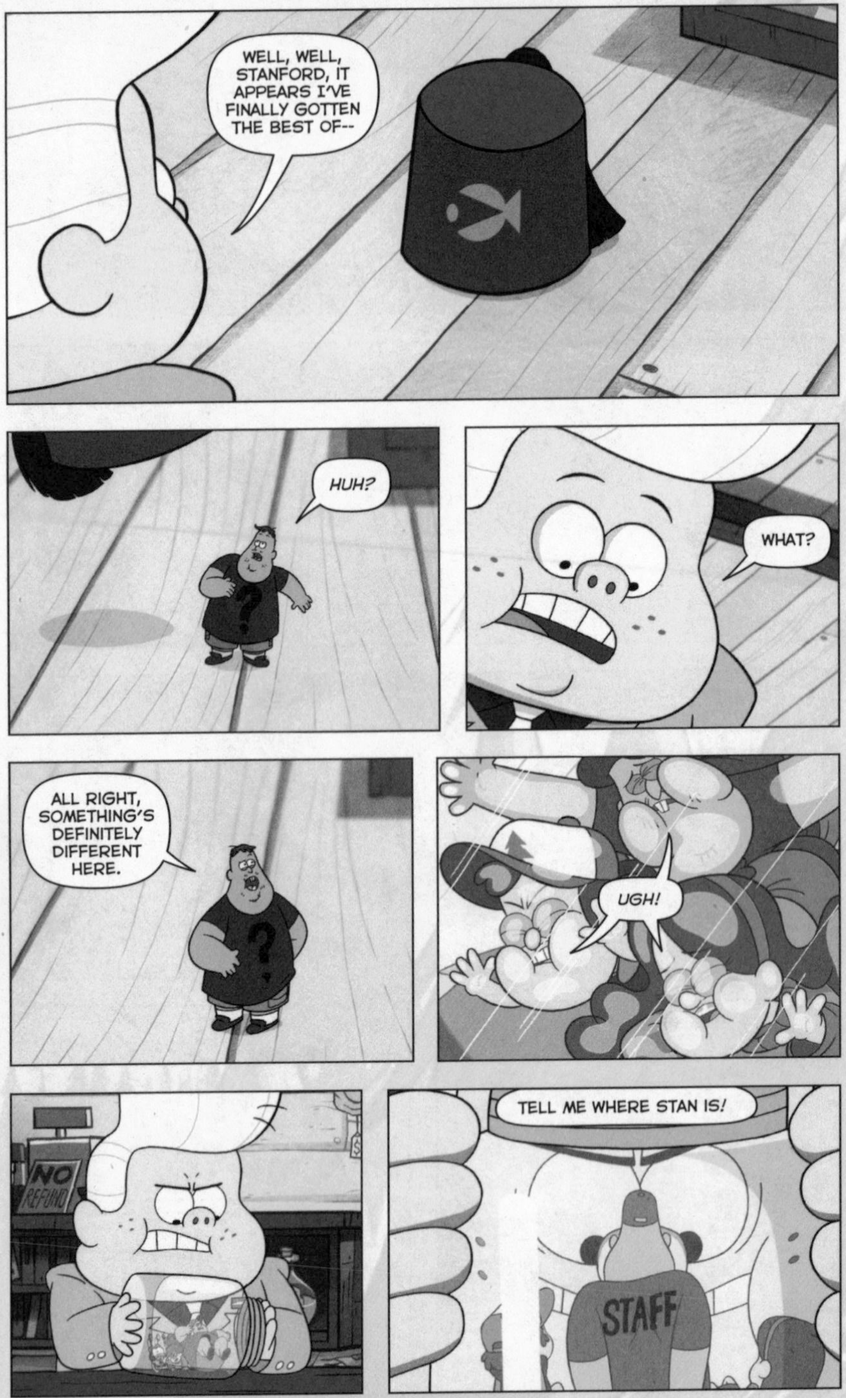
WELL, WELL, STANFORD, IT APPEARS I'VE FINALLY GOTTEN THE BEST OF--
HUH?
WHAT?
ALL RIGHT, SOMETHING'S DEFINITELY DIFFERENT HERE.
UGH!
NO REFUND
TELL ME WHERE STAN IS!
STAFF

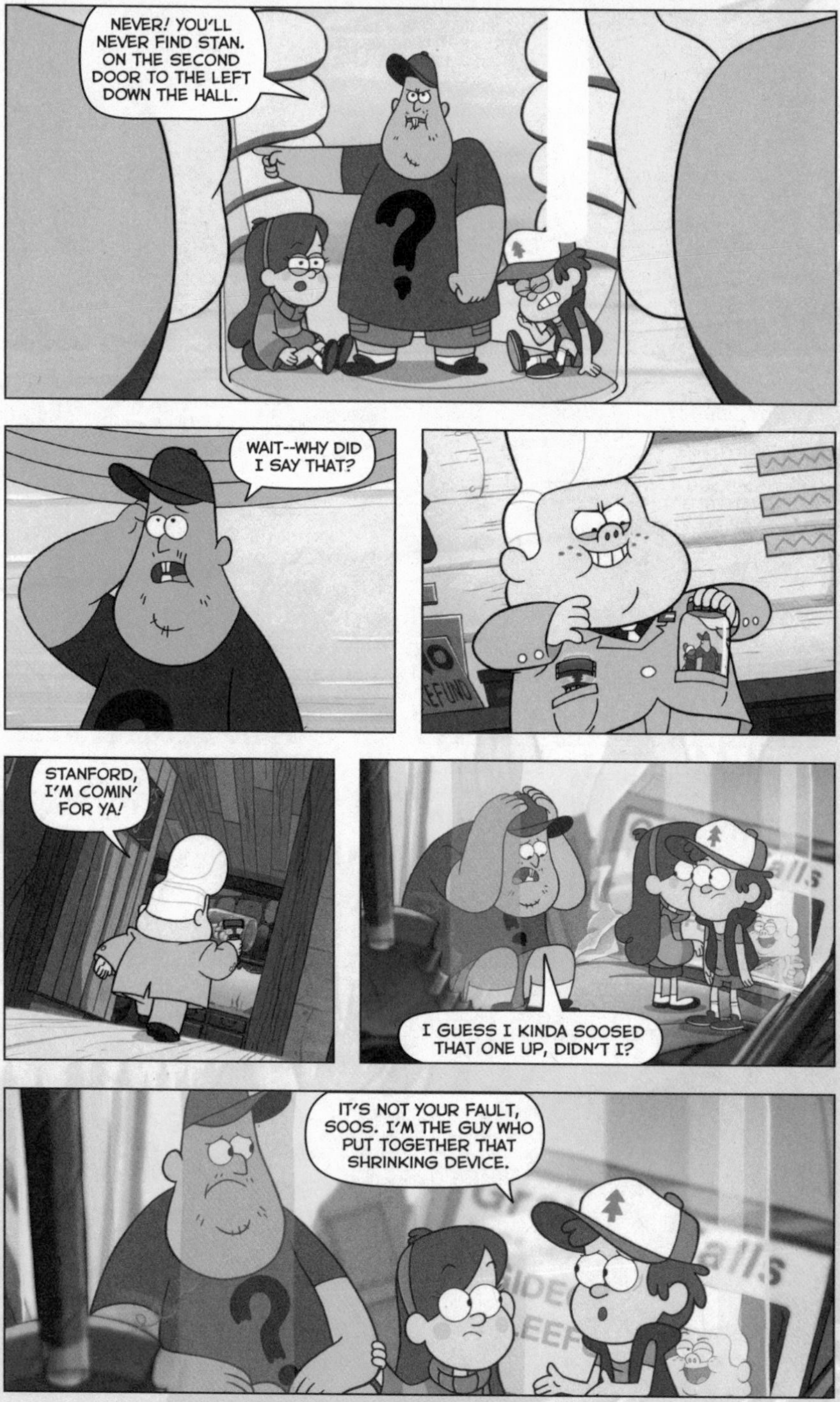
NEVER! YOU'LL NEVER FIND STAN. ON THE SECOND DOOR TO THE LEFT DOWN THE HALL.
WAIT--WHY DID I SAY THAT?
STANFORD, I'M COMIN' FOR YA!
I GUESS I KINDA SOOSED THAT ONE UP, DIDN'T I?
IT'S NOT YOUR FAULT, SOOS. I'M THE GUY WHO PUT TOGETHER THAT SHRINKING DEVICE.

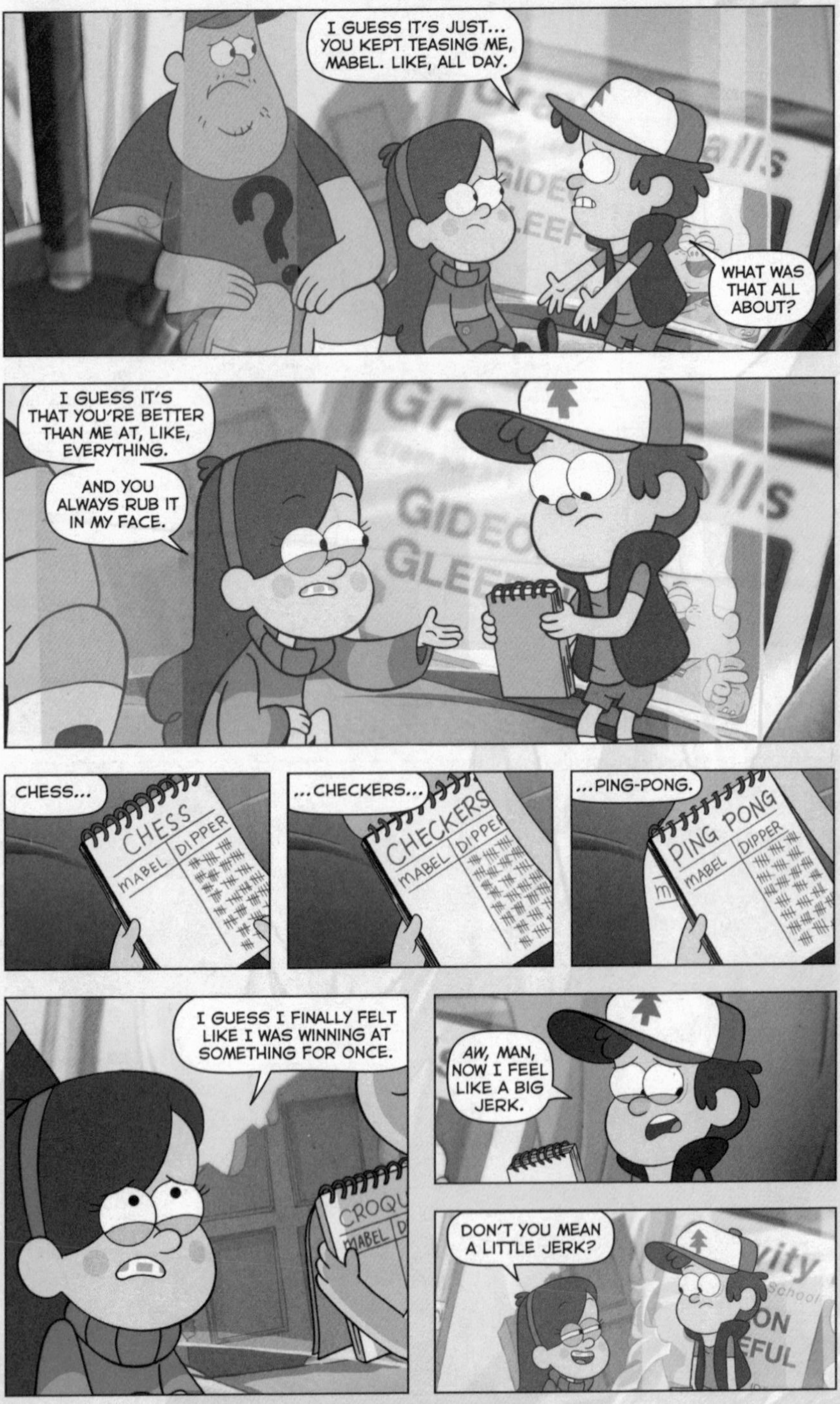
I GUESS IT'S JUST... YOU KEPT TEASING ME, MABEL. LIKE, ALL DAY.
WHAT WAS THAT ALL ABOUT?
I GUESS IT'S THAT YOU'RE BETTER THAN ME AT, LIKE, EVERYTHING.
AND YOU ALWAYS RUB IT IN MY FACE.
CHESS...
CHESS
MABEL DIPPER
...CHECKERS...
CHECKERS
MABEL DIPPER
...PING-PONG.
PING PONG
MABEL DIPPER
I GUESS I FINALLY FELT LIKE I WAS WINNING AT SOMETHING FOR ONCE.
AW, MAN, NOW I FEEL LIKE A BIG JERK.
DON'T YOU MEAN A LITTLE JERK?

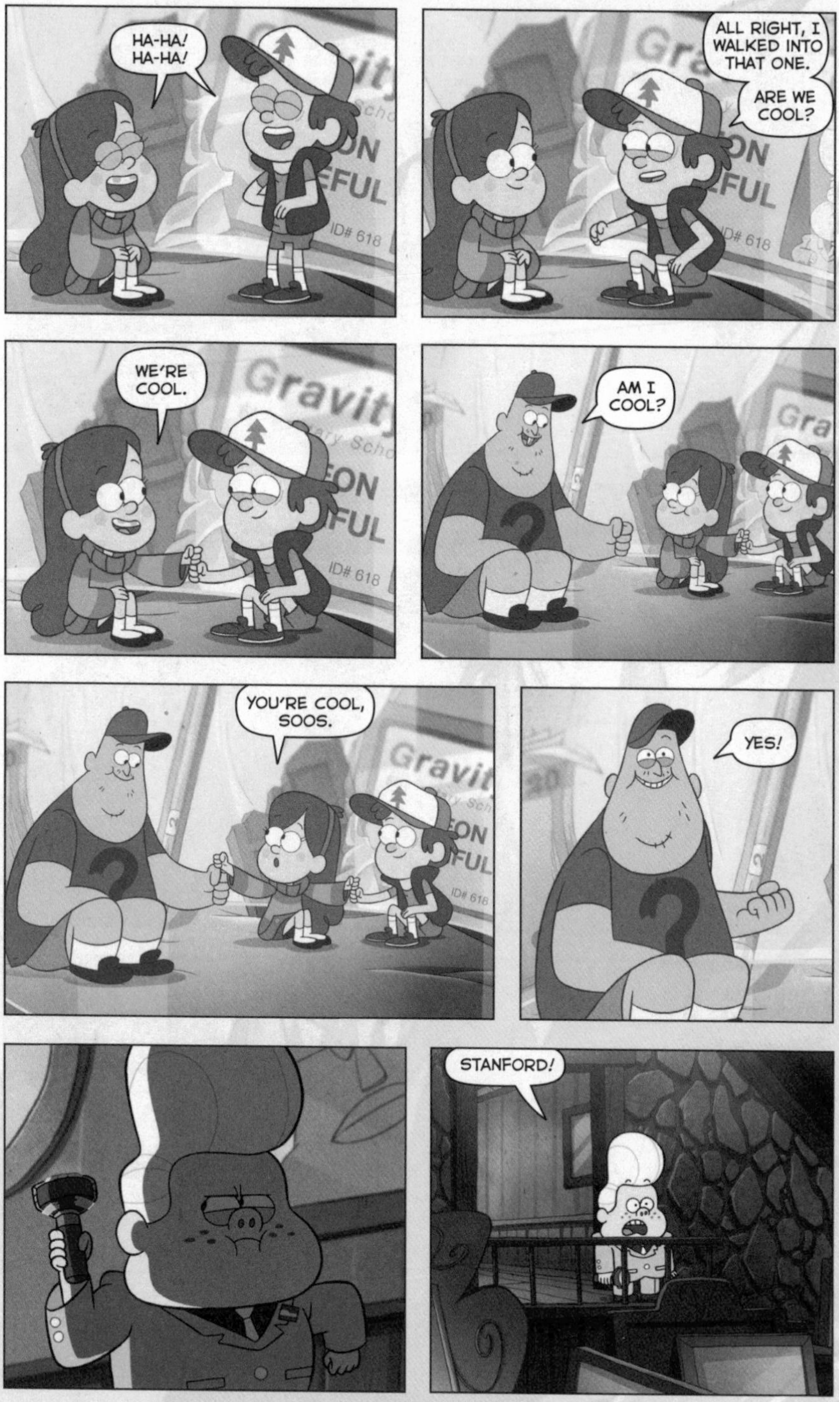
HA-HA! HA-HA!
ALL RIGHT, I WALKED INTO THAT ONE.
ARE WE COOL?
WE'RE COOL.
AM I COOL?
YOU'RE COOL, SOOS.
YES!
STANFORD!

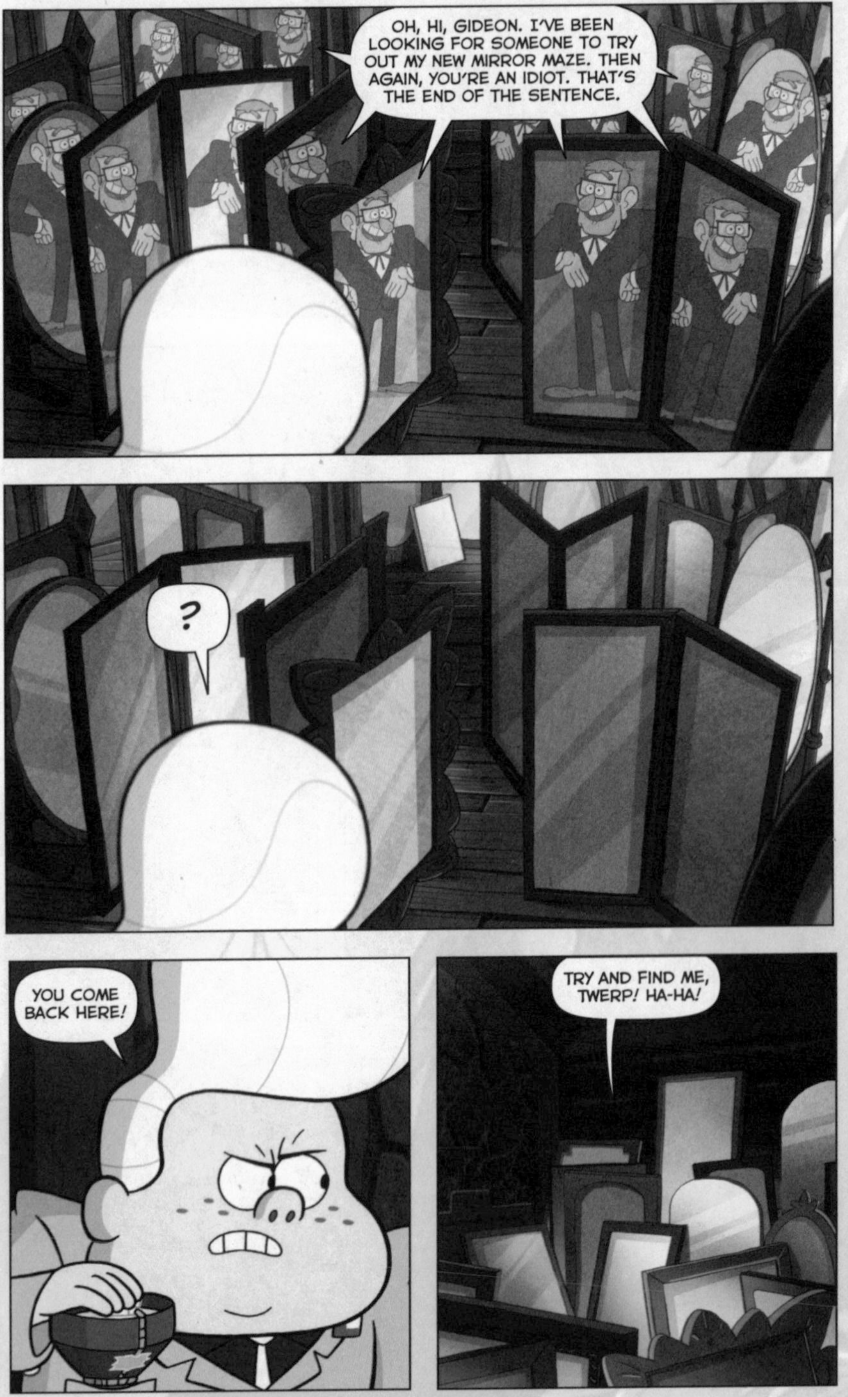
OH, HI, GIDEON. I'VE BEEN LOOKING FOR SOMEONE TO TRY OUT MY NEW MIRROR MAZE. THEN AGAIN, YOU'RE AN IDIOT. THAT'S THE END OF THE SENTENCE.
?
YOU COME BACK HERE!
TRY AND FIND ME, TWERP! HA-HA!

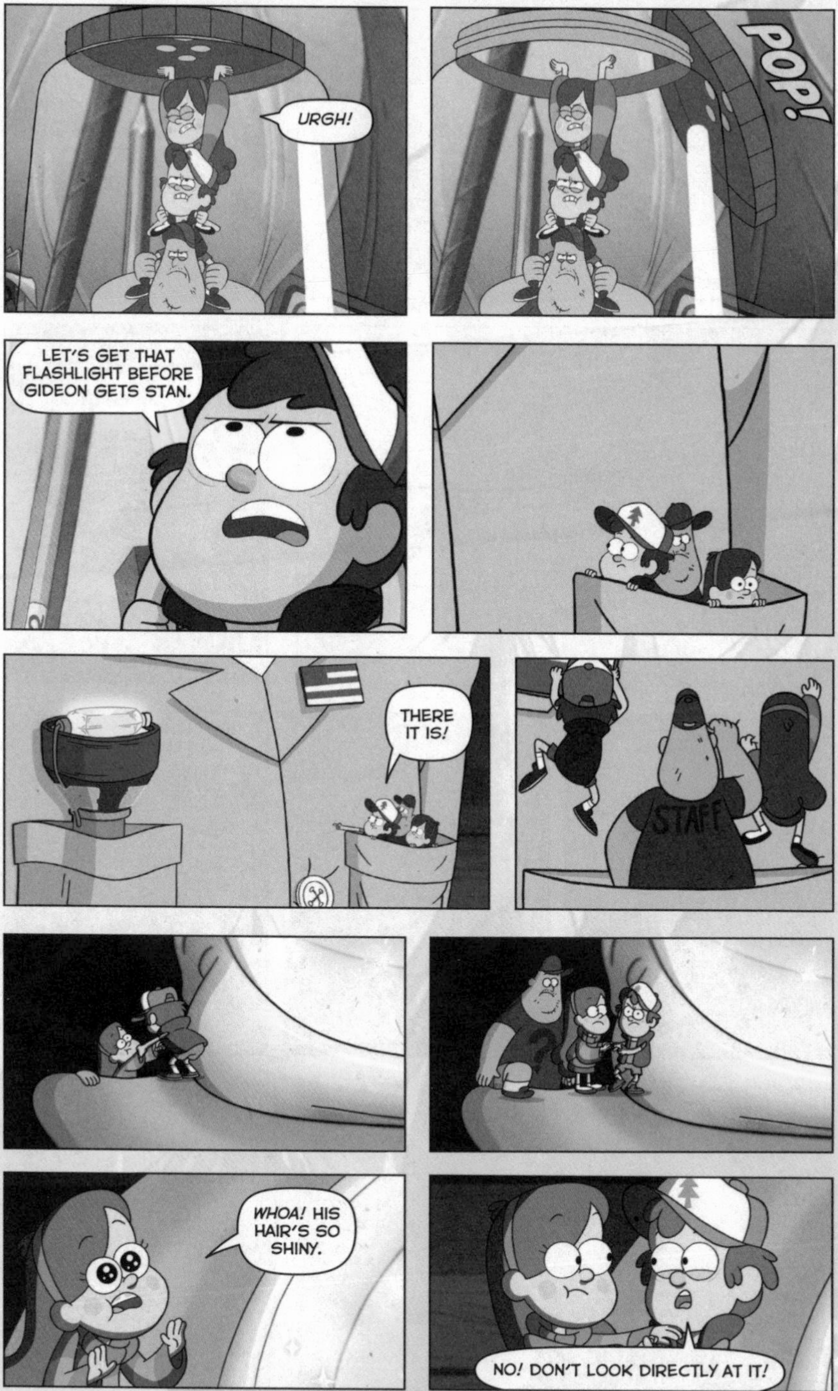
URGH!
POP!
LET'S GET THAT FLASHLIGHT BEFORE GIDEON GETS STAN.
THERE IT IS!
STAFF
WHOA! HIS HAIR'S SO SHINY.
NO! DON'T LOOK DIRECTLY AT IT!

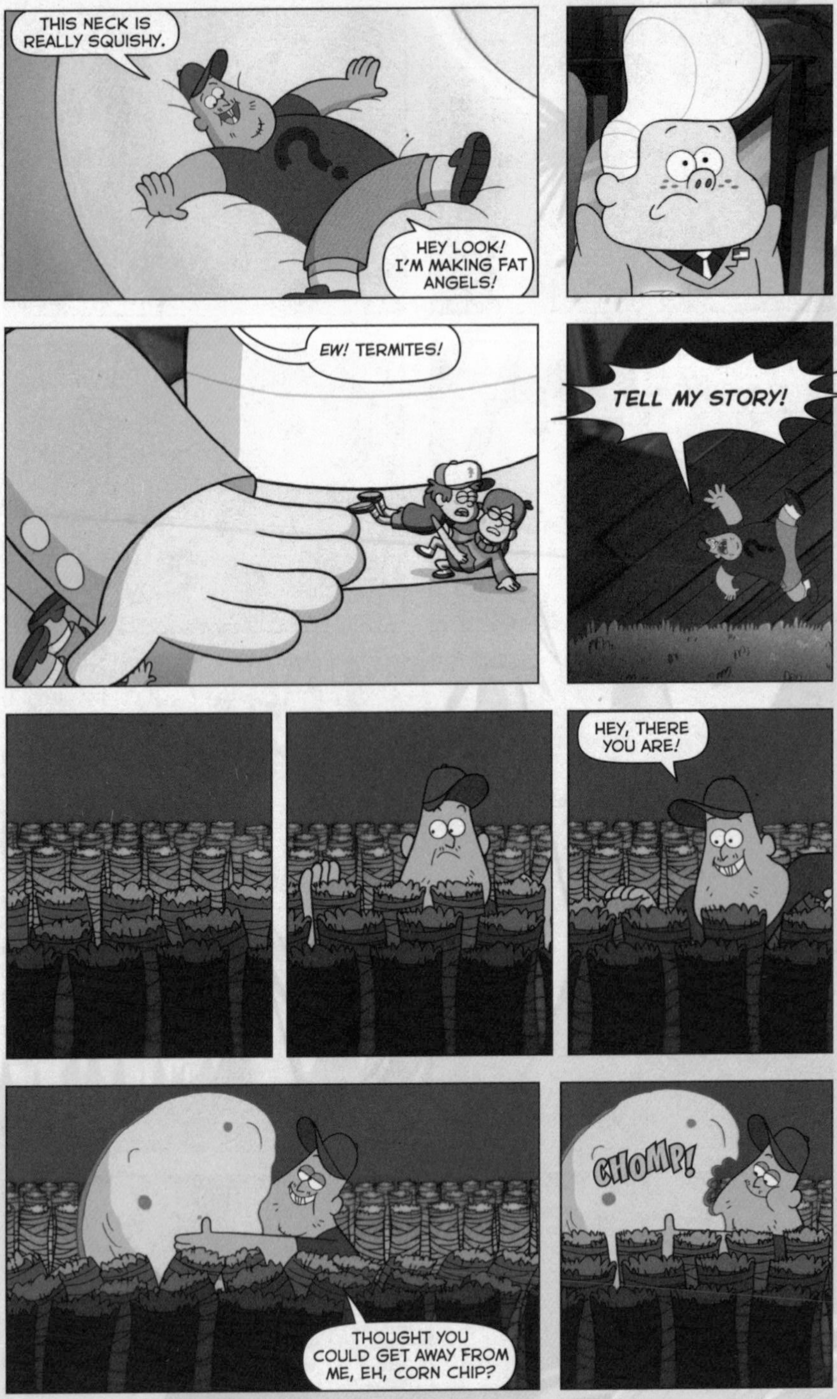
THIS NECK IS REALLY SQUISHY.
HEY LOOK! I'M MAKING FAT ANGELS!
EW! TERMITES!
TELL MY STORY!
HEY, THERE YOU ARE!
THOUGHT YOU COULD GET AWAY FROM ME, EH, CORN CHIP?
CHOMP!

AAH!

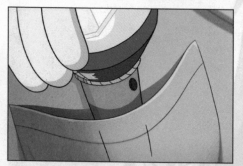

≥GASP!≤

PTEWW!

?

PTEWW!

PTEWW!

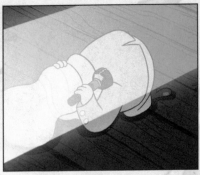

HA-HA!

HA-HA!

HA-HA!

KRRRSSH!!

HEY, WATCH THE MERCHANDISE!

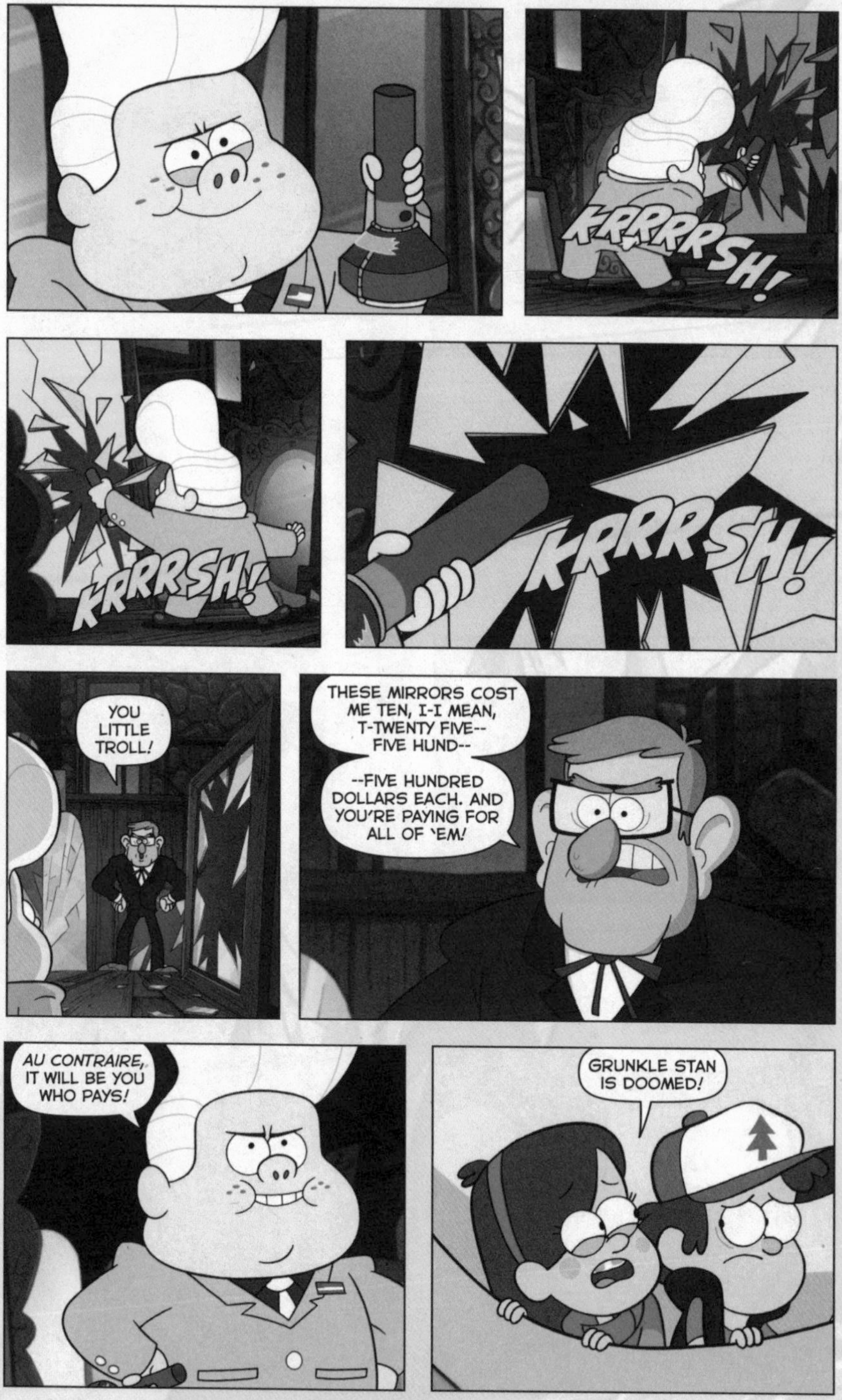
KRRRRSH!
KRRRSH!
KRRRSH!
YOU LITTLE TROLL!
THESE MIRRORS COST ME TEN, I-I MEAN, T-TWENTY FIVE-- FIVE HUND--
--FIVE HUNDRED DOLLARS EACH. AND YOU'RE PAYING FOR ALL OF 'EM!
AU CONTRAIRE, IT WILL BE YOU WHO PAYS!
GRUNKLE STAN IS DOOMED!

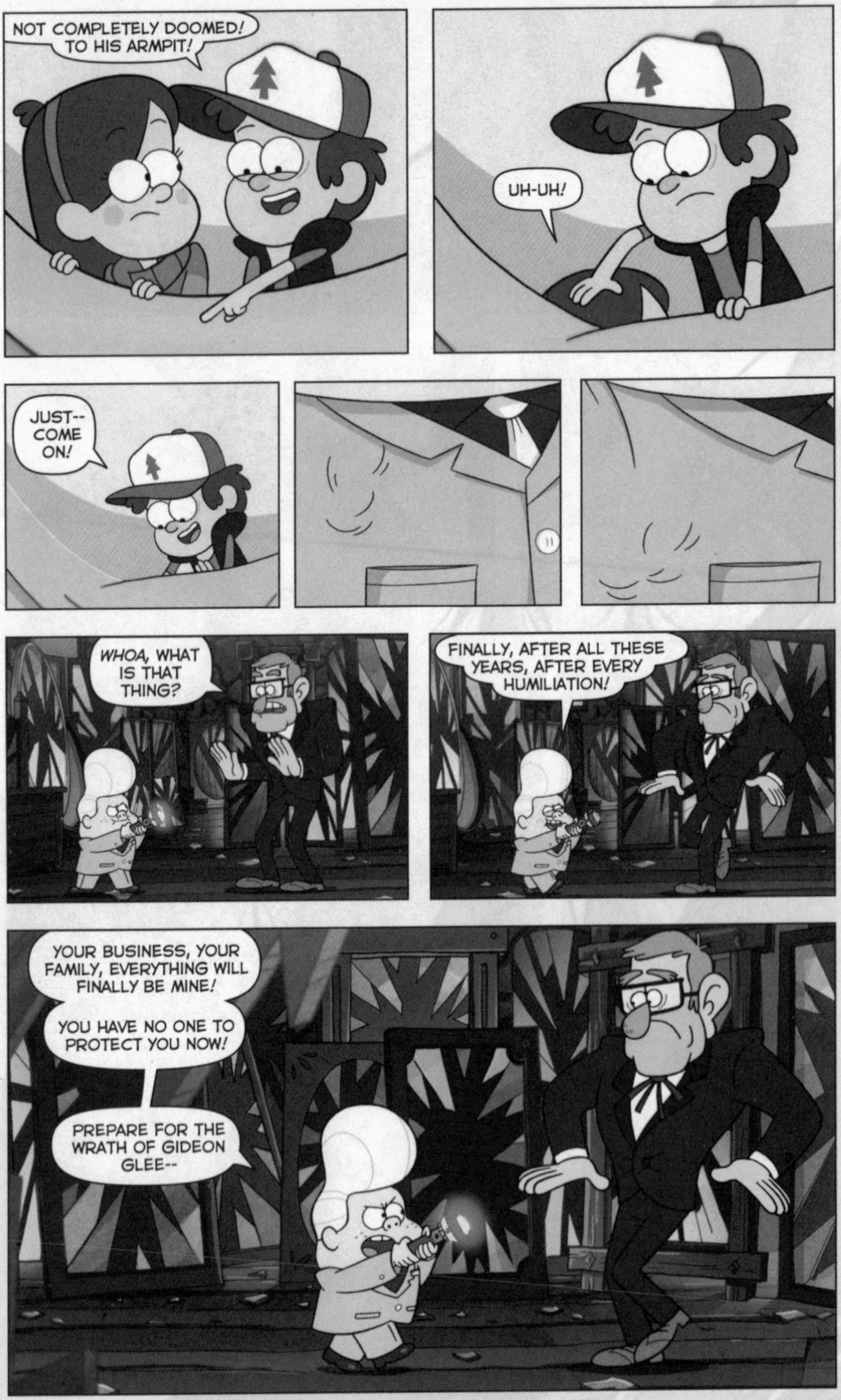
NOT COMPLETELY DOOMED! TO HIS ARMPIT!
UH-UH!
JUST-- COME ON!
WHOA, WHAT IS THAT THING?
FINALLY, AFTER ALL THESE YEARS, AFTER EVERY HUMILIATION!
YOUR BUSINESS, YOUR FAMILY, EVERYTHING WILL FINALLY BE MINE!
YOU HAVE NO ONE TO PROTECT YOU NOW!
PREPARE FOR THE WRATH OF GIDEON GLEE--

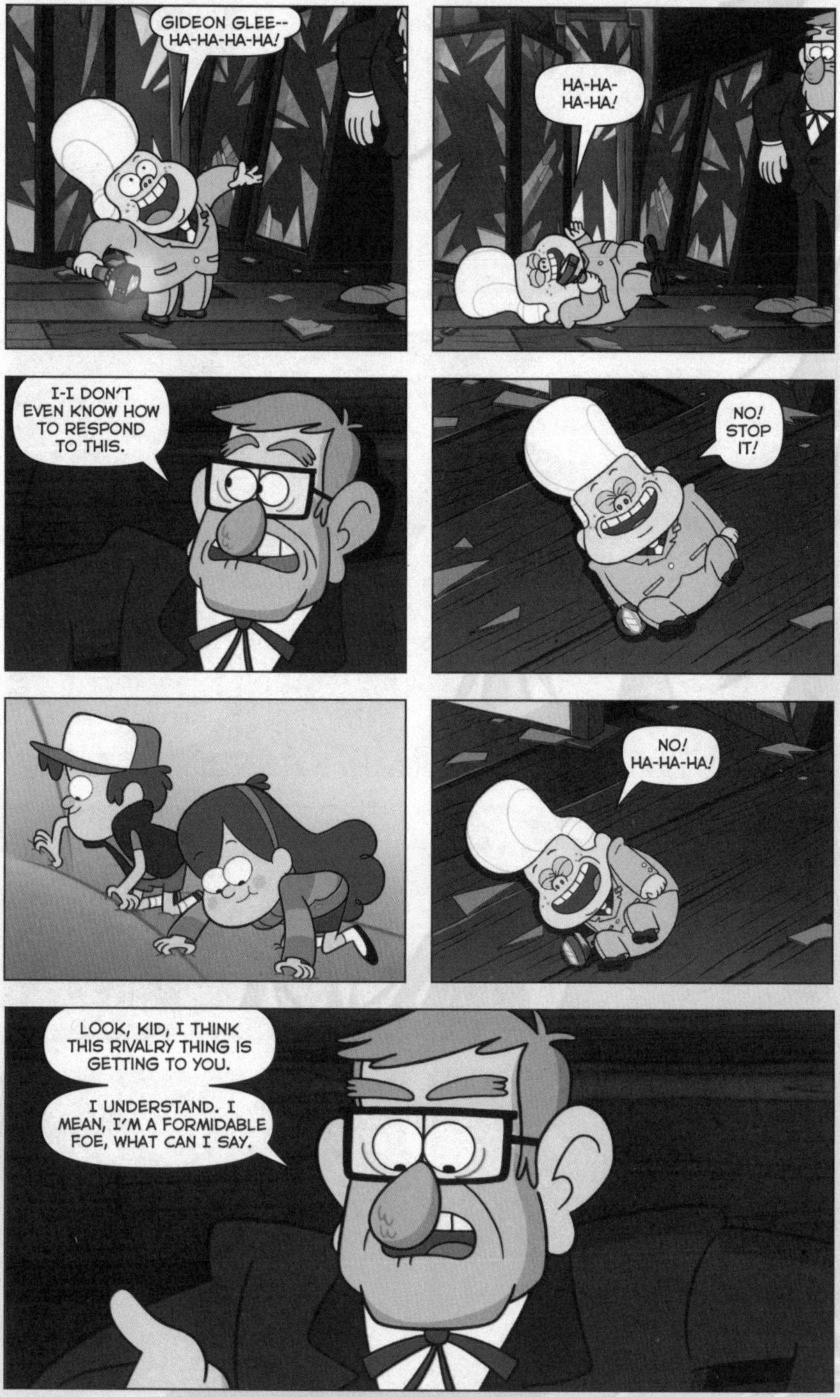
GIDEON GLEE-- HA-HA-HA-HA!
HA-HA- HA-HA!
I-I DON'T EVEN KNOW HOW TO RESPOND TO THIS.
NO! STOP IT!
NO! HA-HA-HA!
LOOK, KID, I THINK THIS RIVALRY THING IS GETTING TO YOU.
I UNDERSTAND. I MEAN, I'M A FORMIDABLE FOE, WHAT CAN I SAY.

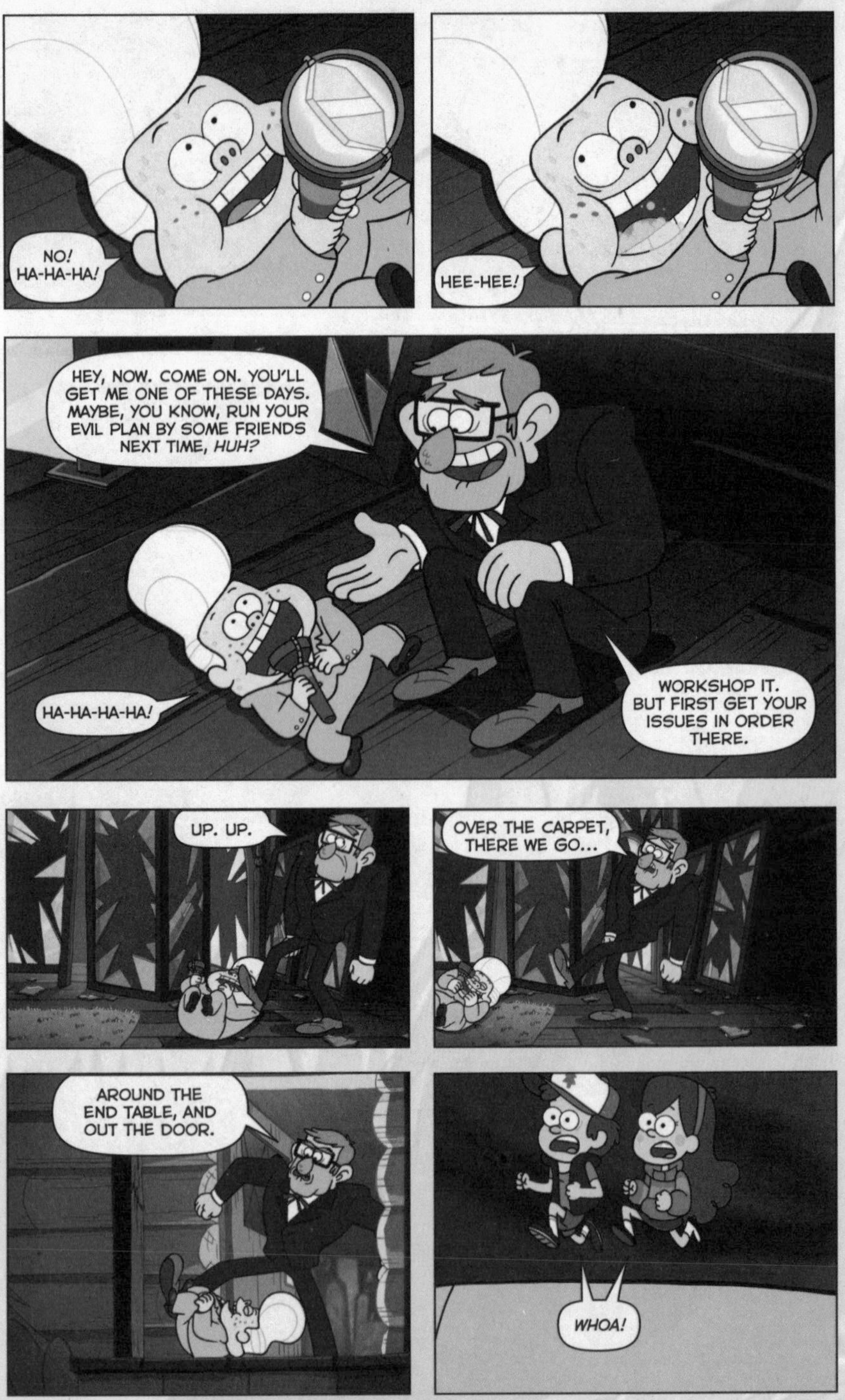
NO! HA-HA-HA!
HEE-HEE!
HEY, NOW. COME ON. YOU'LL GET ME ONE OF THESE DAYS. MAYBE, YOU KNOW, RUN YOUR EVIL PLAN BY SOME FRIENDS NEXT TIME, *HUH?*
HA-HA-HA-HA!
WORKSHOP IT. BUT FIRST GET YOUR ISSUES IN ORDER THERE.
UP. UP.
OVER THE CARPET, THERE WE GO...
AROUND THE END TABLE, AND OUT THE DOOR.
WHOA!

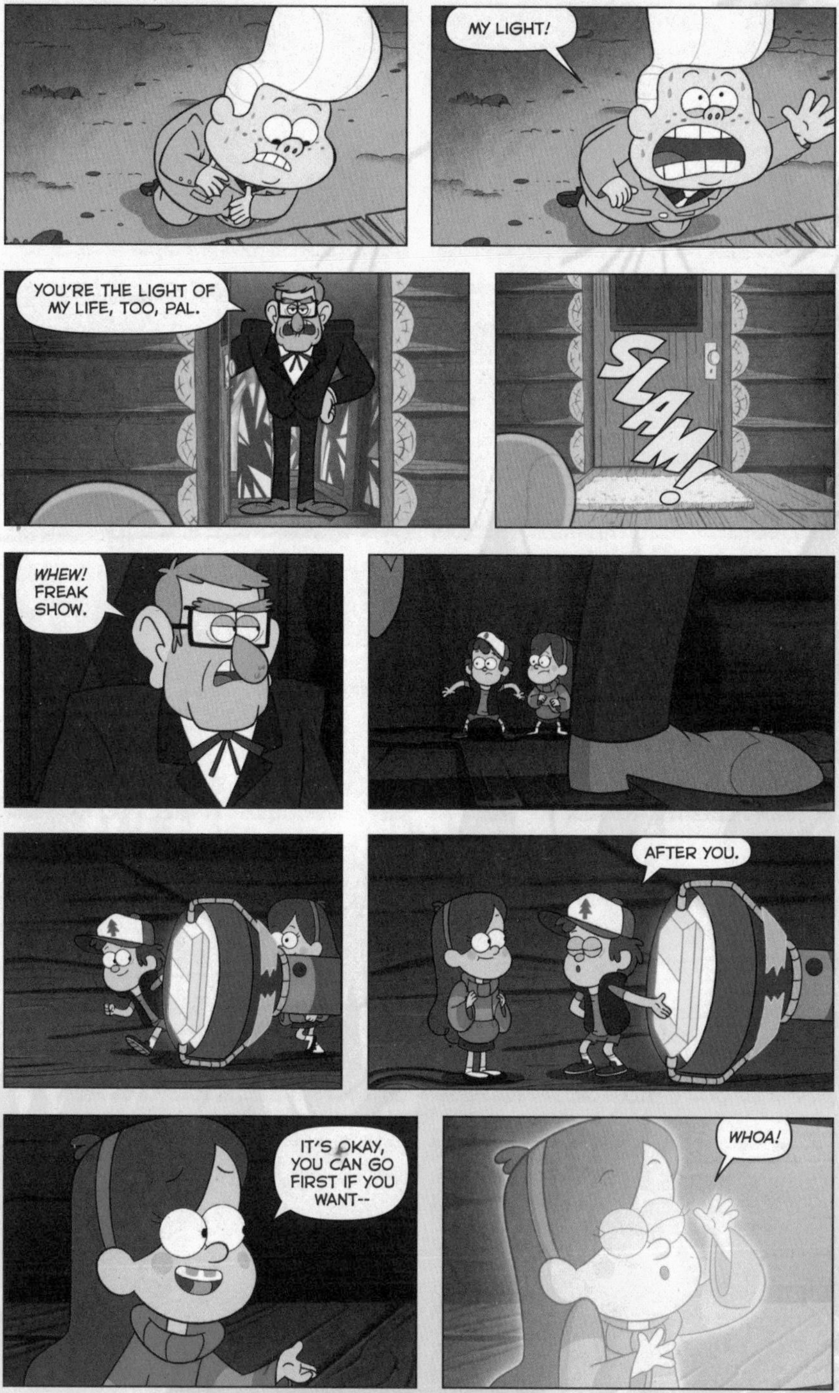
MY LIGHT!
YOU'RE THE LIGHT OF MY LIFE, TOO, PAL.
SLAM!
WHEW! FREAK SHOW.
AFTER YOU.
IT'S OKAY, YOU CAN GO FIRST IF YOU WANT--
WHOA!

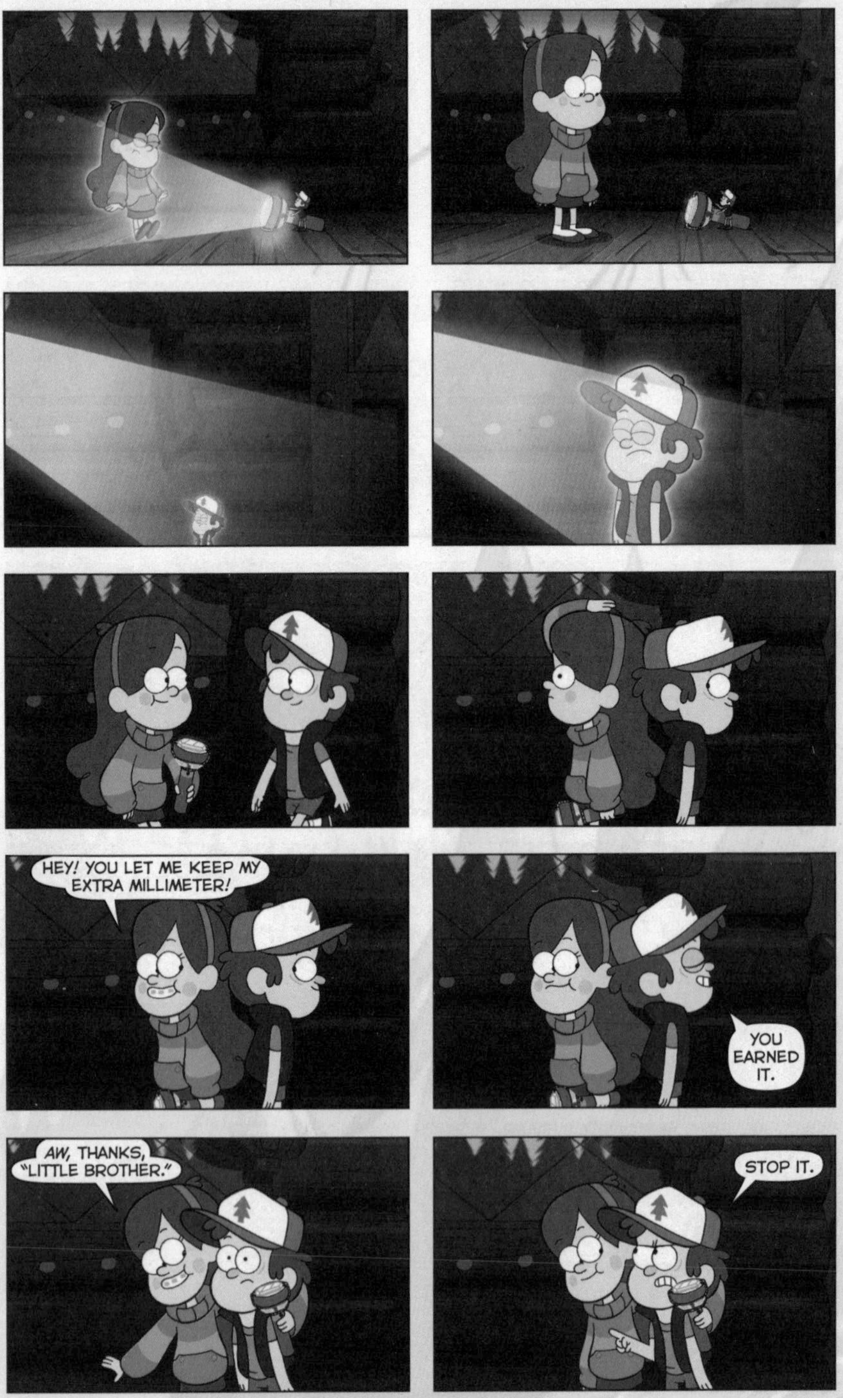
HEY! YOU LET ME KEEP MY EXTRA MILLIMETER!
YOU EARNED IT.
AW, THANKS, "LITTLE BROTHER."
STOP IT.

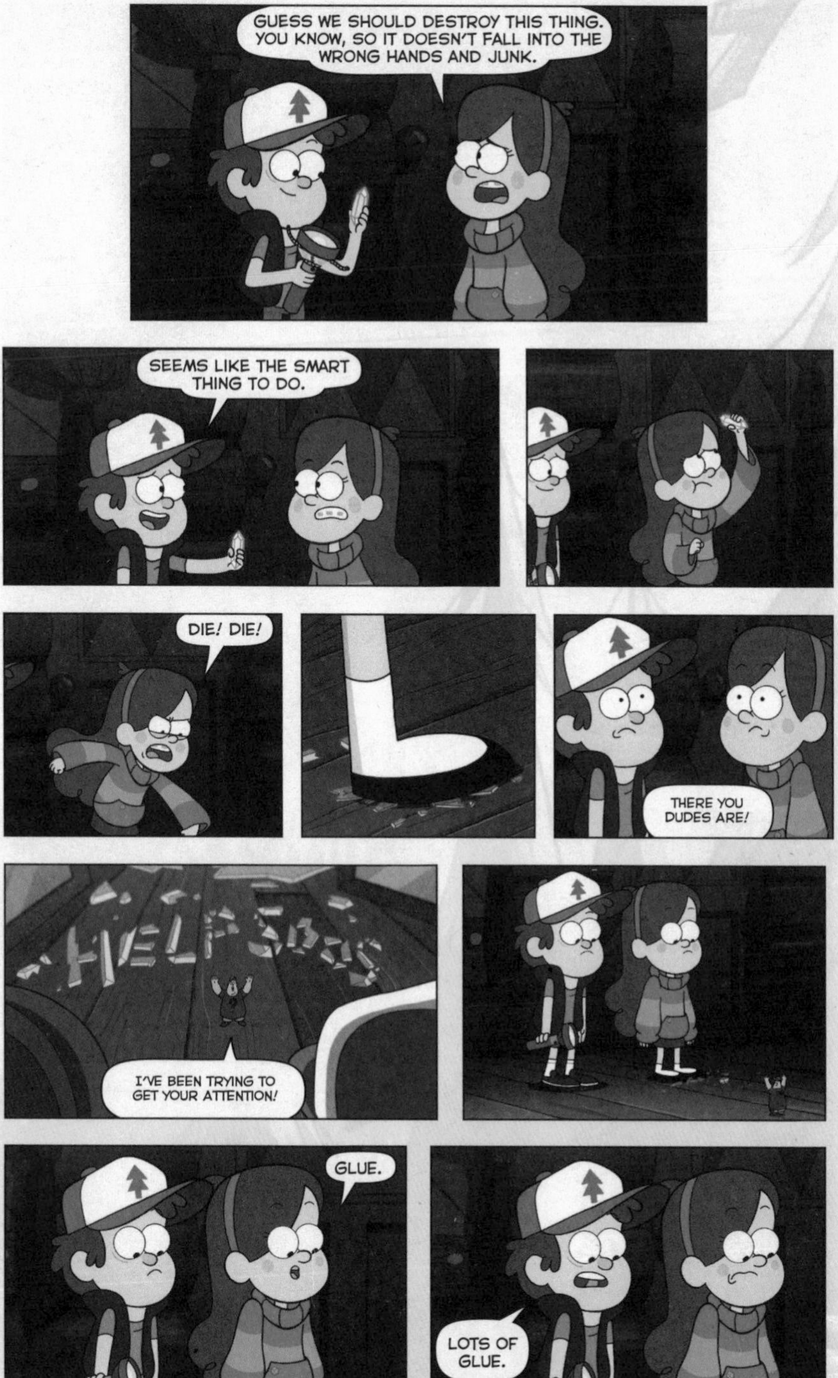
GUESS WE SHOULD DESTROY THIS THING. YOU KNOW, SO IT DOESN'T FALL INTO THE WRONG HANDS AND JUNK.
SEEMS LIKE THE SMART THING TO DO.
DIE! DIE!
THERE YOU DUDES ARE!
I'VE BEEN TRYING TO GET YOUR ATTENTION!
GLUE.
LOTS OF GLUE.

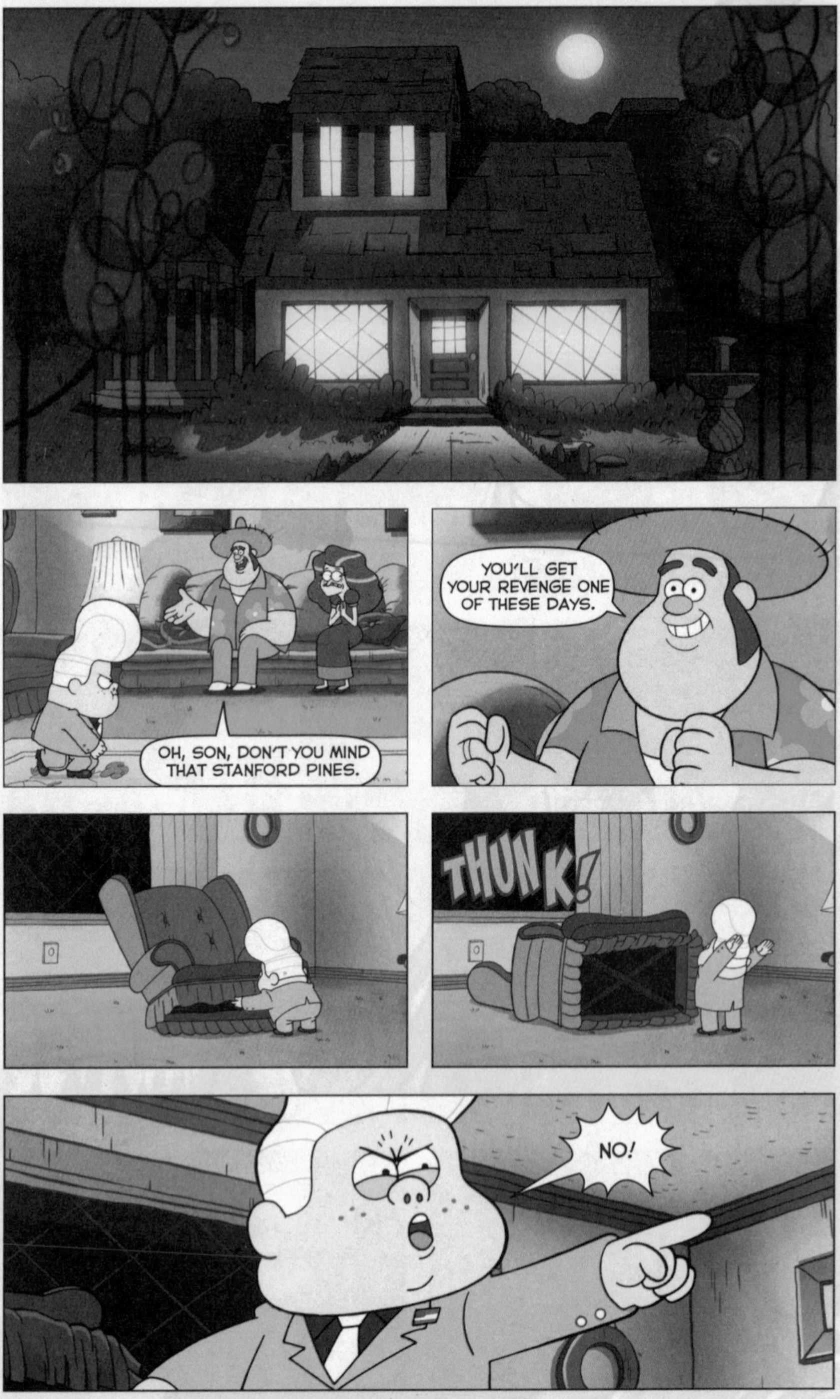
OH, SON, DON'T YOU MIND THAT STANFORD PINES.
YOU'LL GET YOUR REVENGE ONE OF THESE DAYS.
THUNK!
NO!

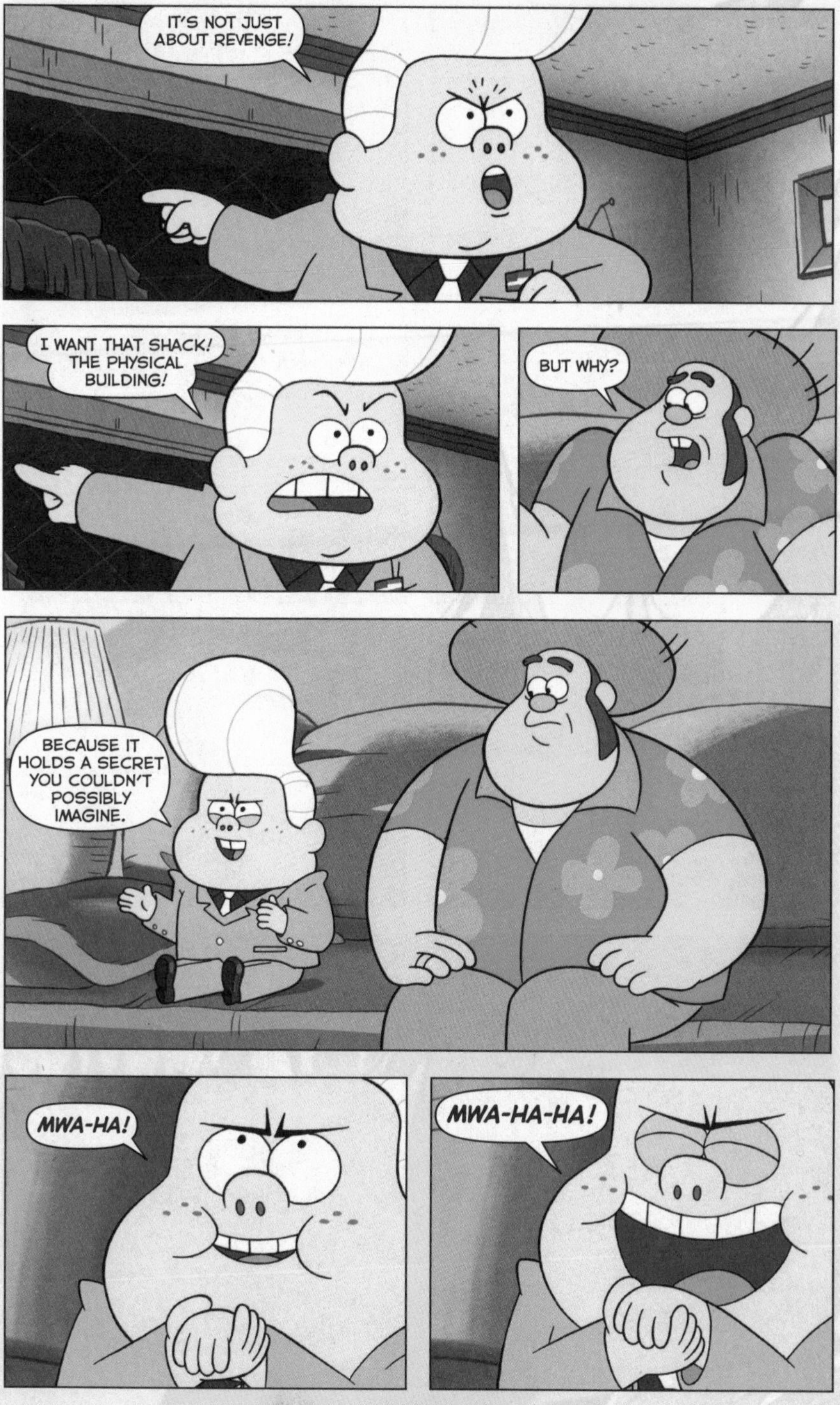
IT'S NOT JUST ABOUT REVENGE!
I WANT THAT SHACK! THE PHYSICAL BUILDING!
BUT WHY?
BECAUSE IT HOLDS A SECRET YOU COULDN'T POSSIBLY IMAGINE.
MWA-HA!
MWA-HA-HA!

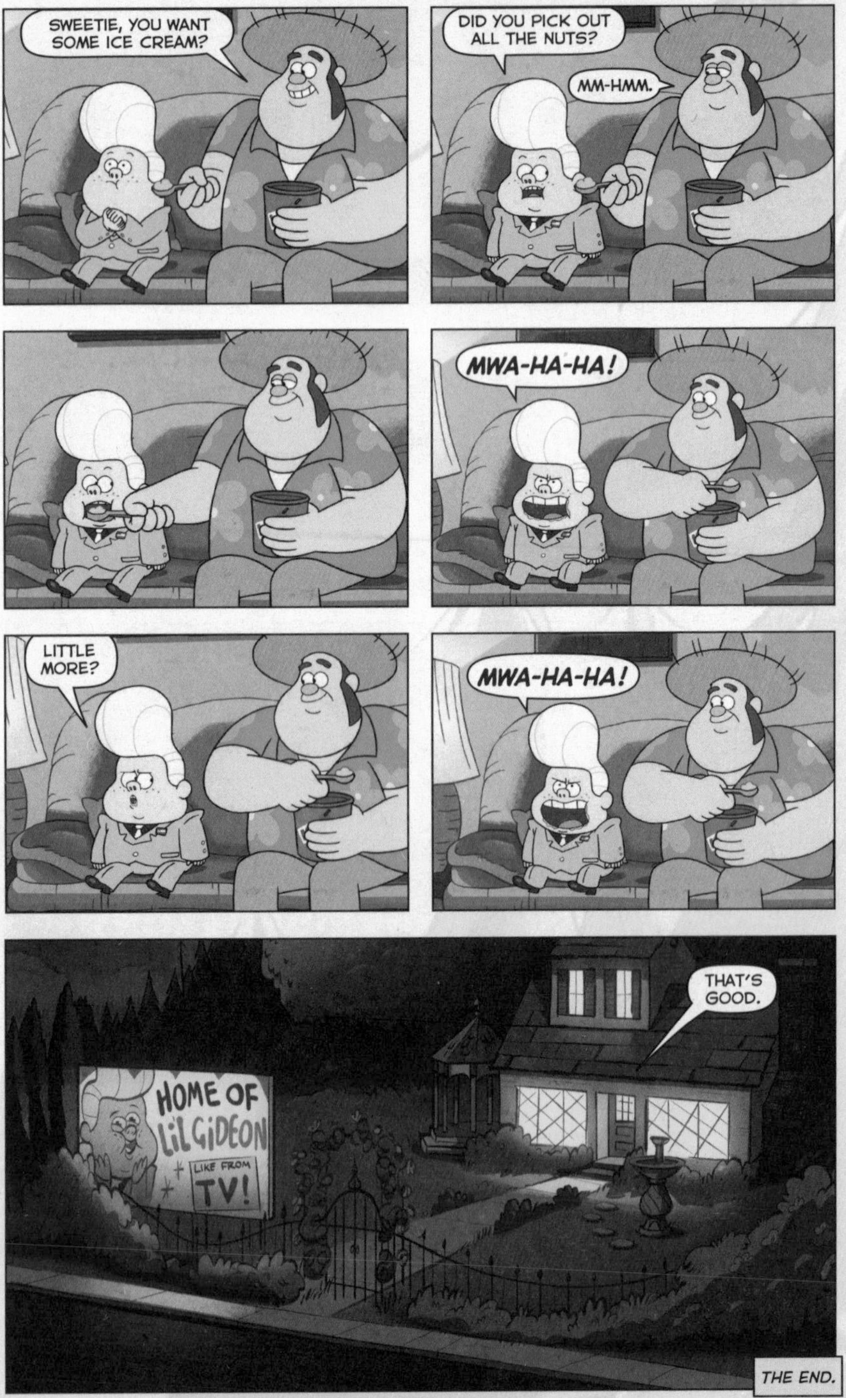
SWEETIE, YOU WANT SOME ICE CREAM?
DID YOU PICK OUT ALL THE NUTS?
MM-HMM.
MWA-HA-HA!
LITTLE MORE?
MWA-HA-HA!
HOME OF LiL GIDEON
LIKE FROM TV!
THAT'S GOOD.
THE END.

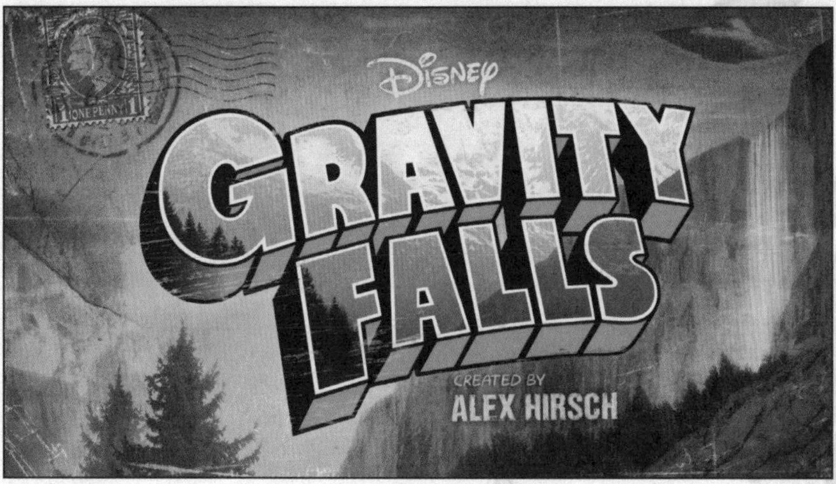
ONE PENNY
Disney
GRAVITY FALLS
CREATED BY
ALEX HIRSCH

SUMMERWEEN
EPISODE 12

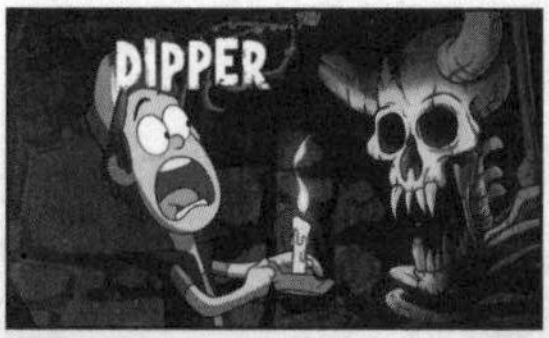
DIPPER

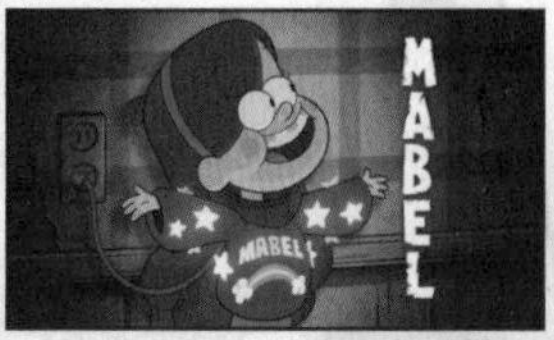
MABEL
MABEL

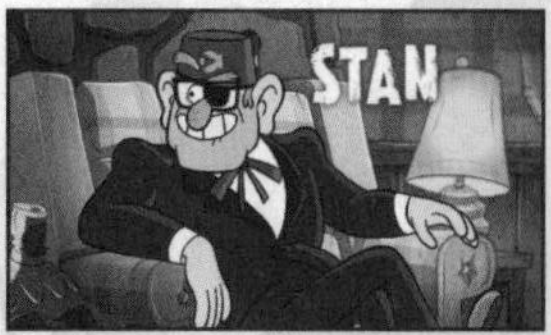
STAN

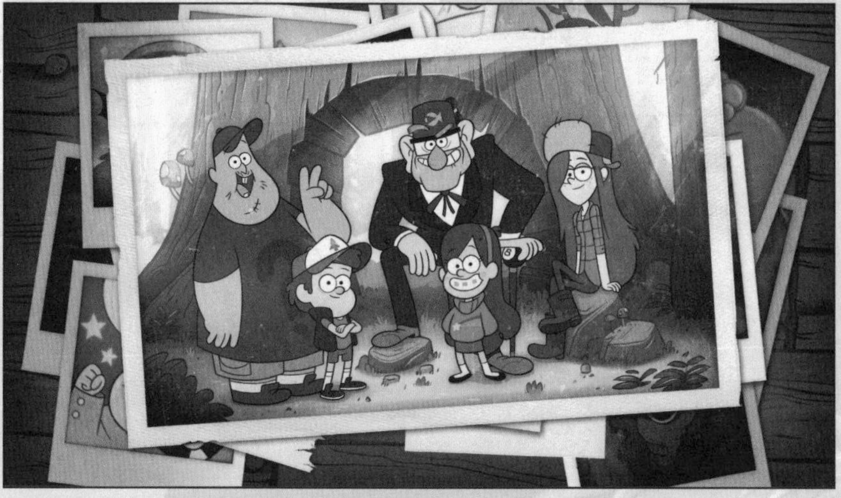

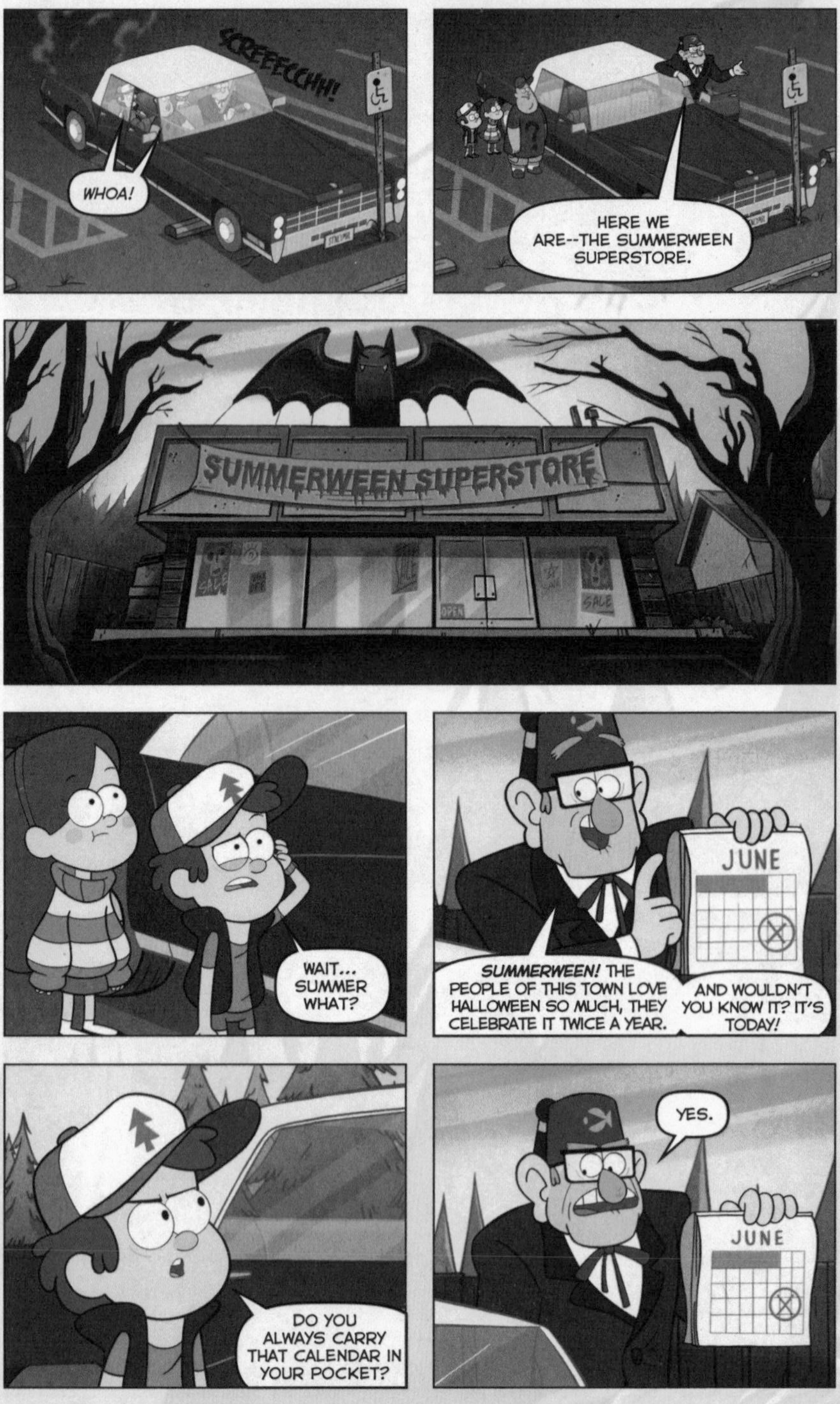

SCREEECCHH!
WHOA!
HERE WE ARE--THE SUMMERWEEN SUPERSTORE.
SUMMERWEEN SUPERSTORE
SALE
OPEN
SALE
WAIT... SUMMER WHAT?
JUNE
SUMMERWEEN! THE PEOPLE OF THIS TOWN LOVE HALLOWEEN SO MUCH, THEY CELEBRATE IT TWICE A YEAR.
AND WOULDN'T YOU KNOW IT? IT'S TODAY!
DO YOU ALWAYS CARRY THAT CALENDAR IN YOUR POCKET?
YES.
JUNE

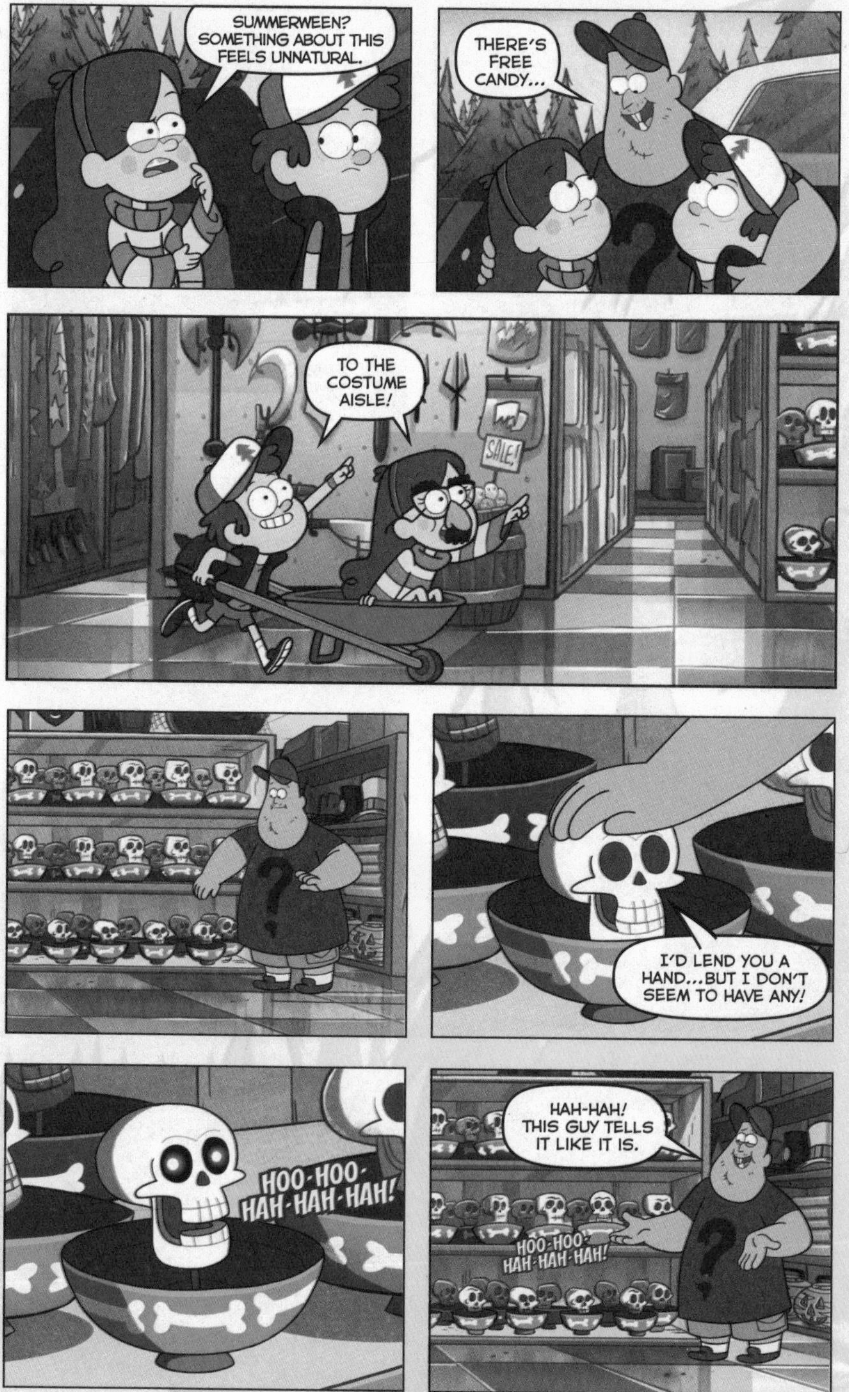

SUMMERWEEN? SOMETHING ABOUT THIS FEELS UNNATURAL.
THERE'S FREE CANDY...
TO THE COSTUME AISLE!
SALE!
I'D LEND YOU A HAND...BUT I DON'T SEEM TO HAVE ANY!
HOO-HOO-HAH-HAH-HAH!
HAH-HAH! THIS GUY TELLS IT LIKE IT IS.
HOO-HOO-HAH-HAH-HAH!

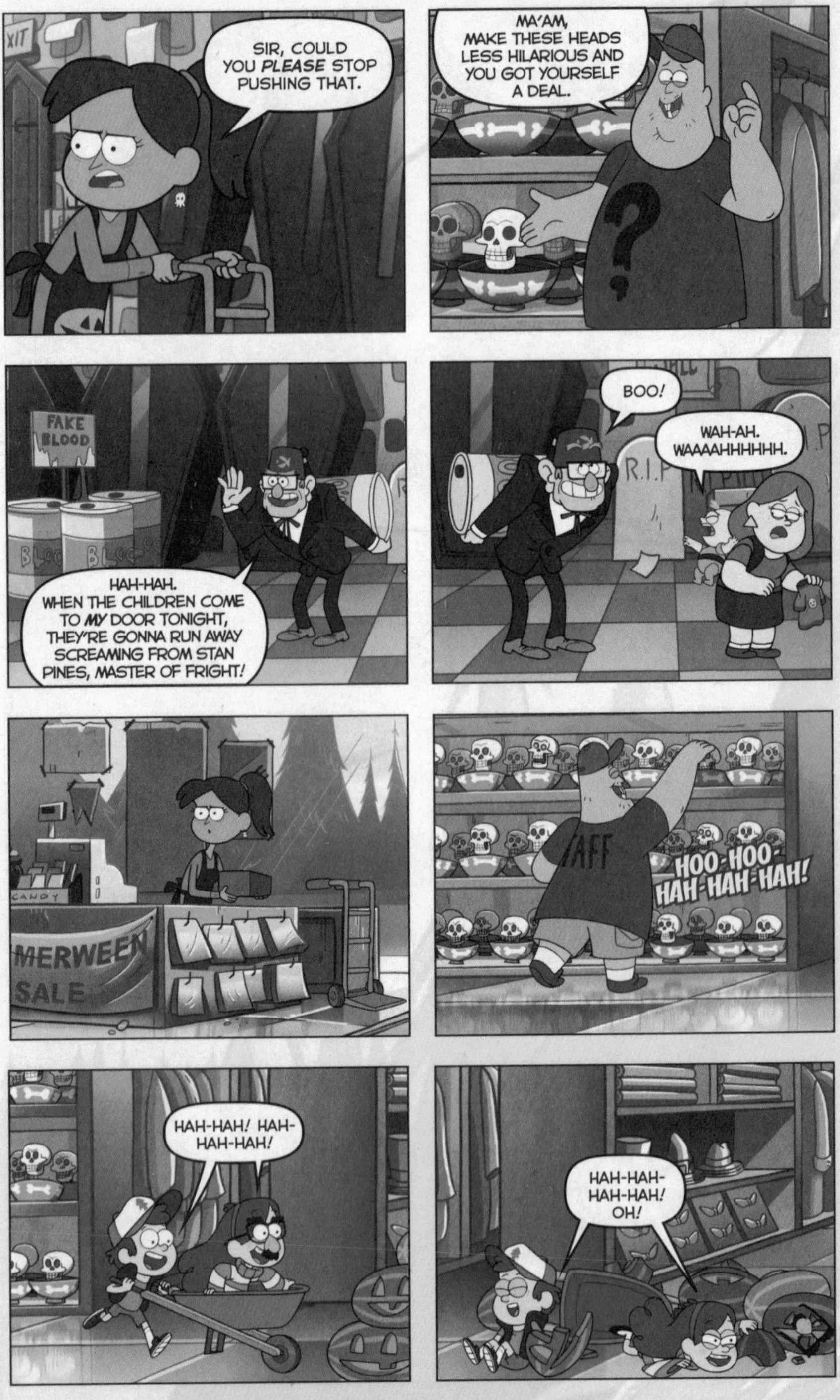
XIT
SIR, COULD YOU *PLEASE* STOP PUSHING THAT.
MA'AM, MAKE THESE HEADS LESS HILARIOUS AND YOU GOT YOURSELF A DEAL.
FAKE BLOOD
HAH-HAH. WHEN THE CHILDREN COME TO *MY* DOOR TONIGHT, THEY'RE GONNA RUN AWAY SCREAMING FROM STAN PINES, MASTER OF FRIGHT!
BOO!
WAH-AH. WAAAAHHHHHH.
R.I.P
CANDY
MERWEEN SALE
HOO-HOO-HAH-HAH-HAH!
HAH-HAH! HAH-HAH-HAH!
HAH-HAH-HAH-HAH! OH!

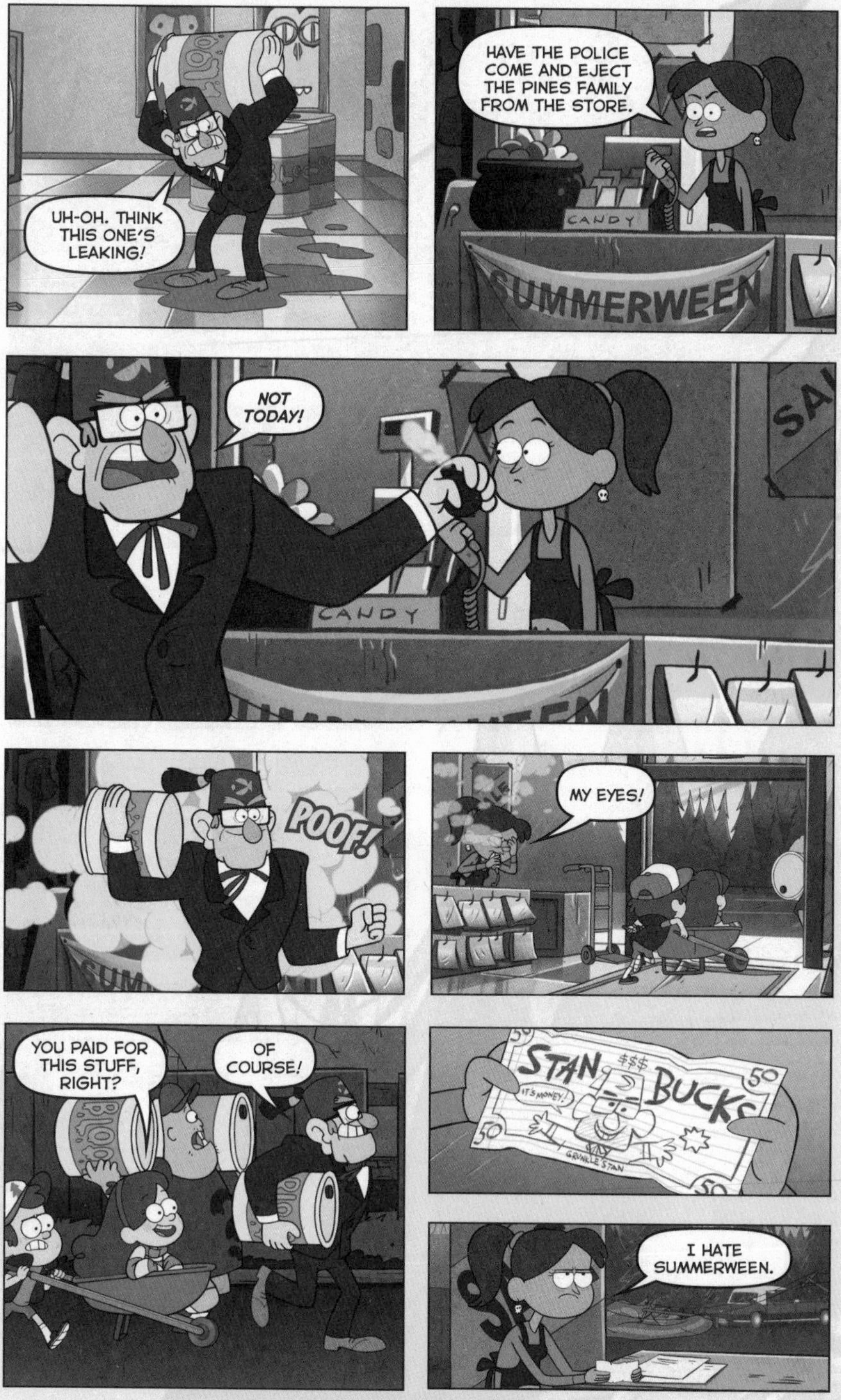
UH-OH. THINK THIS ONE'S LEAKING!
HAVE THE POLICE COME AND EJECT THE PINES FAMILY FROM THE STORE.
CANDY
SUMMERWEEN
NOT TODAY!
CANDY
POOF!
MY EYES!
YOU PAID FOR THIS STUFF, RIGHT?
OF COURSE!
STAN
$$$
BUCKS
IT'S MONEY!
50
GRUNKLE STAN
I HATE SUMMERWEEN.

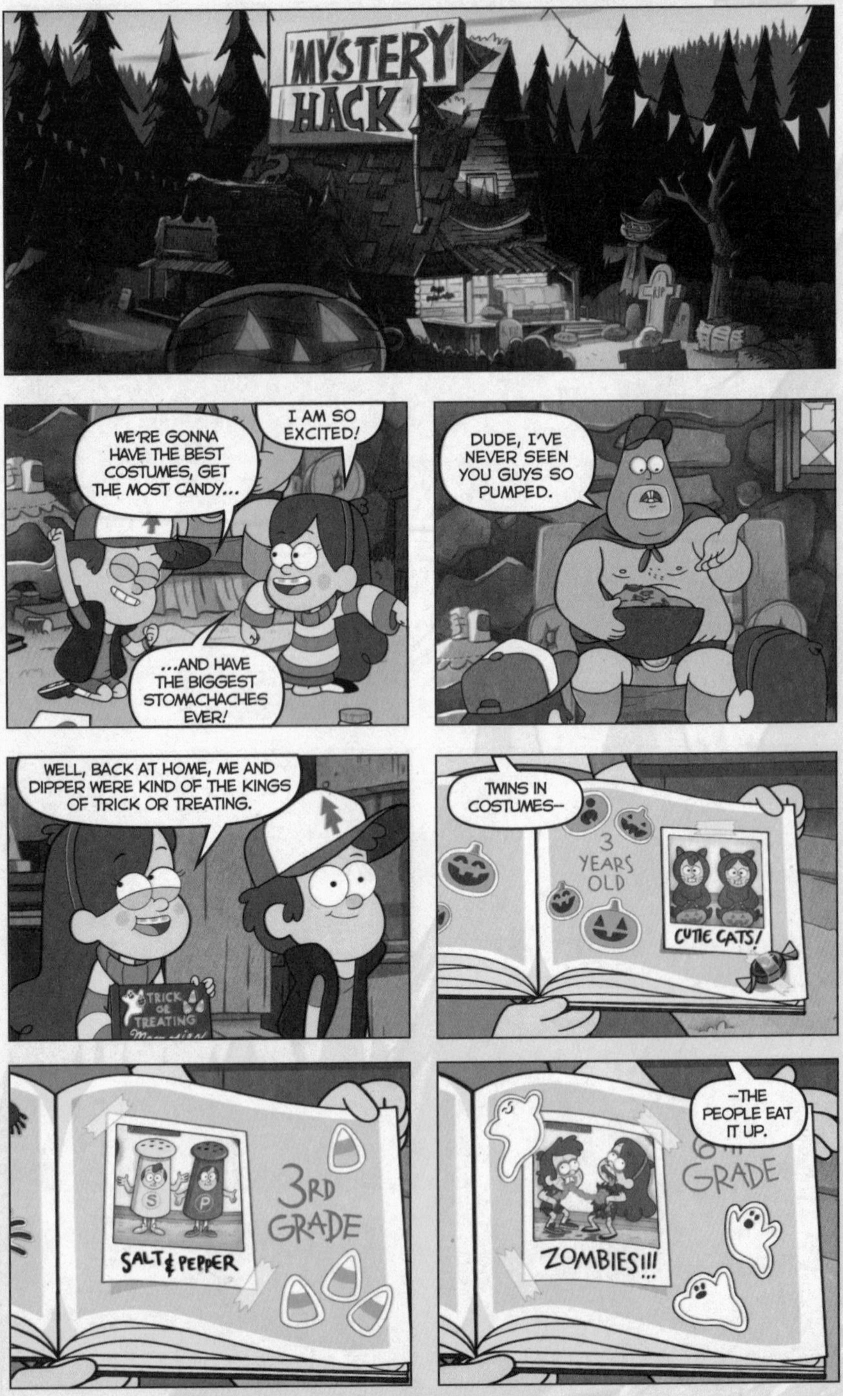
MYSTERY HACK
WE'RE GONNA HAVE THE BEST COSTUMES, GET THE MOST CANDY...
I AM SO EXCITED!
...AND HAVE THE BIGGEST STOMACHACHES EVER!
DUDE, I'VE NEVER SEEN YOU GUYS SO PUMPED.
WELL, BACK AT HOME, ME AND DIPPER WERE KIND OF THE KINGS OF TRICK OR TREATING.
TRICK OR TREATING
TWINS IN COSTUMES--
3 YEARS OLD
CUTIE CATS!
SALT & PEPPER
3RD GRADE
ZOMBIES!!!
--THE PEOPLE EAT IT UP.

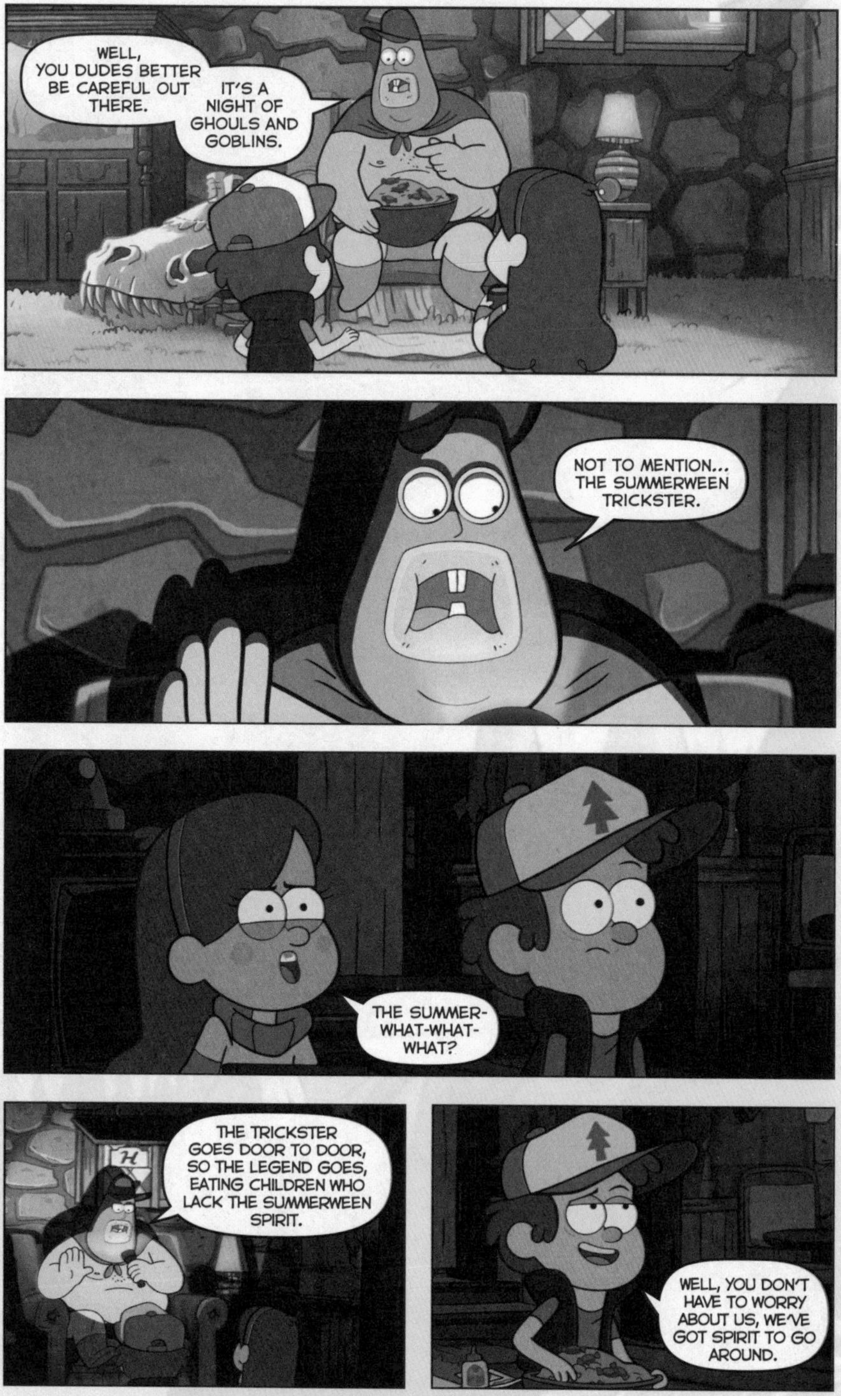
WELL, YOU DUDES BETTER BE CAREFUL OUT THERE.
IT'S A NIGHT OF GHOULS AND GOBLINS.
NOT TO MENTION... THE SUMMERWEEN TRICKSTER.
THE SUMMER-WHAT-WHAT-WHAT?
THE TRICKSTER GOES DOOR TO DOOR, SO THE LEGEND GOES, EATING CHILDREN WHO LACK THE SUMMERWEEN SPIRIT.
WELL, YOU DON'T HAVE TO WORRY ABOUT US, WE'VE GOT SPIRIT TO GO AROUND.

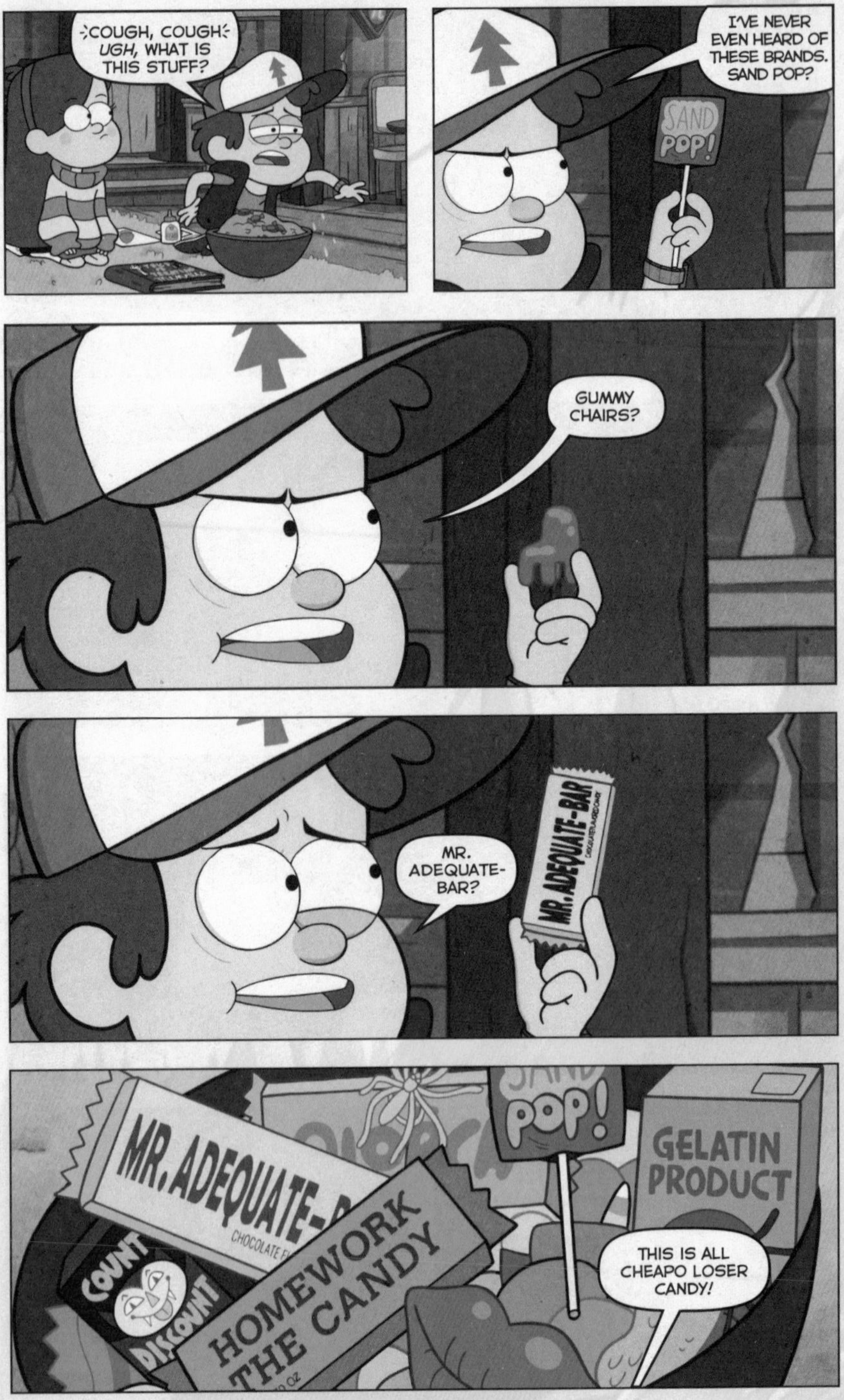
COUGH, COUGH UGH, WHAT IS THIS STUFF?
I'VE NEVER EVEN HEARD OF THESE BRANDS. SAND POP?
SAND POP!
GUMMY CHAIRS?
MR. ADEQUATE-BAR?
MR. ADEQUATE-BAR
MR. ADEQUATE-B
CHOCOLATE F
POP!
GELATIN PRODUCT
COUNT DISCOUNT
HOMEWORK THE CANDY
THIS IS ALL CHEAPO LOSER CANDY!

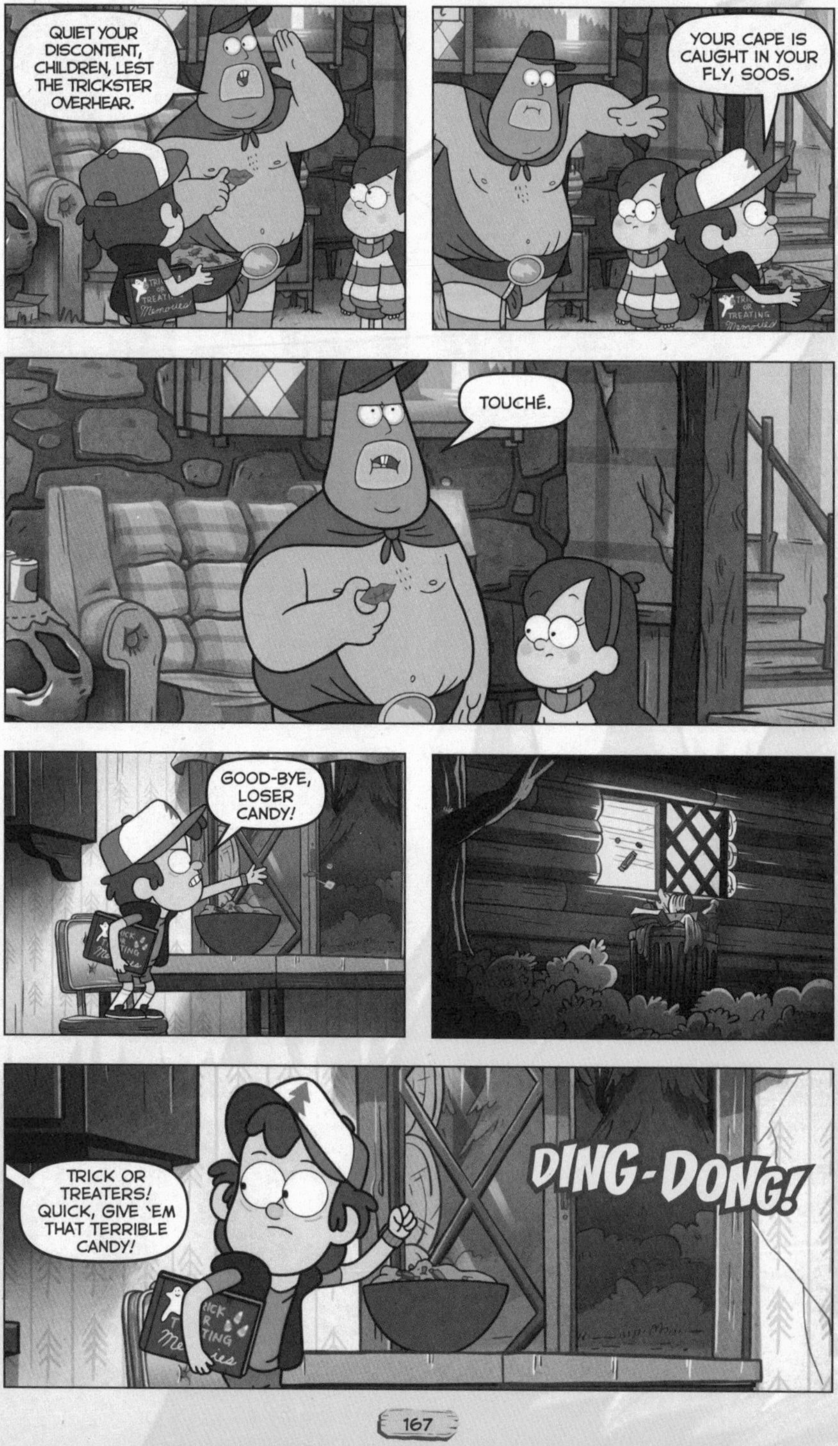
QUIET YOUR DISCONTENT, CHILDREN, LEST THE TRICKSTER OVERHEAR.
TRICK OR TREATING Memories
YOUR CAPE IS CAUGHT IN YOUR FLY, SOOS.
TOUCHÉ.
GOOD-BYE, LOSER CANDY!
TRICK OR TREATERS! QUICK, GIVE 'EM THAT TERRIBLE CANDY!
DING-DONG!

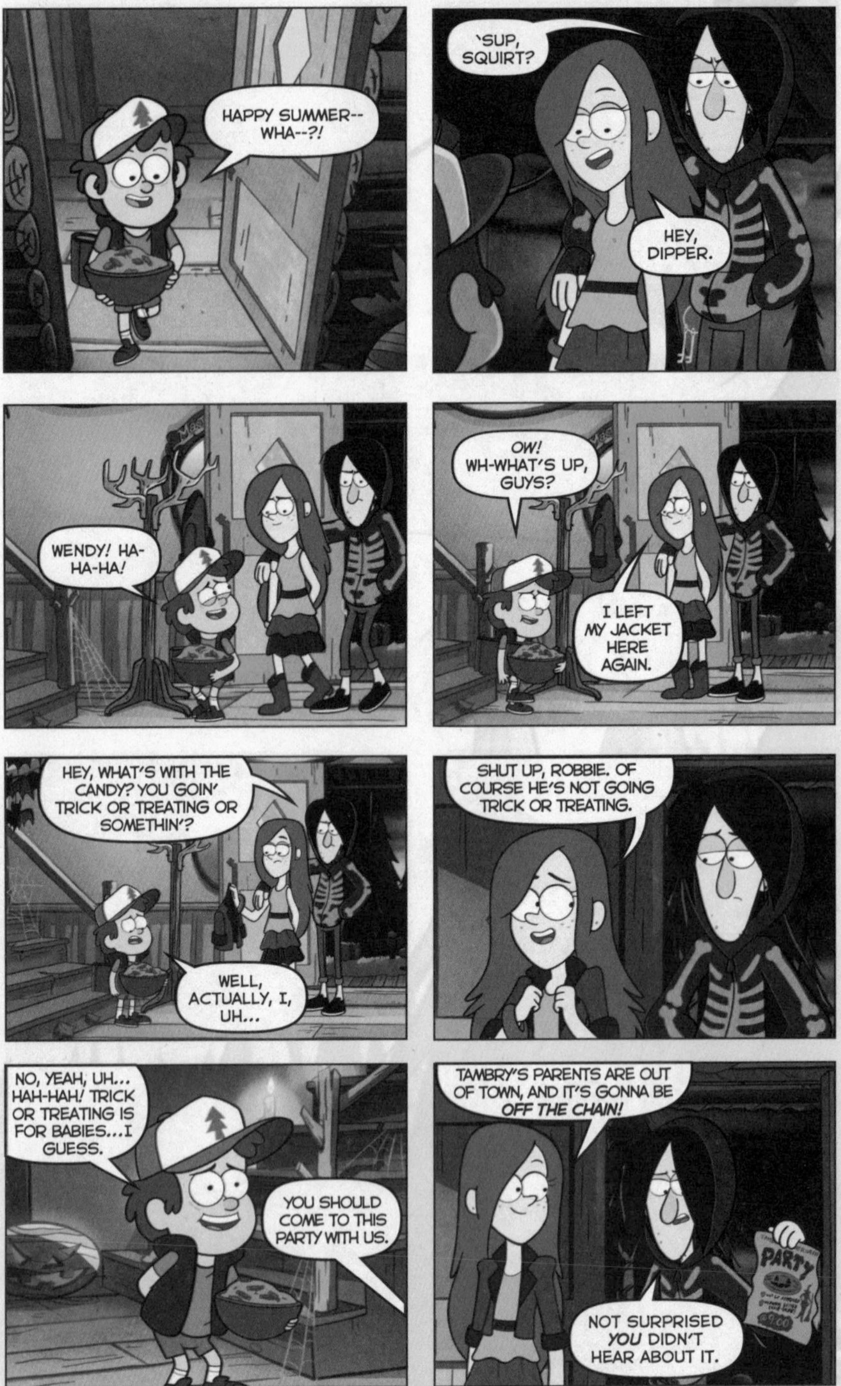
HAPPY SUMMER--
WHA--?!
'SUP, SQUIRT?
HEY, DIPPER.
WENDY! HA-HA-HA!
OW! WH-WHAT'S UP, GUYS?
I LEFT MY JACKET HERE AGAIN.
HEY, WHAT'S WITH THE CANDY? YOU GOIN' TRICK OR TREATING OR SOMETHIN'?
WELL, ACTUALLY, I, UH...
SHUT UP, ROBBIE. OF COURSE HE'S NOT GOING TRICK OR TREATING.
NO, YEAH, UH... HAH-HAH! TRICK OR TREATING IS FOR BABIES...I GUESS.
YOU SHOULD COME TO THIS PARTY WITH US.
TAMBRY'S PARENTS ARE OUT OF TOWN, AND IT'S GONNA BE *OFF THE CHAIN!*
NOT SURPRISED *YOU* DIDN'T HEAR ABOUT IT.
PARTY

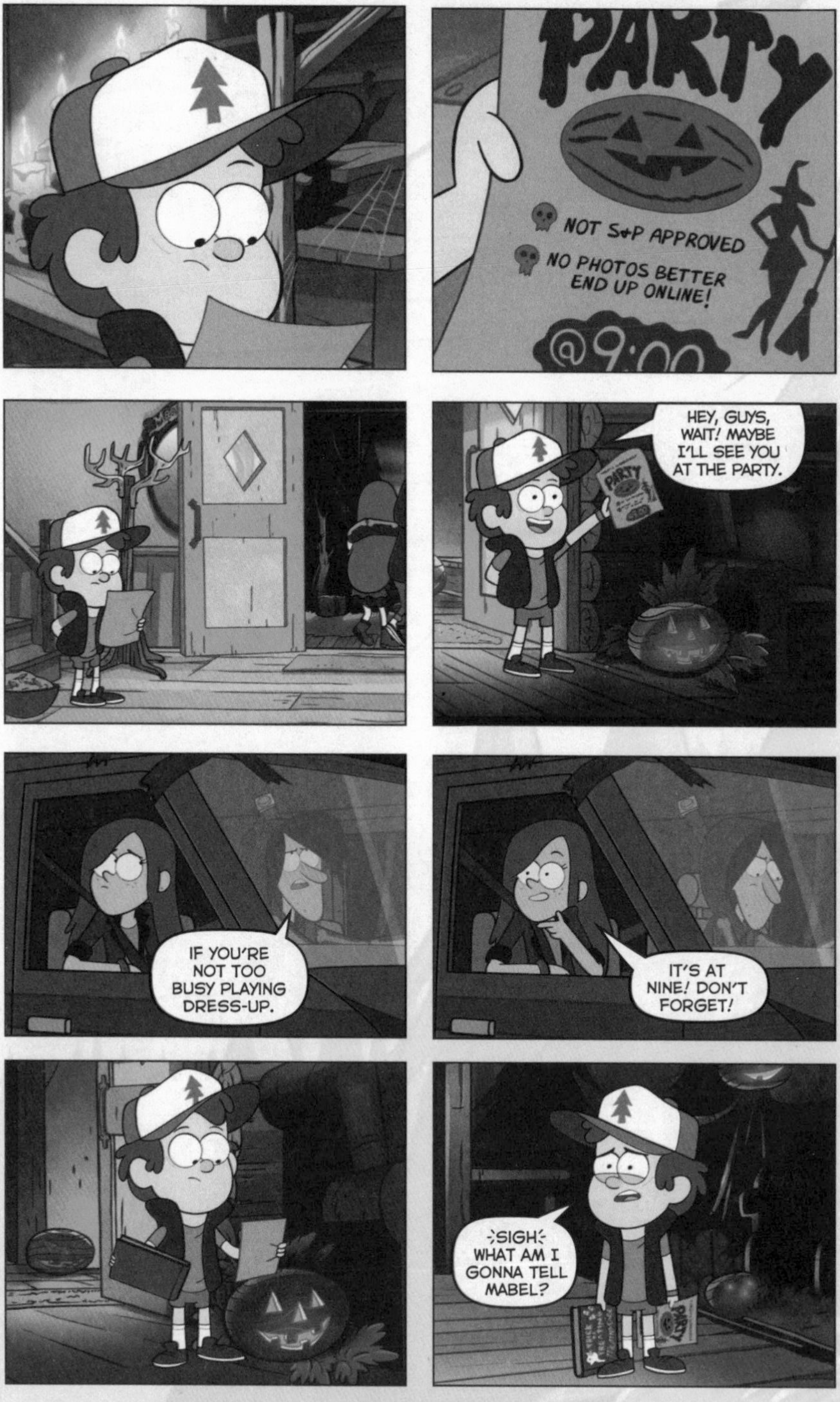
PARTY
NOT S&P APPROVED
NO PHOTOS BETTER END UP ONLINE!
@9:00
HEY, GUYS, WAIT! MAYBE I'LL SEE YOU AT THE PARTY.
IF YOU'RE NOT TOO BUSY PLAYING DRESS-UP.
IT'S AT NINE! DON'T FORGET!
SIGH WHAT AM I GONNA TELL MABEL?

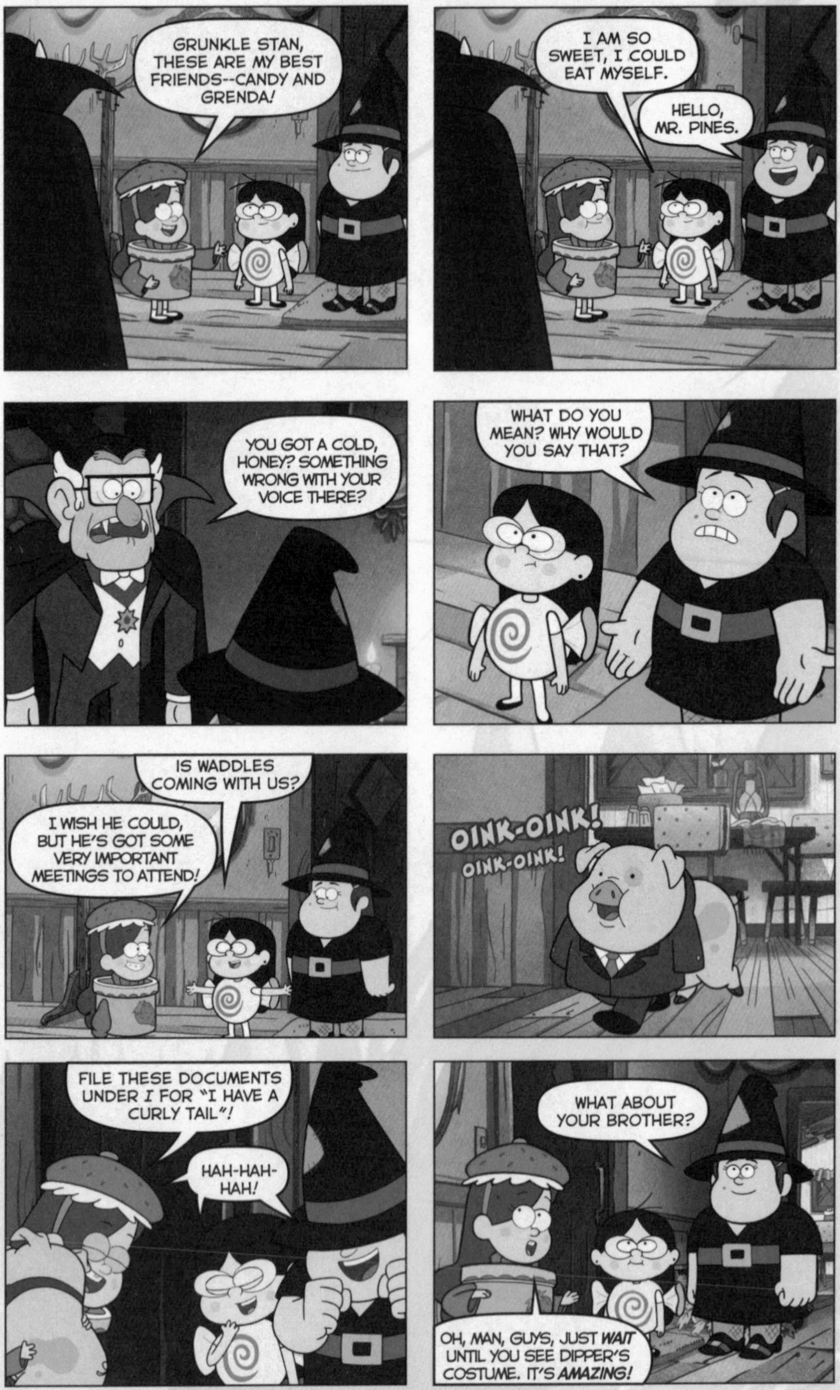
GRUNKLE STAN, THESE ARE MY BEST FRIENDS--CANDY AND GRENDA!
I AM SO SWEET, I COULD EAT MYSELF.
HELLO, MR. PINES.
YOU GOT A COLD, HONEY? SOMETHING WRONG WITH YOUR VOICE THERE?
WHAT DO YOU MEAN? WHY WOULD YOU SAY THAT?
IS WADDLES COMING WITH US?
I WISH HE COULD, BUT HE'S GOT SOME VERY IMPORTANT MEETINGS TO ATTEND!
OINK-OINK!
OINK-OINK!
FILE THESE DOCUMENTS UNDER *I* FOR "I HAVE A CURLY TAIL"!
HAH-HAH-HAH!
WHAT ABOUT YOUR BROTHER?
OH, MAN, GUYS, JUST *WAIT* UNTIL YOU SEE DIPPER'S COSTUME. IT'S *AMAZING!*

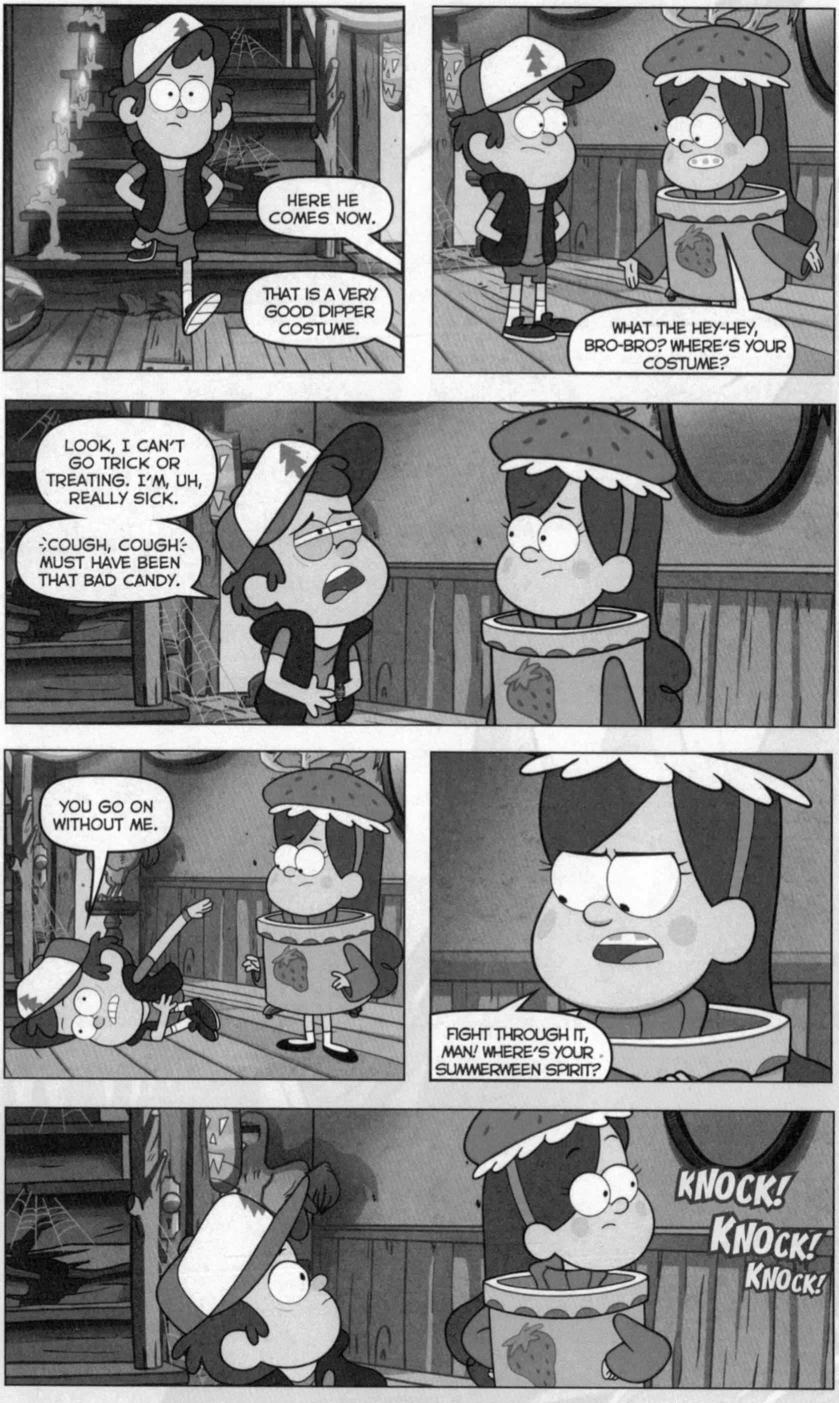
HERE HE COMES NOW.
THAT IS A VERY GOOD DIPPER COSTUME.
WHAT THE HEY-HEY, BRO-BRO? WHERE'S YOUR COSTUME?
LOOK, I CAN'T GO TRICK OR TREATING. I'M, UH, REALLY SICK.
COUGH, COUGH MUST HAVE BEEN THAT BAD CANDY.
YOU GO ON WITHOUT ME.
FIGHT THROUGH IT, MAN! WHERE'S YOUR SUMMERWEEN SPIRIT?
KNOCK!
KNOCK!
KNOCK!

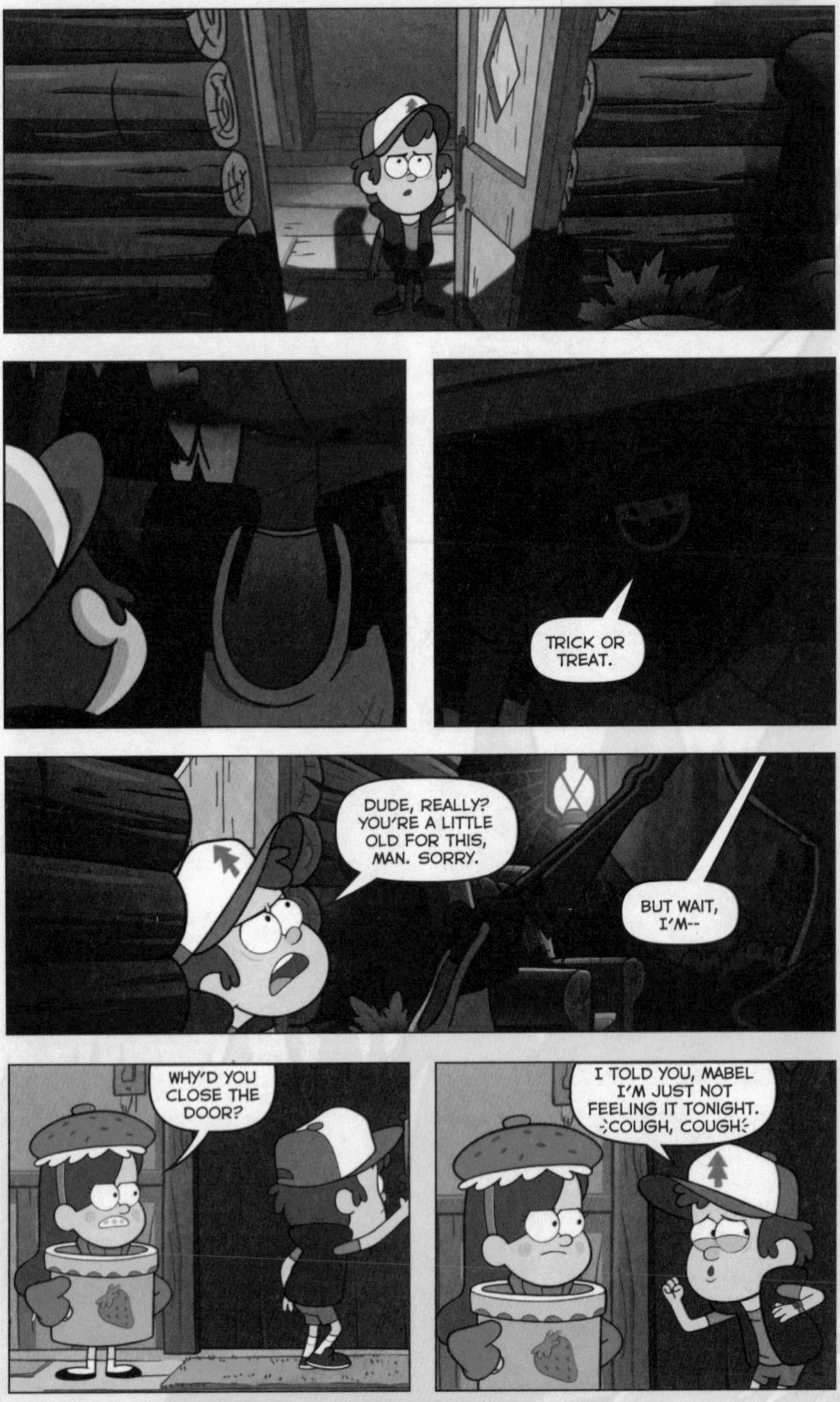

TRICK OR TREAT.
DUDE, REALLY? YOU'RE A LITTLE OLD FOR THIS, MAN. SORRY.
BUT WAIT, I'M--
WHY'D YOU CLOSE THE DOOR?
I TOLD YOU, MABEL I'M JUST NOT FEELING IT TONIGHT.
COUGH, COUGH

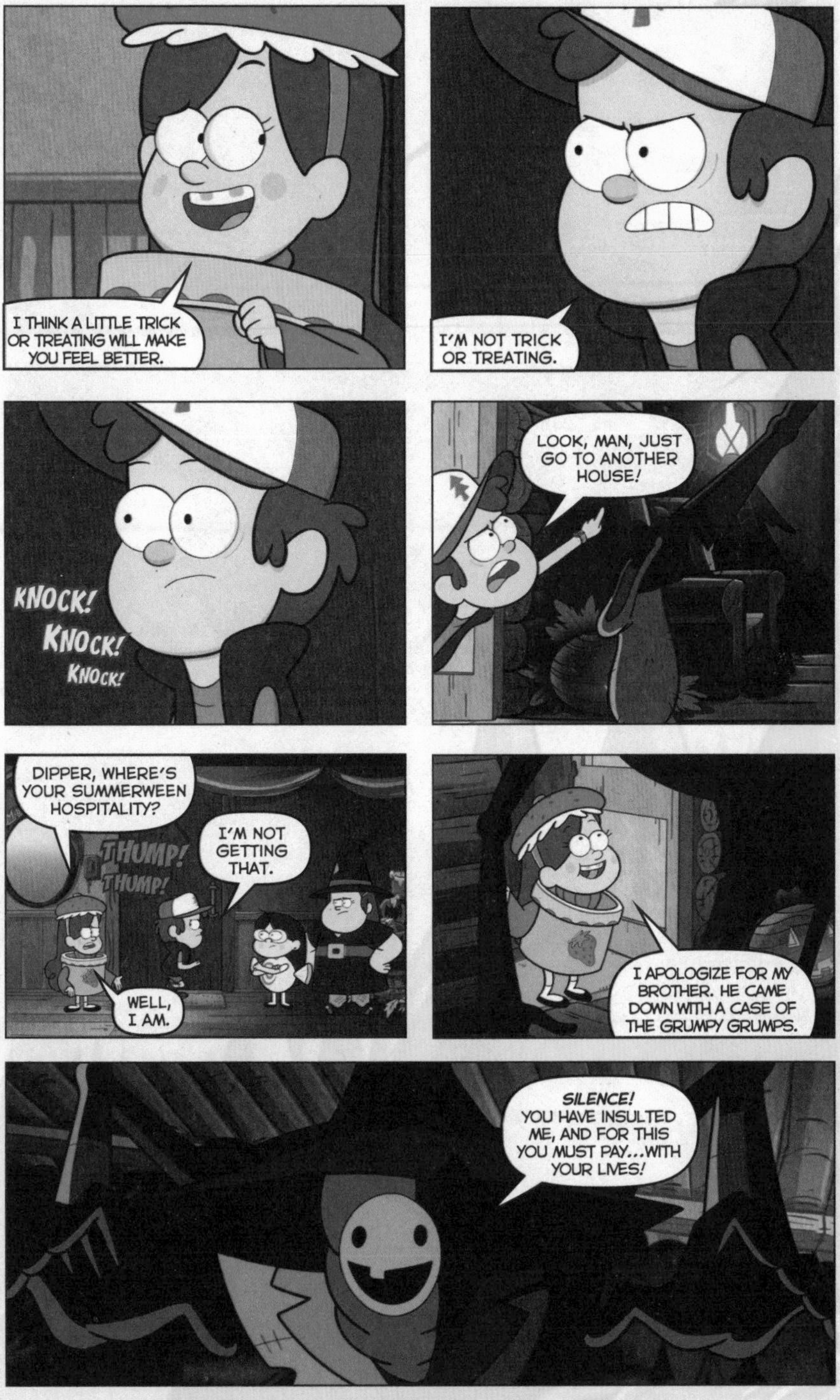
I THINK A LITTLE TRICK OR TREATING WILL MAKE YOU FEEL BETTER.
I'M NOT TRICK OR TREATING.
KNOCK! KNOCK! KNOCK!
LOOK, MAN, JUST GO TO ANOTHER HOUSE!
DIPPER, WHERE'S YOUR SUMMERWEEN HOSPITALITY?
THUMP! THUMP!
I'M NOT GETTING THAT.
WELL, I AM.
I APOLOGIZE FOR MY BROTHER. HE CAME DOWN WITH A CASE OF THE GRUMPY GRUMPS.
SILENCE! YOU HAVE INSULTED ME, AND FOR THIS YOU MUST PAY...WITH YOUR LIVES!

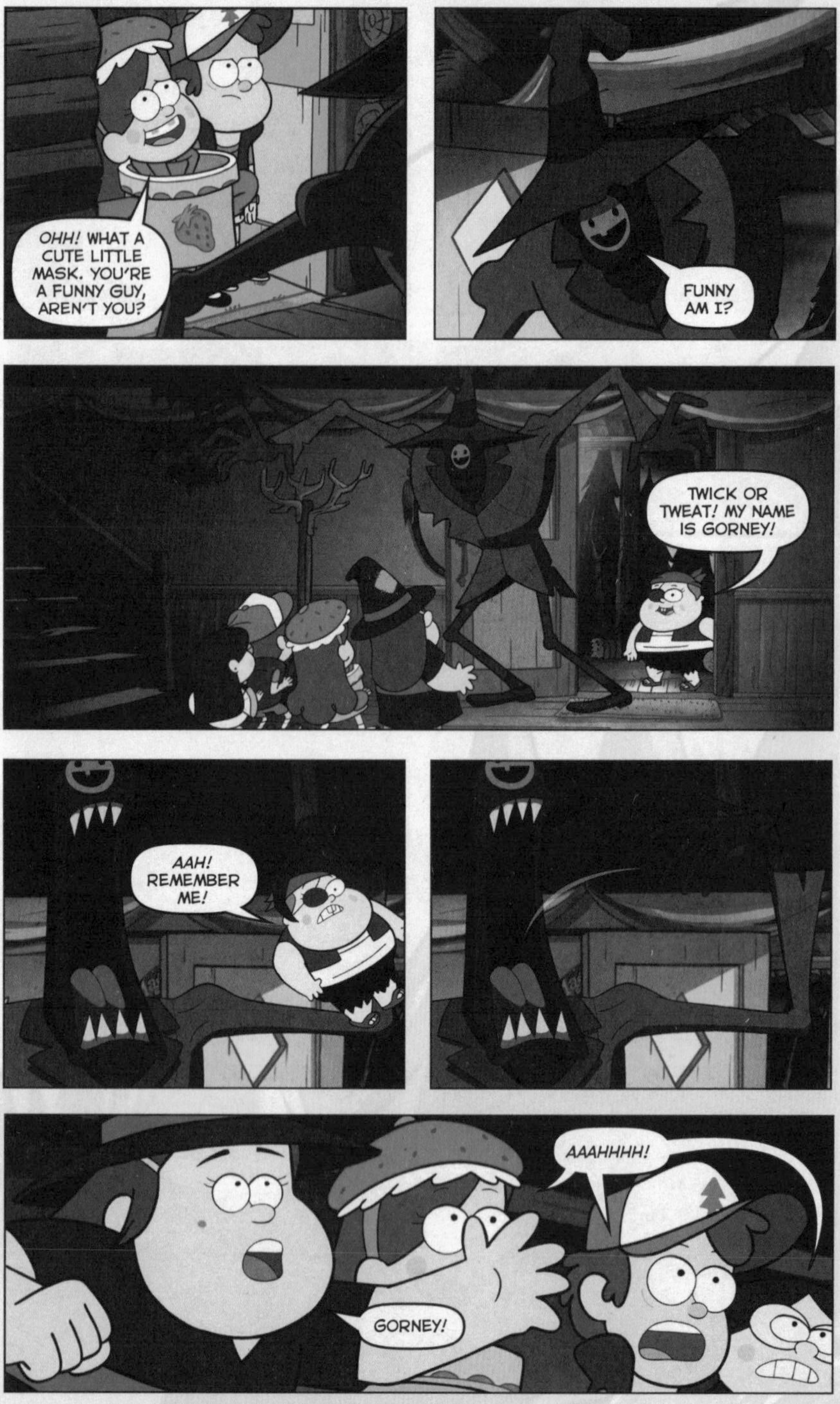
OHH! WHAT A CUTE LITTLE MASK. YOU'RE A FUNNY GUY, AREN'T YOU?
FUNNY AM I?
TWICK OR TWEAT! MY NAME IS GORNEY!
AAH! REMEMBER ME!
AAAHHHH!
GORNEY!

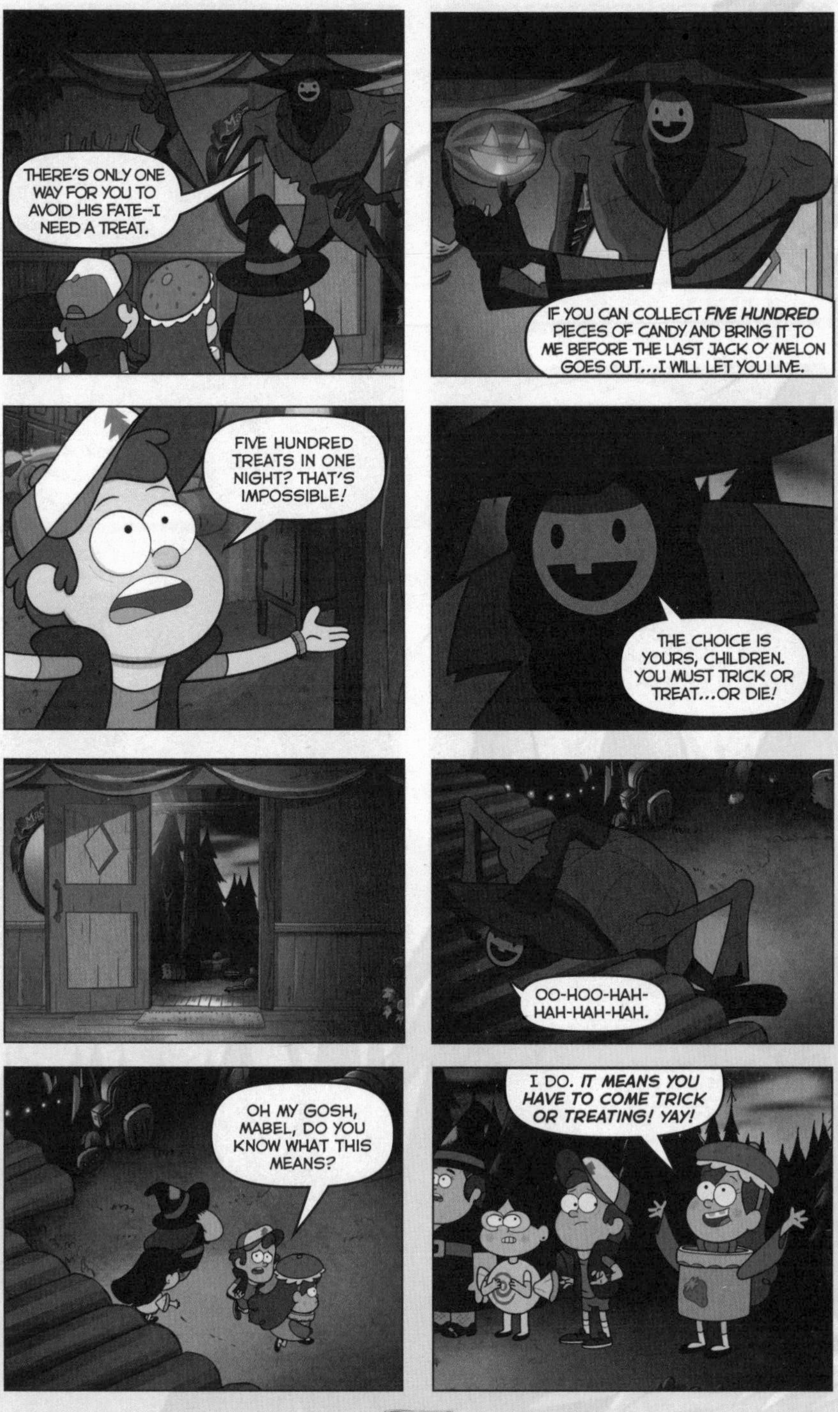
THERE'S ONLY ONE WAY FOR YOU TO AVOID HIS FATE--I NEED A TREAT.
IF YOU CAN COLLECT FIVE HUNDRED PIECES OF CANDY AND BRING IT TO ME BEFORE THE LAST JACK O' MELON GOES OUT...I WILL LET YOU LIVE.
FIVE HUNDRED TREATS IN ONE NIGHT? THAT'S IMPOSSIBLE!
THE CHOICE IS YOURS, CHILDREN. YOU MUST TRICK OR TREAT...OR DIE!
OO-HOO-HAH-HAH-HAH-HAH.
OH MY GOSH, MABEL, DO YOU KNOW WHAT THIS MEANS?
I DO. IT MEANS YOU HAVE TO COME TRICK OR TREATING! YAY!

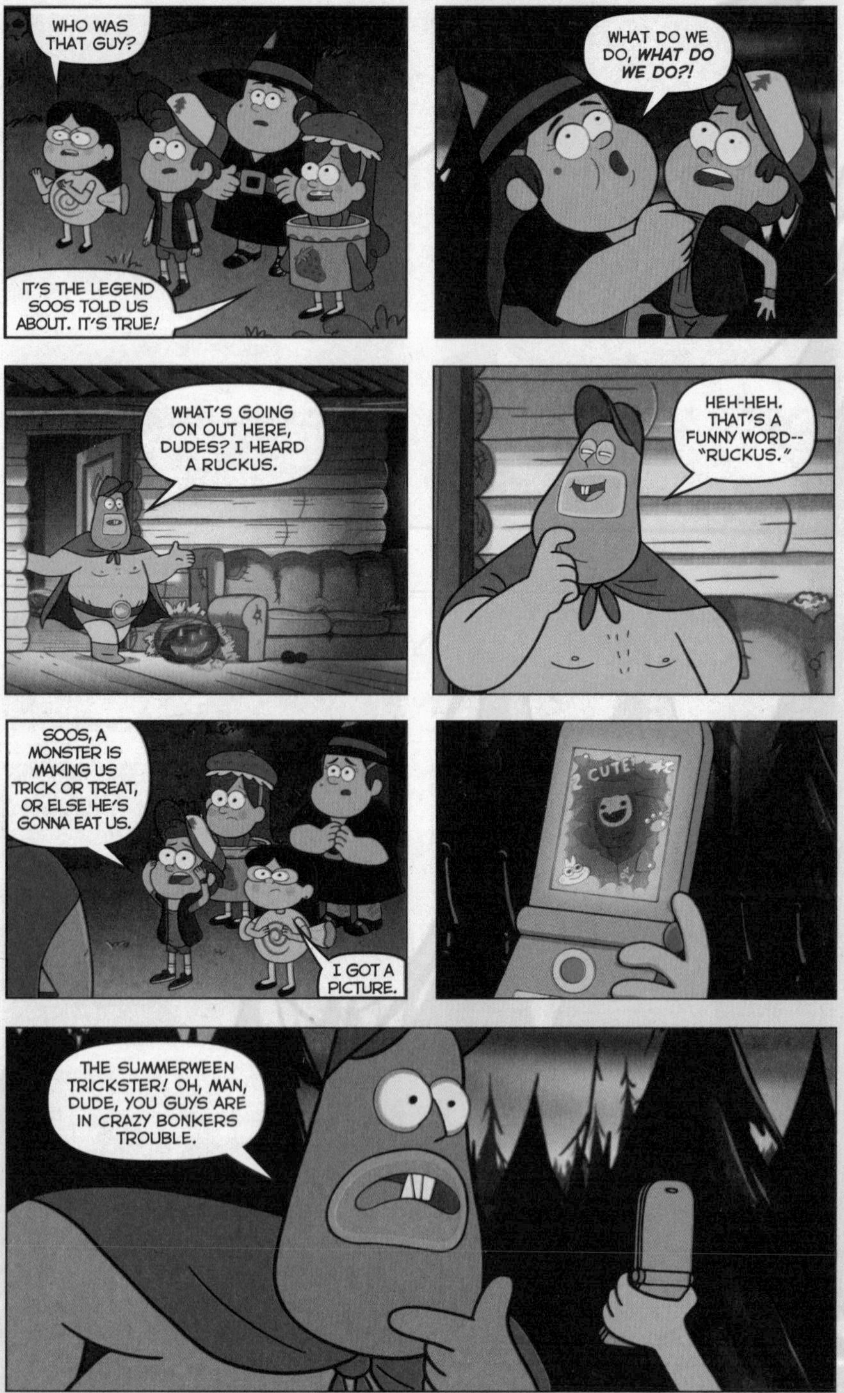
WHO WAS THAT GUY?
IT'S THE LEGEND SOOS TOLD US ABOUT. IT'S TRUE!
WHAT DO WE DO, WHAT DO WE DO?!
WHAT'S GOING ON OUT HERE, DUDES? I HEARD A RUCKUS.
HEH-HEH. THAT'S A FUNNY WORD-- "RUCKUS."
SOOS, A MONSTER IS MAKING US TRICK OR TREAT, OR ELSE HE'S GONNA EAT US.
I GOT A PICTURE.
CUTE!
THE SUMMERWEEN TRICKSTER! OH, MAN, DUDE, YOU GUYS ARE IN CRAZY BONKERS TROUBLE.

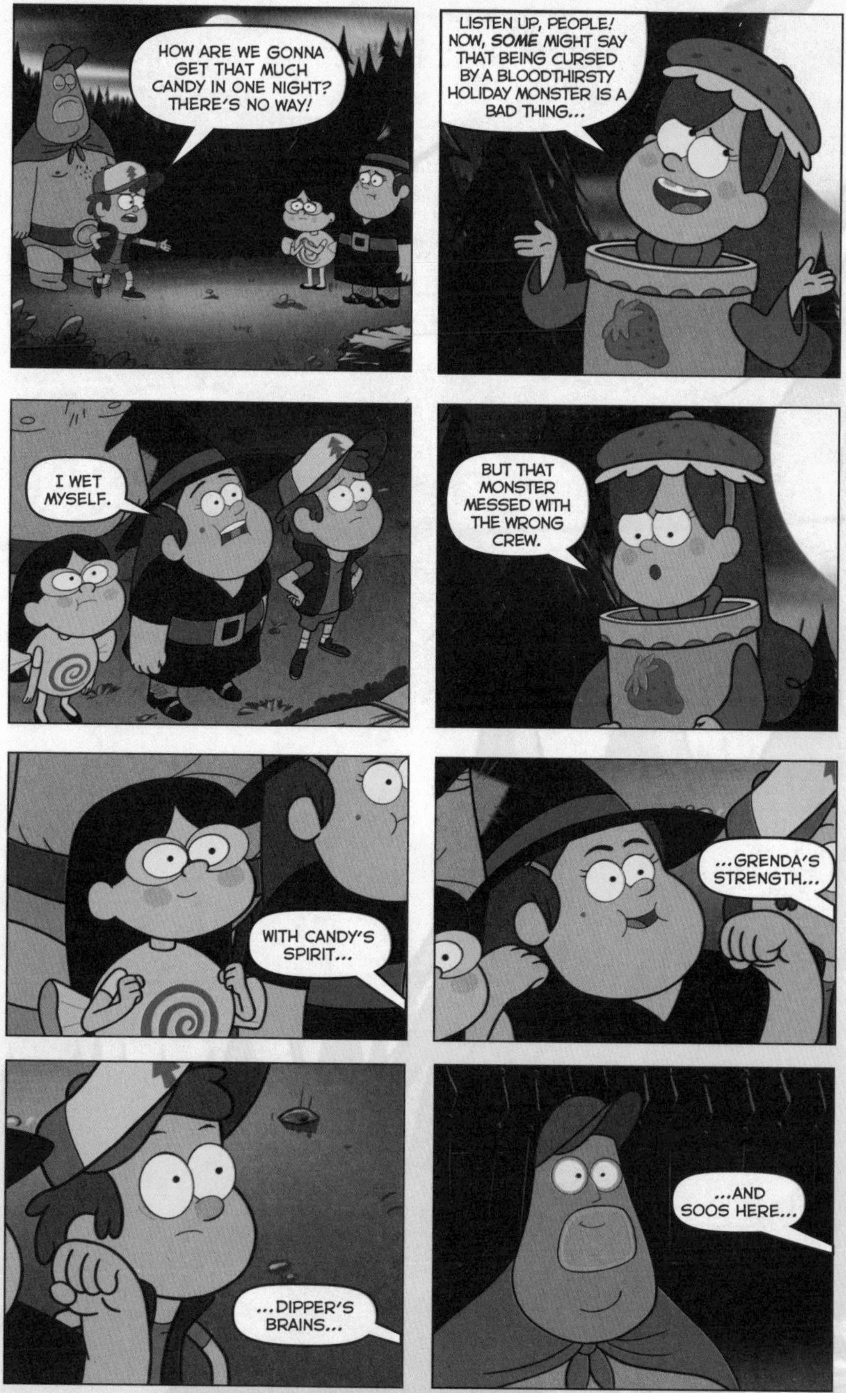
HOW ARE WE GONNA GET THAT MUCH CANDY IN ONE NIGHT? THERE'S NO WAY!
LISTEN UP, PEOPLE! NOW, *SOME* MIGHT SAY THAT BEING CURSED BY A BLOODTHIRSTY HOLIDAY MONSTER IS A BAD THING...
I WET MYSELF.
BUT THAT MONSTER MESSED WITH THE WRONG CREW.
WITH CANDY'S SPIRIT...
...GRENDA'S STRENGTH...
...DIPPER'S BRAINS...
...AND SOOS HERE...

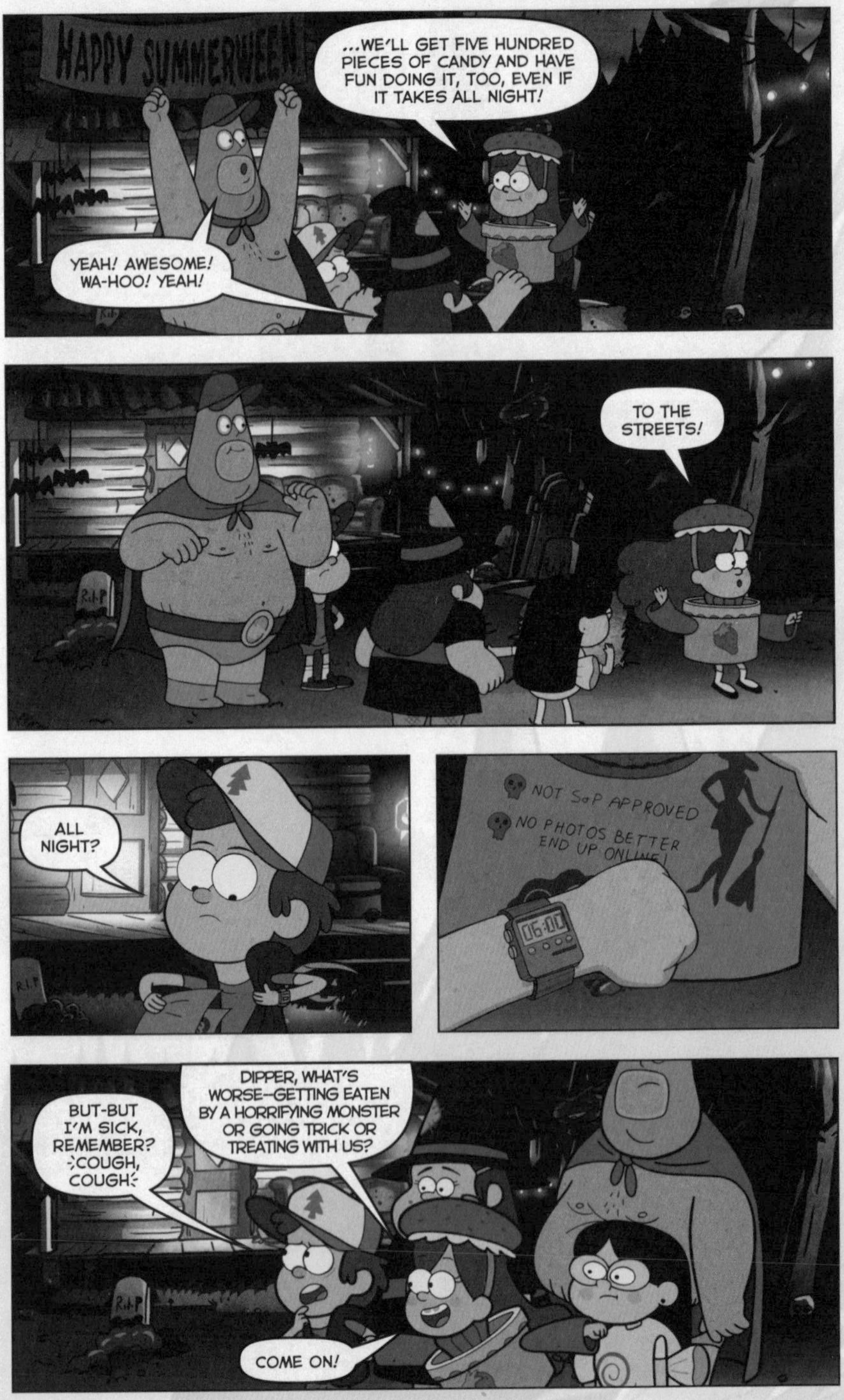
HAPPY SUMMERWEEN
...WE'LL GET FIVE HUNDRED PIECES OF CANDY AND HAVE FUN DOING IT, TOO, EVEN IF IT TAKES ALL NIGHT!
YEAH! AWESOME! WA-HOO! YEAH!
TO THE STREETS!
ALL NIGHT?
NOT S&P APPROVED
NO PHOTOS BETTER END UP ONLINE!
06:00
DIPPER, WHAT'S WORSE--GETTING EATEN BY A HORRIFYING MONSTER OR GOING TRICK OR TREATING WITH US?
BUT-BUT I'M SICK, REMEMBER? COUGH, COUGH
COME ON!

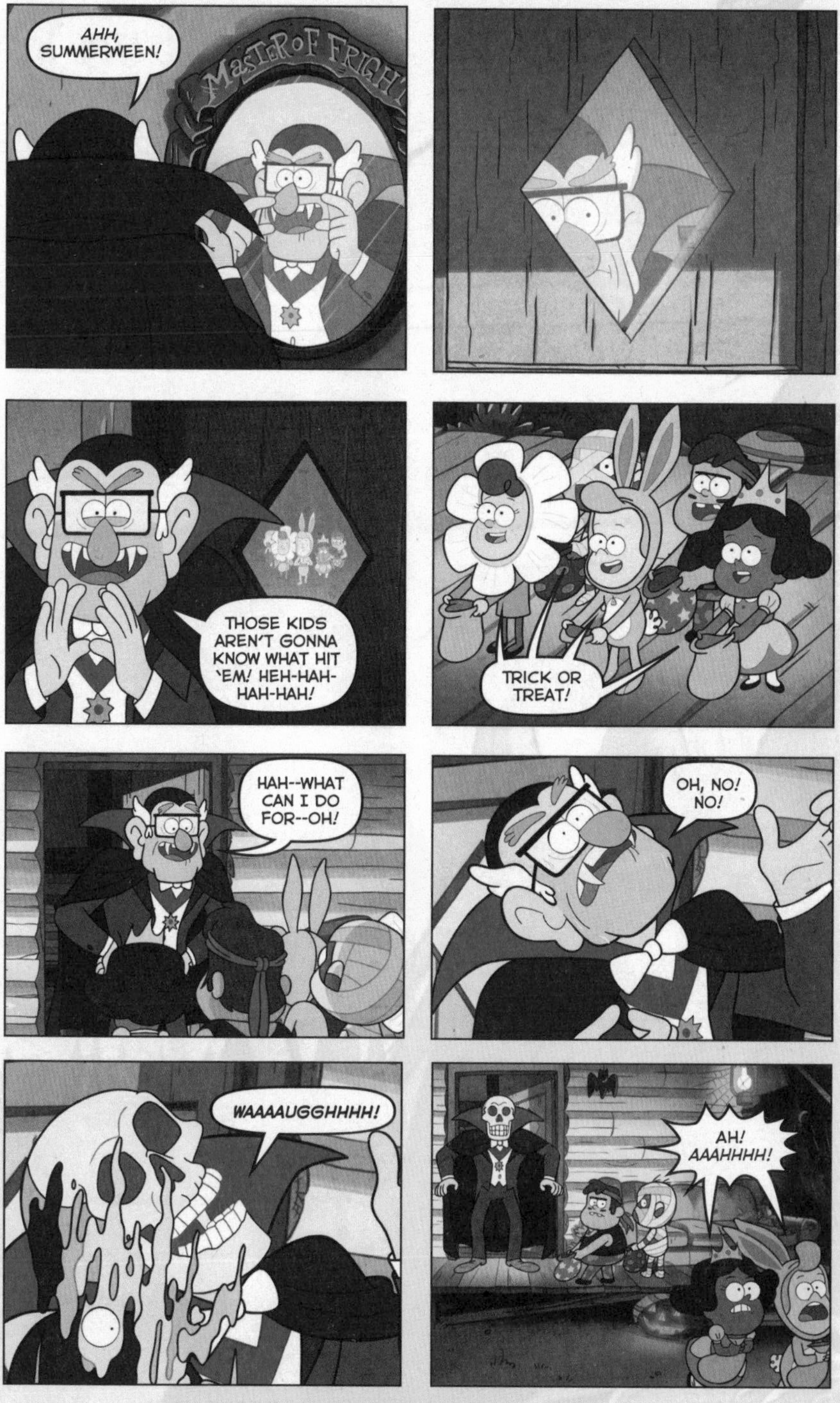
AHH, SUMMERWEEN!
MASTER OF FRIGHT
THOSE KIDS AREN'T GONNA KNOW WHAT HIT 'EM! HEH-HAH-HAH-HAH!
TRICK OR TREAT!
HAH--WHAT CAN I DO FOR--OH!
OH, NO! NO!
WAAAAUGGHHHH!
AH! AAAHHHH!

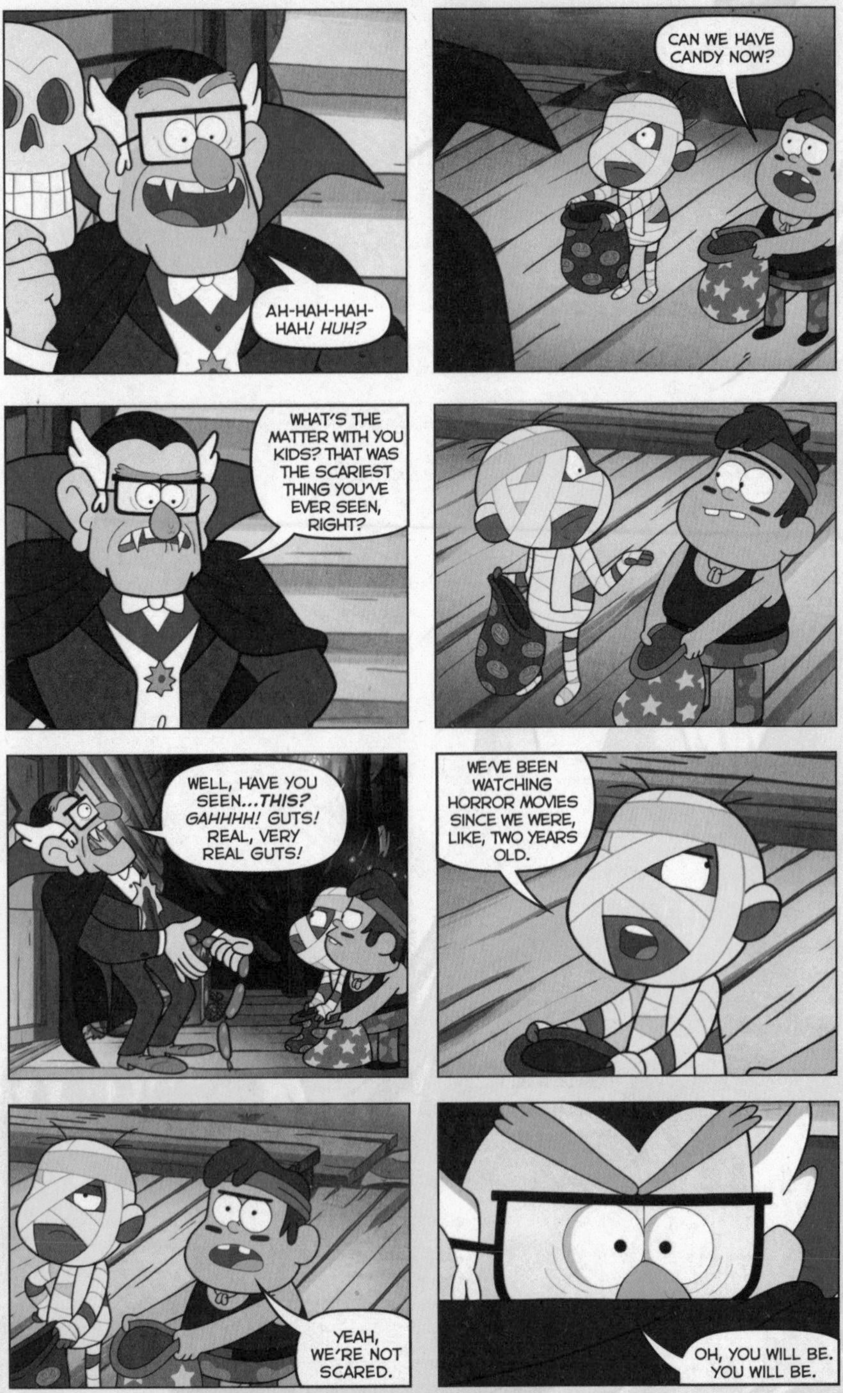
AH-HAH-HAH-HAH! *HUH?*
CAN WE HAVE CANDY NOW?
WHAT'S THE MATTER WITH YOU KIDS? THAT WAS THE SCARIEST THING YOU'VE EVER SEEN, RIGHT?
WELL, HAVE YOU SEEN...*THIS? GAHHHH!* GUTS! REAL, VERY REAL GUTS!
WE'VE BEEN WATCHING HORROR MOVIES SINCE WE WERE, LIKE, TWO YEARS OLD.
YEAH, WE'RE NOT SCARED.
OH, YOU WILL BE. YOU WILL BE.

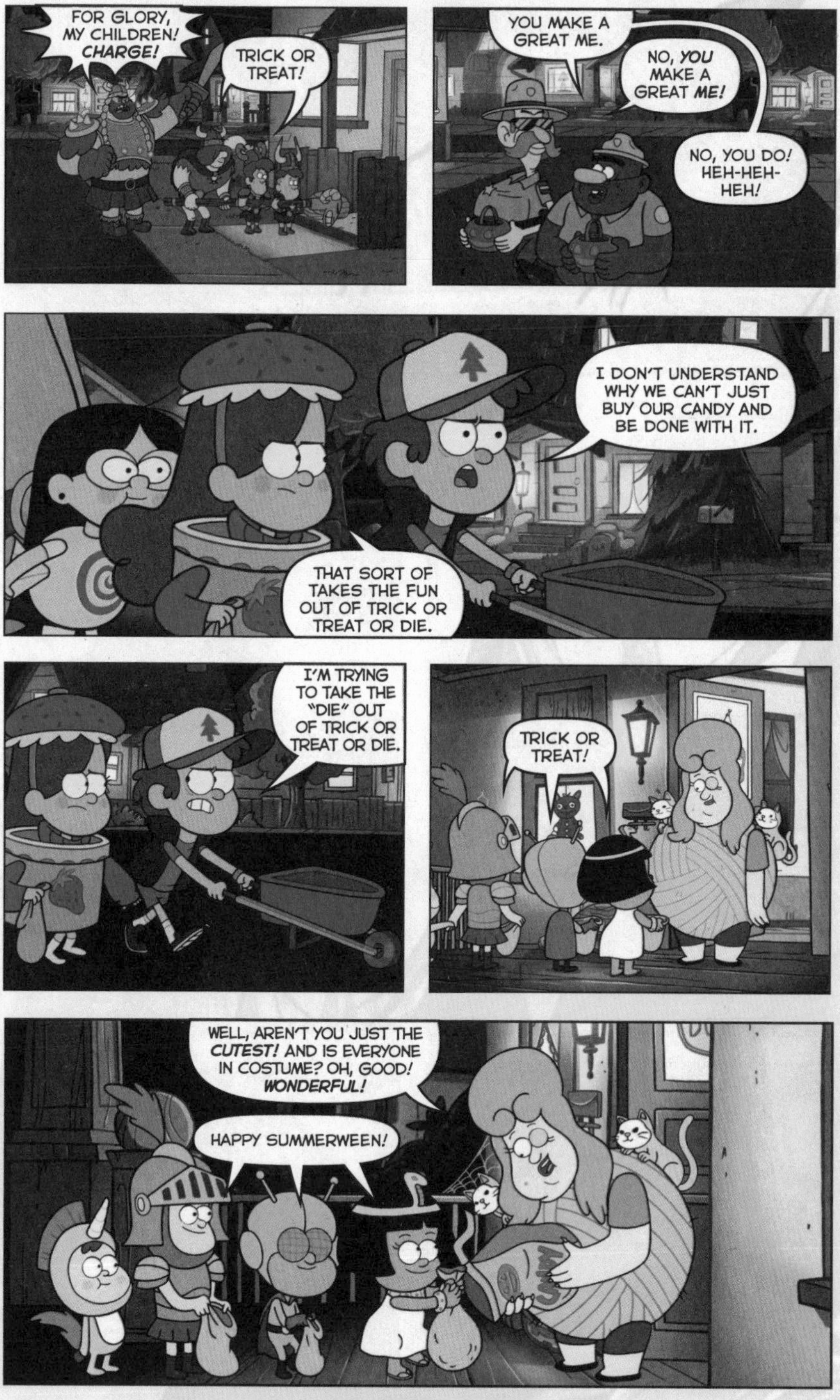
FOR GLORY, MY CHILDREN! CHARGE!
TRICK OR TREAT!
YOU MAKE A GREAT ME.
NO, YOU MAKE A GREAT ME!
NO, YOU DO! HEH-HEH-HEH!
I DON'T UNDERSTAND WHY WE CAN'T JUST BUY OUR CANDY AND BE DONE WITH IT.
THAT SORT OF TAKES THE FUN OUT OF TRICK OR TREAT OR DIE.
I'M TRYING TO TAKE THE "DIE" OUT OF TRICK OR TREAT OR DIE.
TRICK OR TREAT!
WELL, AREN'T YOU JUST THE CUTEST! AND IS EVERYONE IN COSTUME? OH, GOOD! WONDERFUL!
HAPPY SUMMERWEEN!

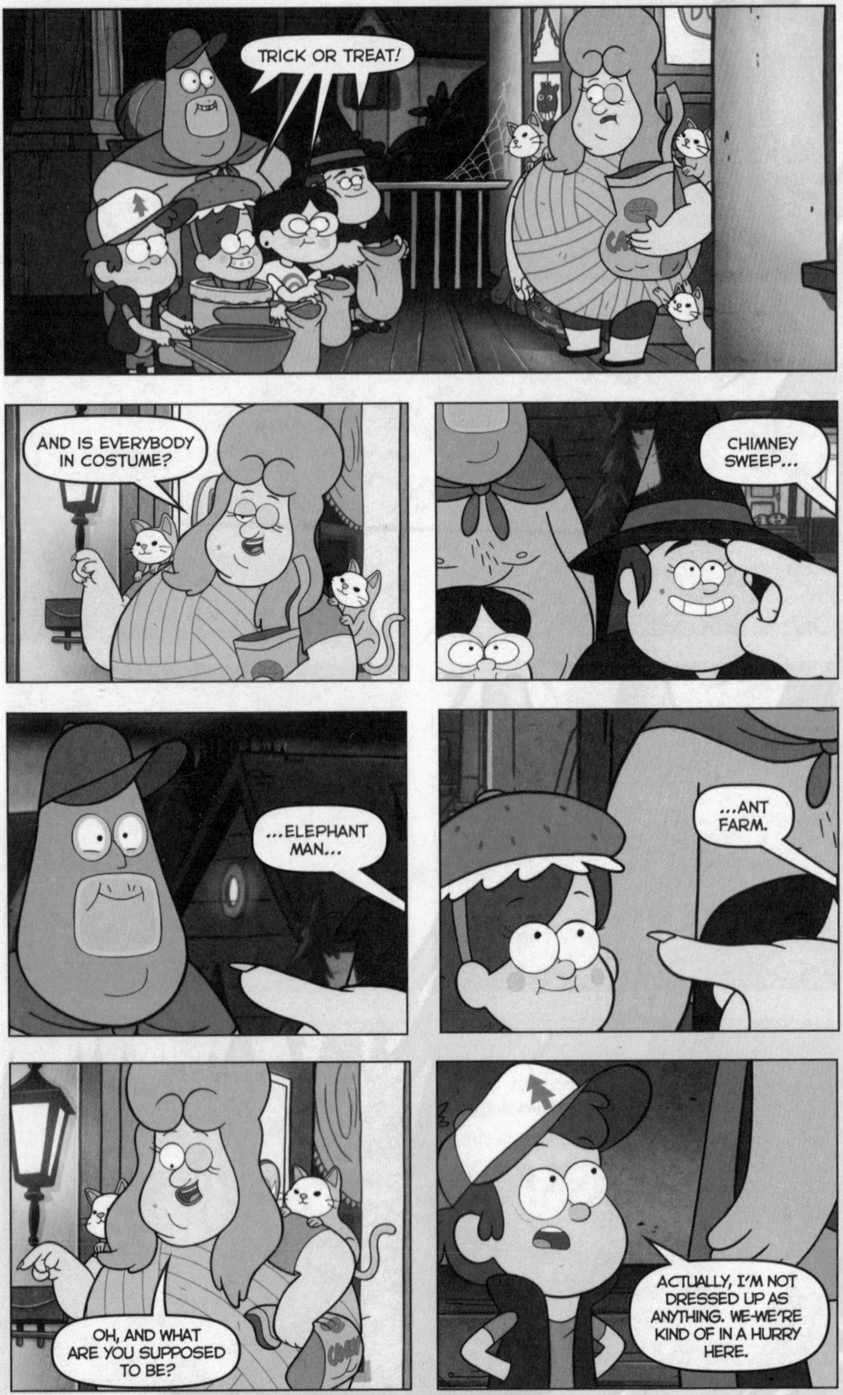
TRICK OR TREAT!
AND IS EVERYBODY IN COSTUME?
CHIMNEY SWEEP...
...ELEPHANT MAN...
...ANT FARM.
OH, AND WHAT ARE YOU SUPPOSED TO BE?
ACTUALLY, I'M NOT DRESSED UP AS ANYTHING. WE-WE'RE KIND OF IN A HURRY HERE.

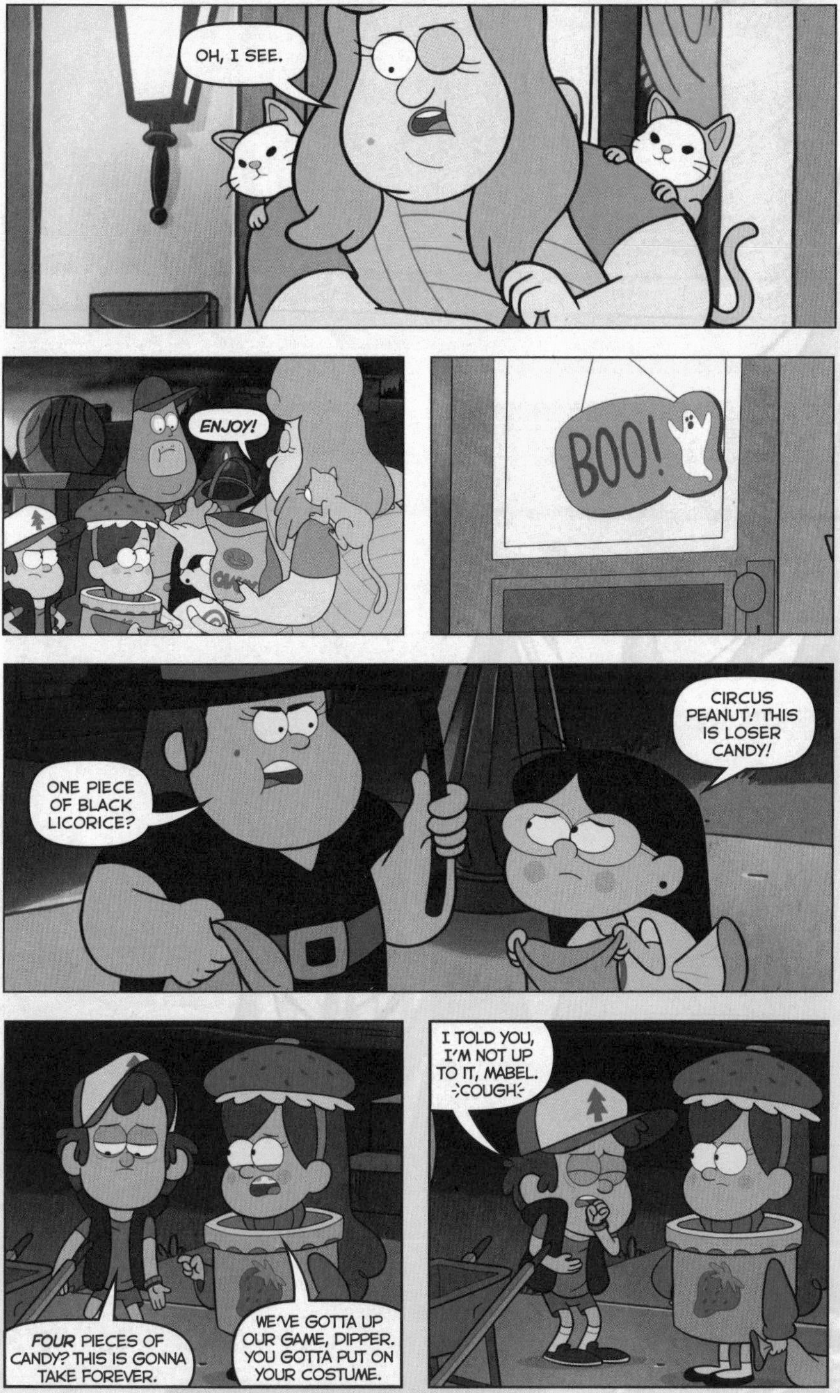
OH, I SEE.
ENJOY!
BOO!
ONE PIECE OF BLACK LICORICE?
CIRCUS PEANUT! THIS IS LOSER CANDY!
FOUR PIECES OF CANDY? THIS IS GONNA TAKE FOREVER.
WE'VE GOTTA UP OUR GAME, DIPPER. YOU GOTTA PUT ON YOUR COSTUME.
I TOLD YOU, I'M NOT UP TO IT, MABEL. COUGH

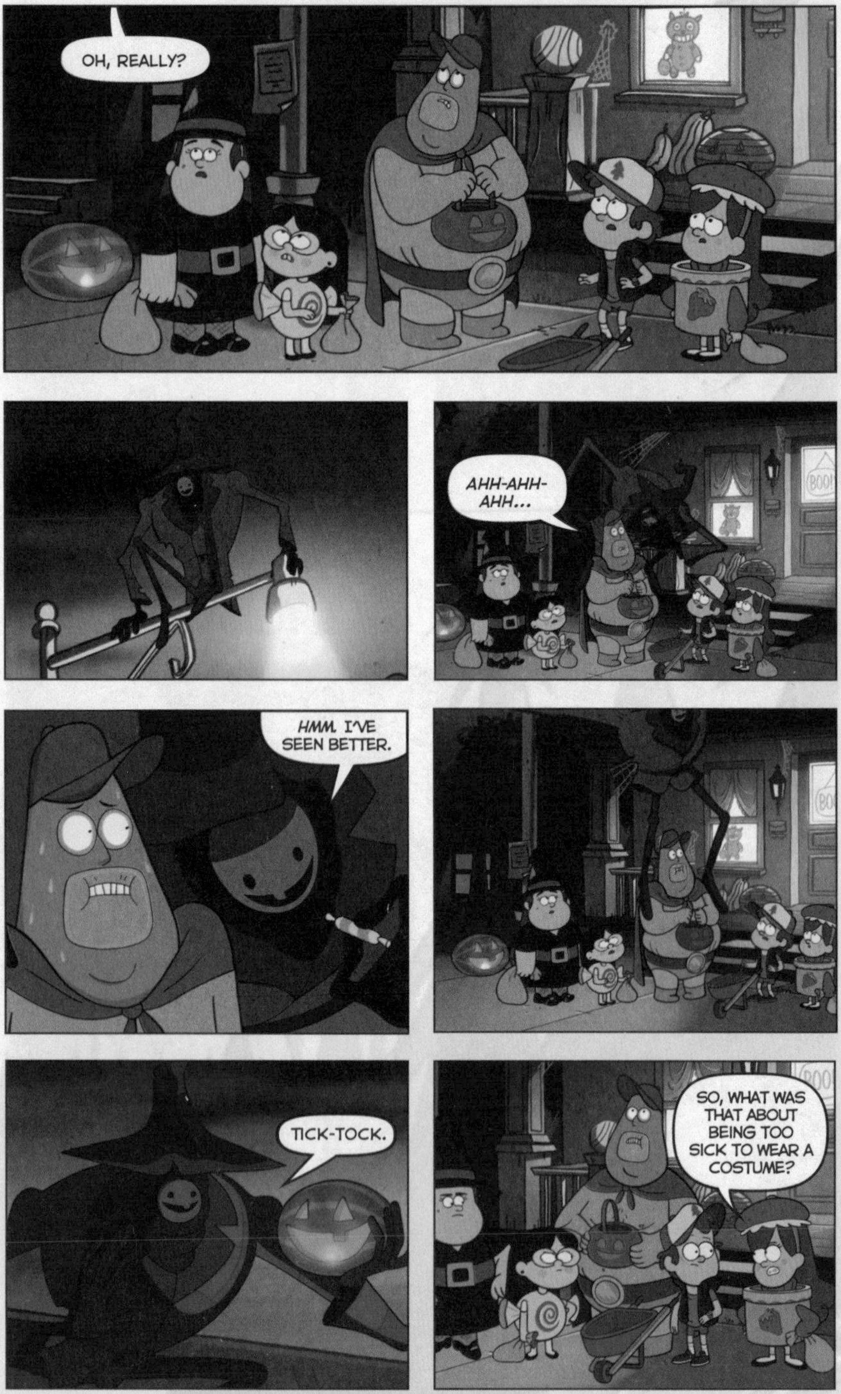
OH, REALLY?
AHH-AHH-AHH...
HMM. I'VE SEEN BETTER.
BOO!
TICK-TOCK.
SO, WHAT WAS THAT ABOUT BEING TOO SICK TO WEAR A COSTUME?

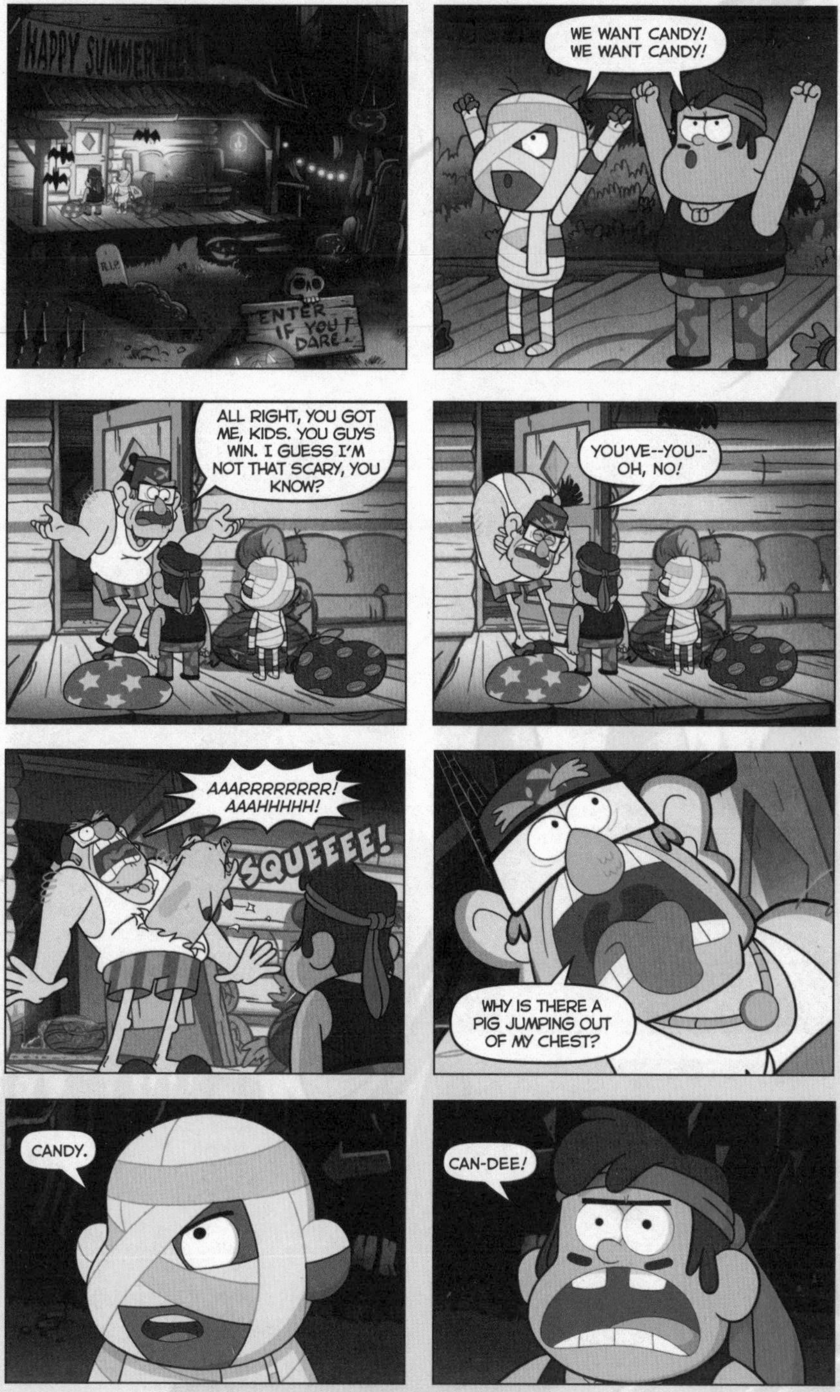
HAPPY SUMMERWEEN
R.I.P.
ENTER IF YOU DARE
WE WANT CANDY! WE WANT CANDY!
ALL RIGHT, YOU GOT ME, KIDS. YOU GUYS WIN. I GUESS I'M NOT THAT SCARY, YOU KNOW?
YOU'VE--YOU-- OH, NO!
AAARRRRRRRR! AAAHHHHHH!
SQUEEEE!
WHY IS THERE A PIG JUMPING OUT OF MY CHEST?
CANDY.
CAN-DEE!

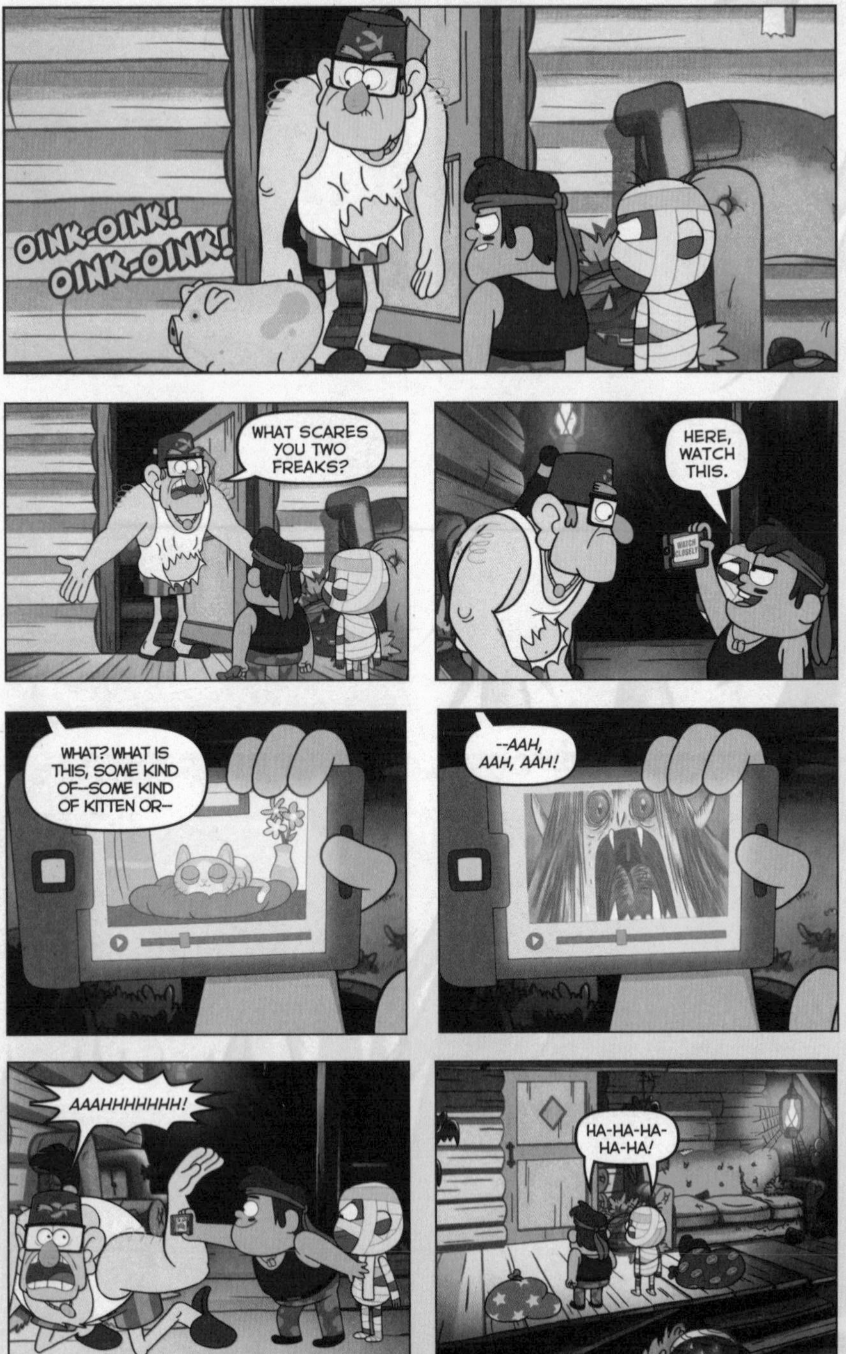
OINK-OINK!
OINK-OINK!
WHAT SCARES YOU TWO FREAKS?
HERE, WATCH THIS.
WATCH CLOSELY
WHAT? WHAT IS THIS, SOME KIND OF--SOME KIND OF KITTEN OR--
--AAH, AAH, AAH!
AAAHHHHHHH!
HA-HA-HA-HA-HA!

WHAT HAPPENED TO YOU, STAN PINES? WHAT HAPPENED?

INTRODUCING, FOR THE FIRST TIME IN PUBLIC, TA-DA!

PEANUT BUTTER AND JELLY!

AWWW!

I WILL MAKE YOU INTERNET FAMOUS!

CLICK!

HEY, ERASE THAT. LET'S JUST GET THIS OVER WITH, OKAY?

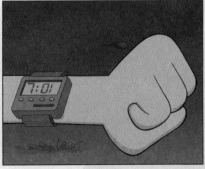

7:01

OVER WITH! OVER WITH!

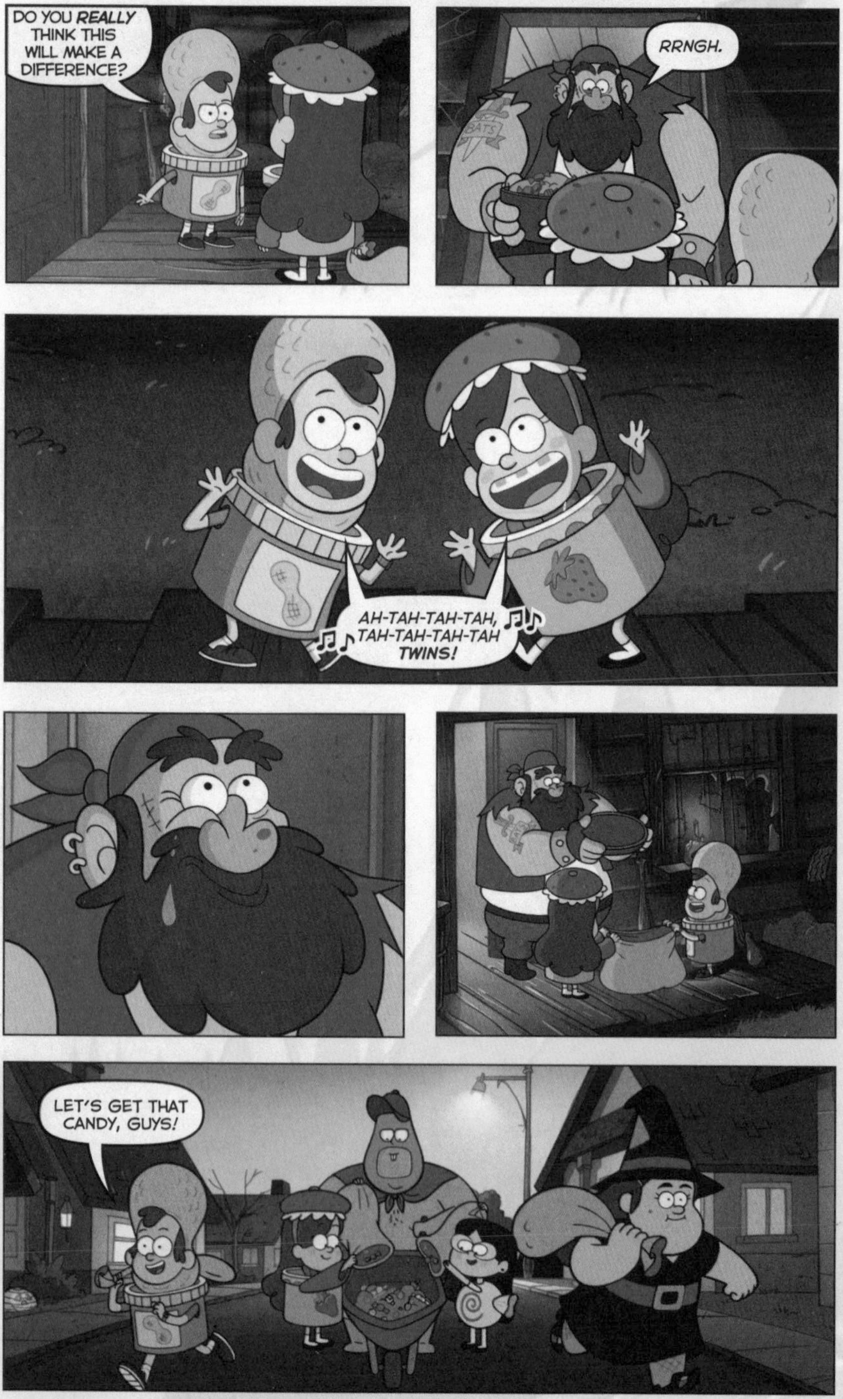
DO YOU *REALLY* THINK THIS WILL MAKE A DIFFERENCE?
RRNGH.
AH-TAH-TAH-TAH, TAH-TAH-TAH-TAH TWINS!
LET'S GET THAT CANDY, GUYS!

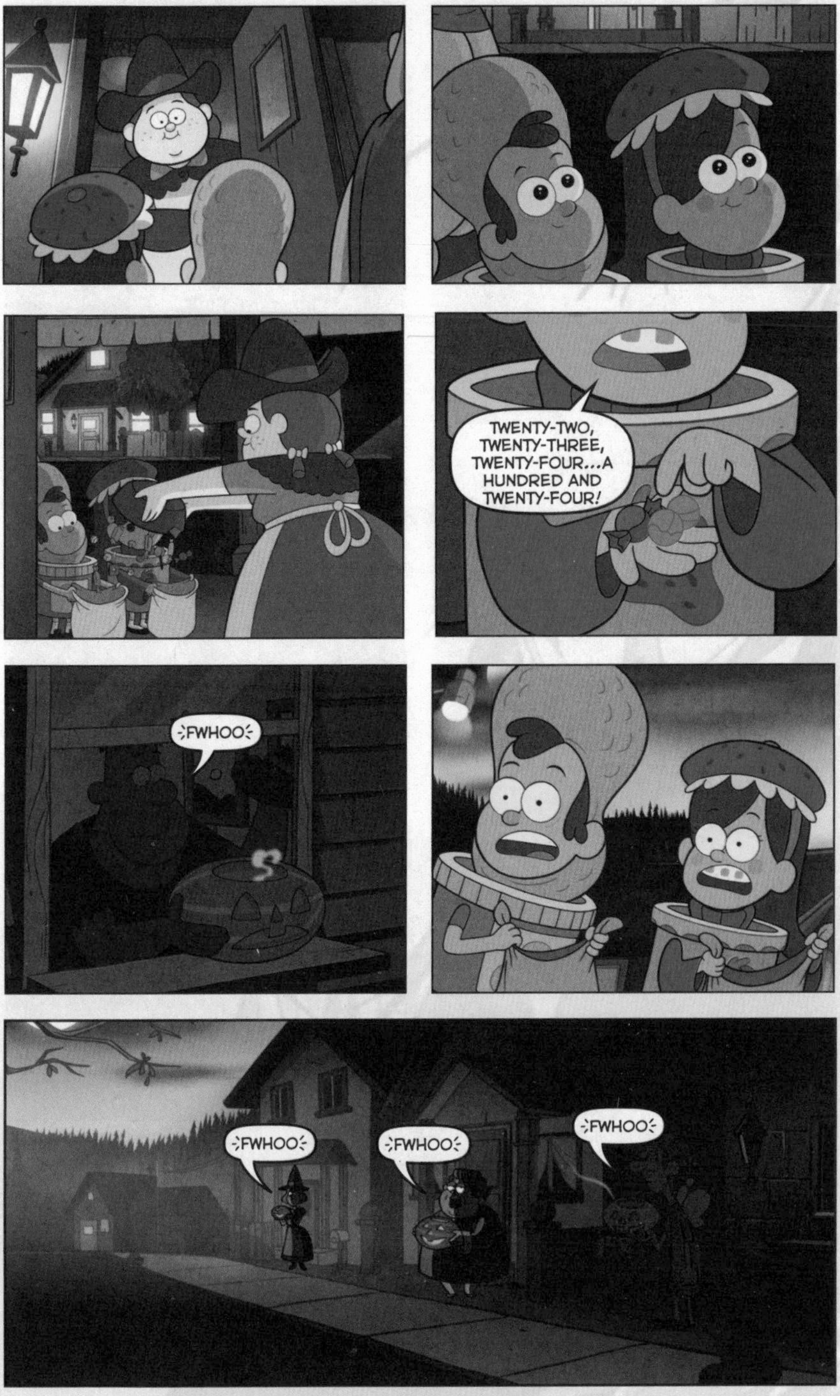
TWENTY-TWO,
TWENTY-THREE,
TWENTY-FOUR...A
HUNDRED AND
TWENTY-FOUR!
FWHOO
FWHOO
FWHOO
FWHOO

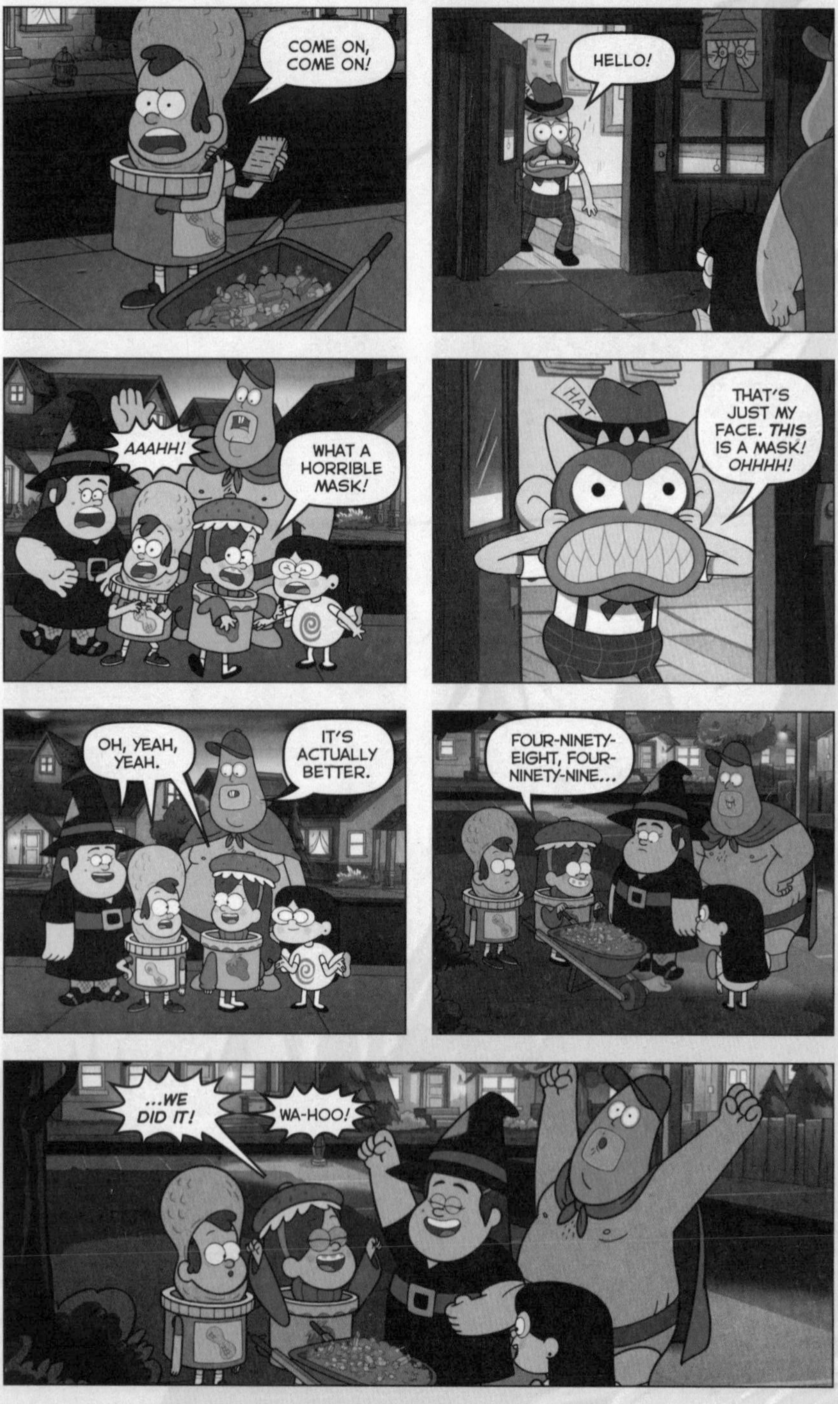
COME ON, COME ON!
HELLO!
AAAHH!
WHAT A HORRIBLE MASK!
HAT
THAT'S JUST MY FACE. THIS IS A MASK! OHHHH!
OH, YEAH, YEAH.
IT'S ACTUALLY BETTER.
FOUR-NINETY-EIGHT, FOUR-NINETY-NINE...
...WE DID IT!
WA-HOO!

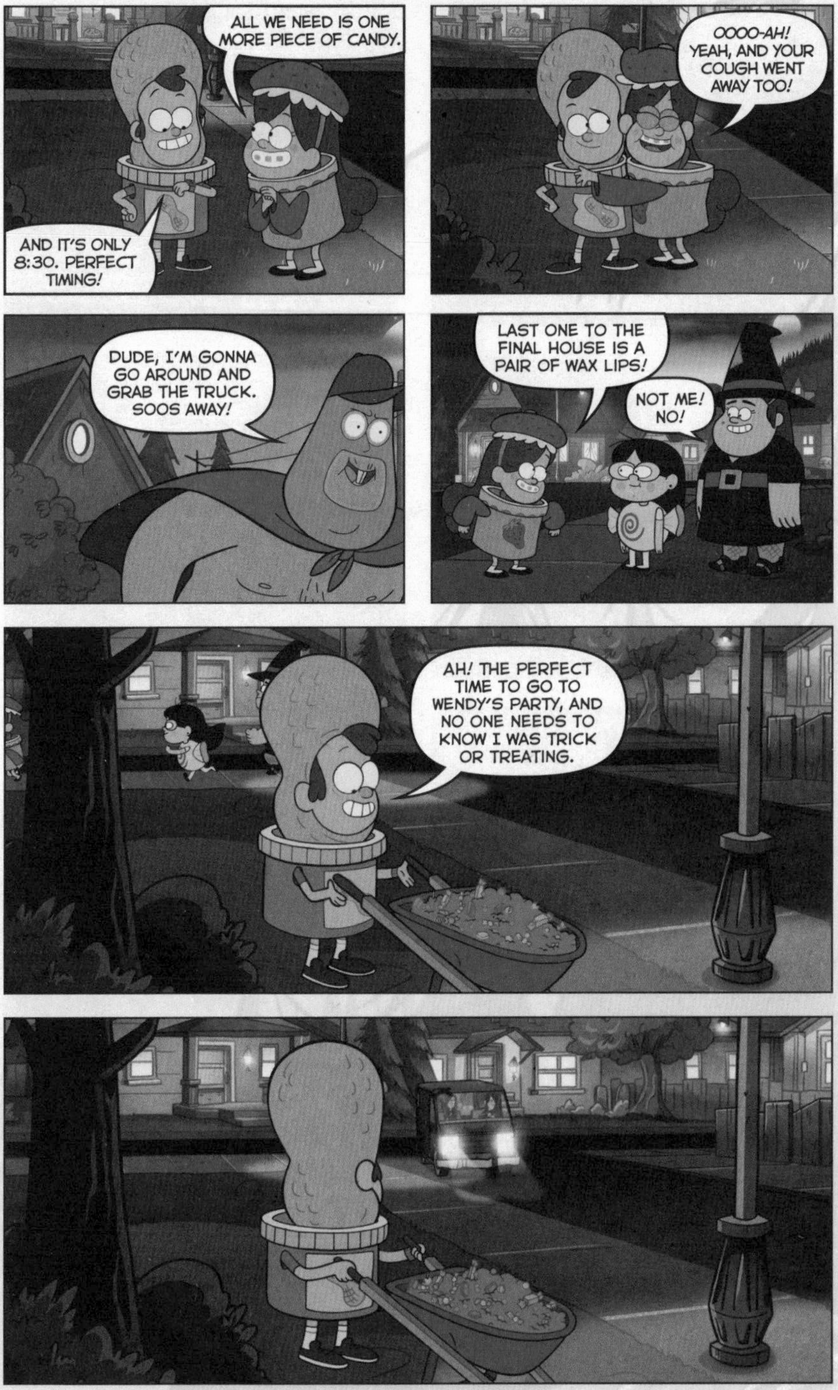
ALL WE NEED IS ONE MORE PIECE OF CANDY.
AND IT'S ONLY 8:30. PERFECT TIMING!
OOOO-AH! YEAH, AND YOUR COUGH WENT AWAY TOO!
DUDE, I'M GONNA GO AROUND AND GRAB THE TRUCK. SOOS AWAY!
LAST ONE TO THE FINAL HOUSE IS A PAIR OF WAX LIPS!
NOT ME! NO!
AH! THE PERFECT TIME TO GO TO WENDY'S PARTY, AND NO ONE NEEDS TO KNOW I WAS TRICK OR TREATING.

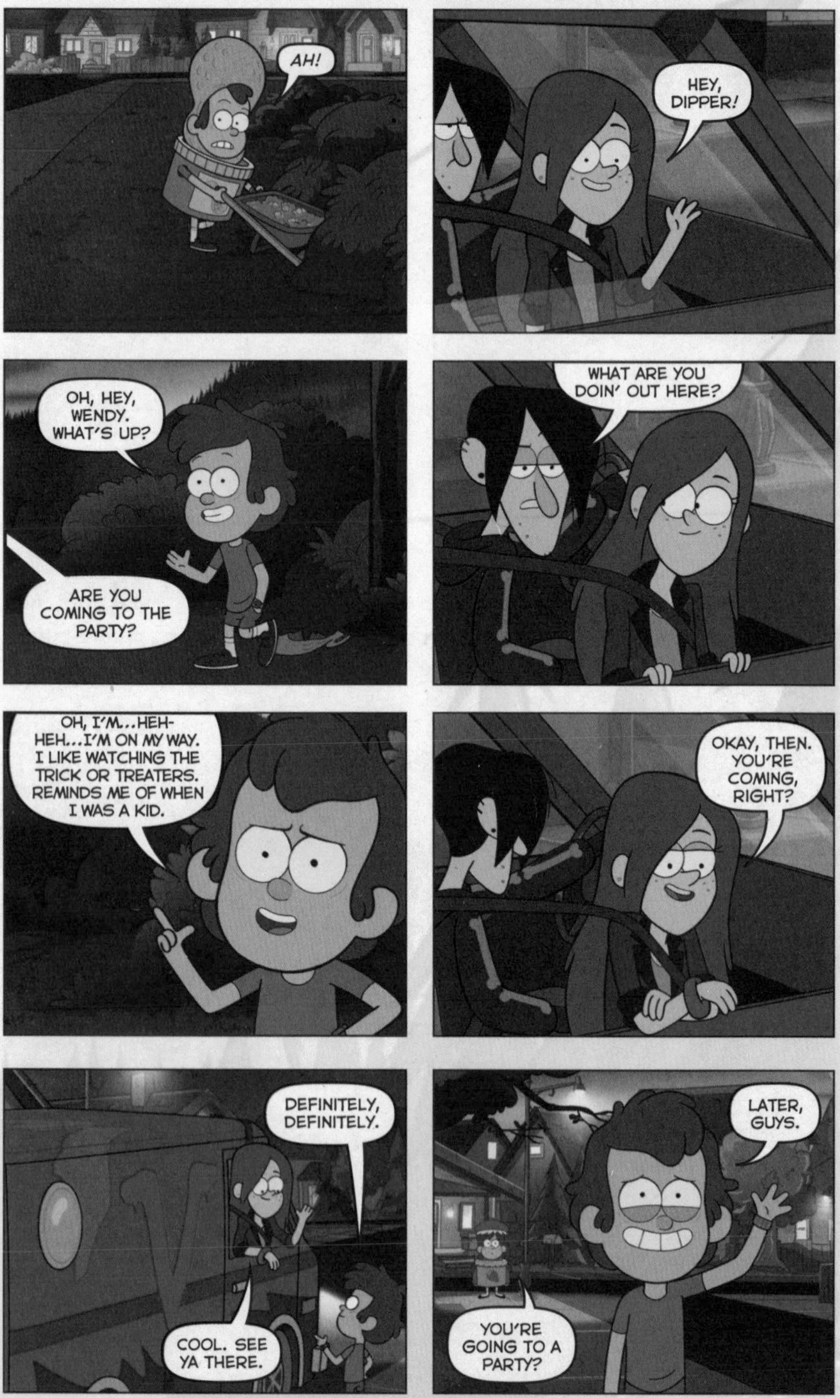
AH!
HEY, DIPPER!
OH, HEY, WENDY. WHAT'S UP?
ARE YOU COMING TO THE PARTY?
WHAT ARE YOU DOIN' OUT HERE?
OH, I'M...HEH-HEH...I'M ON MY WAY. I LIKE WATCHING THE TRICK OR TREATERS. REMINDS ME OF WHEN I WAS A KID.
OKAY, THEN. YOU'RE COMING, RIGHT?
DEFINITELY, DEFINITELY.
COOL. SEE YA THERE.
LATER, GUYS.
YOU'RE GOING TO A PARTY?

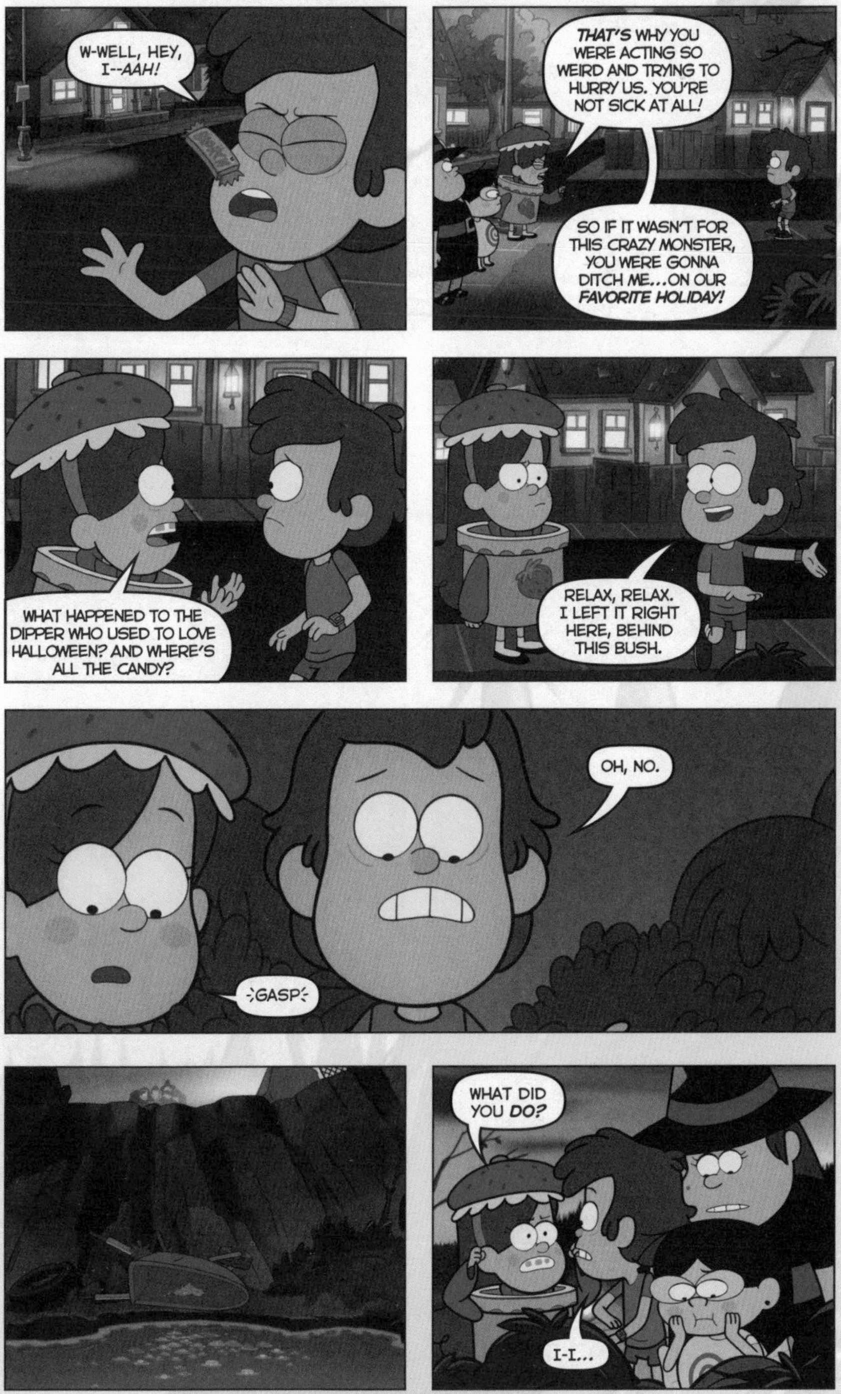
W-WELL, HEY, I--AAH!
THAT'S WHY YOU WERE ACTING SO WEIRD AND TRYING TO HURRY US. YOU'RE NOT SICK AT ALL!
SO IF IT WASN'T FOR THIS CRAZY MONSTER, YOU WERE GONNA DITCH ME...ON OUR FAVORITE HOLIDAY!
WHAT HAPPENED TO THE DIPPER WHO USED TO LOVE HALLOWEEN? AND WHERE'S ALL THE CANDY?
RELAX, RELAX. I LEFT IT RIGHT HERE, BEHIND THIS BUSH.
OH, NO.
GASP
WHAT DID YOU DO?
I-I...

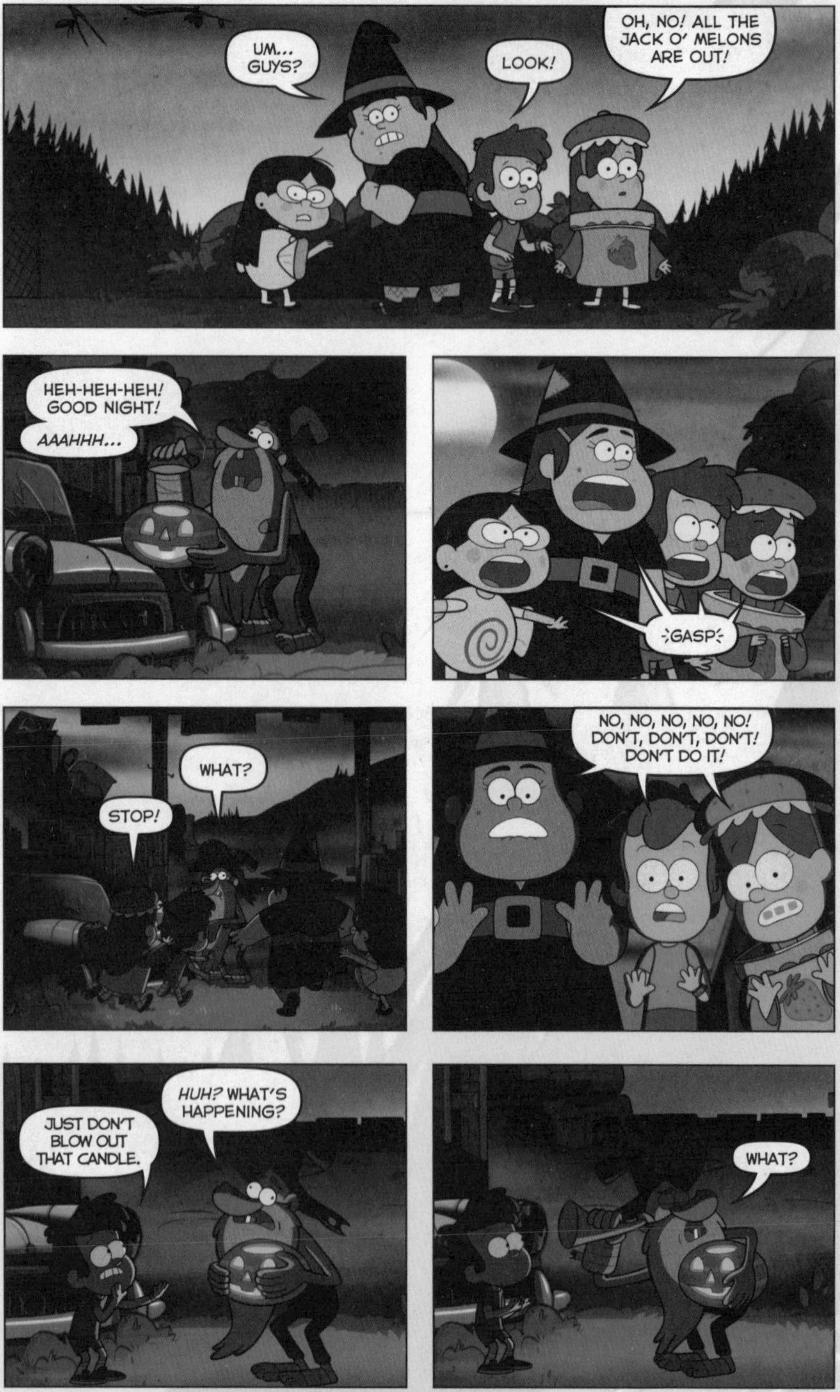
UM... GUYS?
LOOK!
OH, NO! ALL THE JACK O' MELONS ARE OUT!
HEH-HEH-HEH! GOOD NIGHT!
AAAHHH...
GASP
STOP!
WHAT?
NO, NO, NO, NO, NO! DON'T, DON'T, DON'T! DON'T DO IT!
JUST DON'T BLOW OUT THAT CANDLE.
HUH? WHAT'S HAPPENING?
WHAT?

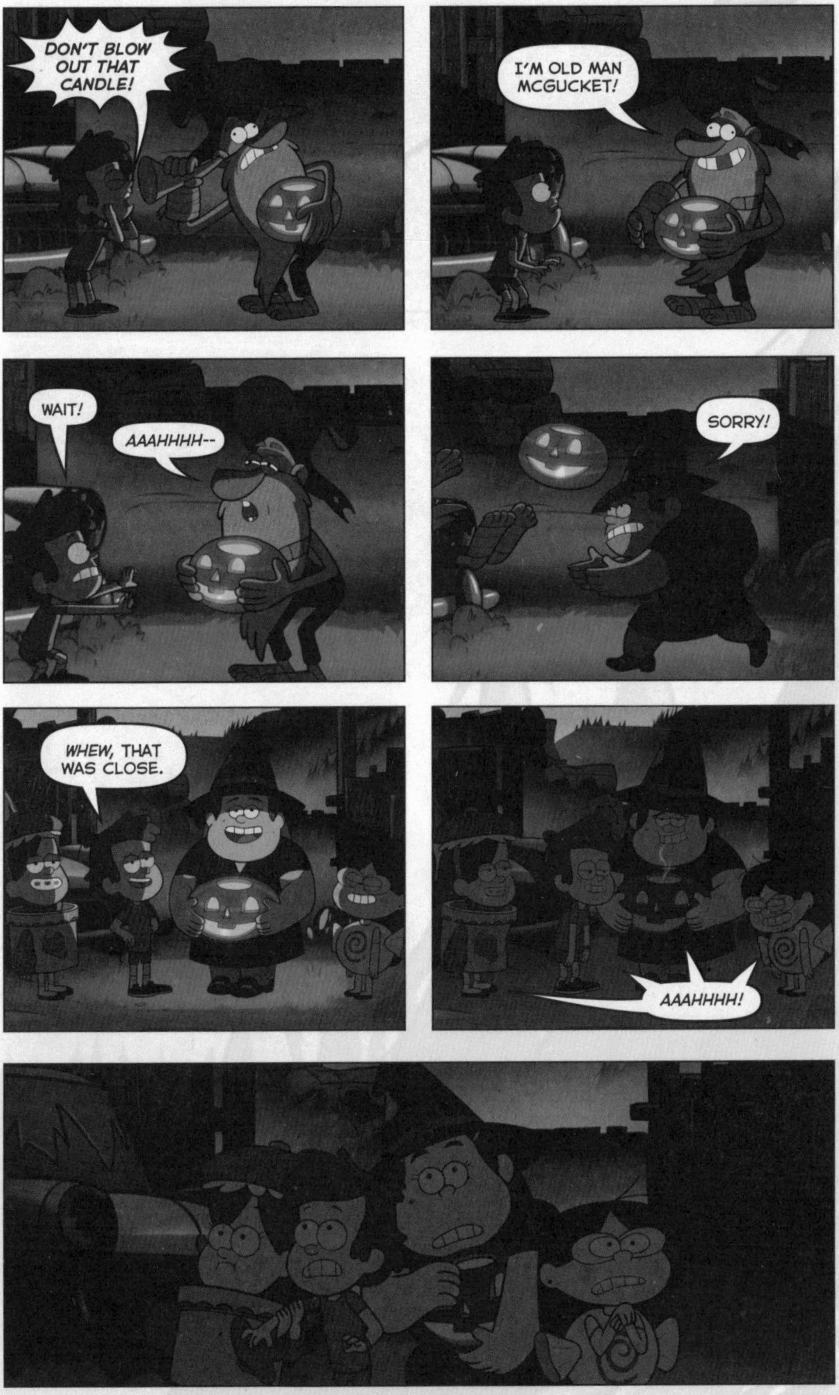
DON'T BLOW OUT THAT CANDLE!
I'M OLD MAN MCGUCKET!
WAIT!
AAAHHHH--
SORRY!
WHEW, THAT WAS CLOSE.
AAAHHHH!

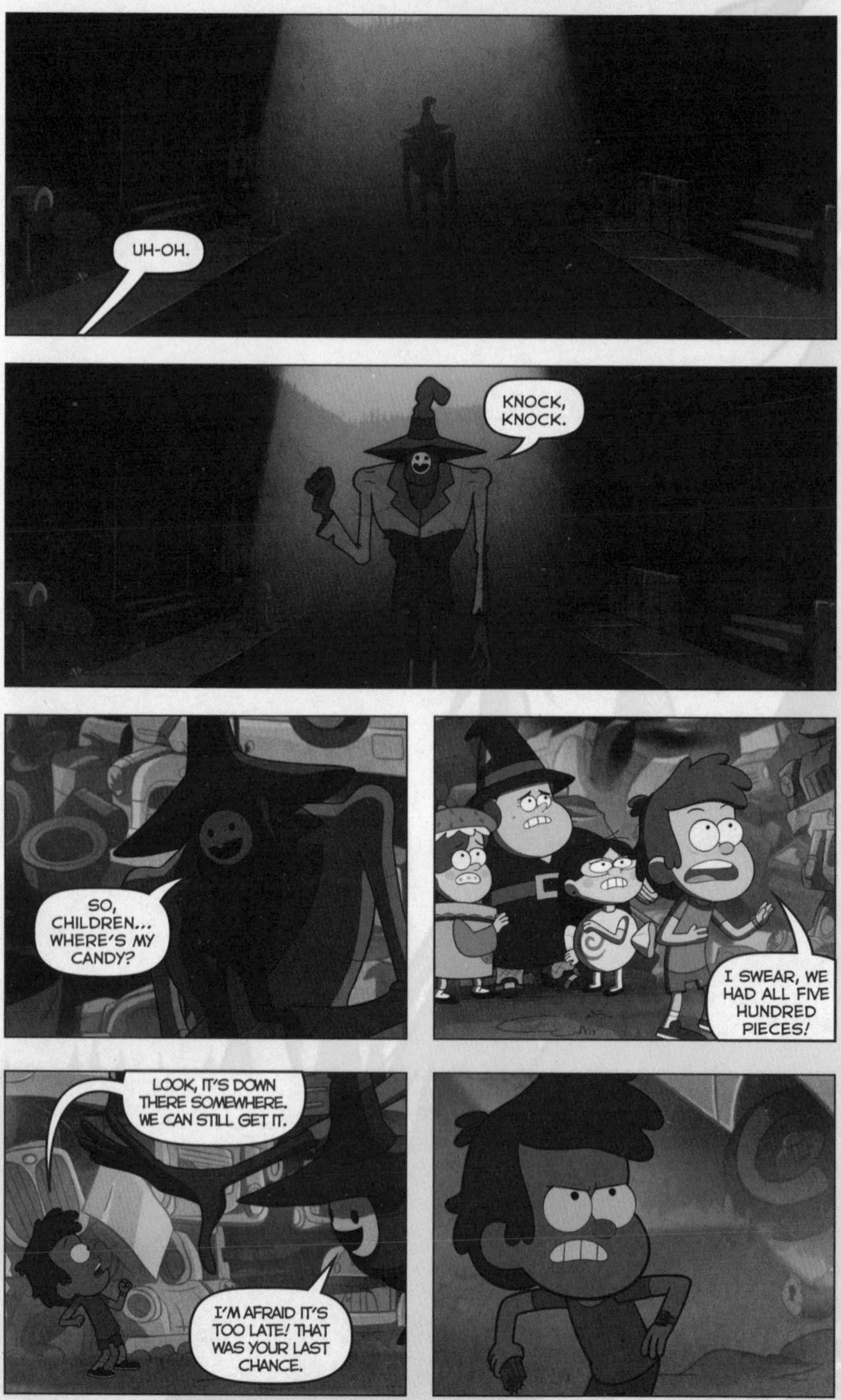
UH-OH.
KNOCK, KNOCK.
SO, CHILDREN... WHERE'S MY CANDY?
I SWEAR, WE HAD ALL FIVE HUNDRED PIECES!
LOOK, IT'S DOWN THERE SOMEWHERE. WE CAN STILL GET IT.
I'M AFRAID IT'S TOO LATE! THAT WAS YOUR LAST CHANCE.

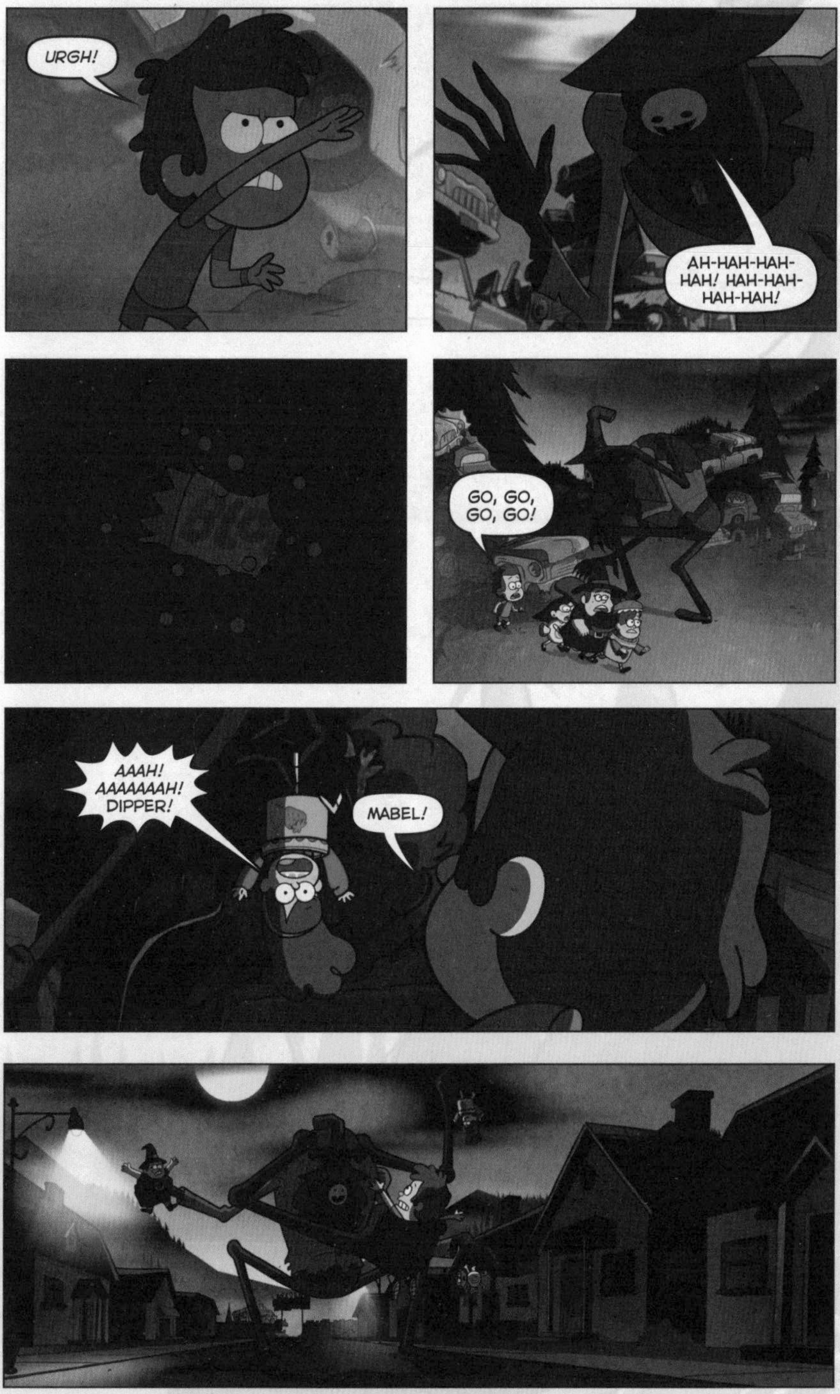
URGH!
AH-HAH-HAH-HAH! HAH-HAH-HAH-HAH!
GO, GO, GO, GO!
AAAH! AAAAAAAH! DIPPER!
MABEL!

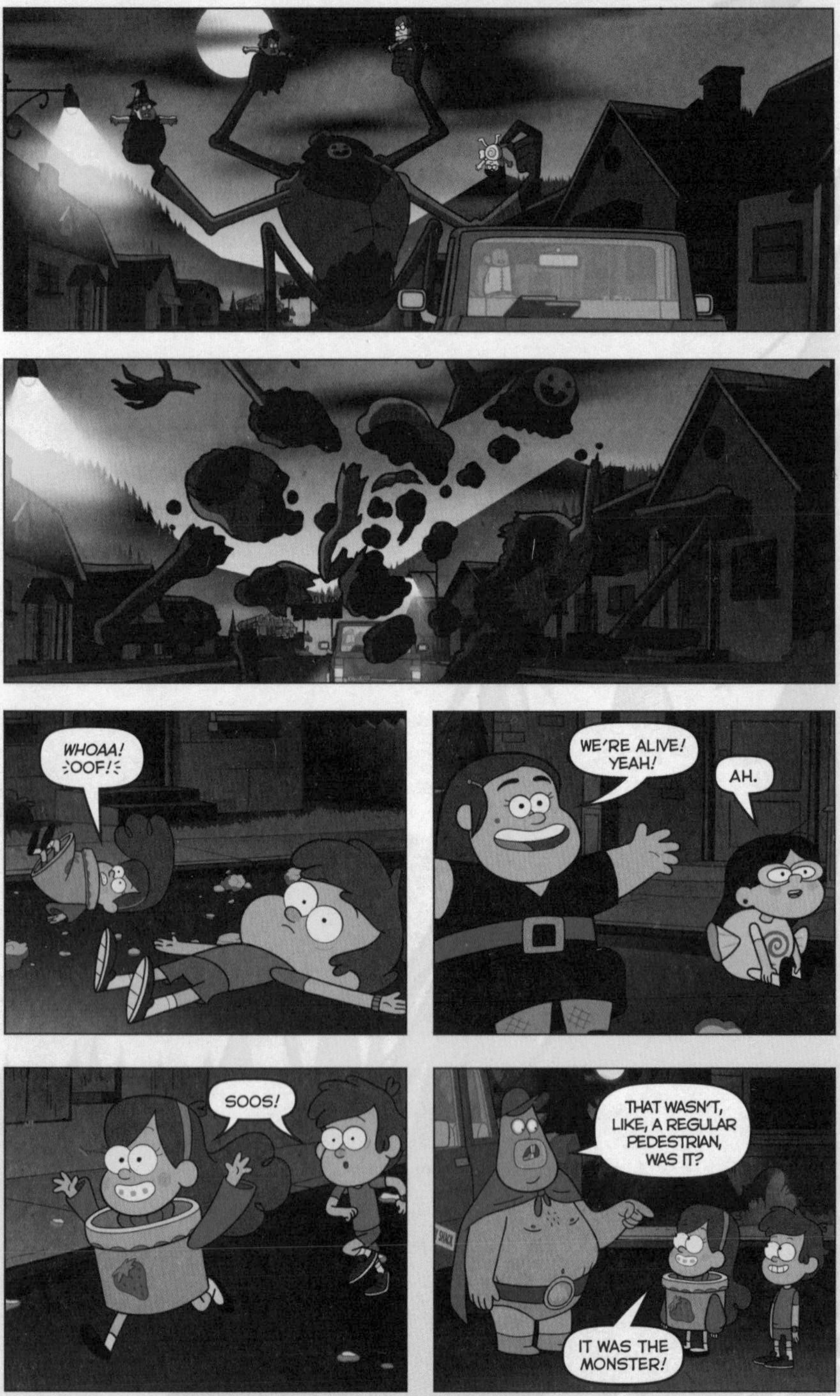
WHOAA!
OOF!
WE'RE ALIVE! YEAH!
AH.
SOOS!
THAT WASN'T, LIKE, A REGULAR PEDESTRIAN, WAS IT?
IT WAS THE MONSTER!

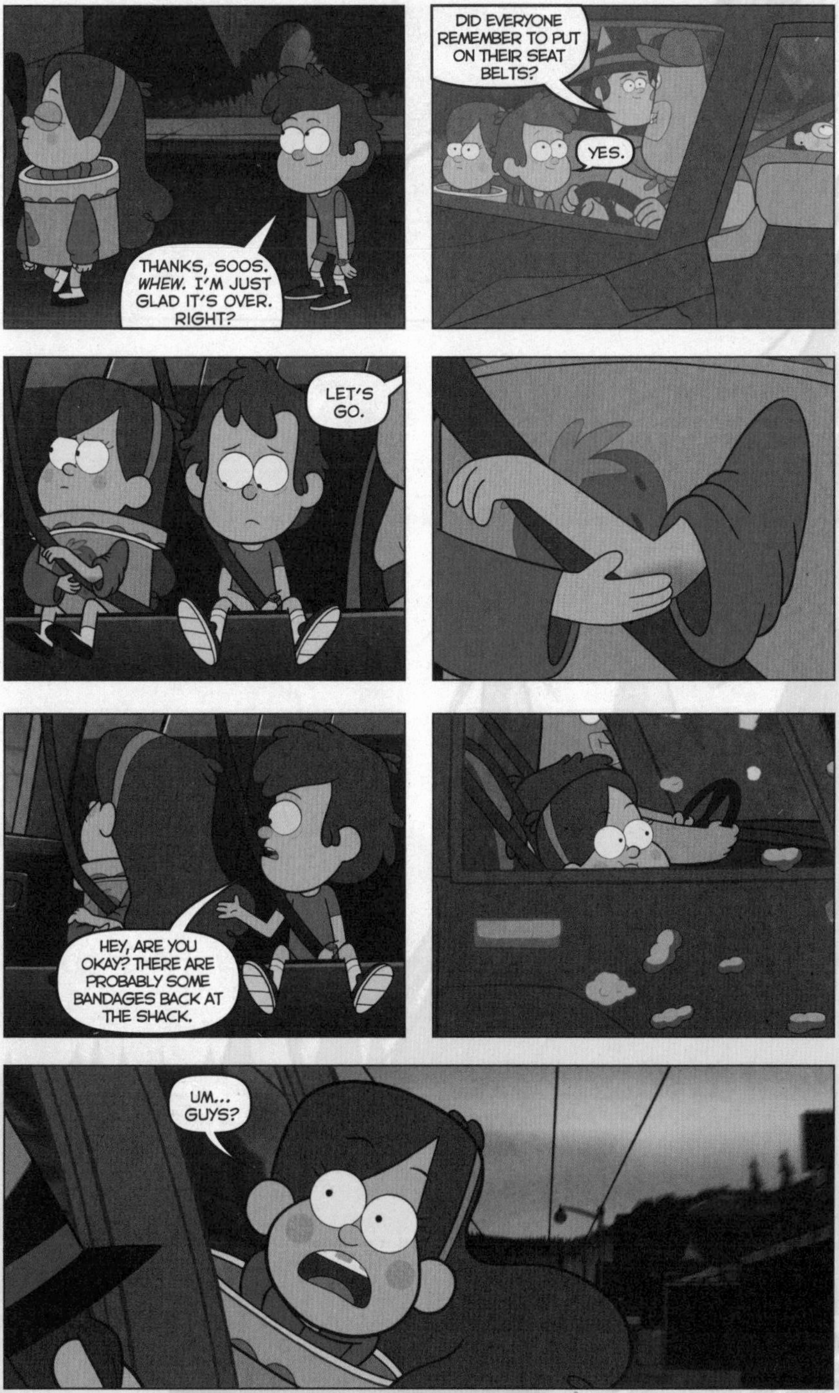
THANKS, SOOS. *WHEW.* I'M JUST GLAD IT'S OVER. RIGHT?
DID EVERYONE REMEMBER TO PUT ON THEIR SEAT BELTS?
YES.
LET'S GO.
HEY, ARE YOU OKAY? THERE ARE PROBABLY SOME BANDAGES BACK AT THE SHACK.
UM... GUYS?

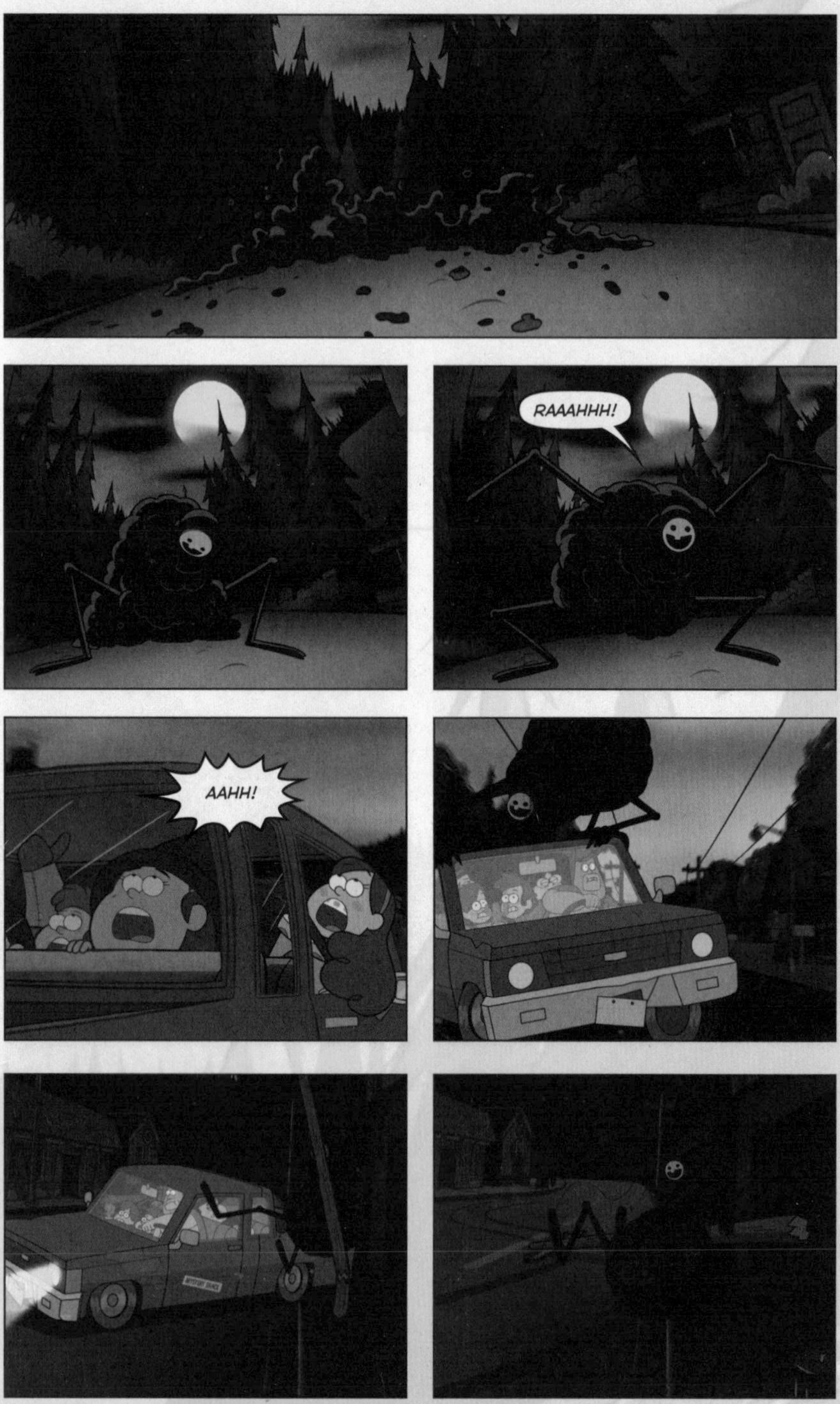
RAAAHHH!
AAHH!

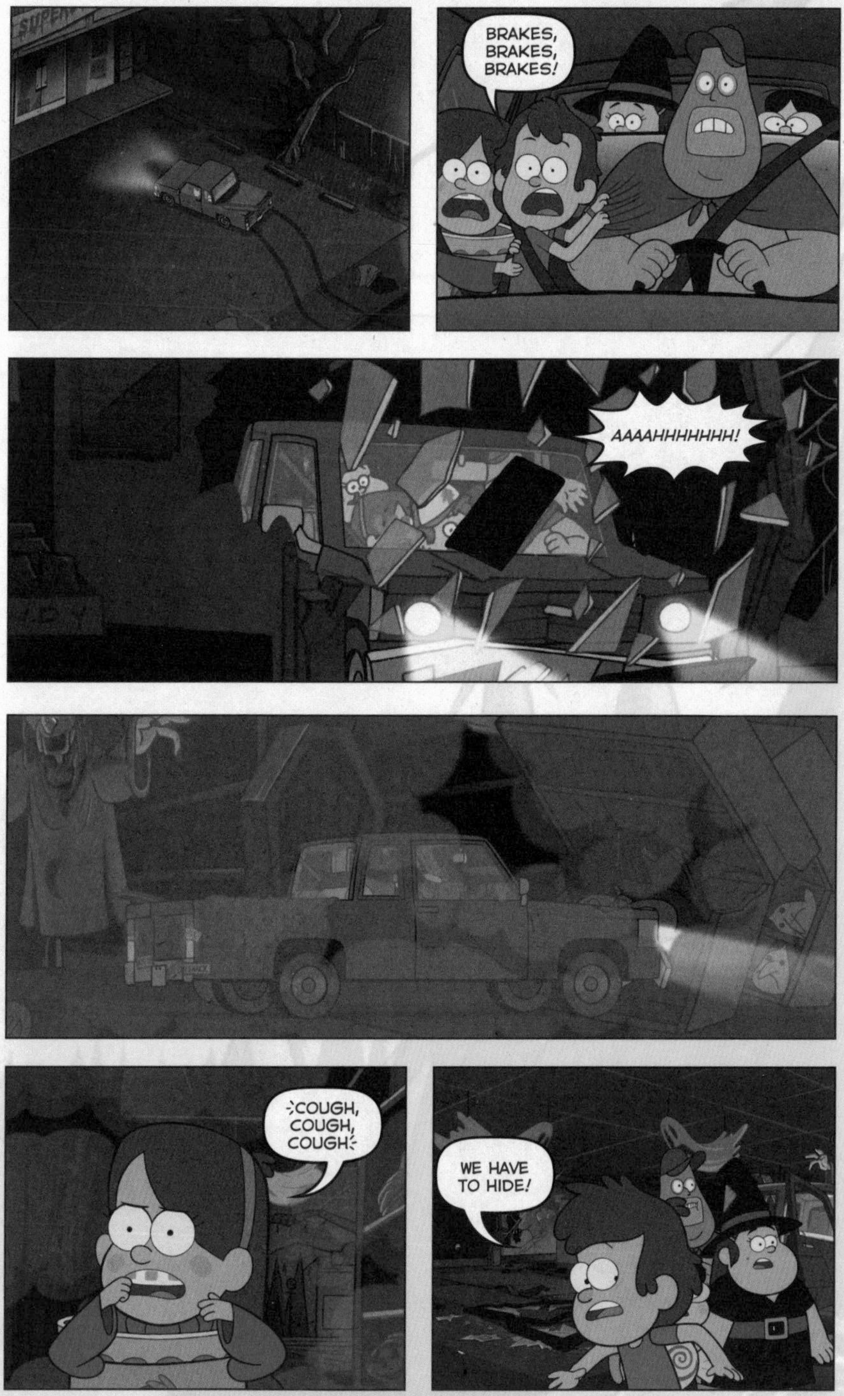
BRAKES, BRAKES, BRAKES!
AAAAHHHHHHH!
COUGH, COUGH, COUGH
WE HAVE TO HIDE!

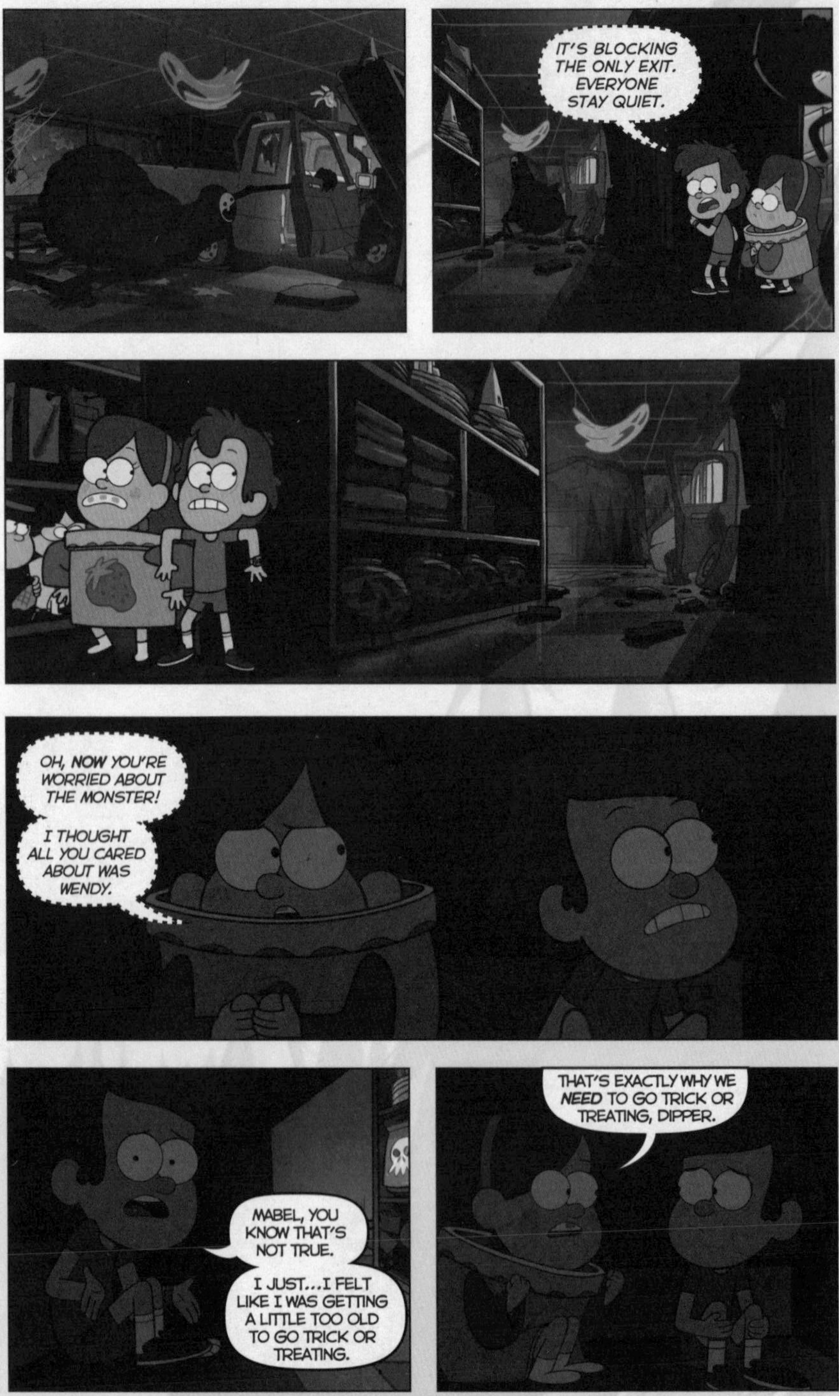
IT'S BLOCKING THE ONLY EXIT. EVERYONE STAY QUIET.
OH, **NOW** YOU'RE WORRIED ABOUT THE MONSTER!
I THOUGHT ALL YOU CARED ABOUT WAS WENDY.
MABEL, YOU KNOW THAT'S NOT TRUE.
I JUST...I FELT LIKE I WAS GETTING A LITTLE TOO OLD TO GO TRICK OR TREATING.
THAT'S EXACTLY WHY WE *NEED* TO GO TRICK OR TREATING, DIPPER.

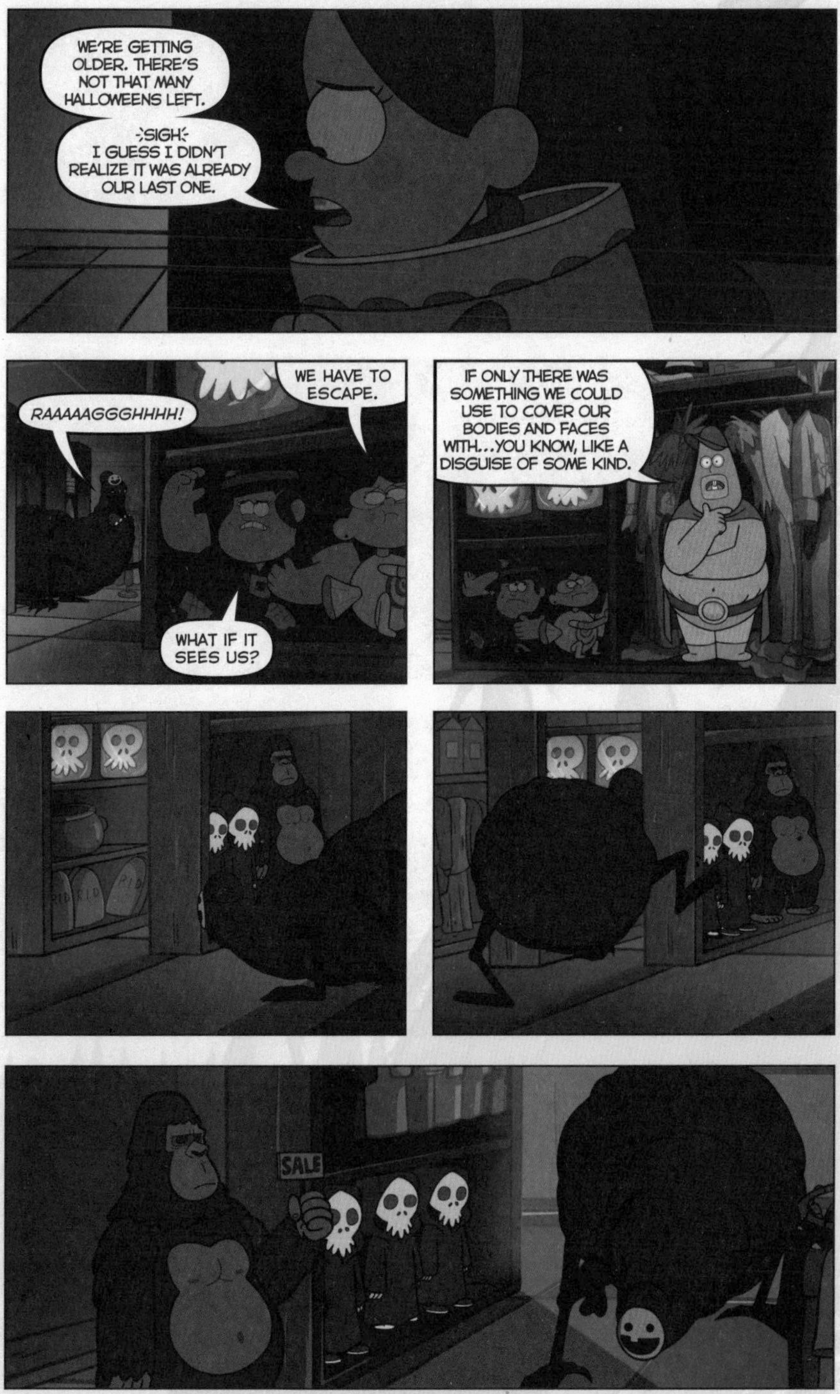
WE'RE GETTING OLDER. THERE'S NOT THAT MANY HALLOWEENS LEFT.
-SIGH- I GUESS I DIDN'T REALIZE IT WAS ALREADY OUR LAST ONE.
RAAAAAGGGHHHH!
WE HAVE TO ESCAPE.
WHAT IF IT SEES US?
IF ONLY THERE WAS SOMETHING WE COULD USE TO COVER OUR BODIES AND FACES WITH...YOU KNOW, LIKE A DISGUISE OF SOME KIND.
SALE

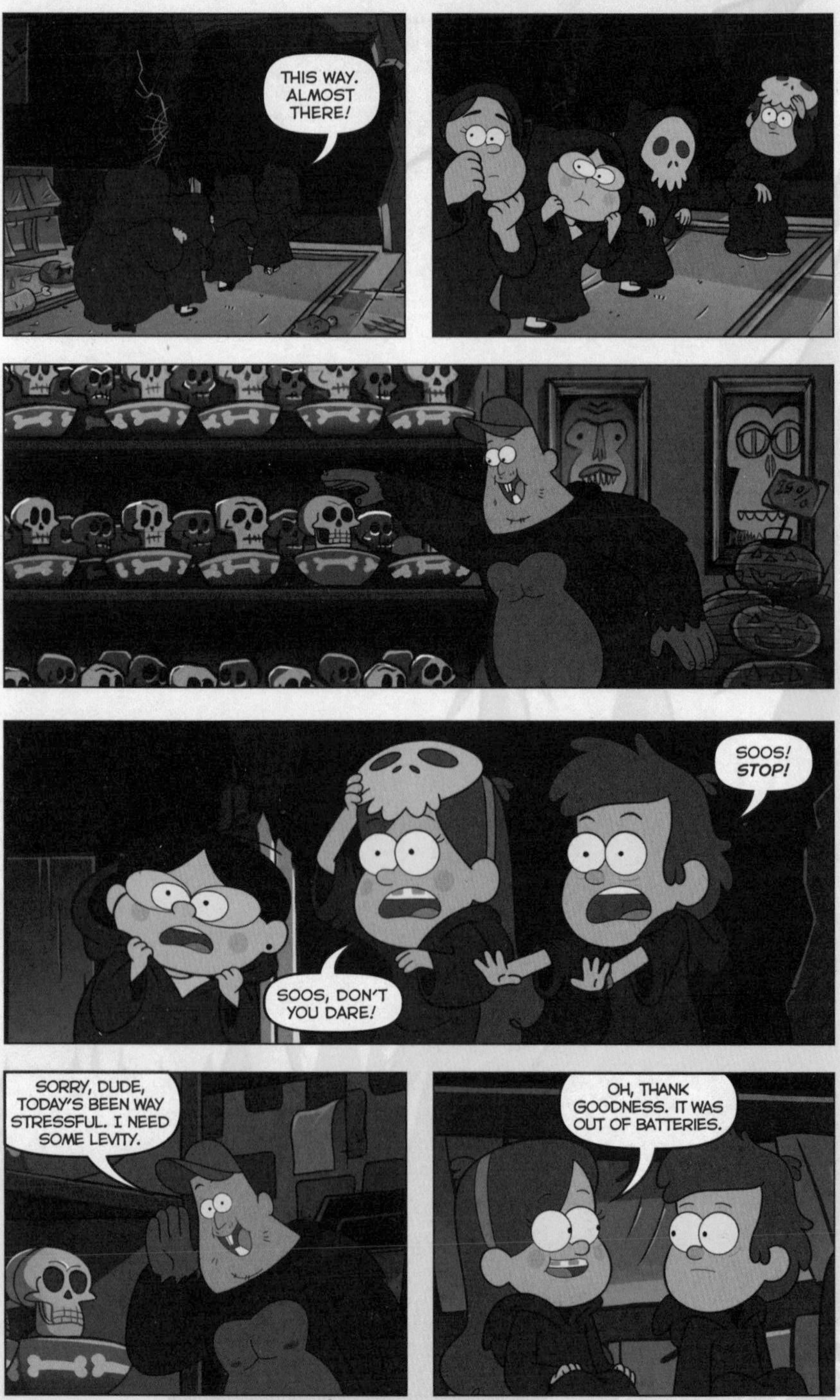
THIS WAY. ALMOST THERE!
SOOS! STOP!
SOOS, DON'T YOU DARE!
SORRY, DUDE, TODAY'S BEEN WAY STRESSFUL. I NEED SOME LEVITY.
OH, THANK GOODNESS. IT WAS OUT OF BATTERIES.

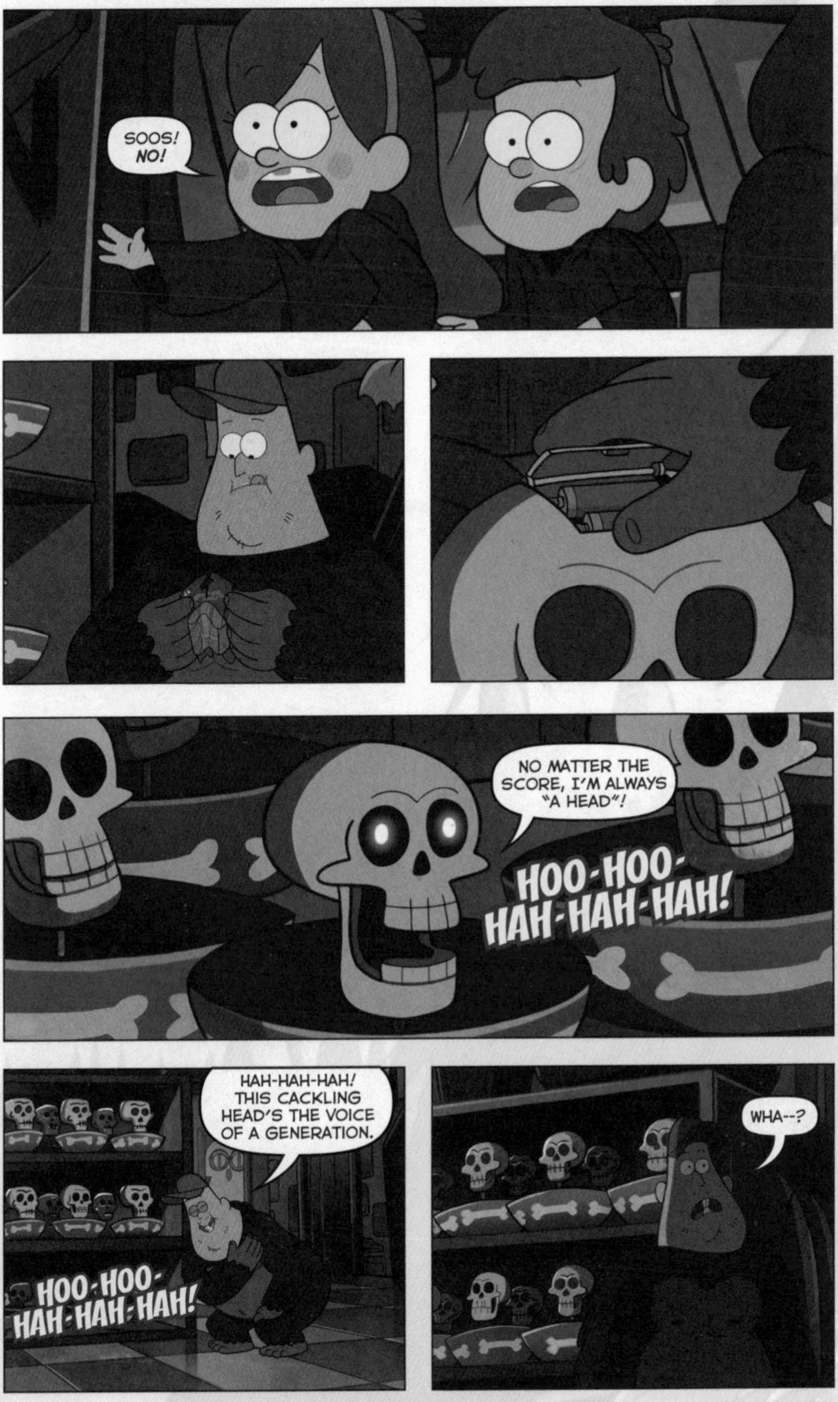
SOOS! NO!
NO MATTER THE SCORE, I'M ALWAYS "A HEAD"!
HOO-HOO-HAH-HAH-HAH!
HAH-HAH-HAH! THIS CACKLING HEAD'S THE VOICE OF A GENERATION.
HOO-HOO-HAH-HAH-HAH!
WHA--?

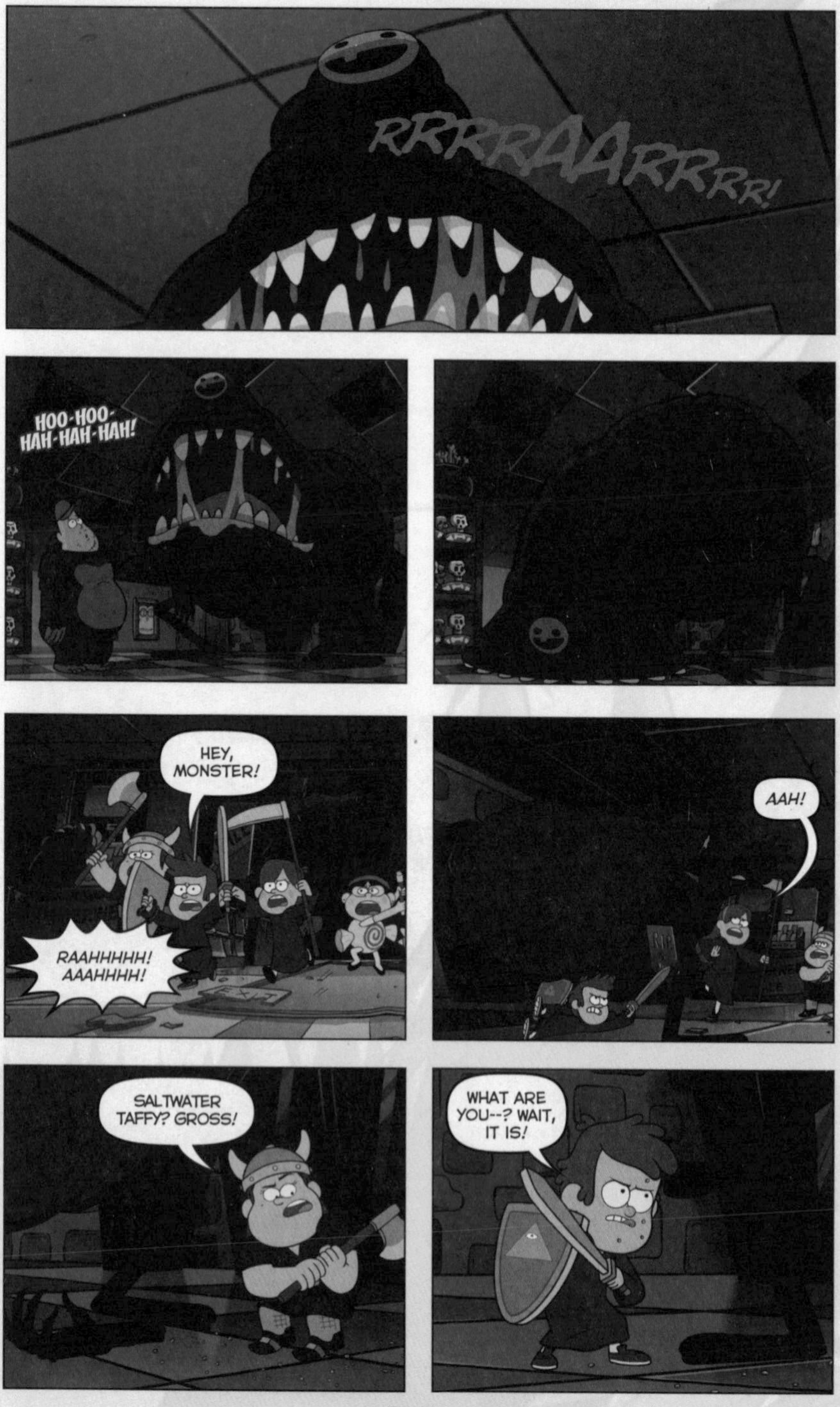
RRRRAARRRRR!
HOO-HOO-HAH-HAH-HAH!
HEY, MONSTER!
RAAHHHHH! AAAHHHH!
AAH!
SALTWATER TAFFY? GROSS!
WHAT ARE YOU--? WAIT, IT IS!

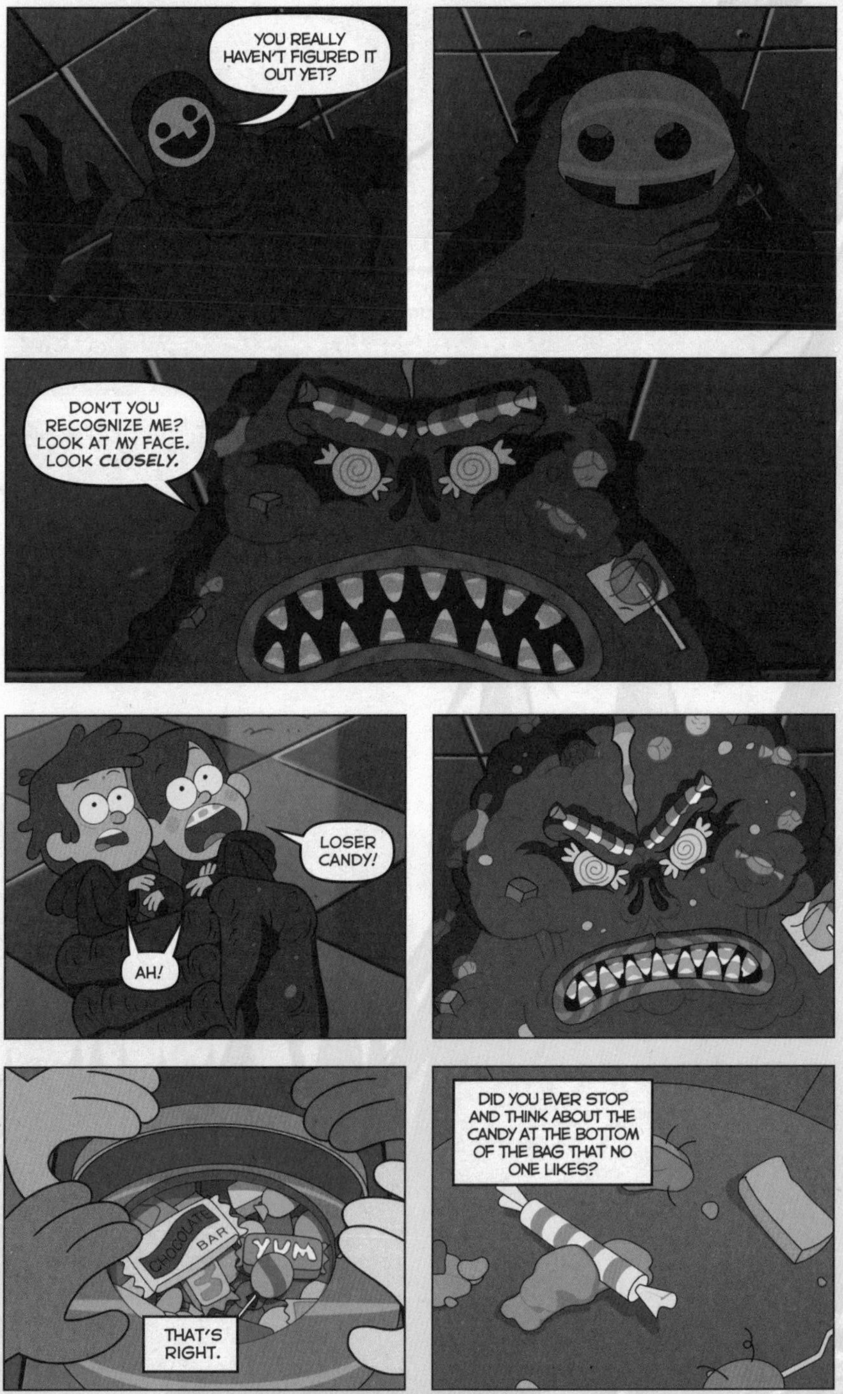
YOU REALLY HAVEN'T FIGURED IT OUT YET?
DON'T YOU RECOGNIZE ME? LOOK AT MY FACE. LOOK CLOSELY.
LOSER CANDY!
AH!
CHOCOLATE BAR
YUM
THAT'S RIGHT.
DID YOU EVER STOP AND THINK ABOUT THE CANDY AT THE BOTTOM OF THE BAG THAT NO ONE LIKES?

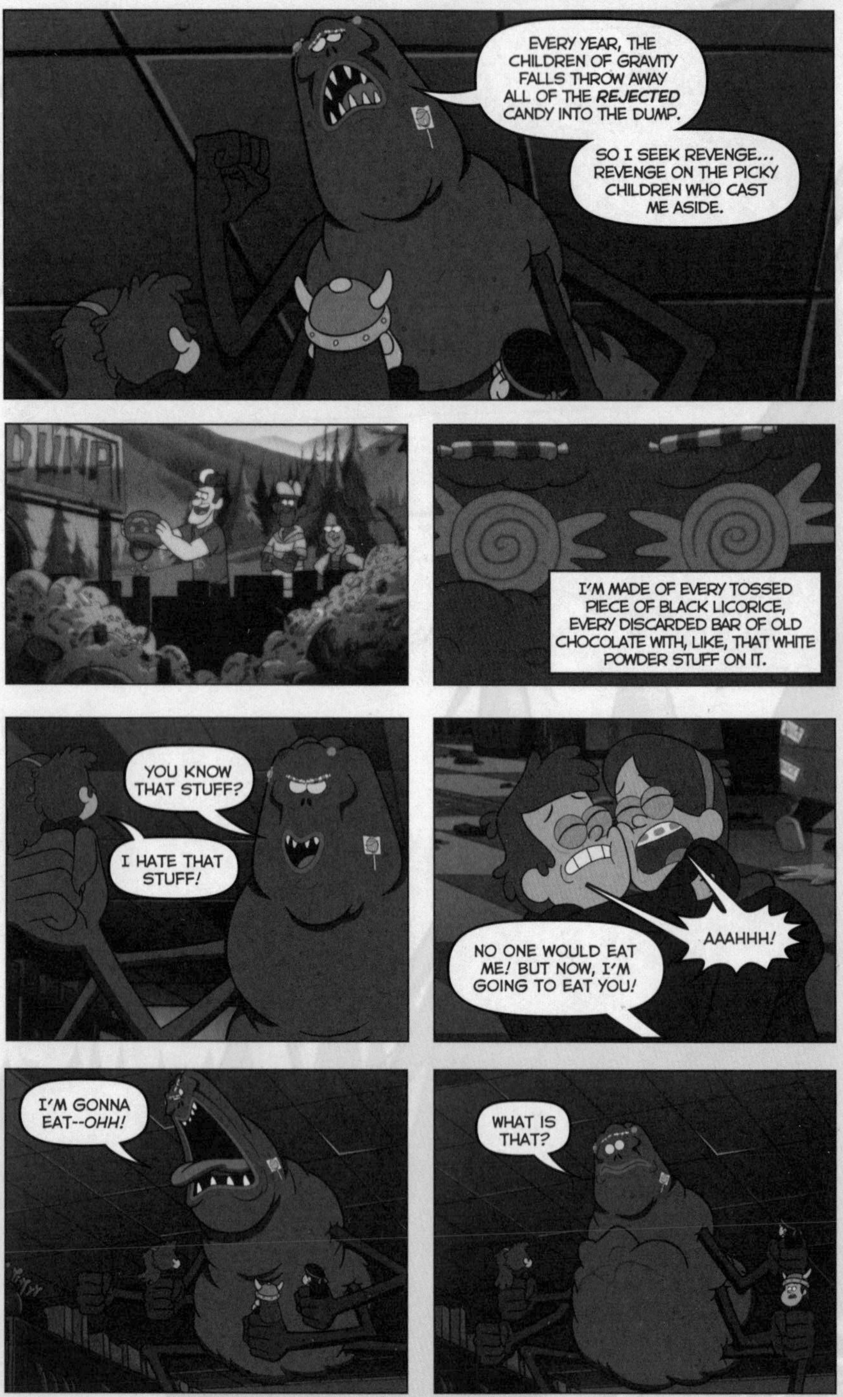
EVERY YEAR, THE CHILDREN OF GRAVITY FALLS THROW AWAY ALL OF THE *REJECTED* CANDY INTO THE DUMP.
SO I SEEK REVENGE... REVENGE ON THE PICKY CHILDREN WHO CAST ME ASIDE.
DUMP
I'M MADE OF EVERY TOSSED PIECE OF BLACK LICORICE, EVERY DISCARDED BAR OF OLD CHOCOLATE WITH, LIKE, THAT WHITE POWDER STUFF ON IT.
YOU KNOW THAT STUFF?
I HATE THAT STUFF!
AAAHHH!
NO ONE WOULD EAT ME! BUT NOW, I'M GOING TO EAT YOU!
I'M GONNA EAT--*OHH!*
WHAT IS THAT?

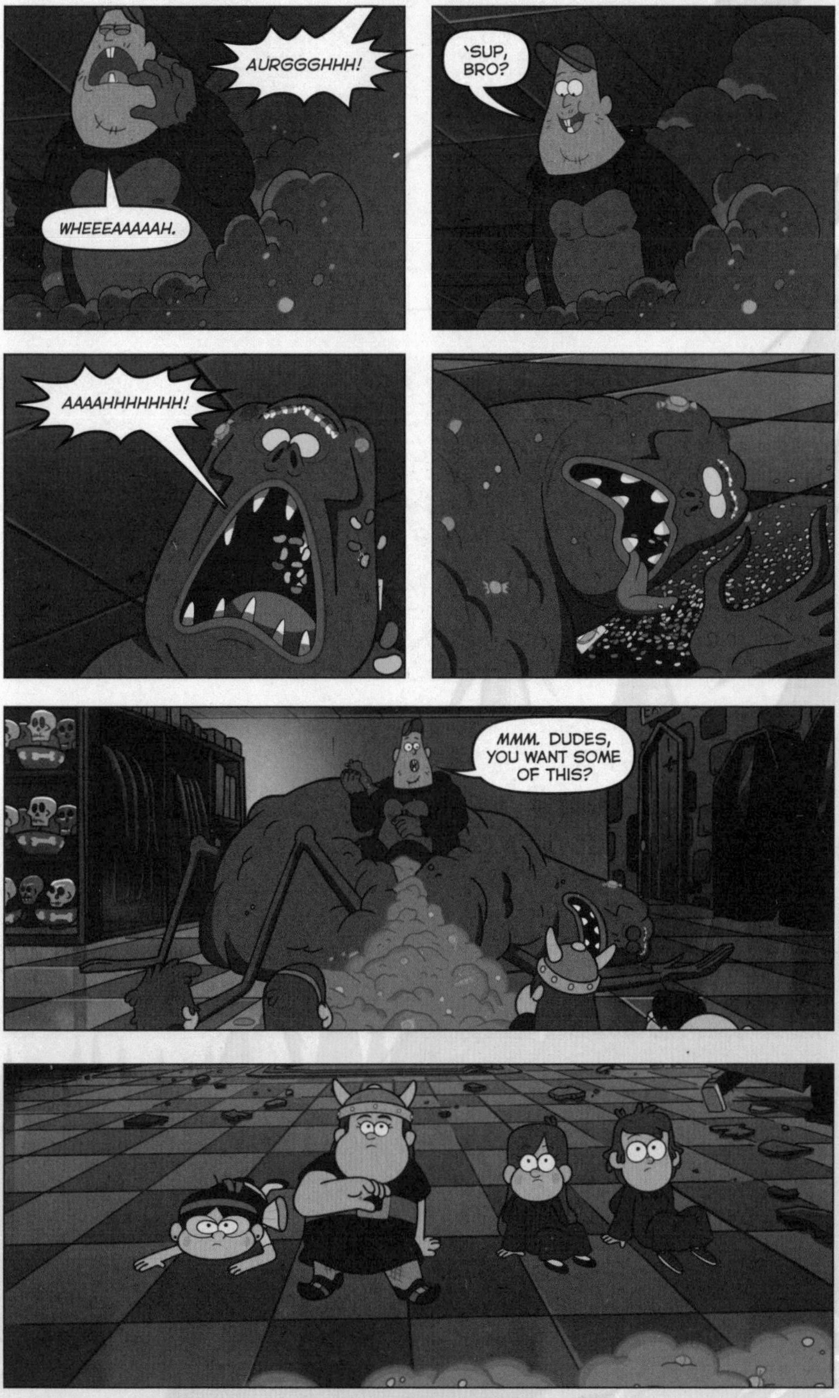
AURGGGHHH!
WHEEEAAAAAH.
`SUP, BRO?
AAAAHHHHHHH!
MMM. DUDES, YOU WANT SOME OF THIS?

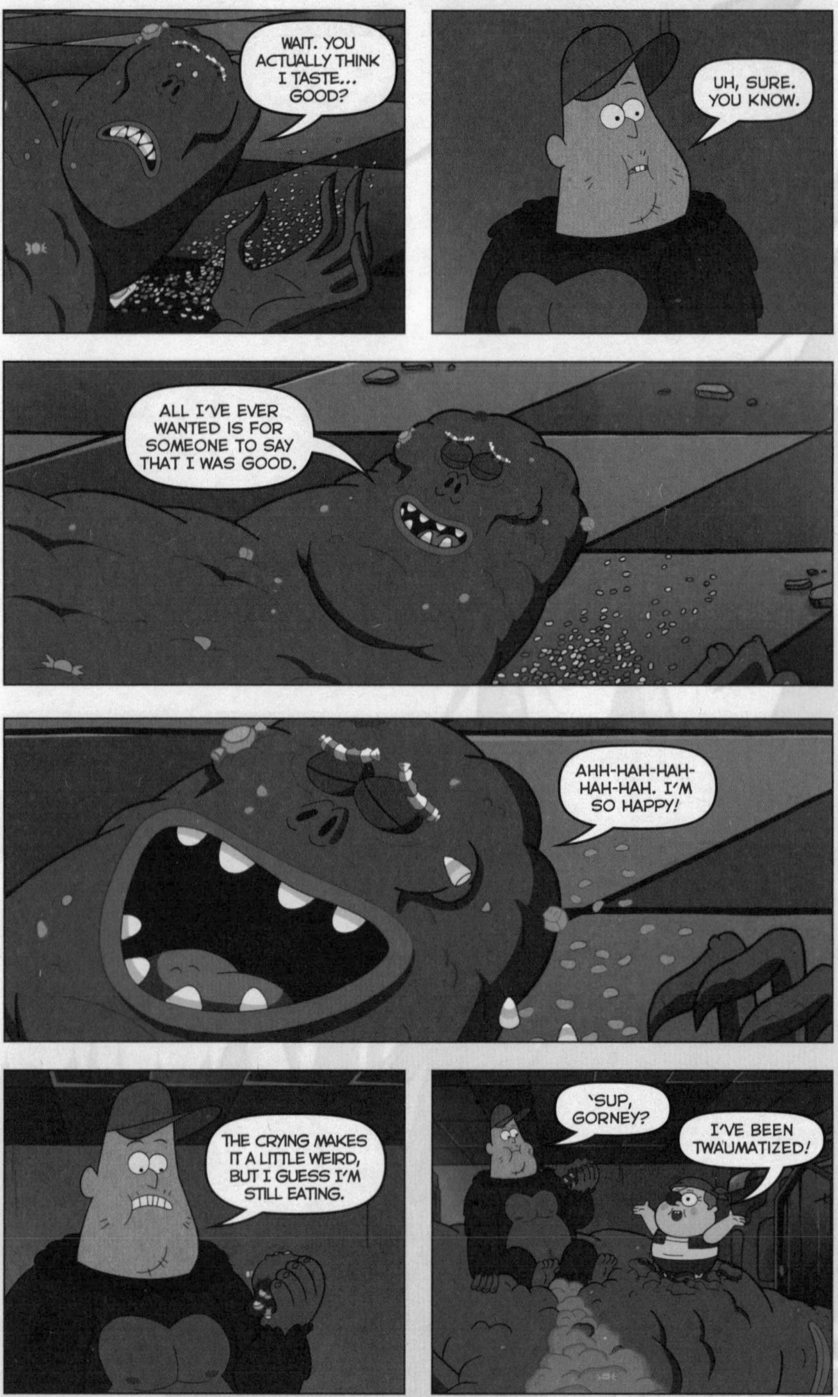
WAIT. YOU ACTUALLY THINK I TASTE... GOOD?
UH, SURE. YOU KNOW.
ALL I'VE EVER WANTED IS FOR SOMEONE TO SAY THAT I WAS GOOD.
AHH-HAH-HAH-HAH-HAH. I'M SO HAPPY!
THE CRYING MAKES IT A LITTLE WEIRD, BUT I GUESS I'M STILL EATING.
'SUP, GORNEY?
I'VE BEEN TWAUMATIZED!

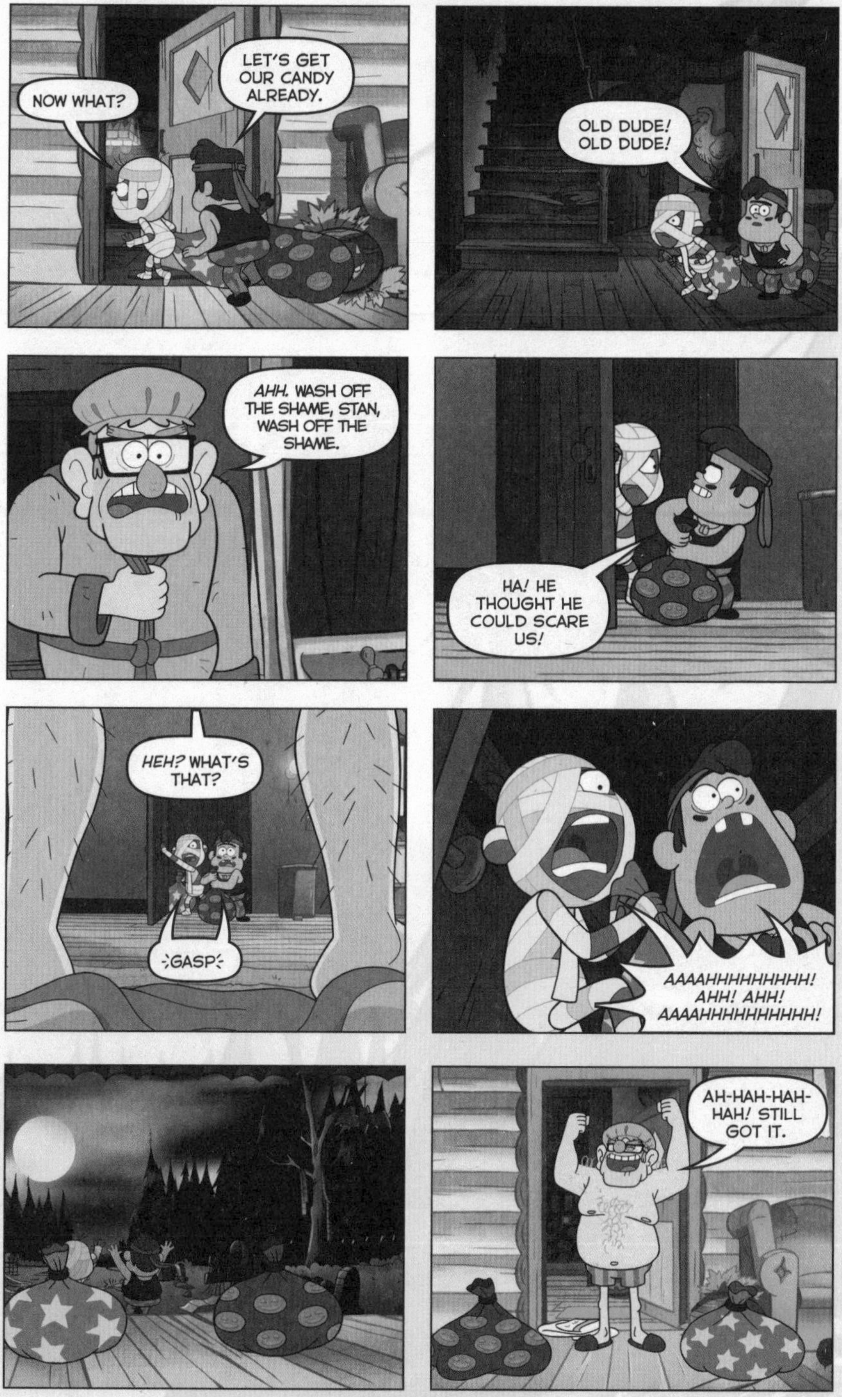
NOW WHAT?
LET'S GET OUR CANDY ALREADY.
OLD DUDE! OLD DUDE!
AHH. WASH OFF THE SHAME, STAN, WASH OFF THE SHAME.
HA! HE THOUGHT HE COULD SCARE US!
HEH? WHAT'S THAT?
GASP
AAAAHHHHHHHHH! AHH! AHH! AAAAHHHHHHHHHH!
AH-HAH-HAH-HAH! STILL GOT IT.

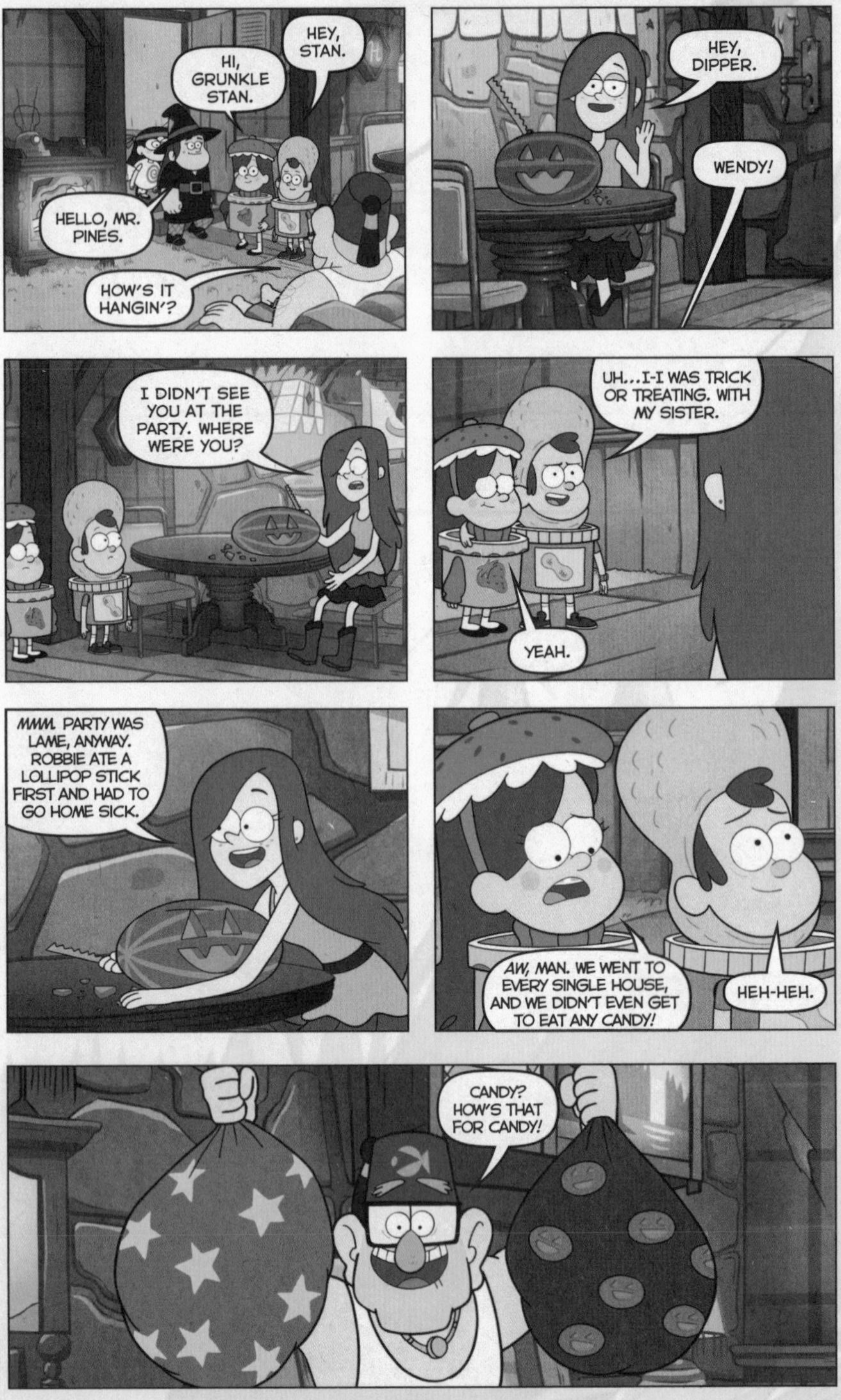
HEY, STAN.
HI, GRUNKLE STAN.
HELLO, MR. PINES.
HOW'S IT HANGIN'?
HEY, DIPPER.
WENDY!
I DIDN'T SEE YOU AT THE PARTY. WHERE WERE YOU?
UH...I-I WAS TRICK OR TREATING. WITH MY SISTER.
YEAH.
MMM. PARTY WAS LAME, ANYWAY. ROBBIE ATE A LOLLIPOP STICK FIRST AND HAD TO GO HOME SICK.
AW, MAN. WE WENT TO EVERY SINGLE HOUSE, AND WE DIDN'T EVEN GET TO EAT ANY CANDY!
HEH-HEH.
CANDY? HOW'S THAT FOR CANDY!

AND NOW BACK TO THE FEAR GUY FROM TERROR TOWN STREET!

NOW BACK TO OUR **SUMMERWEEN** MOVIE MARATHON

AAAAHHHHHH!

AHH!

AHH! AAAHHHHHH!

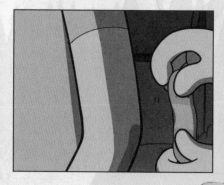

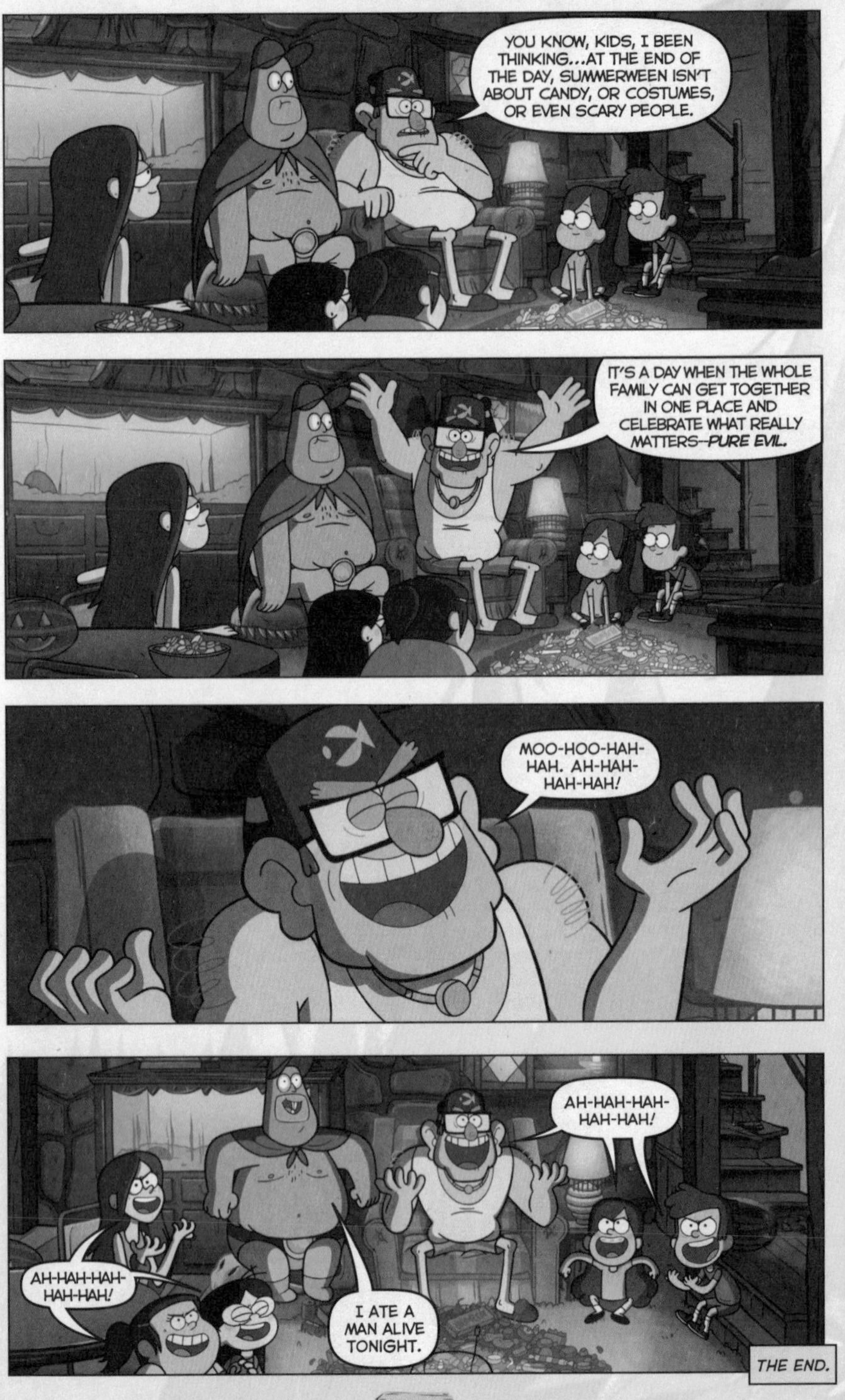
YOU KNOW, KIDS, I BEEN THINKING...AT THE END OF THE DAY, SUMMERWEEN ISN'T ABOUT CANDY, OR COSTUMES, OR EVEN SCARY PEOPLE.
IT'S A DAY WHEN THE WHOLE FAMILY CAN GET TOGETHER IN ONE PLACE AND CELEBRATE WHAT REALLY MATTERS--*PURE EVIL.*
MOO-HOO-HAH-HAH. AH-HAH-HAH-HAH!
AH-HAH-HAH-HAH-HAH!
AH-HAH-HAH-HAH-HAH!
I ATE A MAN ALIVE TONIGHT.
THE END.

CREATED BY ALEX HIRSCH

"Fight Fighters"
Executive Producer: Alex Hirsch
Supervising Producer: Rob Renzetti
Creative Director: Michael Rianda
Art Director: Ian Worrel
Writers: Zach Paez and Alex Hirsch
Director: John Aoshima

"Little Dipper"
Executive Producer: Alex Hirsch
Supervising Producer: Rob Renzetti
Creative Director: Michael Rianda
Art Director: Ian Worrel
Writers: Tim McKeon, Zach Paez, and Alex Hirsch
Directors: Aaron Springer and Joe Pitt

"Summerween"
Executive Producer: Alex Hirsch
Supervising Producer: Rob Renzetti
Creative Director: Michael Rianda
Art Director: Ian Worrel
Writers: Zach Paez, Alex Hirsch, and Michael Rianda
Director: John Aoshima